RACHEL HOBBS

Shadow-Stained

First edition

ISBN: 978-1-5272-5796-2

This book was professionally typeset on Reedsy.
Find out more at reedsy.com

For my husband, who believed in me when I couldn't believe in myself.

In loving memory of Nan, who always cheered me on with unwavering enthusiasm.

Chapter 1

A pulsing entity.

It called out to him from within the torrents of rain, enticing with a promise of unimaginable power, demanding his full attention.

When Drayvex had first arrived and breathed the alien atmosphere, it had nudged against his senses. He'd almost dismissed it. But as he'd lingered at the point between worlds, he'd deduced that not only was the entity moving *towards* him, but its power was on a whole other level.

A low-level demon shot down the cobbled street below him. It took him a second to realise that it was, in fact, his demon.

Drayvex narrowed his eyes from his rooftop perch. Kaelor had followed him through the portal. On top of this, his idea of blending in was truly spectacular. Moron.

The rain lashed around him in waves, hurling itself at him, then evaporating into a fine mist upon contact with his hot flesh. He looked down at the village below, sharp eyes slicing through the downpour, and zoned in on the strange power.

What he saw threw him off his guard.

It was a girl. A human girl emanating a throbbing black aura.

Drayvex relaxed his jaw, allowing the tension to ebb from his taut muscles. She didn't strike him as an unusual specimen. The girl wasn't interesting to look at, nor was there anything about her that stood out. Nothing except

1

that delicious black energy that gathered about her in a possessive miasma.

He watched the girl flee with mild interest, studying her as his minion blocked her path. Would this power weaken and die without its human host? He would soon find out. Kaelor was about to have his way.

As the demon below made to strike, Drayvex's eyes remained on her.

Kaelor pushed off the stones, disappearing in a pop, teleporting with over-dramatic enthusiasm.

Unless, Drayvex mused, watching as the demon materialised in front of her. Unless, she was something *more*. A slick pretender that liked to play human. If that was so, Kaelor would be put in his place, permanently. The ultimate lesson in biting off more than one could chew.

The demon leapt for the kill. The human slashed out with perfect timing, a hidden blade in her hand.

Drayvex stilled. The human had teeth after all.

As the blade sliced into the soft abdomen of his demon underling, Kaelor vanished, fleeing like the miserable coward he was.

Drayvex stared, glued to the diminutive creature standing victorious on the soaked street below. It had been more panic than calculated swipe. A clumsy, last-ditch thrash; but frankly, this girl had the luck of the devil. For one, she'd hit him with her eyes closed.

Drayvex felt his eyes narrow, fresh suspicions emerging. He found himself studying the human with growing intrigue. It was then that he noticed what was around her neck.

It *looked* like a piece of jewellery: a ruby teardrop enshrouded in a delicate silver webbing. It hung on a worn leather cord, with the surrounding silver lattice pulled back on either side to reveal the gleaming face of the stone. The darker line running through the centre gave it the distinct look of an eye. Its slit pupil stared out at the world into which its power bled.

It looked like a pendant, but Drayvex knew better. He stared at the stone in revelation. It was unbelievable.

As the girl walked away with her life, his demon was long gone. Drayvex made a mental note to punish the worthless ingrate. If he'd wanted to be followed, he would have told someone he was leaving.

The pulsing presence lingered in his mind long after her absence.

Old notions of ambition seduced him where he stood. A venture like this would prove to be the best kind of distraction. The kind that would produce hard results.

Bringing up his hands, he studied the curved, black tips of his fingers. These would have to go.

Drayvex clenched his hands into tight fists, and then unclenched them, flexing his fingers anew. He examined the blunt human nails that had taken the place of his claws. Their subtle black sheen was the only thing that gave away his disguise.

His tongue wandered over an array of pointed teeth, and their tips dulled and shrank under its touch. The Lapis Vitae. He, like many others, had assumed that such a powerful object could never be outside the mythos of its own existence. Now that he had seen it for himself, he could confirm that it was everything it claimed to be and more.

The corners of his mouth lifted as he considered his fortunate position. He would do whatever it took to possess it.

*

The words that sprung to mind were 'mangled cat'.

Ruby's feet pounded the puddle-riddled pavements, explosions of water erupting around her. She sucked in breath after ragged breath, the chill catching at the back of her throat with each gasp.

It was one thing to run from danger, to flee for your life; it was another thing entirely to flee from a thing without quite knowing why.

Ruby's heart pounded in her chest. Curiosity buzzed within her like a trapped insect. It was large enough to be a dog, yet its features were distinctly feline. Clumps of fur were missing from its twisted torso and bones jutted out at odd angles, as though someone had pulled the poor animal apart and rebuilt it using the most basic of instructions.

As a child, she had possessed a wonderful knack for finding trouble, often in the most unexpected of places. Now as an adult, the only thing that had changed was that Ruby often found it on purpose.

Her footsteps echoed around her; the sounds magnified tenfold within the enclosed passageway. She knew this village and its secrets inside out. Maybe she could lose the cat if she—

A sharp blow to the middle of her back cut her musing dead.

Ruby gasped, the impact pushing her forward. She stumbled, adrenaline kicking in, and grabbed out at the wall beside her. Her palms dragged across the stone as she caught herself, its rough surface biting into her flesh. Her body reeling, she glanced up.

A jolt shot through her.

The animal was blocking her path. Its sinister silhouette, with its misshapen edges, was unmistakable.

A strong gust rolled down the cobbled passageway, throwing cold rain against her back. Ruby shivered and shrunk into her jacket, bracing herself against the spray. If she stopped running, what was the worst it could do to her?

Soggy ribbons of unnatural red hair tumbled out of her hood, the damp strands sticking to the sides of her face as it fell free. Those teeth alone could cause some real damage.

Stomach churning, she squinted past the cat. The hazy glow of the corner shop winked at her from the other side of the passage, an odd guiding light in the middle of the murk. People. She needed to surround herself with people.

Breathing through her nose, Ruby steeled herself. She would charge at it and catch it off guard. Then, she would vault straight over its head and make a break for the store.

But as her eyes fell back upon the cat, she started.

She hadn't seen it move, hadn't even registered its presence, yet there it was, almost close enough to stretch out and touch. Its twisted body was flat to the floor, yellow eyes fixed on her.

Ruby squinted through the unrelenting rain at the creature, and *it* stared back. Its muddy eyes were large and round, and glowed in the evening dusk.

An instinctual tingle shivered through her. As its lips rolled back into a silent snarl, she noticed its teeth. Its lips stretched back, contorting beyond what was cat-like.

The sound of the persistent rain was like white noise in her stuck mind. Licking her lips, she squeezed her eyes shut. Blinked. As she returned to the smiling cat, they widened. No, smiling didn't do it justice. It was full-on grinning at her.

Ruby stepped back in slow motion, a soft undercurrent of fear oozing through her blood. Her hand gravitated towards her jacket pocket, to the comforting weight of the flick knife, and paused.

The animal bared its teeth in a silent hiss. Then, it sprang.

Ruby screwed her eyes shut in a knee-jerk reaction. A breathy scream escaped from her lips, body tensing for the painful impact.

Her hand closed around the handle and reflex gave way to instinct. That instinct demanded that she fight back.

Still with her eyes closed, Ruby tugged the flick knife from her pocket. She yanked the small blade vertical and slashed out at the space in front of her in one jerking movement.

Her heart sank at the pathetic display. Knife or not, she was *not* a badass.

When she felt the blade connect, she almost dropped it. A terrible hissing swung off to the left. A warm dampness, a contrast to the icy rain, spattered her fingers.

Ruby's eyes flew open. Heart in her throat, she searched the passageway, frantically spinning.

Gone.

She stopped and breathed out. The knife slipped from her fingers, clattering to the ground. Dark speckles dotted the stones at her feet. She'd hit it. Numb, Ruby lifted her hand and studied her fingers. Black.

Her sluggish mind twitched, coming back to life. She'd really hit it, and its blood was ... black?

Heart pounding with the euphoric sensation of being alive, Ruby gazed down the passage towards the hazy lights of civilisation. The cat-shaped thing was gone. And now, like it or not, she would never know its secrets.

*

Drayvex tracked the pulsing entity to a dilapidated building a short way away. Its outdated roof was thatched, and positioned in gold lettering above the door were the words, 'The Golden Spoke'. In the event that one couldn't read a simple sign, wedged into the ground in front was a large, golden wheel.

He scoffed as he approached the door, his steaming skin ebbing as he stepped under the small alcove out of the rain. Humans were predictable to a fault, with their habits and their rituals. Their fear of rejection made them weak and dispensable, and inferior. This was a common opinion among demonkind.

A less common viewpoint—one that involved thinking outside the rather battered box your average knucklehead demon clung to with extreme prejudice—was that at their worst, humanity wasn't so far removed from demonkind at all. Greedy, selfish, violent. Oozing with lust. Rotten at their core. Acknowledging these ties to a species that was best served raw and wriggling was just too much for some.

Drayvex frequently walked that fine line. He violated every rule when he world-hopped on the sly, abandoning his morals to indulge in the simple, sordid pleasures humanity had conjured to keep themselves buzzing in this dismal life. And when he was done, he slipped back into the vicious world that had spat him out and smiled as though he'd never left.

Regardless, he knew how to get what he wanted from these people—specifically, from the girl with his prize. He pushed against the door and stepped over the threshold. This would be child's play.

The girl was sitting alone at the far end of the dim tavern. As before, his eyes were drawn to the stone that dangled at her throat, to its steady sway as she shifted in her seat. As it moved, the air around it rippled and distorted in distracting ways.

The Lapis Vitae. The stone of life. Its power was absolute, sought out by weaklings and powerhouses alike for one reason: it made the claimant untouchable.

Drayvex ran his tongue along the tops of his pitiful human teeth, resisting the change as his fangs fought to emerge in the presence of the stone. The claiming of a Lapis Vitae was more than a one-off power surge; it was a contract. Once sealed, it protected its owner with unflinching loyalty.

The only way it could safely change hands was if the current owner discarded it or died with it. This made it almost impossible to steal.

Drayvex smiled, feeling his ego swell in anticipation of a challenge. Persuading her to cooperate would be simple. Whatever she loved, he could track it down and break it piece by piece until she begged him to take the stone off her hands. Child's play indeed.

It was *too* simple. No, he could think of an even better way to get what he wanted. A method worthy of his time. He tore his eyes away from the stone, and with great reluctance, made himself look at the girl.

She was petite, with a slight frame and bottle green eyes. Her hair fell down her back in a soggy cascade, its rich burgundy sheen a stark contrast against her anaemic complexion. The small stud in her nose, along with the unnatural shade of her locks, appeared to be her small attempt at human individuality. There was something about the way she held herself that made her seem older than she looked. Drayvex narrowed his eyes as he drank her in. Her body language hinted at insecurity, but her sullen pout said, 'bite me'.

As far as humans went, this one would be easy to manipulate. Maybe, when he was done with her, he would devour her. He smirked in response to that last thought and slipped across the room towards her.

The girl was oblivious to his presence as he approached her table. Despite having just battled a demon, she'd already dropped her guard.

He pulled out the chair opposite her, allowing the legs to scrape against the hard-wood floor, and sat down uninvited.

She glanced up at the sound, a smile forming on her lips. It slipped when she saw him.

She was expecting someone. Drayvex folded his arms and lounged back in the chair, making himself comfortable. He gazed at her with open curiosity, picking her apart.

The girl stared back with big eyes. As her blatant surprise morphed into something resembling the suspicion he'd expected, she pulled back from the table, her mouth setting into a sullen line. The corners turned down in the smallest of movements.

Drayvex could almost hear the cogs grinding inside her head as she looked him up and down, her attempts at subtlety falling short. He smirked, careful once again not to trigger the natural sharpening of his human stumps into fangs. It was harder than it should have been.

She broke the silence.

"Can I help you?" The tension was audible in the tightness of her voice. She lifted a hand to twirl a lock of hair around her index finger. A nervous habit?

Drayvex didn't immediately answer, allowing the moment to stretch and distort. A candle flickered in the centre of the glass-strewn table, throwing patches of moving shadow across her unblinking face. The living darkness at her throat throbbed.

When he was satisfied that he'd got under her skin, he leaned forward, resting an arm on the table between them. "Maybe you can."

He smiled, catching and holding her gaze, confident of his abilities. She may be physically untouchable, but Drayvex knew that there was more than one way to crack a nut. She was, after all, only human.

The girl lost her focus for the briefest of moments, her serious mouth falling slack, before bouncing back to its previous shape. She sat upright in one movement, her spine pressing into the padded back of the bench. The stone bounced against her chest and fell still.

"Are you looking for someone?" she asked.

The air around it thrummed. His demon blood screamed in his veins. His teeth throbbed.

Searching for a distraction, Drayvex looked down and noticed again the array of glasses on the table between them. He snagged a stray bottle cap and rolled it between two fingers.

"No." Hearing the new edge to his voice, he blocked out the stone's influence and continued. "I was wondering why you're drinking for two. Are we drowning our problems in whisky?"

The girl gaped at him, her small eyebrows raising, as though every pint-sized human drank this way. Maybe they did. Or maybe he was simply the first to call her out on a bad habit.

"Excuse you?" She moved in to grip the table. "What did you—"

As she leaned in, her arm collided with her current drink, sending it straight off the edge. She gasped and swiped for the glass, her delayed reactions not unlike those of an inebriated troll.

Making a conscious effort not to blur, Drayvex moved with preternatural reflexes. He produced the sloshing glass and placed it back on the varnished surface, sliding it towards her with the push of a finger.

The girl veered to catch it.

"Good save." She laughed once. The sound had a warmth to it, and he found himself wondering how often she genuinely used it. "Thanks. God, I'm a klutz."

Drayvex leaned forward, letting the table take a portion of his weight. Ignoring her gratitude, he picked up the discarded cap and span it on the tabletop. "Have you been stood up?"

She blinked. "*Stood* up?" She laughed again, this time without warmth. "No. I prefer my own company." Her eyes danced to the side of the room and then back. "Not that it's any of your business."

As he watched her stare at an interesting patch of wall, it was obvious that she thought she could lie to him. However, he didn't find it hard to believe that she preferred to be alone. "That so?" he murmured, using his mind to spin the cap. "Well, then you must be good company." He let it wobble and drop.

"Hey, *Rubeey!*"

Drayvex turned and clocked the tall, ginger mop bobbing towards their table.

"Ruby!" The mop stopped to hover behind Drayvex's left shoulder. "How are you, girl? Haven't seen you in ages."

The girl visibly cringed as the boy fixed his attention on her, something that Drayvex took an odd iota of pleasure in watching. "Gary," she said, sounding resigned. "Yeah, I'm fine."

"You wanna join us? We're over in the other corner." The level of hope his voice projected was pathetic.

Drayvex watched the girl named Ruby flounder as the human named Gary mouth-breathed down the back of his neck. Then, after what looked like a fair amount of effort on her part, she smiled back.

"Actually, I—" She paused mid-sentence. Her gaze fell on Drayvex from across the table. "I'm here with someone. Sorry." Her eyes pleaded with him. She didn't *look* sorry.

Drayvex bit down on his lip, fighting to conceal a smirk. He glanced up at the full-length mirror on the wall opposite and studied the boy.

His beady eyes were gawking down, as if he'd just noticed Drayvex sitting there. His clenched fists told a different story. With the red clouds blooming on his cheeks and the indignant bulge of his eyes, he looked as though he'd just been slapped.

Drayvex bristled, his irritation overriding his previous amusement in watching the girl squirm. I'd be happy to slap you, he thought, but I won't stop there. Ignoring the weed, he focused on the girl as she communicated with him using subtle-as-sledgehammer eye gestures. He rewarded her with a smirk. Okay, I'll bite.

"Gary," he drawled.

It took the boy a moment to reply. "Who are you?"

Drayvex smiled without humour. Then, he rose to his feet and turned to face the boy. "I'm busy." He met the boy's gaze and straightened, matching him in height. "In fact, we're both busy. Ruby and I have a lot to talk about, and you're holding us back."

Drayvex moved in closer, putting his mouth next to Gary's ear. "Later," he murmured, allowing his voice to drop in both tone and volume, "we may not talk at all." And just because he could, he winked.

Gary's flaming face glowed as he stared back over at Ruby. She smiled at him, giving him a semi-apologetic shrug that was vague enough to confirm anything Drayvex could have possibly said. It was the final note in a short-lived, ginger opus.

As the boy turned and skulked away, Drayvex smirked, amused at how easy it had been to bait the boy.

Humans really were a cinch.

Chapter 2

*R*uby exhaled as Gary retreated, flame-faced. She glanced towards her new friend, wondering what he'd said to get rid of him. Looking down at her half-empty glass, she decided that she didn't really care. The cool of the rim met her lips, and she took another gulp.

He reclaimed the seat opposite and lounged against the hard wooden backrest, making it look comfortable. This guy, she thought, unable to look away. He would look swank in a bin bag. A grin pulled at her mouth.

The smile slipped as she clocked him watching her back, pinned by those piercing eyes.

Ruby squirmed in her own skin, suddenly conscious of her drowned rat appearance. Her heart pulsed in her throat. They were a strange shade, a powdery blue so pale, they were almost white. It was impossible not to stare. They were striking, and they stood out against jet black hair that she could only describe as organised chaos. His face was cold and handsome with a compelling still, like the calm before a storm. Her breath clouded the glass that hovered at her lips, arm frozen in the motion of pulling it away.

"Friend of yours?" His soft, masculine voice interrupted her reverie. It was smooth velvet and dark chocolate.

Ruby blinked. Where had *that* come from? She felt her face grow warm as she appraised the stranger at her table. She didn't fawn over men.

Taking a moment to ground herself, she licked her lips and replied, "he's a friend of a friend." Of a friend. "A bit clingy, but harmless enough." She owed him at least that much. He had just covered her backside, after all.

His gaze drifted to the wall behind her. When he looked back, he flashed her a smile that briefly touched his eyes. "Ruby, right?"

Ruby fought the ridiculous urge to finger-comb her hair. "Uh, right. And you are?" There was something about him. Something strange that she could see, but *couldn't,* like the faintest stars that you can only see in the corner of your vision. She just couldn't put her finger on it.

"Drayvex."

She nodded. "Well, thanks. It would have been awkward had you got up and left me. And a little sad."

Drayvex hummed in agreement. "The downside to preferring your own company," he said, his eyes lingering on her chest.

Ruby's stomach twisted. "Hey," she yelped, glowering across the table at him. He was a perv. Of course, he was a perv. She should have known that this was what he'd wanted straight away.

Drayvex reacted as though she hadn't spoken. She considered making her escape, and then hitting him over the head *before* making her escape, until a different thought occurred to her. Was he … looking at her necklace?

Taking the charm between two fingers, Ruby stared at Drayvex. His eyes followed it. "Oh. It's a family heirloom." She slid her thumb over the smooth stone. She supposed it was rather pretty. "I don't think it's worth much."

She swallowed hard as the words stuck in her throat. Memories of her gran, still tender, flooded her mind. Her heart squeezed. It was worth a lot to her.

Drayvex had a faraway look as he studied the charm. But as his eyes regained their focus, they flicked up to her face. "I'm sure it's valuable in other ways." He sounded serious.

Ruby stared. Was she that transparent?

Before she could respond, Drayvex rose to his feet. Then, without saying a word, he walked off, leaving her at the table.

Had she offended him? He'd seemed like he had a pretty thick skin.

Drayvex was back before she'd come to an answer. In his hands were two tumblers of golden liquid.

As he reclaimed his seat, he slid one across the table, skimming it through the middle of the empties in a casual display of skill. The liquid inside sloshed up to the rim in a heady, honey coloured wave.

"To dodging life's idiots," he toasted, draining the contents of his own glass in one.

Ruby smirked, unable to disagree with such a simple toast. She picked up her own. "To freedom," she echoed, draining the glass and slamming it down.

The wheezing jukebox sprung to life. Her favourite song drifted across the tavern and the background hum rose to a murmur, matching the song's energy.

Ruby unbuttoned her shirt as the drink burned a trail down her throat. She was starting to feel them *all.*

"You never did say what problem we're ignoring." He flicked a stray peanut across the table, which bounced off her arm. The ghost of a smile played on his lips.

So, they were back to this. She wondered what game he was playing. "You don't even know me. Why do you care?"

"I don't," he replied. "It doesn't matter to me what form your misery takes. I'm just killing time."

Ruby was lost for words. What a jackass.

"But I'm a good listener." Holding up two fingers, he raised his eyebrows at her in an unspoken question. A question that spoke for itself in a place such as this.

Basking in the soft whisky glow, Ruby fell back into the chair and gave a knowing smile. Two more.

Two *rounds* later, Ruby was telling her life story to the charming stranger at her table. She felt oddly comfortable talking to him, albeit with some effort, the drink slowing her tongue into a sluggish stupor.

"We've lived in this place for two years now." Ruby traced the swirls in the rustic table, her mind drifting to days gone by. "Mum and I. We used to live in Callien." When she didn't get a response, she looked up. "You know, the big city a hundred miles from here?" She smiled at his blank expression. "Not a local, then." Not that she'd ever doubted that. No one from around here looked like him.

Drayvex smirked as though she'd said something funny. "No, Ruby. I'm not local."

Ruby frowned. "That's obvious. Crichton is small enough for everyone to know everyone. These people have lived here for a *veeery* long time." She leaned across the table and cupped her hand around her mouth. "There are no secrets here," she whispered, feeling the drink buzz in her veins. "It's kind of creepy."

The corners of his mouth lifted. "I see."

Drayvex got to his feet. This time, he moved towards her.

As he took a seat on the padded bench beside her, Ruby was hyper-aware of him. They were now only inches apart, and despite having just watched him get up and move, the change felt instantaneous. It was an unpleasant sensation, not unlike being snuck up on from behind.

"So, what you're saying is, if someone were to see us here, together …"

Drayvex lay his arm across the back of her seat. This close, he was both glorious and terrifying. Ruby wasn't sure which one was winning. But as he spoke, her eyes were drawn to his lips, and all coherent thought began to slip through her fingers. She wanted those lips.

"… people would talk?"

Ruby leaned in. He was warm—very warm. A soft heat radiated through the thin jacket he wore, as though he'd been standing out in the blistering sun. As he exhaled, his hot breath brushed the base of her jaw.

"Um …" Struggling to hold on to a single thought, she scanned up. Their eyes locked.

Just like that, Ruby was snared. Those pale eyes seemed to contain such depth; a depth a person could get lost in. She couldn't look away. She almost felt like a bird, staring into the eyes of a snake.

Snake.

14

Ruby blinked. Wait, what was she doing?

She pulled back in sudden alarm, sliding away somewhat down the seat. She'd almost given herself to him right then and there.

Ruby placed a hand on the back of her clammy neck. She knew she'd been drinking. She could feel it in her system. The room had that warm, fuzzy glow that only alcohol could offer. But she was still in control and a long way from losing her inhibitions.

"Uh, yeah," she mumbled. "It would give them plenty to talk about." She peeked at him from the corner of her eye.

For a moment, Drayvex didn't move. His gaze continued to pierce through her, and in the eerie hush, Ruby could hear her heart throbbing in her ears.

Then, he threw her a half-smile. "You were saying?" he prompted, relaxing back into the seat.

Ruby breathed out, making the candle flame in the centre of the table flicker and dance. She ran her fingers through her tangled hair. What *was* she saying?

"You're a country girl from the city."

Ruby looked up, triggered by his words. They sounded all wrong.

Perhaps sensing her hesitation, he tilted his head in silent question. "Or, not?" he considered, his softly narrowed gaze making her feel inside out. It was as though he saw right through her.

Shaking her head, she pulled herself together and sat up straight. She was a *city* girl stuck in the country, without a doubt. But for two long years, Ruby had gritted her teeth and sucked up Crichton without complaining, for her mother's sake. Drink or no fricking drink, she'll be damned if she was going to crack wide open for some silver-tongued stranger now.

"No, you had it right. I'm a country girl." She pulled her face into a smile, the muscles in her face feeling tight and wrong. It was Sandra that kept her sane in this small, forgotten place. Thank god for her.

Drayvex smiled back, a small, almost non-existent gesture that spoke volumes. He wasn't buying what she was selling.

Ruby frowned, irrationally annoyed by this. Who the hell did he think he—?

"Ruby. Oh, *Ruby*." Sandra's voice sang out across the half-empty tavern, attracting the attention of the few occupants seated nearby. She weaved towards them, her blond pigtails bobbing as she bounced on the balls of her feet.

About damn time, Ruby fumed, remembering her original reason for being here. She threw a fleeting glance at her new friend and wondered how she was going to explain the man at her table in a way that didn't lead to a thousand questions.

"Rube, I'm so sorry I'm late. I got held up at work. The old hag just *wouldn't* let me go and—hello. Who's this?" Sandra ogled Drayvex. No doubt in a similar way to how Ruby had herself not so long ago.

Drayvex watched Ruby. She knew what he was thinking. She fidgeted in her seat, remembering her earlier protests of not having been stood up.

Ruby ignored Sandra's question. "Why didn't you call? I've been waiting here for over an hour."

"Well, at least you had company." She giggled, grabbing the nearest chair.

Ruby sprung to her feet, jumping straight to damage control. This was a recipe for disaster. "Don't bother, Sand. I've got to get back to Mum." Slipping into a jacket that was now almost dry, she fussed over the material, smoothing out the crumples and folds.

"Ugh, but I've just got here. What were you drinking, the special?"

Ruby started for the door, but then hesitated. Drayvex. She chewed on her lower lip, unsure of how to leave.

After a second's thought, she settled for a rather bland, "It was nice to meet you," before striding for the exit. Sandra would follow if she knew what was good for her. Ruby pushed through the door and stepped out into the cool evening.

Crichton had a certain smell at night. It was delicious and fresh, one of the few things she preferred about the country.

The door swooshed behind her. "I'm sorry, Rube. Forgive me?"

Ruby ignored her, setting off at a leisurely pace, her shoes squelching on the wet ground. It wasn't really Sandra she was mad at.

16

"*Ruby.* Who's your friend?"

She stopped and span, her feet crunching against the stones. She didn't see the point in playing dumb. She did, however, want to make Sandra work for her juicy gossip. "Who was who?"

Sandra sighed, slapping her arms in a dramatic gesture. "The guy," she pushed. "That guy sitting at your table. You know, the one you were talking to when I arrived?"

"Oh," Ruby said lamely. "The guy."

"Yes, you dummy."

"I dunno. He just invited himself over." No sooner had these words left her mouth, than she realised her mistake.

"Oh. Ooh, I seeee." Sandra winked, her blue eyes sparkling. "Maybe he fancied you."

Ruby felt her numb face glow. "Well, he's not from around here. Pretty sure he would have been just as friendly with anyone. You know, when in Rome ..."

They kept going, the two of them walking side by side in silence, their steps falling into perfect sync.

"But he was cute, though, right?"

Ruby laughed out loud, astounded at Sandra's one-track mind. She gave her friend a small smile. "Sure."

The remaining wisps of day lingered on the skyline, painting the streets in varying shades of dusk. She could still see his eyes in her mind. Like looking into a bright light for too long, temporarily blinded and seeing nothing but spots after looking away. It was hard to describe. Her stomach gave an odd squirm, reacting to the memories.

"I wanted to tell you something." A hesitant voice interrupted her thoughts.

Sandra's fingers picked at a loose button on her coat as she spoke, and suddenly, she almost seemed smaller, her naturally tall frame squashed.

"Okay," Ruby said, wanting to make this easier for her. "What is it?"

"I'mmovinginwithmydad."

Ruby was a few paces ahead when she realised that Sandra wasn't with her. She stopped in her tracks.

"I'm moving in with my dad."

Her head felt like a vacuum. But a different kind of emptiness was creeping within her, spreading with each second.

"Rube?"

Ruby turned around, blinking back a betraying dampness. She was leaving.

Sandra sighed and trudged towards her. Stopping a few feet away, she looked down at her perfectly manicured fingernails. "I'm going to work for him. Become his apprentice." Her voice was heavy, thick with forced enthusiasm.

Ruby groped around in her sluggish brain for an emotional response. What she found was an unwelcome throb of panic. "You're leaving Crichton."

Finally, Sandra looked at her. The colour in her face was gone. "I didn't want to tell you until it was set in stone."

"When?"

She opened her mouth, hesitating. "T-tomorrow. But, *but*, everything has happened so fast, and my mother is really keen for me to go, which—"

"But you hate your dad." Ruby was trying to understand, but it just didn't make any sense. "Why now? When was the last time you spoke? Did you even get a birthday card this year?"

"Rube." Sandra grabbed her shoulders and squeezed. "This is what I want."

"But-but why so sudden, Sand? I mean, if you could just give me some time, maybe I could persuade Mum that we—"

"Ruby, this is what I *want*." Sandra's eyes were wide and pleading. It was the kind of look that she often used when she was hiding something and didn't want to explain.

Ruby stared into the big blue eyes of her dearest friend and came to an understanding. This wasn't sudden. Just a well kept secret.

"Please, Rube."

How could Sandra just drop this on her and walk away? It was a low blow, considering all they'd been through. And yet, what kind of friend would Ruby be if she denied her this?

"I'll come back," Sandra said, emphasising with her eyes. "I promise."

Ruby couldn't speak. There was nothing she could say. As Sandra took her hands off her shoulders, the emptiness spread out from her chest. It was too much.

"I'm sorry," Sandra mumbled, spinning around and dashing off down the street.

Ruby watched her best friend flee, the sting of betrayal seeping in. What was she not telling her? Did Sandra not trust her after all this time?

"You're a coward, Sandra Serling," she blasted. Her friend's scarf disappeared around the far corner.

Ruby was alone.

*

Fate: the idea that a higher-power had some modicum of control over his life.

The moon was full and bright, an eyesore in an otherwise pitch black sky. It was a ridiculous notion on many levels. For one, having stood at the top of the food chain for most of his unnatural life, he knew there was nothing out there capable of backing up such a bloated brag. As a being that had both a massive ego *and* the stones to follow through, notions such as fate could kiss his arse.

On the other hand, it was after a day such as this that one had to at least consider it. He breathed out, blocking the moon briefly from view as vapour spewed out into the night air. He was thinking about it.

Drayvex stood on the wasted ground at the edge of the village, his focus clearer than it had been in years. What were the chances that, of all the times he'd escaped to Earth, always with a specific destination in mind, he would screw it all on this one occasion and strike gold? He had ended up in the one tiny spit of a place that was hiding the *stone of life*.

His fangs stirred as he reflected, extending in anticipation. He didn't believe in coincidence. What he did believe in, however, was opportunity. Now, fated or not, the stone and its powers would soon belong to him.

Drayvex crunched across the hard ground, manoeuvring around the mountains of earth in his path. Unlike the rest of this saccharine village, the dump that concealed his portal looked more like the end result of a personal grudge. The kind of grudge that would see him annihilate an entire populace on a whim and leave a smoking crater in its place. It was the perfect place to hide a demonic gateway. Still, Drayvex never left anything to chance.

Raising a hand towards a particular hunk of crumbling concrete, he reached out and hovered the hand within an inch of its surface. Drawing power from his core, he sent it down his arm to the tips of his fingers. When he felt it burn, he stopped. Then, inching his hand forward, he placed it on the concrete.

The portal shifted at his touch, throwing out judders of protest as it fought against his wishes. Drayvex held fast, absorbing the impact. Everything bent to his will eventually. It was only a matter of time.

The concrete rippled and pulsed one last time, and fell still.

Drayvex inspected the rubble, satisfied. Nothing else would arrive this way. Nothing with any real power, anyway.

He turned and slipped into the shadows, his business here complete. Any demon with a scrap of ambition would want the Lapis Vitae for itself. The stone, after all, gave life. Power. Granted finite creatures their maximum life potential and protected the most incompetent fool from unforeseen demise.

He licked his lips, his form slipping as he thought of the chaos to come. For a powerful demon, such as himself, the stone offered so much more than protection. For a being with a *in*finite lifespan, it was immortality.

Immortality and an infinite reign.

The stone would soon be his. And eventually, she would bend to his will too.

Chapter 3

Ruby sucked in the dewy morning air, absorbing country calm into her pores. Sandra was moving to the city. Today. Her best friend, moving on to pursue the bigger, better things of this world, while Ruby remained in sad little Crichton. Not a big deal.

Her lips formed an 'O' as she puffed out a slow stream of breath. It really wasn't. Really, Ruby should be congratulating her. Patting her on the back for achieving what Ruby herself had been trying to accomplish since she got here: getting out of Crichton.

Ruby grabbed the earbuds that dangled from her jeans and shoved them into her ears. A quiet walk was her favourite way to unwind. Even when she had no music playing, they worked like a charm. No one bothered her, and that was the way she thought best.

She moved through the village at a brisk pace, blanking the rows of quaint little cottages on both sides. Within their first week, Ruby and her mother had truly learnt what it meant to live in a village.

If she were to look up the dictionary definition of 'village', Ruby was sure that it would read, 'a network of gossips that feed on steady diets of Chinese whispers and homemade apple pies'. They were especially interested in her mother, who said little and never smiled.

Ruby had done all the talking. Of course, they meant well. But having only lived in the city, where strangers remained strangers and there was no such thing as mandatory small talk, it was still more than she was used to.

Spotting two women having a chinwag on their doorsteps, she waved as she passed, on autopilot. She needn't have bothered. They looked straight through her.

Rude.

Ruby balled her hands in her large hoodie pockets. She didn't want to be selfish. But the hard truth was, Sandra Serling had always been her safety net. She'd even followed them to the country when Ruby's mum was put on indefinite leave for her health.

Her feet slowed, becoming almost weighted by her thoughts. It wasn't unreasonable for Sandra to want out of this small, no prospect place.

'I'll come back. I promise.'

What hurt most was that Sandra didn't trust her. At least not enough to be honest with her. Instead, she'd kept her in the dark until the very last moment, causing them to part on bad terms. Well, she hoped her dad was worth it.

Ruby broke into a jog, following the curve of the pavement as it wound towards the park. Crichton Park was the pride and joy of the townsfolk. Like a rose amongst a bed of weeds, it stood out against the faded buildings on the other side of the fence. Its natural beauty was bewitching on the gloomiest of days, and none more so than the lake in its centre. Its glistening depths were clear and inviting, with the sun reflecting off its surface like a giant mirror.

Ruby jogged through the grounds, hearing the trees and bushes whispering their secrets around her in the morning breeze. Their colours were a treat to the eye at this time of year. Vivid and enchanting, seasonal fruits and berries crowded their branches, tempting those who walked by.

The village beyond was a different story. The locals had long given up on using their gardens, simply because nothing ever grew. It was the 'Crichton curse', a running joke that made tourists smile.

Today, Ruby was ignoring it all. She was on a mission that would be far from easy. Get her and her mum out of the country and back where they belonged. To the city. To *any* city, in fact.

She exited the park and kept going, heading for the boundaries of the village. Enough. Was. Enough.

All of a sudden, Ruby slammed into something, hard. Her earbuds were ripped from her ears as it launched her backwards. Her thoughts scattered like rabbits. Throwing out her arms, she flailed and caught her balance.

He was tall and lanky, with blond scruffy hair that reached his shoulders, and as her brain caught up with her eyes, she cringed. It was the paper guy.

Cheeks burning, Ruby waved in apology. "I'm so sorry," she panted, breathless. He'd come out of nowhere. She smiled at him, fighting her unwilling features. "I really should—"

There was enough time to throw out her arms, to bring up a knee. But Ruby didn't move. She didn't understand.

He slammed into her for a second time, his elbow meeting her stomach.

Air exploded out of her lungs as it connected, sharp and painful. She stumbled backwards, heaving as her stomach squeezed. Black specks danced at the edges of her vision.

The paper guy lurched after her, moving like a man possessed. "You *bitch!*" The words he spat at her from between his teeth were sharp and shocking.

Ruby's head snapped back as he yanked her closer. Her teeth clashed, catching on the side of her tongue. Seconds later, she tasted her own blood.

His movements became rough and urgent, his wiry fingers digging under the folds of her jacket. It was in that moment that she knew what he wanted. It hit her like a bucket of ice water. He was going to violate her.

Ruby twisted in his grip, fighting him with renewed strength. Adrenaline surged through her, bypassing her terrified brain. Not today, screamed her frantic mind.

Diving for her pocket, she reached in for the knife, but came up short. Wrong jacket.

Kicking herself, she brought up her hands and shoved them into his face. The man blocked her advance, knocking her aside with ease. As he slapped away her flailing limbs, his eyes were focused on her chest.

Panic throbbed in her veins. She was the daughter of a policewoman. But she couldn't throw him off to save her life.

23

Ruby scanned the space around her, looking for someone, anyone. What she saw was the far outline of old number twelve at her window.

Scream, pushed her adrenaline-fuelled thoughts. Make a scene.

Ruby screamed from the pit of her stomach. "Help! Help, Mrs T—"

Her attacker's hands flew to her throat, scrabbling with sharp nails at the base of her neck. "Shut up. Fucking stay *still*."

The curtains of number twelve twitched and fell into place over the window. Ruby could hardly believe her eyes. She'd ... been abandoned?

She pulled back, desperate to get away from his pawing hands. Her heart squeezed. Sandra had been right. Old hag, indeed. "Get-get *off me!*"

He didn't let go. Ruby's top popped open as the buttons were stretched to breaking point. Her necklace tumbled out from behind the folds of fabric.

Her attacker froze, her wrists locked in his large hands. His gaze slid back down to her chest and lingered on her exposed necklace.

Ruby fell still, first in trepidation and then in spreading horror as she noticed the greedy glean reflected in his eyes. He wasn't interested in her. He was a thief, and he wanted her grandma's necklace.

Fresh fire blazed through her. She swung up her knee, hard and fast.

The attacker twisted away from the contact, blocking the worst of the damage with his hip. But it was enough to loosen his grip.

Ruby twisted, giving herself a friction burn. She cried out, ignoring the sharp pain it brought, and kept going. There was no way she was going to let this scumbag steal the one thing she had left of her gran. No way in hell.

She threw herself forward, and at the same time, pulled with her arms. As he lost his balance, she pushed him as hard as she could, using their momentum against him.

It worked. Ruby ripped herself free as he fell backwards. She turned to flee —

—not fast enough. Ruby choked as the necklace was pulled taut, digging into her windpipe. A strangled whine escaped from her lips as he dragged her backwards. She couldn't get away.

"Give it to me!" he barked. His hand grabbed her shoulder and twisted her around. Just like that, Ruby was back facing those hard, greedy eyes.

One of his hands remained on the cord as he pulled at the stretching, faded leather.

"No. Please, stop." She heard the desperation in her voice, but she didn't care. He was going to break it. "It's not real. It's not worth any money. You can't— "

Just then, the man shuddered. He cussed and dropped the necklace, reacting as though it had given him an electric shock. A moment later, he was grabbing for it again, yanking at the cord.

"*No*, damn you," Ruby screamed, swiping for his eyes with her nails.

She missed as he dodged, though not completely. Her fingernail raked down the side of his face.

Suddenly, his eyes rolled to the back of his head. He stopped mid-grapple, the whites of his eyes filling the space. His pupils were swallowed. Ruby watched as blood welled in the little grooves between his lips. Was he having a seizure?

Her attacker blinked, his pupils reappearing. He tugged on the cord again, and the blood spilt over, running down his chin in a bright trail.

As his free hand fumbled at the back of her throat for a non-existent clasp, Ruby screamed at him from the pit of her stomach. "You'll never get it," she hissed, striking out for his eyes again. It belonged to *her*.

Unperturbed, he leered at her, teeth red and glistening. "You little—"

"Need some help?"

Ruby stiffened as a second male voice spoke behind her. It was an ambush. She was surrounded.

Before she could react, the earphones that dangled at her leg were snatched from her pocket.

Panic. "Hey, w-wait a sec." She braced herself for a second attack.

Quick as a whip, the thin wire slipped out from behind her and looped around the paper guy's throat.

He gave a choked grunt, one hand still gripping her necklace, as the wire bit into his flesh. His free hand shot to his throat. It was only then, trapped between the two men, that Ruby registered the heat at her back. A fleeting memory of a warm stranger teased at her thoughts.

25

The wire tightened further, turning the victimiser to victim in the blink of an eye. Her rescuer, as it turned out, pulled the thief backwards. Ruby was pulled with them both. The paper guy's grip on her slipped, and the street span as she slipped free from between the two tussling bodies.

Ruby hit the ground, her hands sliding against the rough gravel as it broke her fall. A wet warmth burst across the soft skin of her palms.

Sounds of struggle bounced around her. Kneeling in the middle of the road, Ruby let her buzzing head hang. She needed to move. She held up her throbbing palms for inspection and winced. She didn't have the energy to run.

Without warning, the area fell silent. Eerie silent.

Ruby stared at the ground, unwilling to discover the outcome of the brawl. What if it wasn't her new friend at all? What if it was someone worse? She tensed, readying herself to run.

"Still in one piece?"

The sound of his voice sent a jolt of alarm lancing through her. She jerked her head left and right, scanning the isolated roadway.

A pair of strong hands secured her from behind. Ruby stiffened as she was pulled her to her feet. She staggered forward, spinning on the spot.

When she saw him, she breathed out. It *was* her new friend. Thank god.

Drayvex was smiling, but it didn't touch his eyes. He folded his arms, watching her as she caught her breath.

"Yeah, I guess. I … damn." Ruby shook her head, glancing down at her stinging palms. They were a mess. "Your timing was impeccable." She attempted to collect her thoughts. She felt fragile, self-conscious. But she was definitely still in one piece.

She studied her rescuer, looking for signs that he'd been hurt. He wasn't visibly bleeding, and he didn't look like he was in pain, but …

"Did he hurt you?" Swallowing, Ruby looked around for the paper guy.

"It takes a lot more than that to hurt me."

Her gaze snagged on the shape just behind Drayvex's shoulder. The guy was lying on the floor several feet away. He wasn't moving.

Breathing out all at once, she allowed herself to relax. Out cold. She

26

returned the smile, drawn in by a gaze that was somehow both warm and cold at the same time. His melted chocolate eyes gleamed with unspoken secrets, flecks of green splashed within the brown.

She blinked. Brown? Their eyes remained locked, dark strands of hair falling across his eyes from the scuffle, and without understanding why, she knew she couldn't look away even if she wanted to.

He broke the stare, and she was freed.

Ruby's head span. His eyes had been blue the other day. Hadn't they? "Well, thanks. So much." She hoped she sounded as grateful as she felt, not as awful as she felt. "I owe you one."

Drayvex tilted his head to one side, his eyes narrowing as he watched her shuffle out from middle of the road. It was almost as though she'd said something he wasn't used to hearing. "My pleasure."

As her mind settled, her thoughts drifted back to the scuffle. Ruby's hand flew to the cord at her neck. She grabbed it between two fingers, feeling along its length for any kinks or breaks in the leather. It was fine.

She puffed out in relief, a soft chuckle escaping from under her breath. "I thought he was going to break it," she said, explaining. "But it survived just fine. Lucky." She didn't know what she would do without it.

"Very," said Drayvex, without a trace of humour.

Something squirmed in her stomach. She'd taken an elbow to the gut, and now she felt sick. "I suppose I'd better call the police." Ruby frowned. She'd much rather leave him on the floor.

Drayvex flashed her a smile. "I'll deal with it." He held out his hand towards her in offering.

Ruby suppressed her discomfort, irrationally unsettled. She was traumatised. She needed to rest. Her gaze dropped to Drayvex's outstretched hand and lingered there.

He was offering her earphones, woven through Drayvex's fingers. Once a source of joy, now, a weapon.

*

The mess at his feet groaned.

Drayvex looked down on the soggy remains of the human boy, the onset of a growl building deep within his chest. A pitiful specimen if he ever saw one.

He watched the boy continue his fruitless mission of dragging himself through the secluded passageway. The trail his body smeared across the cobblestones stretched from one end of the alley to the other in gory map, with vomit-stained points of interest marking the highlights of his suffering.

For the umpteenth time in the short period since Ruby's departure, the blond boy stopped. "What's ... hap-happening?" He heaved, his damaged organs shutting down.

Drayvex watched the subject crawl for a moment longer before his irritation peaked. Whipping forward, he plucked him off the ground and dangled him by his throat.

The boy struggled in his grip in feeble protest. Drayvex studied him with clinical interest. The stone had destroyed the boy from the inside out. And yet somehow, he was still squirming. This one *really* wanted to live.

He had known that the stone would protect her. What he hadn't predicted was just how powerful its defences would be for a mere human. Subtle, but deadly. This boy was toast.

Drayvex bared his extending fangs and struck. Plunging them deep into the soft neck, he clamped down, his fangs lubricating with venom.

The body in his grip shuddered in violent spasms as he ripped the throat open wide. A warm wave spurted upward, soaking him.

Drayvex dropped the body in a lifeless heap. He took a deep breath and pushed it out, feeling his irritation subside. Ruby was by no means a trusting person. Whatever secrets she was hiding, she wasn't giving them up so easily.

But all he needed was a crack in that door. And easy just wasn't worth his time.

The watery sun glinted off the crimson-stained street, revealing the series of macabre trails that trickled towards the drain from the body at his feet. Blood ran down his jaw as he licked his lips, dripping down to the puddles below.

What a glorious mess. It was almost a shame he had to hide it. Still, once he was done with Ruby, there would be no need to hold back.

Drayvex smirked. The boy had been easy to manipulate. He hadn't needed to use much power to convince him to steal the stone. He'd already been rotten. The do-gooding neighbours were equally pliable.

After Drayvex had set the pieces in motion, everything had fallen neatly into place. Ruby had been so grateful for his intervention, it hadn't even occurred to her that he might be the cause of her troubles.

The girl and the stone would soon be his. That necklace couldn't protect her from him forever.

Chapter 4

Ruby perched on the edge of the bed, weaving her fingers through her hair. This morning's shift had been an endless string of rude customers and sarcastic remarks, the latter courtesy of her boss.

Weary, she puffed out her cheeks, sliding her work bag under the bed with a foot. They wouldn't have to be here for much longer. Not if she had anything to do with it.

Her feet sunk into the carpet as she crossed the room. Ruby had always known that she was unusual, not least because she was drawn to unusual things. Her bedroom was a showcase of mysterious objects and broken things, collected over the years. Their strange, exotic shapes had been fuel for many a fantastical daydream.

As she passed the dresser, her fingers brushed over the soft curves of the black-skulled candle, its six carved faces all looking out around a thick, black wick. Car boot sale, three years ago. It still gave her pleasant chills.

Pausing to gather her wits, she hovered at the bedroom door, before pulling it open and heading downstairs. This was going to be interesting.

The cheap kitchen radio was churning out the latest pop catastrophe, filling the room with its repetitive background drone. She heard it but didn't process the words. Sandra hadn't even told her where she was going. Was Ruby supposed to wait for her to remember her friends and get in touch?

Old hinges creaked. Her mother shuffled into the room, slippers sliding on the linoleum floor. "Are we in a better mood today?"

Ruby's knife hovered over the bread as she processed those words. Placing it on the counter, she sucked in a breath. Out of the many ways to make peace with someone, starting with 'are we in a better mood today' was not one of them.

"I'd much prefer to be friends."

Ruby fixed on an interesting mark on the cupboard at eye level. "Have you considered my proposal?" Her nails tapped with a life of their own against the counter.

Chair legs scraped against the floor behind her. Ruby waited for the usual arsenal of excuses her mother saved for their feuds about Crichton life.

"Ruby Peyton, if you think this is a conversation that is going to end well, then you've got another thing coming, young lady."

She turned to stare at her mum, her mind reeling. She couldn't believe what she was hearing. "You're shutting me down, now? That's not how this works."

She watched her mother, her flyaway curls hiding everything but the tip of her nose as she avoided eye contact.

Ruby sighed. She knew she shouldn't bite back. It wasn't helpful, and it wouldn't get them out any faster. She moved around the large circular table until she was opposite the woman seated there. "Ignore me," she pleaded. "Work was tough."

Her mother looked up, her face all hard lines and soft expression. "Life is tough," was her response.

Ruby groaned and headed for the lounge.

The room was in darkness. As she walked in, she stubbed her toe on a hard object. Blind and cursing, she tumbled forward. She caught the sofa with her raw hands and hissed in, the fabric making them throb afresh.

Ruby ripped the curtains open, bathing the room in light—and froze.

The room looked as though it had been ransacked. Papers were scattered about the floor, boxes lay on their sides, contents spilling out across the room. Every drawer and cupboard was open.

"Mum?" Ruby raised her voice. "Mum!"

Her mother stuck her head into the room a moment later, squinting against the light. "What?"

"What is this?" She gestured around the room.

Her mother stared vacantly at the mess. "I was looking for your grandma's lighter."

Ruby blinked. Smoking again.

She ran her fingers through her hair. "Why?" Ruby whispered. "You quit years ago." Sandra would know how to deal with this. She was a negotiator.

"*The* lighter. You know, your grandma's silver one. Where is it, Ruby?" Her mother's voice was accusing and highly strung. "What have you done with it? It's important."

"Me? Why would I need it?"

"Don't play games with me, I have a blinding headache. Where have you put it?"

Stay calm. "I don't have your bloody lighter, Mum. You're delusional."

"Ruby Peyton, if you're going to speak to me like that, you can get out."

"Fine. I can't do this any more."

"How many times do I—"

"You can stay. I'll pack my bags."

A heavy silence pressed down on them. Neither moved.

Without another word, Ruby scooped her bag up from the floor and stormed past the hunched figure in the doorway. Her stomach squirming, she headed for the front door. This wasn't happening.

As she passed the telephone table in the hall, a flash of silver caught her eye. It was the lighter. A hot wave of petty anger washed over her, and as she passed by, she swiped it from the surface.

She'd fix this later. Right now, she just needed to be alone.

Her mother was a damn good policewoman. She was compassionate and stood for no nonsense. She was *good* at her job.

Before the incident, Ruby had been a personal assistant to a rising young artist. It wasn't her first choice of job, but life was interesting, sometimes challenging. Since moving to Crichton, her career had been put on indefinite hold.

Ruby watched the sunrise from her clifftop perch, huddled into herself. A shudder ran through her as the morning chill bit through her thin jacket. This village was eating away at her. The isolation. The mundane repetition. Every day, it seeped into the edges of her mind, like a slow but persistent leak.

The rising sun was her favourite thing in the world. It was the dawn that brought the hope of a new day. It had always had that magical feel to it, as though in that small window of time, you could accomplish anything.

Even the sunrise had lost its power, of late.

Her fingers combed the soft grass beneath her as she sat, lost in her own mind. She didn't blame her mother for their new life. She blamed the thug who'd shot her mother for a few handfuls of cash. Ruby had given up everything to help her recover and she would do it again in a heartbeat.

Still, the thought of working at Brinley's Bed and Breakfast month after month, with no end in sight, was more than she could stand.

Ruby breathed in the cool morning as she gazed out at the endless sea. Calm and still. One day, she would pick a spot and sail until she found somewhere new. Moving on because she could, taking nothing with her but her wits, and enough food and water to survive.

That day was not today.

Ruby pocketed her numb hands and froze as her fingers brushed against metal. She pulled the lighter out of her pocket and studied it, chin resting on her knees. She squirmed, regret already pooling in the pit of her stomach. That one was going to haunt them both.

She popped the old lighter, summoning its light—and frowned.

She flicked the button again, and then again. Its empty click was the only sign of life. Wrinkling her nose, she bounced the lighter off the ground beside her. A spark popped where it landed, making her jump.

"I'm sure the grass would prefer *not* to feel your wrath," said a voice behind her.

Sitting bolt upright, Ruby glanced around her, trying to locate the voice.

"Drayvex?" Patting the grass for the lighter, she twisted towards his voice.

A shape emerged in the soft morning glow and became a person, details sharpening as he stepped into her immediate space. "When this place goes up, *I'll* know who to blame."

Ruby looked up, squinting at Drayvex against the painted sky. His voice was light, teasing. She looked back out to sea. "Then I'll have to buy your silence."

Drayvex sat on the grass beside her, and she immediately felt his warmth. Like the embers of a dying fire. She frowned.

"Can you afford my price?" His voice was low. Compelling.

A shiver of something not entirely unpleasant ran down her spine. "Of course. Name it." Hand finally landing on the lighter, she grabbed it and held it upright.

Something popped sharply next to her. Ruby jumped and turned towards the new light.

Drayvex was holding his own flame, the flickering tongue illuminating his face. "I see. Well, in that case, I'll take your soul."

His face was serious. Ruby stared at him, her stuck mind empty of witty comebacks. "My what?"

Drayvex smirked. His smile was fleeting, but traces of humour lingered in his eyes. "You drive a hard bargain. I suppose I'll settle for an IOU."

Ruby smiled back, despite the weight in her stomach.

"So, what's a city girl doing in a small country hole?"

His words caught her off guard. Of course, he'd figured her out. "Well, I ..."

Drayvex's eyes lingered on her face. He seemed genuinely curious.

The same tired old lie hung on her lips. *Why would I want the stress of the city when I have this carefree place?* The words never came. She was homesick. And so tired of pretending. "I do miss it. A lot. This place doesn't compare."

Bottled frustrations bubbled to the surface. "I miss the noises, the smells. I miss my old job. My friends. The night life. The pulse of the city itself." She paused. "But ... –"

Drayvex was the picture of still. "But?"

Ruby hesitated. It wasn't a secret that she mourned for the city. Anyone who knew her would say this. But the fact that she wasn't coping? That part wasn't so public.

"My mother had an incident at work." Ruby reached out towards the flame in his hand, barely even seeing it, lost in her own thoughts. Her finger skimmed over its tip. "Moving here was supposed to calm her nerves. Help her forget about things for a while. Now she's stopped caring about anything, and she doesn't want to leave."

"What about you?"

Ruby shrugged. She couldn't stay here indefinitely, but could she really just move on and leave her mother to it? "I just, I can't do this without her."

Drayvex was watching the horizon. "Who?"

Ruby looked out to the sea. "My best friend. The person that made living in this place bearable." The last sliver of darkness hung on the edge of the new day, clinging to the night as though it could bring it back through sheer will. "One day, we're great. The next, she up and leaves without a word of explanation. The only thing she gives a damn about is herself."

Drayvex looked around, triggering an uncharacteristic shyness. "Right. But if *you* don't give a damn enough to change your life, then why should anyone else stick around?"

Ruby felt those words sink in. "I—that's not ..." They stung. Sandra was out there, doing something with her life. She, Ruby, was serving coffee and indulging her mother's new hermit lifestyle. "You certainly have a way with words," she said, the lingering bitterness in her voice sounding like sarcasm.

Drayvex smiled, a sly look illuminated by the firelight. "I'm keeping a tab. This doesn't come free, you know."

"Ha, ha, ha." Funny guy.

The flame in his hand flickered, shivering in the morning breeze. Ruby stared at it, hypnotised. She couldn't remember the last time anyone had been so direct with her.

Making up her mind, Ruby took a deep breath. "Do you think I should move on, too?" It was a question that she wrestled with on a daily basis. She had yet to find the answer.

Drayvex looked up, meeting her gaze. His expression was unreadable, but as the seconds ticked by, something changed in his eyes.

After a moment, he smiled, a small smile that pulled at the edges of his mouth. "Is your freedom more important than your mother? If so, why wait until tomorrow, when you could be a hundred miles away by dusk?"

Ruby bit her lip. She knew it. She *was* being selfish.

Drayvex's smile slipped as he studied her. An odd expression flickered across his features, before they settled on cool indifference. There was something about him. He was hard and soft, all at the same time, just like her mother.

He was watching her back. Watching her every move, as though she was some rare specimen of insect. Just like at the tavern.

"What about you?" she jabbed, keen to shift the focus. "Surely, you must have ties of your own back home?" She was doing all the talking.

Drayvex's eyes gleamed with untold secrets. "Irrelevant."

She couldn't tell if he was laughing at her or enjoying a private joke. "Irrelevant?"

"Any ties I may have bear little significance to my actions. I'm here now because I want to be. The very word 'tie' describes a compulsion to carry out an action against your will. I never do anything I don't want to do. Therefore, these *ties*, as you put it, have no power over me. Their existence is irrelevant."

Ruby studied her mysterious new friend. His expression and body language were devil may care.

As she processed his brazen words, a bitterness crept through her. It must be nice to wake up and go wherever you want, whenever you want, she thought, squashing the stab of jealousy that followed.

Taking a deep, cleansing breath, she made a decision. "Well, my ties are waiting for me back at home. I suppose I'd better salvage what I can."

Drayvex gestured to her with a slight nod. "Seize the day."

Ruby smiled.

*

The small, green house was exactly the same as all the others in its row. Its rooftop was red and the door identical to its neighbours, right down to the last saccharine swirl—with one exception. *This* one contained the Lapis Vitae.

Drayvex probed the house with mental feelers, not bothering to contain the power he knew would fill the vicinity as a result. There were two humans inside the building; one on the upper floor, one on the level below. He didn't need to probe any deeper to decipher which was Ruby.

He shifted in the pseudo darkness, his pinpoint focus drawn to her. The delicious black aura that surrounded her had been distracting at first. Its perpetual presence teased at his demonic nature, tempting him out of hiding behind its human shield.

Drayvex lingered on the aura for a moment more, before delving deeper, to the girl herself. Her heart pumped blood around her body, its beats strong and even. Her breathing was slow and shallow, her body resting. Normal processes for a normal human.

As he probed her, a menagerie of scents overwhelmed him, triggering the sharpening of his teeth, the lubricating of his venom ducts. Appearing as someone Ruby classed as normal was a constant battle against nature. He needed her to trust him, which wasn't going to happen if he grew fangs and claws mid-conversation.

Quelling his desire to feed on the girl was part of the job. But ignoring the tantalising lure of the Lapis Vitae had proved to be more of a challenge than he'd anticipated.

As he brushed his power over her, she stirred, her heart rate spiking.

Pulling his probing strands back a touch, Drayvex moved to the ground floor, continuing at half the power. It was no matter. Since committing himself to the pursuit for immortality, he'd discovered a new trick. Not only could he enhance his senses to ridiculous levels, as he already well knew, but he could also shut them off. This was a new experience, even for him.

Drayvex couldn't recall a single moment of his unnaturally long life where making himself weaker was had been a game-changer. As a Demon Lord, power was everything. Strength was paramount. And having more of both than anything that challenged you was key in maintaining his ungodly status back home.

But here he was. Dulling his senses to gain Ruby's trust.

As a low-level demon moved into his immediate vicinity, his attention was pulled away from the house. He identified the intruder immediately.

"You have five seconds to explain yourself." He spoke to the spot where his minion's aura thrummed against his active power. Worthless ingrate.

The silence stretched.

Drayvex felt what little patience he possessed unravel. "You know better than to keep me waiting, Kaelor."

The demon materialised under the sprawling lamplight a few feet away, cowering on the spot like a wounded animal. "My Lord," he rasped, bowing his head. "Forgive me. I hardly recognised Your Greatness in this form."

Drayvex glared down at the demon, breathing out through his nose. "Speak. *Now.*"

The demon crouched low to the floor, but his eyes rose upward. "My Lord, the lands become restless in your absence. The throne that grows cold is—"

"That's why you're here?" He lowered his voice, letting ice drip off his every word. "You ignore a direct order and compromise my plans—plans beyond your minuscule comprehension—to bring me back against my will?"

Kaelor opened his mouth. Nothing came out.

"No, don't speak. Listen." Drayvex crouched down until he was face to face with his dense but devout familiar. "I am here because I wish to be. I will remain here until I see fit. You will not follow me. You will not make demands and you will not question my decisions."

"Yes, of course. But—"

"This is your only warning, Kaelor. A warning that you do not deserve. Try me, and you will meet the same fate as any other worm that gets in my way." Drayvex rose and grinned, revealing a full mouth of fangs. "Do you understand?"

The demon nodded, mouth firmly glued shut.

Satisfied, Drayvex looked back towards the little house and narrowed his eyes in thought. Just a little more pressure was all it would take. The girl that had weakened Ruby's resolve may as well have held the door open for him. She was easier to manipulate when she was broken.

"I'm close to something big, Kaelor. Can you feel it?" His mouth twitched. Of course he couldn't. He was no better than the girl in that respect.

"Feel it? I-I leave such privileges to Your Grace."

Drayvex scoffed. He needn't think flattery would get him anywhere. Still, he was useful in other, more interesting ways. "I want you to do something for me. Do you think you can manage that?" He heard the patronising intonation in his voice and watched the demon at his feet squirm. This one had always been easy to mould. Regardless, this wasn't why he kept him around.

"Of course. Your orders, My Lord?"

Drayvex let his eyes rise to the top left window of the house across the street. "There," he said. "I want you to work on the girl in that building. Do what you do best, then bring what you reap back to me. Is that understood?"

Kaelor looked up towards the window, his long tongue dangling from the side of his mouth. "The girl. Consider it done, My Lord."

"You are not to touch her, and you are not to be seen. Is that clear?"

"Of course, My Lord. The little human is prickly. Kaelor doesn't need to be told twice."

"Oh, and Kaelor?" He paused, waiting until the demon's focus had switched back to him. "You're a cat, not a bloody dog. *Act* like one!"

"Um, yes. Affirmative."

Drayvex glared down at the demon. The idiot had no idea what he was talking about. "Go." He turned his back on Kaelor, and heard the pop of his exit. That wasn't one he would win tonight.

Drayvex lingered outside the house for a period more, mulling over his next few moves. Her weakness was her mother. She was the chain around Ruby's ankles. His gaze slid down to the first-floor window, the only one that had any light. Perhaps it was time he paid this mother a visit.

He smiled, slipping towards the house. Tomorrow, he was going to get his way, and by nightfall, he would have everything he wanted.

Chapter 5

*T*he front door was unlocked.

Drayvex stepped over the threshold of the green house, and closed the door behind him. Really, they were all but inviting him inside. Who was he to refuse such an offer?

He walked into the first room, tracking the non-Ruby presence. As he entered, he stopped in his tracks.

His first thought, as he scanned the room and its contents, was that something had beaten him to the punch. Got here before him, ransacked the place and taken anything remotely useful. No sooner had this thought entered his mind than he dismissed it. No demon looking for valuable information would make such a spectacular mess without breaking anything.

"You must be Ruby's mother," Drayvex said, speaking to the far end of the room.

The small woman had her back to him. She was hunched over a desk, motionless, as though absorbed in what was on top.

Drayvex wasn't fooled. Her heartbeat was quick, her postured stiff and ready. She knew he was there. "I've heard so much about you. I feel like I know you."

Her breath hitched.

Drayvex approached the woman, stepping over the cluttered assortment of objects around his feet. He moved slowly, deliberately, allowing her to track his footsteps.

By the time she reacted, he was right behind her.

The thin woman whipped around, putting a handgun in his face. "Stay back," she demanded in a quiet voice. "It's loaded." Her heart raced, but her aim was steady. A near-perfect still. "What do you want?"

Drayvex smiled, unperturbed. "I'm a friend of Ruby's. Speaking of, does your daughter *know* of her mother's spirited way of greeting guests?"

The woman stared at him with hard eyes that hinted at an impenetrable exterior, and pink swollen rims that suggested otherwise. A contradiction of a creature if he ever saw one. He narrowed his eyes, studying her. She had a thin, wiry frame that boasted an active lifestyle, but her pallor and posture were anything but healthy. *Used* to be active.

"She … that's not …" The fear in her features was masked by an air of sullen defiance. Drayvex caught a glimpse of Ruby in her face, which quickly disappeared.

She aimed the gun at him for a few seconds longer, before lowering it a fraction. Her mouth set into a thin line. "It's the middle of the night." She shook her head, the corners of her eyes creasing. "Tea?"

Drayvex put his hand on the barrel of the gun and pushed it down to face the floor. "No."

The woman's breathing evened, slowing as seconds passed. She looked back down at the gun in her hand.

"Where did Ruby get her necklace?"

A clock ticked on the mantelpiece. Slow, heavy. "Her grandma. Coffee?"

"No. And where did Grandma get it?"

The gun raised a fraction. Drayvex took her wrist, immobilising her arm. The crazy mare would wake Ruby any minute now. That wasn't going to happen.

She shifted in his grip, her glare boring into him. "I don't know," she said, raising her voice. "It looks old as hell. It's a part of the family now. Who did you say you were, again?"

Drayvex watched her eyes as she spoke, measured her pulse, her facial movements. She wasn't lying. She was utterly clueless.

"Ruby's in bed. Come back later."

A flash of annoyance flared inside him, brief but destructive. Maybe she knows something she doesn't know she knows, he thought, glaring down at the feeble woman still in his grip.

"Later," he said, putting his free hand on her shoulder. She tried to step back, but Drayvex held firm. "I'm afraid that just doesn't work for me."

He struck out at her in a psychic attack, pushing his way deep inside her mind. He met staggered resistance. The woman struggled in his grip, letting out a soft whine as he hit her mental barriers. Drayvex pushed harder. *Be still*, he projected.

She complied, falling limp. The gun clattered to the floor. Her walls fell at his touch.

Drayvex set to work, recalling memories from the past five minutes. He combed through her responses to his questions, analysing her private thoughts and triggered memories.

Nothing. There was nothing new. Hell.

Drayvex pulled out sharply, causing Ruby's mother to shudder. She was pale, her eyes unfocused. If he pushed her any harder, he might as well just kill the woman.

He debated it, running over various schemes in his mind that might involve Ruby's defunct mother. If he killed her, Ruby would have no reason to stay in this miserable place. He'd be doing her a favour. Making his own life more difficult.

Making up his mind, he looked straight into her eyes and prepared to wipe her mind of his presence. The woman was more trouble dead than she was alive. Drayvex scoffed, somewhat amused by the irony.

Still, he mused, pushing his way into her mind once again. She may be useful yet. She was certainly worth a lot to Ruby.

Drayvex stopped. Something wasn't right.

He tried again, threading strands of power within the corridors of her mind. They hit a snag, a block of interference that diluted his strands upon contact. Drayvex pulled back, intrigued by the mystery this human's mind presented. Why could he influence her, but not wipe her recent memories?

He recalled more memories, going back further, to before their recent meeting. Twelve … twenty-four hours.

As he hit his limit, he paused in thought. Her life was mundane. Human. And yet, it was almost as though something had …

Drayvex promptly withdrew. It all made perfect sense. This wasn't her first contact with a demon. No, at some point in her short human life span, something had been here before him. Something powerful and *damaging*.

He paused, staring at the human in his grip. She stared back, her eyes glassy and distant. So, he couldn't make her forget. But his earlier conclusion still stood. Ruby's mother was worth more to him alive than dead.

Drayvex manoeuvred the fragile woman round to the right, then let her go. She dropped, collapsing onto the cushioned chair behind her. He turned his back on her, disgusted. Useless.

"Ruby … doesn't have friends … like you."

The defiant mumble that floated from the chair stopped him in his tracks. He stood, his back to the chair. After a moment's debate, he turned back to face the woman, curiosity winning over.

She lay slumped in the chair where he'd dropped her. But as he narrowed his eyes at her in thought, her shadowed eyes rose to meet his.

"If you go near her again … I will kill you."

Drayvex watched the broken woman who, quite frankly, had been at death's door before he even got here, threaten his life, and smiled. Despite himself, he found a grudging admiration for this weak creature with balls of steel. If Ruby was half as strong-willed as her mother, she may hold his attention for more than five minutes *after* he'd taken the stone.

As he made for the exit, he thought about Ruby. If her mother had had a mental tussle with a demon elite at some point in her past and lost, then what was *Ruby's* story? What was she hiding?

Switching trains of thought, he stepped back out into the night. If it came to it, the girl would have to decide whose word was strongest. Who would she believe; the person who had protected her, listened to her, who had proved to be dependable? Or her poor, demented mother who greeted people with cold metal and blabbed about demons?

Drayvex smiled. Tomorrow, it wouldn't even matter who she believed. Tomorrow, he would take the stone. And by the end of the day, he would be holding the key to the ultimate power play: immortality.

Morning, noon or night, the village of Crichton was unchanging in its simple tedium.

Drayvex glowered at the smattering of shrivelled bushes by the roadside, his already dismal mood plummeting. "What is it?" he snapped, irritated by the morning sun. "You can't possibly be done already."

A tangle of bony limbs and matted fur tumbled out of the thorny snarl, landing in a graceless heap on the pavement. Kaelor's bulbous eyes slid up to meet his, before shooting down to his boots. "My Lord, this is not about the—"

"*Get* up, Kaelor. Cats don't bow." Why the hell did he keep this idiot around, again?

The demon stood, wincing at his tone. "Of course. Apologies."

Drayvex narrowed his eyes, allowing his tight control to slip for a fleeting moment, and knew that they would be red. "Well?"

"I come not about the girl, My Lord. This is in regards to the portal."

The portal. Drayvex tapped his foot in a slow, thudding rhythm.

"Th-there's been activity. Demons passing through, not so long ago. One or two, no more."

Drayvex stilled. Through the sealed portal? Then they were weaklings. Still, his claws responded to his mood, the tips pushing through his human disguise. It didn't hurt to be thorough.

"Drayvex?" Ruby's voice interrupted his violent contemplation. "Is everything okay?"

Drayvex turned. She was standing right behind him. He stood on the spot, staring stupidly back at her. How had she caught him off guard like that?

"Are you okay?" she repeated. "What are—oh!"

He followed her gaze down to the sorry excuse of a creature at his feet and cursed. Kaelor was taking a large dump on his plans. Again.

Ruby's eyes grew wide. "That cat," she whispered. "I've ... seen that cat before." She sounded more like she was talking to herself than him.

Yes, you have. That was a mistake, too.

Drayvex glared down at his familiar and watched him curl in discomfort. At least *she* thinks you look a cat, he thought, giving him a black look. He would have to fix this. Now.

"Really? I'm surprised." He glanced at Ruby, flashing her a grin. "This flea-bitten stray doesn't look like it has long left for this world. I'd even go as far as to say that it's at *death's* door." He heard the icy undercurrent in his own voice and looked down at his familiar on those last words.

Kaelor understood the subtle threat. His eyes bulged, body crouching low, as though torn between fight or flight.

Drayvex narrowed his eyes. Kaelor bolted.

Ruby's eyes lingered. "I don't think it agreed with you," she said, her voice light and distant.

No, but it knows what side its blood is buttered on. He watched her as she chewed on her lip, her gaze dragging from him to the path where Kaelor had fled and back again. She looked like she wanted to follow the demon.

Drayvex folded his arms, studying Ruby for signs of mistrust or scepticism; anger, fear. He found none, which meant that she hadn't had a heart to heart with mother dearest.

"Where are you headed?" he said, fishing for her attention. He couldn't allow her to linger on this. Not when he was so close to getting what he wanted.

Ruby looked away. She gathered her loose hair over one shoulder, running her hand along the back of her neck. Her complexion was pale, her eyelids heavier than normal. Alcohol—or dare he think, something else? It was almost as though she'd had a *bad* night's sleep.

Drayvex smiled.

"I'm just off to the caf." She stared at him, her eyes glazing over as she took him in with drowsy calm. "Maybe I'll see you around."

She waved at him and left.

The caf. Drayvex watched her walk down the road, allowing the aura of the stone to tease at his senses. Weaklings or not, the demons would wait. It was time to make his move on the stone.

Drayvex loitered in the doorway of the small café, leaning against the worn frame. He scanned the room with vague interest, wondering how a place named 'The Cosy Corner' could look any less inviting. The furniture was faded and worn, with threadbare chairs that may have once passed for comfort, but now looked more itchy than inviting. Finances were clearly squandered elsewhere. But he supposed 'The Skinflint Corner' had less of a ring to it.

Once again, it took him less than a second to locate the pulsing beacon in the room. She was sitting at a window table, her nose buried in a book.

Drayvex watched Ruby through the eyes of a predator. Her delicate skin was almost translucent in the morning sunlight, her flushed cheeks a contrast to the rest of her milky complexion. Skin like that would surely show every mark he made, every bruise he would leave behind in his wake, like a canvas.

It would give her something to remember him by.

He started towards her, moving in slow strides. Maybe in the morning, if she was still alive and oh so lucky, he would let her live. Mercy wasn't in his nature, but on a good day, stranger things had happened.

Ruby looked up from her dog-eared book as he approached. "Hey." Her eyes flashed with a cheeky gleam. "Are you following me?"

Drayvex raised a dramatic eyebrow as he took the seat opposite her. "Am I—? Ruby," he deadpanned, "do I not strike you as someone who enjoys coffee?"

She chewed on a thumbnail, her smile vanishing and then returning after a moment. "I don't know."

He watched her as she adjusted to his presence. Demons *didn't* do coffee. Coffee was a human creation, and therefore unclean. Basal. Drayvex did coffee like a junkie did crack.

Ruby closed her book, disturbing the fine hairs resting on her shoulders. "This is the last place I would expect you to hang, though." She giggled at the admission, her green eyes lighting up.

"Right. Because I'm spoilt for choice." He allowed a touch of humour to creep into his voice.

"Ah. You mean Crichton's lack of anything remotely useful or modern." Pausing, she tucked a section of hair behind her ear, and stared at him with solemn humour. "I'd say you get used to it, but you don't."

Drayvex mirrored her, giving her his best poker face. "You don't say."

As he watched her swig her drink and lick the froth from her lips, he found himself picking her apart, trying to figure out what made her tick. His charged thoughts slipped back to the mother, his sprawling mind making connections. Was Ruby aware of the demon world, of the power she wore around her neck? Or was she a victim of happenstance?

The smell of burnt coffee filled the room, mingling with the array of scents emanating from the human across from him. He could smell the blood rushing through her veins, the unique scent of her skin, stronger than any other in the room. Coincidence? Or maybe he was losing his mind as he was denied the Lapis Vitae, again and again.

As soon as he opened himself to this assault of the senses, his body began to react. His teeth sharpened, lengthening inside his mouth unchecked.

Drayvex shut them out.

Patience, whispered a conceited voice in his head. She will come to you.

His gaze drifted to the stone dangling at her throat, and lingered there. This time, he didn't bother to conceal his interest.

Ruby followed his gaze, her own bouncing down to her chest and back. She clutched at the pendant in a subconscious gesture and traced a finger down one side of its length. "You like this?" She sounded surprised.

A slow smile spread as he tightened his focus, moving back up to her face. "It's unique." He leaned towards her, moving with weighted urgency. "May I see it?"

Ruby's breathing faltered. She stared at him, lips parted. Her fingers twitched, her internal struggle playing out over her person.

After a moment, she smiled. "Yeah, if you like." The conflict disappeared from her features but remained in her eyes as she lifted the necklace over her head. "I've had it since my gran died."

As Ruby held out the stone towards him, it swung like a pendulum, leaving a shadowy blur in its wake. Drayvex fought the temptation to snatch it out of her hand. Centuries' worth of experience told him that this would be an incredibly stupid move. Demon stones were known for being highly unpredictable, and indiscriminate when dealing out punishment.

He reached out with barely controlled compulsion and took it from her by the cord, careful not to touch the stone itself. The stone would react to his touch, and he in turn would react to *it,* giving the entire room the shock of their lives.

Drayvex eyed the impressive object dangling from his grip, feeling it pulse in reaction to his proximity. He smiled, triumphant.

Ruby wasn't paying him any attention. She was gazing out of the window with a faraway look on her face. Still, he made doubly sure that his eyes didn't give anything away. The eyes were the windows to a demon's soul. Most of the time, they were as black as his heart. On occasion, they would change to reflect a particular fleeting mood; but maintaining the blue eyes which she believed him to have was a challenge at the best of times.

Ruby's attention switched back to the necklace. "I don't think it's worth much. It's just ..."

Drayvex tuned her out. Now that she'd been freed from the protection of the Lapis Vitae, he would be able to do whatever he desired with her.

He studied the girl, watching as she twisted crimson ribbons of hair around a finger as she spoke. Ruby Red. What *did* he want with her?

Her eyes glowed with excitement as she enthused over her topic of choice. He wanted to devour her.

Drayvex felt the corners of his mouth twitch. But he was in a good mood. And girls like her were easily replaced. Common, even, in the cities.

Today was her lucky day after all.

Drayvex moved with precision and speed, rising from the table and placing his hands on either side of Ruby's head. He secured her before she had time to react, pushing his way into her mind. The minimal barriers she had in place fell apart at his touch.

You lost it, he pushed. *Your necklace came loose in the long grass just beyond this village. Clumsy of you; but you'll never find it now.* Planting the idea firmly in her mind, he slipped back out again.

She blinked at him, her blank eyes gazing straight through him.

Taking advantage of her brief stupefaction, Drayvex released Ruby and made his exit.

Lingering outside, Drayvex listened to the bustle and inane chatter that came from inside the building. His fangs pushed down, unrestrained at last, and he revelled in the simple moment, in the victory and the inevitable rapture.

Ruby didn't move for a full five minutes. He hadn't pushed her hard—he hadn't needed to. She'd been wide open to him when he'd accessed her mind. The stone, however, would have shown her no mercy upon release.

He could feel the Lapis Vitae thrum in his pocket. It yearned to be a part of him, and he welcomed the friction that burned in his veins. It fought to merge with his true nature through the thin barrier of his jacket pocket, and the result made him shudder with vindictive pleasure.

The sound of Ruby's voice floated through the glass.

On autopilot, Drayvex focused on her voice, and on the unfamiliar second. A persistent male was forcing his company on her, the seat squeaking under his weight.

Curiosity piqued, Drayvex turned to eyeball the helpful stranger through the window.

The man opposite Ruby was slight, but well built, with thick, blond hair that was shorter at the sides in a confused display of ego.

A frown flickered across Ruby's features as she struggled against the mental barriers he had put in place. "No, I was just with someone ... I think. I don't know where he's gone, though." Her hand wandered to her neck. Finding it bare, she ducked under the table.

"Well, why don't I wait with you? Jus' so you're not on your own." The man extended a hand and waited until she ceased her futile search for the necklace. "Sam."

"Ruby." She hesitated, before reaching out to take his hand.

Drayvex stood at the window, watching the blond boy's transparent attempt to win Ruby over. She was distracted and oblivious. It didn't deter him.

Why are you still here? nagged a voice, pulling at the back of his mind. You got what you wanted.

He wasn't sure what held him as he stood planning his next power play. But as he watched the human rat try to creep his way into Ruby's bed, he found himself wanting to eradicate the plague that had infested in his absence.

Drayvex watched the pair through narrowed eyes, judging the pitiful boy. If Ruby was naive enough to welcome in whoever came her way, she would learn fast.

Putting the café behind him, he left with the stone. It had been a good day. And now, nothing would stand in his way.

Chapter 6

*T*he knife fell to the floor with a clatter.

"What's going on in there?" The muffled voice of her colleague floated through the door.

A drop of blood splashed onto the white kitchen tiles. Shocked, Ruby checked her finger. A garish droplet oozed from the slice in her fingertip, spilling over. Springing up, she grabbed a handful of paper towels and pressed them against her finger. Crap, crap, crap.

"Ruby?"

Ruby dropped to the floor and soaked up the spilt blood with more towels. "Everything's good, Lyla," she called, grabbing the knife. "I'm fine."

'Fine' was relative. Her fingers wandered over her chest, searching in vain for the necklace that should hang there. How could she have lost something so special?

Dropping the knife into the empty sink, she removed her apron and hung it on the rack. She'd been here long enough. The walls were starting to close in.

Outside, she ditched her makeshift bandage. Sleep-deprived and moody, she could now add super-klutz to the list. It didn't help that every time she closed her eyes of late, she had the same recurring nightmare. It was a childhood special, but for one reason or another, it was back.

The walk home passed in a disengaged blur. Before she knew it, she'd hit the steady slope of the homestretch and was passing through Whittal Walk.

Ruby felt naked without that strap around her neck. The necklace had been a gift from her grandma on her deathbed. Since she'd passed away, not a day had gone by when Ruby hadn't worn it. It was irreplaceable.

For the umpteenth time that day, her fingers drifted to her chest.

She ripped them away as grief and anxiety swallowed her. For a few long seconds, she drowned.

Ruby tried to pull herself together. She would probably never see it again. That was life, and there was nothing she could do to change it. As this thought smothered her, something niggled at the back of her mind. It was a sort of knee jerk reaction. The long grass, just beyond the village. Was it there? Ruby lingered at the front door to the house, chewing on her nail. That was odd. Why did she think she'd lost it there? Shaking her head, she twisted the door handle and gave it a push.

The house was in darkness, but the clatter of pots and pans from the kitchen could be heard from the other side of the house, and her stomach squeezed in kind. Their stupid tiff had dragged on for too long. She hoped she could reverse the damage.

Ruby crossed the hallway and pushed into the kitchen. Her mother was rummaging through the cutlery drawers, digging with both hands. A large pot steamed on the stove and several more were piled up on the surrounding counters.

"What are you doing?" Ruby reached out, grabbing the top of her mother's arm. "Mum, stop. What is this?"

Her mum stilled, her thin frame motionless under the dim kitchen lights. "Mum, say something."

Her mother span towards her, her face serious. "I know I haven't been the mum you deserve in a good while." Her voice was raw, vulnerable. Ruby didn't like it. "God knows, if you have to leave, then I can't stop you. But I thought ..." She paused, stopping to run a hand through her flyaway curls. "Well. I thought that if I started cooking for you a little, then you might want to stay here, with me."

Ruby squirmed, hating herself. How could she do this to her mum, the one person in life who'd always been there for her?

Without another word, Ruby stepped forward and threw her arms around her mother's shoulders. "I'm sorry," she mumbled, squeezing. "I was being selfish. I didn't mean what I said."

The figure enveloped in her arms shifted, before wrapping a responding pair of arms around her. "You're not—"

"I'm not moving out." Not by herself, anyway. "I just miss Sandra. Her absence bothers me more than you can know."

Suddenly, Ruby was pulled back and held at arms length. Her mum gave her a meaningful look. "Is that all?" She squeezed Ruby's upper arms with surprising strength. "There's no *other* reason that you'd want to get away from Crichton?"

Ruby blinked. She seemed so serious. "I—no." What was she getting at? "Of course not. Why?"

Her mother licked her lips. They inched apart, as though she was about to speak.

Ruby mithered over the figure opposite. When did her mother get so pale? She looked almost ill.

Just then, her mum smiled, her eyes crinkling in that soft, motherly way that Ruby often missed as she blinked. "Good. Well, I'm glad we're okay."

As her mum reached out and tucked a stray lock of hair behind her ear, Ruby found herself smiling back. They were going to be okay. That lighter would never find its way into those twitching hands.

"Oh, but Ruby, dear. Sandra called for you while you were out. Why don't you have a chat?"

Sandra. Ruby's stomach fluttered. "What time?"

Her mum let her go, stepping back to rest a hand on her hip. "She said that she'd be near her laptop for the next few hours."

Ruby frowned at her mother. That didn't answer her question.

"Go and speak to her. It might make you feel better."

No, it probably wouldn't. Ruby made herself smile and kissed her mum on the cheek on her way to the stairs. "Okay, Mum. But no more cooking."

Her mum laughed, a short bark, before flicking her with the tea towel on her way out.

Dragging her body upstairs, Ruby headed into her room and fired up the laptop. The old machine wheezed through its start-up rituals, then sat on the desk, waiting for further instruction.

Ruby pulled off her shoes and dumped them in the cupboard. Then, she grabbed the laptop and carried it over to the bed. Despite their last awkward parting, there was a part of her that couldn't wait to hear her best friend's voice again. It felt like a lifetime since they'd seen each other.

The call rang out, and Sandra's anxious face appeared on the screen.

For five long seconds, neither of them spoke. Ruby licked her lips. Was this a bad idea?

Then, without warning, Sandra beamed, pulling her face into an overly cheery grin. "Ruby, there y'are. Talk about keep a girl waiting!"

Sandra looked well. She'd ditched the pigtails for a more sophisticated look. Grown-up, but still the bubbly, fearless Sandra she knew and loved. She was closer to her dad now, although their time together had been far from a father-daughter bonding success. She was learning feng shui and had a small dog named Tito. Ruby had to feign excitement at that point; her fear of dogs ran deep.

"But enough about me. God, why do you let me blab so much? I want to hear about *you*." As it turned out, they were both equally pro at pretending their problems didn't exist. "Tell me something good. Give me some juicy gossip."

"Juicy?" Ruby pulled a face, and Sandra giggled. "Are you forgetting where I live?"

Sandra pouted. "But this is *you* we're talking about. There's always something going on with you."

Ruby didn't know how to take that. But as she gazed at the face on the screen, she found her thoughts wandering into Drayvex territory. Oh well, that would certainly pass for 'juicy' in Sandra's eyes.

"You know that guy I was with the last time I saw you?" She gave a half-smile, running her hand along the duvet crinkles. "I've seen him again since. A few times, actually."

The brief pause that hung between them was followed by a squeal. "Tavern guy? Oh my god, Rube. You've been holding out on me."

Sandra may look grown up, Ruby thought, rubbing the back of her neck, but that was where it ended.

Ruby found herself telling Sandra more than she'd meant to. But once she started reiterating the past few days, it was hard to stop. Sandra had always been a good listener, at least for Ruby, and she always took her seriously.

Ruby's finger made soft circles over the enter key as she spoke. "Since he disappeared the other day, I haven't seen or heard from him. So I don't know where we stand. I don't even remember him leaving."

It was like a mental block. They were there at the caf, and then they weren't. "Maybe he told me why, and I spaced out."

Sandra snorted. She adjusted the bangles on her wrist then gave Ruby 'the look'. "Please. Even *you* would remember a conversation like that. Is it possible that this is all just a misunderstanding?"

Ruby thought about it. She looked at Sandra on the screen, the cogs of her mind turning. "Yes."

"Then talk to him. You know, communication? With your mouth?"

There was something else, though. Something that had been bothering her since the tavern. When she'd first met Drayvex, her instincts had pulled her in two different directions. Despite his recent kindness, there was *always* a part of her that was on edge in his presence.

Ruby shook her head. "I will," she said, pushing the negative thoughts to the back of her mind. Drayvex had been good to her. He deserved better than this.

"Atta girl. Hey, where's your necklace?"

*

Drayvex dangled the alluring object from a curved black claw, examining it in meticulous detail. The stone itself was a dull red. It wasn't remotely close to full power.

He winced as the fine strands of silver caught the sun and flashed, searing his eyeballs. Although, he debated, watching it rotate above the thirty-foot drop, a Lapis Vitae carried by a human would naturally see far less bloodshed than power demanded.

He shifted, adjusting his position on the roof of the archaic church. It was tall enough to provide him with a view of the pint-sized village in its entirety. Despite this, he wasn't up there for the view. He merely got a kick out of his ironic choice.

The wind changed, blowing the lingering scent of the girl towards him. Drayvex's trail of thought slowed. Ruby. He ran his tongue along a row of razor teeth, their tips extending in response to her strong human scent.

"It's impressive, My Lord. What is it?"

Drayvex took a moment to appreciate the scent, before switching it off. "This, Kaelor, is raw, unadulterated power." He glanced through the corner of his vision at his buoyant familiar, before returning to the stone. "That is all *you* need to know."

"Of course. Quite, My Lord."

Slipping the stone back into his pocket, he chewed over his next move. How much would be enough?

He narrowed his gaze, his shifting his focus to rest on a spot on the far horizon. He couldn't use the humans for this. Not that he didn't appreciate a slow, steady body count. He could leave a trail of bodies from one city to the next; a sporadic line of chaos encircling the globe, with violent ripples of backlash fanning outward alongside the trail's end, bringing him back to the place where it all began. But he still wouldn't have what he needed. And time was not on his side. He needed to think *bigger.*

Drayvex sprang off the roof and dropped, landing heavily outside the entrance to the church.

A pop to his left signalled Kaelor's arrival, his ability to teleport reducing the risk of him becoming a demon pancake.

Thrumming with power, Drayvex started to shed his human skin. Now, where had the stone been, he wondered, during his first decade on the throne? Where was it when he'd annihilated the entire warrior fae race, their dying throes saturating the air with power, going to waste as they drew their last agonising breaths?

Total annihilation. Almost. Are we counting the bitch that slipped through your fingers, these days?

Drayvex felt his mood darken. He ignored the voice. The timing would have been glorious.

"Looking, looking. They have no idea. Your Lordship has outsmarted every single one of them."

Drayvex paused, suspending the power within him that thrummed on the verge of a violent shift. He span around, flooring the scrappy demon with one look.

The lopsided grin slipped from the demon's mouth, his jaw hanging loose as their eyes met. He looking down in hasty submission. "I was only saying, My Lord, that they have no idea that the power no longer lies with the girl. They look, but they don't use their eyes."

The demons that came through the portal. "What did you see, Kaelor?"

"My Lord has outsmarted them." Kaelor grinned again, the glee apparent in his voice. "Kaelor saw demons, chasing their tails. Round and round they go, but their prize is always just beyond reach."

Drayvex frowned. The idiot never said what he damn well meant. Fortunately, Drayvex had learnt to speak moron long ago. Rogue demons were tracking the Lapis Vitae. And somehow, it was leading them back to Ruby.

He ran his tongue along his half-formed fangs. Could the Lapis Vitae still be somehow connected to its previous owner? If so, did it truly belong to him? The Lapis Vitae was now in *his* possession.

He watched the demon prance at his feet. Regardless, the stone's aura would be masked by his own powerful one, misleading any who sought to claim it. Ironically, it was the perfect set-up.

"Are we leaving, Your Grace?"

Ruby's face flashed through his mind. The demons would be attracted to her like a beacon. She wouldn't stand a chance.

"My Lord?"

Maybe *Sam* would protect her. He sneered. "You are. Leave me."

Kaelor knew better than to argue. Without a second's hesitation, he disappeared, a lifetime of servitude kicking out in an ingrained reflex.

The girl wasn't his problem. Her life meant nothing to him. Besides, she could be any—

'Your necklace came loose in the long grass just beyond the village. Clumsy of you. You'll never find it now.'

Drayvex shut his eyes, incredulous. Surely not. She'd have to be utterly moronic to look for one piece of junk in a sea of grass when she could just purchase another like it.

He opened his eyes, his gaze rising up to the dismal sky as he recalled her possessiveness, the way she stroked its edges when deep in thought. No, that's where she would be. Exactly where he'd sent her. Stupid girl.

Drayvex scowled, looking into the distance. Well, more fool her.

*

The last time she'd been here, the grass had been below her knees.

Ruby frowned. If it had been so long, then why was she here looking for her necklace? What a stupid thing to think.

She waded through the unkempt grass, letting her fingers glide over the tips of the yellowing blades. This was going to be harder than she thought. To top it all off, the sun was setting. She was on the clock.

Pulling back her hair, she dropped to the ground. It was pointless of her to come now. Deep down, she knew this. But waiting until morning would wear her out. She ran her hands along the damp earth, using her fingers like feelers. Admitting to Sandra that she'd lost a family heirloom would have only led to a nice long lecture on 'keeping things safe'. These lectures were worse than her mother's.

She stood, feeling for solid objects with her feet. Besides, Ruby already knew how it would have ended. *'Well, what are you still doing here, Rube? Go find it!'* Ever the optimist.

A sharp rustle sounded to her far left. Ruby stared at the patch of grass that had moved. Nothing.

Dismissing it, she continued her slow and strange tap dance through the field. Maybe she should go back to using her hands.

Another rustle broke through her musings, this time from her immediate right.

Ruby stopped walking. There were probably rabbits living nearby. She breathed out, running a hand through her hair. She couldn't afford any more distractions. The sun was setting fast, and soon she would be in darkness.

Another rustle came. And another. Ruby span on the spot and caught movement behind her. Was this whole field full of rabbits?

The grass just ahead parted. Something was moving towards her. Something big enough to flatten the long blades in its path. It sliced through them like a shark through water. Ruby's eyes were glued to the rustling trail. It was going to attack her. A weasel, or a stray dog, or a—

Her arm flew across her face. Stupid.

A crack echoed and resounded through the wide expanse of field. The rustling stopped all at once.

Ruby lowered her arm. The grass at her feet was flattened and bent.

Her heart pounded as she blinked at the ground. If something had been there, it wasn't any more.

*

Crack.

The demon's body shattered as it collided with the tree. Birds exploded from its branches. The surrounding trees undulated as the edge of the field shook with smaller blasts of life.

Drayvex abandoned the twitching body and focused on the second demon. He slowed, and without breaking momentum, allowed himself to unravel.

His form became a thick, black vapour. A pulsing miasma.

The somewhat dog-like demon panicked and scrambled, abandoning the girl as a bad job.

Drayvex floated with a menacing slow towards its face. It whined as Drayvex entered, sliding in through the nose. Its eyes snapped wide, its body growing rigid.

Now, Drayvex purred inside the demon's head. *We can do this the easy way, or the hard way.*

He could feel its fear, the surging panic of having its own body used against it.

Why are you here? And I don't want that pre-rehearsed shit about bringing me back to reign. If that were so, they'd send their best.

Inside its head, the dog-demon struggled, trying to regain some kind of feeble control of its tongue. Drayvex relinquished his hold a touch, allowing the demon to speak.

"For—for *you*, My Lord," it choked, attempting to find its legs.

Wrong answer, Drayvex blasted, snapping its head back. He felt a surge of pain course through his host body. *Why?*

The dog-demon whined in agony. "It's more than my life's worth." It tried again to break through his hold.

Drayvex pushed harder. *You know, some things are worse than death.* He filled its head with vivid pictures, the smorgasbord of suffering that he had at his disposal, even so far from home.

The demon's eyes bulged. Drayvex took advantage of its weakness. Springing his new puppet to its feet, he led it away from the field and its oblivious occupant, into the patches of darkness under the trees. And for dramatic effect, he inched its jaws open.

The demon panicked as it glimpsed what he was planning.

Yes, the hard way is a lot more fun. For me. Are you hungry? His voice became deep and monstrous, echoing inside the demon's head as he switched gears. *I can make you devour the meat on your bones. We'll start with the legs. One ... two ... three ... four. Then we'll eat your stomach, and watch as the chewed remains of your legs fall out of the gaping holes.*

"Okay," said the demon in a pitiful screech. "It's the stone. He wants the stone!"

Drayvex stopped and fell silent.

"Please. Have Mercy."

Who wants it?

The demon didn't respond.

Drayvex felt his host's fear once again. But this fear was inspired by something else. *Someone* else. He wondered who, aside from himself, could inspire that level of fear without being present.

Fine, he said, growing impatient. Drayvex span its head, snapping its neck

61

with a sharp crack.

He slid out of the demon's mouth, changing back into his human guise. He knew that the Lapis Vitae's attracting of unwanted attention had been inevitable. It had whispered to him not so long ago, taunting him with the tremendous power it promised. It had just been a matter of time before something else found it.

The question was, who?

Drayvex slipped into the darkness of the trees, his mind in overdrive. Someone not willing to get their hands dirty, that much was clear. Someone with influence. And power.

Chapter 7

*F*ate, it would seem, was not yet done with the girl with the demon stone necklace.

Drayvex leaned beside the coffee machine, trying to separate the smell of the heady black sludge from any demons in the immediate area.

He lay in wait in a shadowed corner, coiled for a fight. Exactly how he'd found himself back in this sad excuse for a café was something of a mystery to him. What he did know was that Ruby was now top quality demon bait.

This made her his unwitting siren call.

As the lanky waitress stepped across his line of vision, besmearing his view, Drayvex threw her a dirty look. She shuffled towards the high counter, knees bent as though the tray was weighted with lead. The stacked cups clinked as she dumped the tray on the only clutter-free surface.

"Move it or lose it, woman," he murmured, focusing on Ruby's steady breathing on the other side of the room. Deaf to his idle threat, the waitress cleared her entire tray before moving off, his words bouncing off his earlier influence.

Ruby was sitting by herself at the far window table. Preoccupied with whatever floated inside her head, her coffee was cold, and her gaze told him that she was present in body alone. She had been this way for the past hour.

Drayvex picked up a small, blunt knife with his mind. He snorted at the pathetic utensil, spinning it in the air in front of him. Only a human could put a weapon like the knife to such ridiculous uses as slicing food. The blade glinted under the cheap, fluorescent light as it span, and as he watched it flash in a steady pattern, his thoughts slipped to darker matters.

Any being that craved ultimate power would go on to crave ultimate status. His status. Therefore, if someone other than himself was making a move on the stone, it was only a matter of time before they made a move on *him*. And Drayvex made an effort to get know his enemies, intimately.

The waitress weaved between tables, swaying under yet another tray of steaming mugs. Drayvex had long ago memorised each of the small mundane rituals playing out before him. He never slept. But should he ever need to engage in such a pointless activity, he was confident that simply recalling these memories would see him through.

As if in challenge to his silent protest, two unexpected things happened one after the other, breaking the previous hour's pattern.

First, the lanky waitress tripped on her over-sized feet, sending an entire steaming tray sliding into the nearest booth.

Second, Drayvex intervened.

Dropping the knife, he reached out—a subconscious reflex to Ruby's imminent peril. Power shot down his arm, and with a mental push, he nudged the base of the tray.

Ruby half jumped, half slid down the booth, her inferior reactions sluggish and confused. She brought up her arm, shielding her face from the misdirected mugs as they flew through the air.

Several crashed across the table, hot liquid spewing uncontained. One smashed to the floor, exploding against the tiles. One went the wrong way.

Drayvex grabbed at the escaped mug, securing it with strands of power—and then caught himself. Why in Hell's name was he still protecting her?

For a fraction of a second, he suspended the precarious mug above her, searching for an answer. The clarity he found was unwelcome.

With a vindictive flick, Drayvex redirected the mug and withdrew his power, sending it back towards the feckless waitress in one swift action. The mug and its contents hit the waitress, who squealed in a strangled whine, her pointless fumbling pushing her further into the splatter zone. Ruby gasped in chorus, knocking her cold cup of java over herself.

Drayvex summoned the discarded knife, a vicious stab of anger surging through him. He resumed its spinning at a choppy pace. It had been an automatic reflex to protect her.

A nosy hum filled the room, the mutterings of rat-eyed observers picking for the scraps of the scalded waitress's dignity, killing the brief vacuum of silence.

His mind raced. For the time it had taken him to win Ruby's trust, he had catered to her petty human needs, fabricating for himself the necessary role of her protector. It had been a heavy contributing factor towards his success.

The lanky waitress fussed over her startled customer despite her own state, the sound of her profuse apologies rising above the background murmur. Ruby seemed at a loss for words.

Drayvex glared at the girl, his flesh searing with the responding heat that flared deep within him. He knew it was irrational to blame her for his own negligent behaviour. But the longer he stared, the more her presence irritated him, like an itch under his skin that couldn't be assuaged.

If you treated a pawn like a queen for long enough, the lies would eventually start to stick. *She* was a pawn. A basic piece to be sacrificed at a time of his choosing. That time was fast approaching – and—yet he was still treating her like a queen.

The waitress dashed back over to the counter next to him, a mortified grimace plastered across her face. She grabbed for the pile of towels at the sink, oblivious to his presence.

"Is there anything you *can* do?" he spat at her, regretting his earlier decision to influence her co-operation. "Oh, more coffee. Good. Are you going to piss this up the wall too?"

The large metal cylinder began to whistle, heating as she rushed off with dry towels.

Drayvex dismissed the bustle of bodies, focusing once more on the girl at the window table. He probed her aura, curious as to what he'd find with the stone now gone from her person. It was no longer black, but purple, and streaked with slices of darkness. Now *that* was interesting.

"Ruby? Hey, it's me. How's it hanging, love?"

He was surrounded by idiots. *Snack*-sized idiots.

"Sam?"

Sam. The name triggered a connected memory. Yes, the helpful stranger from his café victory.

Ruby fussed with her hair as he swaggered over to her table. "I … didn't think I'd see you again. Did you miss your coach?"

Drayvex narrowed his eyes, judging the unremarkable specimen that was making for her table. The boy couldn't have got what he wanted from her the first time around. That, or he was playing the long game.

Sam reached the table where she sat and paused, folding his arms in an exaggerated manner as he looked down on her. "You're wet. Didn't think it was raining." He grinned, looking pleased with himself, and waited for the laugh he clearly expected to follow.

Ruby obliged, smiling despite being the butt of the joke. "You know what, Sam? It's really not my week. Are you, uh, sitting?" She wrinkled her nose, as though this were a particularly awkward question to ask.

The blond boy took the seat opposite her. He didn't waste any time, leaving small talk behind from the moment he sat down. He proceeded to work on her with an expertise far beyond that of a simpleton who couldn't tell if it was raining.

Drayvex span the knife in the air as he analysed the boy, keeping a slow but steady pace. His body language played the part of the fool, but his eyes remained cold. detached. They told a *different* story. They were the eyes of a predator; a liar.

Takes one to know one, said the voice in his head.

He stopped the knife dead. It glinted and thrummed in the grip of his mind.

Drayvex continued to observe the pair, watching with the patience of an experienced hunter as the human named Sam wormed his way into Ruby's good graces. Loathing squirmed in the pit of his being, hot and fresh.

Isn't that what you were doing not so long ago, pushed the snide voice? Manipulating a vulnerable young girl for your own well deserved cause?

Drayvex considered it. Yes, it was. So what?

Ruby giggled, this time with more feeling.

"Why don't we go find a *real* drink? Would you like that, hon?" The boy reached across and took her hand, stroking it with his thumb.

Ruby flinched at the contact. As she stared at their intertwined hands, she looked taken aback. "Well ..." She gazed up at her captor. "Fine, okay. Why not? I've got nowhere else to be."

"Great."

They stood, their chairs scraping against the floor one after the other.

Drayvex watched them leave, teeth extending inside his mouth. He flicked the knife, sending it slicing across the room. It landed in the softwood of the window's table with a thud. The handle quivered, blade embedded in the spot where their hands had just been.

Yes, he had manipulated and exploited fragile young Ruby. He'd been doing it for days. He'd been here long before this puke stain had arrived, and if anyone was going to screw her over, it would be him. *He* was the stronger, faster and all-round better predator.

And Drayvex didn't like to be challenged.

The tavern was full of dark corners. So much so that even without trying, Drayvex was just another faceless form in a bar.

Ruby seemed agitated, her drinks lasting five minutes in the glass. Drayvex pitied her liver. Clearly, her previous indulgence was not a one-off.

"What's wrong, love?" asked Sam, doing a passable job of sounding concerned.

"My necklace is gone," whispered Ruby, her voice barely audible to the human ear.

"What? Your breakfast?" His beady eyes flicked down to her empty glass across the table. "Let me get you another drink."

The Lapis Vitae throbbed in his pocket, sensing his reaction to the unexpected change of topic. Patience, he thought, caressing the outside of the pocket. Soon, he would have his way. Then, there would be nothing else to hold him back.

Drayvex lingered, cloaked in shadow as the day began to give way to evening. He contemplated ways he could make the boy suffer. Did a human really need all those innards? His bet was no. The question was, which ones were vital and which weren't? It was so easy to forget. He smiled.

Time passed with rigid structure, as it always did on Earth. Minutes, hours—such details didn't concern him. If he *was* keeping track, though, he could measure it by the growing collection of glasses on Ruby's table.

At some point within that time, her mood did a one-eighty degree turn.

"So, how come I've never seen you around before, 'en?" The boy leaned into her as he spoke, his weight pushing her into the side of the padded seat. His glassy eyes wandered down to her cleavage.

Ruby span to face him. She smiled as he breathed whiskey fumes down her neck. "Well, Sam," she said with alcohol-fuelled enthusiasm, "I've only lived here for two years. So, I'm easy to miss if you don't come here often."

His arms snaked around her waist as he pulled her roughly into him. "Then, in future, I'll have to make sure you're my first stop."

Drayvex suppressed an impatient impulse, an impulse that wanted to abandon stealth and rip out the boy's throat in the middle of the tavern. His fangs bared in a snarl, the tips moist and black, as he watched her mould into his arms.

He was going to enjoy killing this one.

Ruby giggled, her head lolling onto the boy's shoulder as he gripped her against him.

Something stirred in the pit of Drayvex's stomach. It burned, leaving a bad taste in his mouth. It was unfamiliar, and left him with one restless thought: *kill* him.

Ruby was semi-conscious. But as the boy lifted her chin with two fingers and crushed his lips against hers, she responded to his needs. He slid his hands up her body, stopping to rest a hand on her breast.

What are you waiting for?

Sam trailed his filthy mouth down her neck, stopping to graze the skin at her throat with his teeth. Ruby lifted her head and pulled back, attempting to sit up straight. He pulled her back down, grabbing at her with a depraved urgency.

Are you going to let that maggot steal your prey?

Ruby whined in his grip, struggling in feeble jerks as he continued to have his way with her.

Bang!

Ruby screamed as the lightbulb above exploded, covering her face with her hands. Tiny shards of glass rained down on the pair as they were plunged into shadow.

"Crap." Sam shot up from the table like a flayed dog, stumbling backwards. "What the bloody 'ell …?"

He cursed, brushing shards from his jacket, squinting up at the ceiling as he swayed on his feet. "Be right back. Need a cig." He patted his pockets, then stumbled for the door.

Drayvex slipped past the table, unnoticed by the girl who sat by herself in the gloom, and out through the door behind.

The remaining light of the day barely touched the grimy pit at the back of the tavern. His night vision was second to none. But even blind he would have smelled this lowlife for miles off, with the mingled stench of whisky, cigarettes and sweat a physical barrier around him.

The boy leaned against the faded brickwork, breathing clouds of nicotine into the air. Drayvex smiled as he approached, a slow grin that revealed the glistening array of teeth behind it. His black claws extended, curving to become an extension of his fingers.

As the prey turned, he did a double-take. "What the f—" His eyes flicked up, then down, and fell upon Drayvex's mouth. He regarded those teeth with fear in his eyes. "P-please, don't hurt me. I ain't got nothing." And then under his breath, "Crap."

Drayvex shot forward, clearing the space between them in an instant. The boy yelled in surprise and flailed, his back hitting the wall. "Please!" he begged, louder this time. "What the ... what the hell are you?"

Drayvex pushed in closer, ignoring the cries of the pitiful specimen. He could see his own gleaming red eyes reflected in the boy's; eyes that, unlike earlier, were now anything but dead. Drayvex revelled in the utter terror swimming in those eyes. "Sam, is it?" he purred, dropping his smile. "Can I call you Sam?" He dragged the tip of a claw along the exposed skin at the boy's throat, leaving a deep, oozing trail. Blood trickled down his collarbone, seeping into the material of his shirt.

Sam gasped at the contact, hissing through clenched teeth.

"Oh, do you not like these?"

The snivelling boy shook his head, his eyes glued to the claw hovering closest to his face.

"Well, you see, Sam, I have a problem." Drayvex leaned in closer, embracing the stench of his recreational habits. "I would love for us to have a bit of fun—you, me and *these*." He gestured, twitching the claw nearest to the flesh.

Sam flinched. He whimpered, his thin veneer of bravado long gone.

"But I despise you. And I really don't think I have the patience to keep you alive for more than ten seconds."

It took Sam a moment to process his words, before plunging straight into begging for his life. "Nonono. No. Oh, please, don't. I have a wife."

"Five," Drayvex spat, feeling the tenuous guise of his semi-human shape struggle to contain him.

"Wait, *Wait!* What do you want? I-I can give you anything yer like. Money?"

Drayvex stilled. "Money?" He laughed. It was a hard, mocking sound. "Oh, Sam." Leaning closer still, he moved so that his mouth was close to the boy's ear. The quivering body beside him tensed. His breaths were almost nonexistent. Drayvex trailed his mouth down the boy's filthy neck, stopping to graze the soft skin at the throat with his teeth. "The satisfaction of extracting your last scream is worth far more to me than money."

He smiled. "One."

Drayvex slashed open the screaming Sam, causing him to double over.

The boy clutched in vain at his open stomach, fumbling over the wound.

Snatching him from the floor, Drayvex sunk his fangs into the neck and ripped. Torrents of blood spurted from his jugular, painting the ground.

Dropping him, Drayvex stood, watching the human twitch and writhe in the expanding pools.

Yes, *he* was the better predator. Better on every level. And if there was one sure way to get yourself killed, it was to steal from those far, far above you.

Chapter 8

Ruby lingered at the B and B's entrance, enjoying the morning drizzle against her face. The light breeze was just as welcome. It made her feel almost human again.

Her head throbbed in a cruel reminder of last night's events. Yes, she had drunk too much. But being abandoned by not one, but two men in two days was a record for her, even if the last one had turned out to be a pig.

Her pocket buzzed. Ruby pulled out her phone and checked the screen. "Hey, Mum."

"Honey. Are you busy?"

She was busy not being busy. She bit her lip. "Not really. Why?"

Pause. "We're running low on a few things. Can you shop?"

Ruby didn't answer. In other words, they were out of food, and someone had to fill the shelves. She closed her eyes, pressing her fingers to her thumping temple.

"Are you with your new friend? He was looking for you the other day." Her voice dropped, gaining a strange new edge. "Ruby. Are you still seeing him?"

Seeing? She wasn't seeing any—

Ruby tensed as a sudden understanding struck her. It could only be one person. "Who?"

"The one with the dark hair. Look, I don't want you seeing him anymore.

Is that clear?"

Drayvex. He had been looking for her, and she didn't even know it. "When was this, Mum?" She hadn't seen him in days. And when the hell had he met her mother? And, wait. "You don't ... want me seeing him?" Had he offended her? Or was this the overprotective mother routine that she had come to know and expect?

A clang echoed down the phone as her mum dropped something on the other end. "Ruby, please. Just trust me. I'm your mother, and I know a bad egg when I see one. You know, he was very interested in that necklace of yours, which is none of—"

Her mother's voice cut off mid-sentence.

Ruby pulled the phone away from her ear and stared at the screen. Her fingers were squeezing it. Her knuckles were white. Making a conscious effort to relax her grip, she redialled her mother. Paused. Cancelled the call. She opened a fresh text.

'Am alone. Will pick up tea. See u later. X' Ruby stared at the text a moment longer, then pressed send.

Adjusting her mental journey, she set off. For the first time since losing her grandma's necklace, Ruby felt calm. Eerily so.

She paced through the village, letting the country hush clear her mind. Her mother was already so against him. Ruby's nose tingled in indignation. She wanted to defend him in his absence. But what did she really know about the stranger she'd befriended at the pub?

She stopped, her feet crunching against the gravel. He was good in a fight.

Ruby stood on the spot, staring blankly at the tops of the trees ahead. But he had *saved* her that day from—

The realisation smacked her over the head. From the thief who tried to take her necklace. Dear god.

She cracked her knuckles and wet her dry lips. When had she seen it last?

The field of long grass immediately sprung to mind. She'd lost it there. No, she hadn't been there. Why did she keep coming back to that field?

Okay, new question. When had she last seen Drayvex?

Ruby crossed the road and followed it round towards the park. The last time she remembered seeing him was in the café. He'd sat with her, chatted about nothing. She approached the grounds and paused at the main gates. Her hand hovered over the handle. She'd given it to Drayvex because he had wanted a closer look.

An elderly couple came up behind her and Ruby dropped her arm. She stepped aside to allow them past, barely aware of her movements. She'd given it to him. Now it was gone. She rested her forehead against the cool metal. Her memories were fuzzy from that point on.

Ruby stood motionless, relishing the feel of cold metal against her clammy skin. She didn't want to believe it. For one, it didn't make any sense. It was a piece of junk, almost certainly worth peanuts. Yet, her thoughts warred, he was looking at it. That first night they met.

She cast her mind back further, reluctant to accept that she'd been used. She would search the Cosy Corner before jumping to any more conclusions. It was the least she could do—if only for her own peace of mind.

*

Drayvex slipped through the recesses of the old theatre, his gaze fixed on the cluster of humans below. They were arguing amongst themselves, oblivious to the danger they were in. Creating enemies with their own twisted minds.

He smiled, running his tongue along sharpened fangs. Humans were so easily corrupted. They may as well have big red X's on their backs.

Drayvex stepped towards the edge of the balcony, analysing the testy group of humans below.

"So, Nielson. What's it like to have the worst turnout in this place's history on *your* hands? Hmm?"

"That's *Mr* Nielson to you, spiteful brat!"

"Dahlings, don't fight, now—"

"Piss off, Grandpa. Move over. Let someone young pump the life back into 'er."

Drayvex placed a hand on the balcony rail, grazing a claw along its glossy surface as he scanned the pits below. Simultaneously, he watched the balconies opposite. He was looking for a specific kind of predator. He could feel its presence polluting the air, see the effects of its hunger playing out on the humans below in all its volatile glory. It was close.

Drayvex waited, watching the situation unfold. It was only a matter of time before the wraith chose to feed, and these humans were ripe for the picking.

Idle, his mind cast itself back to the previous night. The light bulb had been a convenient ploy. He could take credit for the simple idea, but he couldn't deny that it had been just as much a surprise to him as to the prey.

He ran his tongue along a canine, unsettled. He couldn't recall the last time he'd lost control. Things exploded around him when he willed it so, when he directed power their way. *Had* he ever lost control?

The young male shoved the withered man, sending him toppling into a tower of chairs.

"Dai, leave him!"

The old man bounced off the stack. He hit the floor and fumbled for a weapon, grabbing at a long piece of wood. He sprang back to his feet with surprising gusto. "Argh! You arrogant—"

The young male took a blow to the head and veered off to the left.

Drayvex felt the corners of his mouth lifting as he monitored the spectacle below. Now, that was one power he *didn't* possess. The ability to manipulate emotion. This was unique to wraith-like species. Then again, his meals were rather more substantial than ill will and petty human jealousy.

As the feel of the air around him changed, Drayvex's split attention merged. Every fibre of his being became hyper-aware of the creature uncloaked on the balcony opposite.

He slipped around the edge of the theatre in silence. Sounds of the humans killing each other bounced off the circular walls around him, their screams music to the ears of their malevolent conductor, pulling the strings from the shadows.

The light bulb was a stain on his spotless control. He could explain what had happened. The light bulb had exploded upon contact with his power. What he didn't know was why.

The smell of fresh blood drifted up his nostrils, sticking in the back of his throat. He ignored it, his focus fixed on the wraith. If he didn't know any better, he might argue that as he'd lurked in the shadows, plotting the boy's demise, watching her respond to his depraved needs, a part of him had been jealous. However, Drayvex did know better. It wasn't just implausible. It was impossible.

He slowed, eyes fixed on the creature dead ahead. Demons were devoid of all but the most basic and pure of emotions. Anger, fear. Pleasure. They were selfish creatures, incapable of caring about anything that didn't directly affect them, and Drayvex was the epitome of selfish. What did he care who some ordinary human girl gave her affections to?

The wraith turned as he approached, breaking away mid feed. Six feet five inches of malevolent, pulsing darkness. Both the predator and the prey.

Drayvex smirked, satisfied, as he felt the air around it crackle. Yes, this power would jump the stone to a whole new level.

As the wraith coiled like a dark, glistening serpent, Drayvex reached out with black tendrils. The wraith sprung at him.

Darkness clashed with darkness. Drayvex whipped out the stone, seizing the moment. "Nothing personal," he drawled, holding the necklace by the cord. "Your power is simply divine."

The wraith struggled like a trapped animal, fighting the Lapis Vitae's pull. It was a wasted effort, and within seconds, the wraith had been pulled into the pendant.

The stone flashed a dull crimson, before fading.

Drayvex registered the single heartbeat left in the room, then dismissed it, his attention turning back to the powerful object in his grip. It wasn't enough. Of course, it wasn't enough. It would take a good five *hundred* wraiths to make something like himself immortal. He'd known this from the start.

He stared at the cord wrapped around his fingers. The leather was a human addition. The girl had used it this way, as though it were a piece of jewellery and not the most sought after piece of lost demonic power in existence.

Drayvex scoffed, running a thumb over the cord. It *was* useful, though. It gave him the ability to pick it up at will without breaking his cover.

"Oh ... oh, no, no, no. What ...?"

He slid his gaze down to the lower floor. The smell of blood was thick in the air. Blood and fear. His fangs lengthened, the points extending down to prick his tongue.

His persistent thoughts lingered on Ruby, like an itch just beyond his reach. The stone was still in her system, clouding her aura. Did she still have a claim to the stone?

Drayvex sprang, jumping over the balcony rail and dropping straight down to the pits. Inconvenient as it was, being right was something that he never tired of.

*

Ruby trudged down the aisles of the corner shop, grabbing whatever happened to take her fancy. Her necklace hadn't been at the cafe. The staff hadn't seen it. And now, she had to do the damn food shop.

She paused, staring at the rows of coloured packets in front of her. She'd never been an organised shopper. Her usual trick was to wait until the cupboards contained only sauces and dried fruits. Then, hungry and resigned, she would buy enough for a small army as her every passing fancy ended up in the basket.

She smiled, remembering her mother's old tight fisted shopping trips. They used to take it in turns. Between them, they wouldn't know balance if it smacked them in the face.

Her smile slipped, her heart aching from the fond memories. Not anymore.

Ruby grabbed two tins of tomato soup from the shelf and dropped them into her basket.

So, Drayvex.

She frowned, fiddling with the items in her basket. Drayvex had been to her house, cased out the joint, made an enemy of her mother and—what? Decided that the only thing they had worth stealing was the necklace at her throat? She shook her head. Ridiculous. But maybe he'd asked her mother about her necklace, and her mother had used all the right words. Family.

Old.

Her breathing faltered as she considered this. She didn't want to believe it. Drayvex had been good to her. He'd been a friend just when she'd needed one most. But now, red flags were popping up all over the place. Had he met her with the intention of making some quick cash? What else was missing that she didn't know about? How much of what they'd shared was real? Did he even like her, or had it all been an act?

She couldn't stop herself from going there. Digging deeper and deeper. Her thoughts were out of control.

Ruby jumped as the shelf edges bumped against her back.

Smash! A jar of sauce burst at her feet.

Ruby squeaked, jumping backwards. A second jar followed her, moving as though it had a mind of its own. It narrowly missed her head, bouncing off her arm. It smashed against the floor in a thick, red wave.

She opened her mouth to scream out in pain, but nothing happened. Shock had seized her voice. Her arm throbbed in a dead sort of way, as though someone had swung a punch.

"Excuse me?"

Ruby dropped her basket and squeezed her arm. What was wrong with her?

"Miss? Are you hurt?"

Her face grew warm as a shop attendant started towards her. She couldn't deal with this. Not today.

"Miss, can you hear me?"

Her stomach twisting, she abandoned her basket and made a break for the exit.

You're an idiot, Ruby, she thought, wishing she could have at least kept the paracetamol. It was shameful, smashing and running. But right now, running away from her problems was all she was capable of.

Ruby quick-marched through the village, avoiding anyone that might slow her down with chatter. Everything around her was falling apart. She'd already lost her best friend and her grandma's necklace. Today, she could add her dignity to that list.

Suddenly, she stopped. She could have sworn someone had spoken her name. Tugging her collar up, she pulled her jacket tighter around her. But the road was deserted.

"Oh, she has it alright. I can smell it on 'er."

Ruby turned and eyeballed the big skips at her back. The rough male voice had come from behind them.

"Then, the girl named Ruby must die," said a second male voice, softer but deadlier. "She will give it to us. Or we will take it from her corpse."

Panic flooded her veins. *Run,* screamed her instincts.

Run. The word bounced around inside her skull as her feet pounded the ground. The village raced past her in a blur.

She'd gotten a head start, but it took them seconds to catch up. She could hear them laughing at her. Screaming maniacally.

Ruby's mind was working on overtime. She weaved through the streets, trying to attract the attention she'd shunned only moments ago. It felt like a sick joke. She was running for her life, but none of it felt real.

As she passed the laundrette, she caught a glimpse of her pursuers' reflections in the window, and a scream stuck in her throat.

Her mind spiralled. Stretched, leather skin. Bulbous eyes. Nightmarish claws and teeth. They weren't men—they were monsters.

Ruby darted into the road, dodging a wailing jeep, and shot down a small passageway. They were like no animal she'd ever seen.

Somehow, the voices made it worse. Like some low budget horror film that scared you for all the wrong reasons. She turned the corner and ran straight into Drayvex.

Ruby's mind did a backflip.

"Drayvex. Run!" She grabbed for his arm and tugged it. "Monsters are coming this way."

Drayvex stared at her, his face a picture of composure. "Get behind me." He didn't look scared or even surprised.

Ruby stared at him. In that moment, she wondered if he actually believed her. But in shock, she obeyed.

As they charged into the passageway, Ruby threw her hand over her mouth. There was no mistaking those horrific creatures. They were the ugliest mothers that she'd ever encountered.

The two creatures slammed on the brakes, the first skidding to a stop a few paces away. The second was slower to react. The creature crashed straight into the first, taking them both out in a face-meets-floor manoeuvre. If she hadn't been paralysed with fear, Ruby might have doubled over at the sight.

"Move, human. Or I'll go *through* you."

Ruby's heart jolted. It was talking to Drayvex. Thief or not, she wasn't okay with that.

The second fell to its knees. "L-Lord Drayvex," it stuttered, bowing flat to the ground

The first pulled a face, its vile features twisting. "What are you—oh, fuck." Its face fell, and then it was on the floor too. "My apologies! I didn't recognise—"

"Shut up, you idiot."

Ruby felt a cold shock reverberate through her. *Lord* Drayvex? Her stuck mind tried and failed to put the pieces together.

"We don't want no trouble, My Lord, just the girl. If you give her to us, then we'll be on our way."

"Yes, My Lord. If anyone asks, we ain't never seen you. Nuh-uh."

"Never."

Ruby's capacity to be shocked was long-since broken. But in this moment, she found herself hoping with all she had that Drayvex was on her side. She couldn't see his face. But it was clear, as she studied the cowering creatures, that he wasn't phased by the bizarre situation. In fact, they seemed to be scared of *him*.

Drayvex turned his head, his gaze inching towards her. The look on his face sent a chill down her spine. It was as though he was weighing up his options. But no, he wouldn't, she reasoned, frantic. He wouldn't hand me over to monsters. Would he?

As he turned back towards them, an unsettling smile grew on his face. He was dragging out the moment; making her squirm before he handed her over to her death. He was in league with them. He —

"No."

A silence filled the space. "My Lord?" An uncertainty flickered in the depths of their pitch black eyes.

"No. You can't have her." His tone was unflinching and had an authoritative ring that she'd never heard in a voice before.

Ruby felt as though a large weight had been lifted off her chest. She breathed out, relief flooding through her.

It was short-lived.

The monsters exchanged uncertain glances, before sinking into a crouch, their looks of doubt replaced by grim determination; and malice.

Drayvex turned and met her gaze.

Ruby stopped breathing. She didn't understand. Help me understand, she pleaded mentally, clinging to the shared look like a life raft.

He broke it, turning back to face the creatures.

Suddenly, to Ruby's horror, she noticed that Drayvex was changing. She teetered on the verge on unconsciousness, watching as vicious, black claws grew down from where his nails used to be. Ruby fought to cling to reality. The world span. Black specks clouded her vision.

The monsters threw themselves at him.

The last thing she saw before darkness claimed her was a severed head hitting the wall beside her.

Chapter 9

Drayvex scanned the small passageway, admiring his handiwork. Two demon corpses lay twisted and broken at his feet. Garish streaks smeared the walls in abstract patterns, and scattered limbs sat in expanding puddles, relinquishing juices they would no longer need.

He lifted a claw and ran his tongue along its dripping length. They'd been out of their depth, cannon fodder at best. They'd had a lot to give, though. He smirked. It was a macabre masterpiece.

He looked down and noticed the unconscious girl sprawled amid the carnage, and remembered the reason for the bodies. He'd been caught up in the moment, forgotten all but the ripping, and albeit brief, the agony. Now, he had been left with the problem of what to do with Ruby.

The girl's no longer of any use, bled the vitriol inside his head. Move on.

Drayvex ran his tongue along his teeth, removing any stains. He *wanted* to move on, to leave her unprotected, unconscious, at the mercy of whichever nasty thing came for her next. And they would come for her.

He watched the rise and fall of her delicate chest, the fragile skin stretched over her bones, her bare throat. The steady thump of the one thing keeping her alive. But in this one distorted moment, he was hyper-aware of how vulnerable she was. It shouldn't bother him, but it did. And he couldn't bring himself to walk away.

Drayvex snarled, consumed by a sudden blinding anger. He'd taken her precious trophy, and she'd failed to stop him. Life was a bitch. Game over was game over.

He lunged at the comatose Ruby, landing heavily beside her. Fuelled by both instinct and petty resentment, he struck out, sinking his teeth deep into her neck.

Her blood hit the roof of his mouth and the back of his throat, satisfying his carnal appetite. It tingled in his mouth, a minuscule jolt of electricity.

"Well, thanks. So much."

Ruby jerked in violent spasms. Her eyes rolled to the back of her head as his venom travelled through her network of small blood vessels, turning them black in its wake.

"I owe you one."

Drayvex paused, his fangs still embedded in her neck. Her blood coated the inside of his mouth, and her fragile body began to fall into shock beneath him.

His anger, like the dribbles of demon dripping down the drain, slipped through his fingers. As he tasted her blood on his tongue, Drayvex felt a twinge of disgust at his sudden flare in temper. He found himself overcome with an alien sensation as he stared at her dying form: doubt.

It was so unexpected that he was thrown by the sheer force and surprise of it. Did he really want to kill her? He was no longer sure.

When no immediate answer came to him, he worried over her fading condition. Ruby shuddered beneath him, her icy skin brushing him briefly as she jerked.

Drayvex made an impulsive decision. Moving swiftly, he pulled his fangs out of her neck. He made a further incision, before proceeding to suck her venom laced blood. Again, it tingled as it slipped down his throat.

When he was satisfied that he had withdrawn all traces of poison from her system, he focused, and let his form go.

Drayvex came apart piece by piece, unravelling, losing solidity. His form flowed as a black vapour, and he slipped inside her.

Demons didn't have healing powers. When you were made of darkness itself, such powers of light lay far beyond your reach. He could heal himself, of course. But as far as anything else went—forget it. Despite this, there were always loopholes to exploit, *if* you knew how.

Drayvex flexed her fingers, testing his control over her unconscious form. He didn't need her co-operation, her permission. He didn't need access to her mind, just her physical body. This was enough.

Focusing on her wound, he sent a small amount of power to the area. He willed it to heal, treating this body the way he would his own. The area heated with concentrated power. It seared for a moment, before cooling and slipping away into the atmosphere.

Drayvex slipped out of Ruby's body and studied her, taking wicked pleasure in the trickery. It worked.

He ran a meticulous finger over the tiny mark on her neck. This one wasn't going to go away. Technically, Ruby had now been marked by a demon, although that was never his intention.

He curled his lip.

Drayvex paced over to the space opposite her and sat with his back against the wall. He glared at her through suspicious slits, unblinking. As he did, the remaining anger and hatred he had clung to trickled away. No matter how hard he tried, he couldn't stay angry with her, and eventually, he stopped trying.

In that moment, he found himself slipping back into old suspicions, humouring his previous paranoid theories. The girl was a witch. Her blood was off. She knew exactly what he was, *who* he was, and was luring him in to use his blood, his organs, for her depraved spells.

Or she was a demon hunter, biding her time. Capturing the infamous Demon Lord would set her up for life. She was just playing her hand close to her chest.

Drayvex scoffed as he scanned over her sprawled form. If she *was* biding her time, she was either as twisted as he was, or had no regard for her own life. She was lucky it was him she'd been bitten by. If another demon had gotten to her first, there would have been nothing he could do for her.

Somewhere between painting Ruby as a cunning viper and scoffing at those theories, he realised she was going to be terrified of him when she woke. If she had any sense, she would run away screaming. And he was going to help her along the way. He'd let this whole debacle go far enough, and tonight it would end.

When Ruby came around, he was ready for her.

Drayvex idled a few feet away, picking flakes of dried blood from his claws. He watched her from the corner of his vision, his extended teeth gleaming like razors in the weak midday sun. His eyes were two black pits.

He knew he was overdoing it. If Ruby was as clueless as she had him believe, she wouldn't need any of this to scare her witless. But Drayvex liked to be thorough.

It was time to force her hand.

The semi-conscious Ruby gripped her head as she sat up. Dragging her hands down the length of her face, she took a groggy look around. Her initial response was one of utter bewilderment. But her blank features morphed into horror as she processed the murder scene around her.

Drayvex watched her, aloof.

She blinked. "You."

"And the memories come flooding back."

She sat, frozen. "W-what is this?" Her eyes were fixed on him.

Drayvex raised his eyebrows at her in an arrogant expression. Yes, she was scared. He smiled, and he knew his face would show a look of triumph. He was winning, and he wasn't even trying.

Ruby scrambled to her feet. It was as though she had seen the challenge in his eyes. "You're one of them." It wasn't a question, but the way she said it begged to be proved wrong; to be told that it was all a sick joke, and of course, that he was as human as anyone. That hope was a lie.

He laughed out loud for her benefit. "Yes, I'm one of them."

"I don't understand." She took a step backwards. "You're a monster."

Drayvex took that as an invitation. He surged forward, appearing in front of her in a blink.

Ruby screamed in a piercing blast. She turned to run, to find the splattered wall at her back.

"You have no idea," he snarled, digging his claws into the brick on either side of her head as she spun back to face him. "*Monsters* have nightmares about me." As he spoke, he pushed his face even closer to hers, his fangs hovering inches away from her fragile throat. The mark he'd made earlier sat under a slick layer of blood, the irony of his current threat not escaping him. Having just saved her from himself, he wasn't about to rip her open all over again.

Ruby stared, the colour draining from her face all at once. Drayvex wondered if she was going to faint on him again, but instead, she closed her eyes. "I thought we were friends."

It was no more than a whisper. But the words themselves were heavy and thrummed in his head as though she'd screamed them. "No, Ruby. I *used* you." He emphasised each word with cruel nonchalance, a growl forming in a soft undercurrent as he spoke. "To get close enough to steal your necklace."

Ruby's eyes widened, a look of understanding registering on her face as his words sunk in. Her chest rose and fell, and as though he'd flicked a switch, he saw her change.

She moved in a sudden burst. Digging into her pocket, she whipped out her small blade.

Drayvex felt the corners of his mouth twitch. As he watched the knife quiver in her hand, slivers of begrudging respect rose, despite himself. He grinned, a patronising sneer. "What are you going to do with that toothpick, Ruby Red?" he said in a dangerous purr. "Are you going to teach me a lesson?"

"It was you all along."

"You'd better make it a good one. Because I. Don't. *Miss.*"

Ruby stopped breathing. She opened her mouth, hesitating, her words caught on her tongue.

Drayvex lowered his voice, all humour gone. "If I see you again, I will kill you." He met her gaze. "Do you understand?"

He'd finally found her limit. In a burst of action, Ruby slid out from where she was pinned and tore off down the passageway.

She didn't look back.

Drayvex stared at the spot where Ruby had disappeared. Humans ran from demons. It was the natural order.

He leapt into the air and changed into a bird, letting the breeze carry him high into the darkening sky. He no longer wanted to think. Drayvex took control of his wings, keeping his eyes open for somewhere he could do some mindless killing.

Now, she was on her own.

*

Ruby had never ran so fast. Unwilling to look behind her, she charged through Crichton. Head rushing. Heart racing. She didn't want to see that face again. Those soulless eyes sucking her into the darkness. Those monstrous teeth that—

A realisation hit her like an invisible bruise. Drayvex had invited himself into her home. Her life. She'd trusted him, opened up to him over a friendly drink. Now, she was running for her life.

The world passed her by in a blur. Her lungs ached, her deadening legs screamed. None of it felt *real.*

She reached the house in record time, falling over the doorstep in her haste to get inside. She slammed the door shut behind her, before twisting the key and sliding the chain across. Would a locked door really stop him?

"Ruby, you look exhausted. Is ev—Ruby?"

Ruby span to face her mother, the tone of her voice pulling at her fraying nerves.

Her mother's eyes grew wide as they scanned her. Her face paled. "Ruby. You're hurt. Who attacked you? Are you—?" She stepped forward, her hands outstretched in a grabbing motion, before stopping short. "I'll get help."

Ruby's stuck mind jolted. How did she know?

No, she *couldn't* know. "Whoa, whoa, whoa." She grabbed for the hands that were stretched out towards her. Don't panic. Don't panic. "Mum, what's wrong?"

Her mother pulled her closer. "Ruby, you're bleeding!"

Ruby froze.

"Who attacked you?"

She prised her hands from her mother's iron grip and looked down. Blood. On her chest, her shoulder, her arm. Stunned, she ran her fingers over the sticky substance on her skin. Was it hers? "I, um ..."

Ouch. Ruby winced as her fingers found a tender spot on her neck. Attacked.

"God. Hold on, honey, I'll phone for help."

Ruby's fingers probed her neck. Was she the collateral damage in a three-monster scrap? Or had *he* attacked her?

"What did they look like? How many of them were there? Be specific."

She doubted anyone would be able to help her.

"Mum, stop." She reached out for a second time and grabbed at mother's hand. What if the help ended up getting torn into little pieces? Her stomach turned.

Ruby pulled gingerly on the hand, guiding it away from the phone. Heart thumping, she took a deep breath. "It's okay, Mum. Everything is fine." Here we go.

"Ruby, it's okay. You're safe now—"

"It's not my blood. I wasn't attacked." She forced herself to laugh, then stopped. She sounded mad.

"But the blood. Where did the blood come from?"

"The blood? It was, uh, a cat."

"A cat. Honey, please. Whoever you're protecting isn't worth a damn."

"What? No, no, Mum. The cat was attacked—hit, I mean. Hit by a car." Her mum had been bang on about Drayvex all along. And as much as that sad fact pained her, it wasn't Drayvex she was trying to protect.

"And ... you—"

"And I tried to save it. Hence the blood."

Her mother's eyes flicked to the locked door and back. Ruby's hair stood on end. Neither of them were safe. "I'm *fine*," Ruby said, making eye contact and cringing inside. "Just do me a favour?"

Her mother breathed out, as if trying to steady her nerves. "Of course.

What is it?"

"Don't unlock the door. Don't let anyone in." Was that contradictory?

"Ruby Peyton, what's going on? I'm calling the police."

"Just trust me, please. Nothing is going on." She gave her mother a pleading look. "Mum?"

Her mother met her gaze. She looked as though she had a few choice words to say. But instead, she shook her head wearily. "You know where I am."

Ruby didn't wait to be dismissed. Frantic and wired, she took the stairs two at a time.

When she was safe inside her bedroom, it didn't feel enough. Her door didn't lock, so she closed it, and slid a chair underneath the handle.

Ruby took a deep, slow breath, trying to steady her pulse. Blood.

Her eyes fell upon the mirror on the dresser table. She padded over to it, unsure whether she wanted to see what she looked like.

She didn't. She put her hand over her mouth, taking in the horrific sight. No wonder her mother had panicked. The girl in the mirror was pale and dishevelled, with wide, fearful eyes—and she was covered in blood. Some of it was almost black. Some was a deep red, lightening as it dried. Her fingers hovered over the tender spot she'd found on her neck before she dropped her arm. She couldn't do this right now.

Ruby moved to the window. Shutting the curtains, she enclosed herself within the warm darkness of the safe and familiar space of her room. Then, she stood in the silence, strangely vulnerable in her inaction. Her shoulders sagged. Her body curled inward. The shot of adrenaline that had kept pushing her forward was ebbing away.

Jet black eyes flashed without warning through her mind.

Ruby kicked her shoes off and headed for bed. Crawling beneath the sheets, she drew herself into a ball and lay in the silence, waiting for her pulse and mind to settle.

As her body began to relax and warm, it occurred to her that both her *and* her mother had been right about Drayvex. That bastard had stolen her Grandma's necklace.

She didn't know how much time had passed, but after an unknown period, Ruby emerged.

She stared at the glow of the dark stars on the ceiling, sorting through the thoughts that whizzed through her mind. Drayvex wasn't human. That explained a lot.

Ruby fiddled with the duvet, lost in thought. The words sounded ridiculous, even in her head. If she hadn't seen it for herself, she would have laughed at anyone who'd said that the charming stranger was a monster in disguise.

Still, the truth was like a light in a dark cave. And she found herself shining it on all those small mysteries that had niggled away at her.

Whenever she'd looked into Drayvex's eyes, she'd felt small and weak. Now she knew why. It was because she *was* small and weak. And when he stared at her, she couldn't look away from those strange eyes. Eyes that you could fall into and be swallowed whole by.

Ruby closed her own. Memories, vivid and fresh, flashed across her mental vision. The blood-splattered passageway. The creatures inside it. Nailed to the inside of her eyelids.

Ruby sat up and wrapped her arms around her legs. The last thing she remembered before passing out was Drayvex, defending her against the monsters that wanted her dead. She'd been grateful to him, and terrified for his life; until claws had burst from his fingers. That's when the darkness had claimed her.

She knew he'd killed them. Sliced them open, decorated the walls with their entrails. She'd woken up covered in their blood, because *surprise*, he was just as much a thing as they were.

A hysterical laugh bubbled up her throat and escaped through her lips. She was talking about monsters as if they were real. Which they were, but even having witnessed their existence first hand, the ingrained adult part of her denied it still.

Drayvex was a *thing*. But here was where it got complicated: if he was one of them, then why had he opposed them? He could have easily handed her over with zero effort on his part.

She licked her lips, stopping to tug at the thin skin with her teeth. He had defended her and killed his own kind to give her a chance. Then, as if remembering that he was supposed to be a monster, he had scared her witless and threatened to kill her himself.

Ruby's hand wandered to her chest, fingers stroking the place where her necklace should be. It was clear now that Drayvex had never been her friend. He had used her. And Ruby, the fool she was, played right into his hands. The realisation of this hurt a surprising amount. He'd marked her from the very beginning. His words of comfort had been empty. His concern a polished act. How could she have been so needy?

Ruby shuffled her feet under the duvet, her mind drifting back. As it did, something heavy settled in the pit of her stomach. Had that really all been an act? Why bother, when he could have just taken it by force long ago? There would have been nothing that she could do to stop him.

Just then, the truth hit her square in the face. She swung her legs out of bed, her pulse racing. Here she was, sitting in the dark, waiting for Drayvex to come and finish the job. Drayvex had already passed up several opportunities to kill her. If he wanted her dead, he would have done it by now.

Right?

Ruby breathed out, slowly. Drayvex had told her with no reservations that if he saw her again, he would kill her. But something curious inside her couldn't let this go. She needed her necklace back. And she needed to know where they stood.

She needed to find Drayvex again.

Chapter 10

The Lapis Vitae pulsed in time to the throbs of his power, emanating a deep red hue in the starless night and bathing him in its unearthly glow. Drayvex watched it flex, admiring its savage beauty. Even at a fraction of its potential, it was a beacon of true power. An object worthy of his boundless, Demon Lord ambition.

"You called, Your Eminence?"

Drayvex narrowed his eyes before tearing his gaze from the stone and glaring down at his feckless familiar. "I called you a long time ago," he said, quelling the urge to separate the demon's tongue from his head. "What, I wonder, is more important than your pledge of servitude, and thus keeping your head on its bony little shoulders for another day?"

Kaelor squirmed under his gaze. As he sunk down to the gravel, he paused, eyes drawn to the rippling portal forming in the wall at the tips of Drayvex's fingers. Drayvex expelled his serpentine tongue in a whip-like flick.

"The human girl, My Lord. It hasn't left its tiny castle in a while. Breaking its routine, no?"

Drayvex tensed. Hell. He should have pulled Kaelor from Ruby-watch days ago. He glanced back at the stone, its curved face throwing patches of crimson light across his person.

"Not that it provides any protection. The human that sheds its own blood needs no enemies to slay it."

His concentration slipped. The stone flickered and died.

"Forget the girl," Drayvex snapped, his irritation peaking. Mercy. Never mind the demons; Ruby would kill her own damn self long before they caught up with her. He grimaced, suppressing his brittle mood, before adding, "The human is no longer of any relevance."

"Of course, My Lord."

Drayvex held out his free hand, palm facing upwards in expectation.

Kaelor stared for a moment at his empty palm. Then, he hunched over and retched. The demon vomited onto Drayvex's outstretched hand, dropping onto it a glistening, grizzled lump.

Drayvex spun the shimmering ball of cack in his fingers. Ruby's dreams. A useless by-product of a successful plan. He stowed it in his pocket for future disposal. "Good. Now shut up and let me think."

The crunch of gravel sounded in the darkness behind him. "My Lord—"

"Or better yet, piss off." Drayvex stared ahead at the portal but spoke to the matted creature behind him. The last thing he needed was Kaelor distracting him with his verbal diarrhoea.

A tiny pop confirmed that his minion had indeed pissed off. Drayvex resumed his mission.

A current of power buzzed down his arm, travelling along his fingers and hitting the bricks with a thrum. The key to his endless reign as the current and last Demon Lord there would ever be was in the palm of his hand. He could simply dismiss his competitor as the loser he clearly was and enjoy his newfound power.

But anything capable of tracking down the legendary Lapis Vitae and sending other demons to do his dirty work was also capable of acquiring *other* means of power. A being that would ultimately challenge him for the throne. Because there were millions of degenerate beasts crawling on that steaming rock he reigned over, and every single one of them wanted to tear him down.

Drayvex lifted the pulsing stone and enveloped it in his power. Precision was key here. If he was overzealous, he would advertise the Lapis Vitae's whereabouts, not only to those within the boundaries of Crichton, but to every power-hungry overlord and their underlings within a million-mile radius. And that would really slow him down.

The portal in front of him rippled in response, at first fighting his will, then relenting to it.

The answer was quiet. Too quiet. He scanned the surrounding rubble, combing the darkness with feelers of power. No response to the stone's siren call.

Drayvex increased the charge a fraction. His arm glowed with unnatural heat, rising off his skin in steaming waves.

Suddenly, a new presence caught his attention. It was a speck on his radar, small fry at best—but it had responded nonetheless.

Drayvex turned towards the source, anticipation pulling at the corners of his mouth. Showtime.

*

The smallest things around her were working her up. A leaf skittering on the pavement, a twig snapping under her boot, the occasional stirring of chilly night air, tickling the back of her neck.

She wandered through the village at a snail's pace, looking for unusual things, for signs. She didn't know where Drayvex was staying, or if monsters even needed a place to crash for the night. Maybe he'd moved on by now, taking her Grandma's necklace with him.

What are you going to do with that toothpick, Ruby Red?

Right on cue, a warm sensation rose up in her chest, making her eyes prickle, hot and fresh. Ruby pushed it down. That bastard would not get a rise out of her. She needed to keep her head, and not least of all, she needed to keep his appendages far away from her. Picking a fight with a monster was not how to stay alive. But oh, how she wanted to wipe that smug grin off that perfect face.

As this thought entered her head, she realised how truly blasé she was being. It was stupid to assume that she knew him in any way, shape or form. The human pretence she'd come to know was just a pretty veneer. Now all bets were off. And it was possible that she would not be breathing tomorrow.

Ruby wandered through the main square, feeling exposed. She double-scanned the darkest corners and crevices, the dark places not even the moonlight could penetrate. What creatures were waiting for her there? Why did monsters want to kill her? Did Drayvex know?

A bright light flashed in the corner of her eye, scattering her thoughts like rabbits. She blinked once, searching for the source, and looked up.

The sky had been lit by a brilliant red beam. It pointed upwards in a thin straight line, like a laser lighting effect on pause. It was so unexpected that for a moment she forgot what she was even doing. She followed the light downwards.

A twig snapped in the darkness behind her. Ruby span on the spot, heart hammering in her chest. Something was following her.

She licked her lips and turned her head, inching back up towards the light. The sky was black again.

Her breaths came short and fast. The old barn on the edge of the village. That was where the light had come from. She was sure of it.

Ruby faced the disturbance, listening hard. The local nightlife chirped in chorus.

The light could have been bored city kids. Or drunk visitors, messing with things that they shouldn't. Or maybe, Drayvex was still here after all.

She hoped he was in a good mood.

Throwing caution to the wind, Ruby tiptoed through the village, towards the little abandoned shack. There was one way to find out.

*

The demon that had entered his web was a crossbreed. With the leathery physique of a fire hag and the eyes and mouth of a soul sucker, it was a level two mash-up for hire.

Drayvex lingered on the creature below from his position on the ceiling, disgusted by its dual form. Its very existence made a mockery of demonkind. Well, by the time he was done here, there would be one less piece of mutated vermin infecting this planet.

He trailed it through the creaking barn, his demon flesh blending into the night. He basked in the cold nothing that ran through his veins, the sweet darkness that oozed out of his every pore. After almost a full week of being human, a touch of sadism was a welcome change of pace.

Drayvex dropped down in silence, landing on all fours behind the creature that was about to tell him everything it knew. As he touched the dubiously stain-splattered floor, he uncoiled, becoming a mass of roiling, liquid darkness, rising upward in a towering pillar to brush the ceiling that contained him.

Three … two …

At the last second, it sensed him. Head snapping around, it tensed and screeched. The fine cracks in its leathery hide erupted into molten lines. Flames burst from the cracks in a short blast.

Drayvex dropped. He crashed over his unsuspecting victim in an inky wave, smothering its entire form with his. The demon fought him, thrashing inside his living walls. Drayvex held for a few seconds, before coiling around its limbs, restraining his captive's movements further.

Nearby objects sparked and flickered to life, caught in the spreading trails of hungry flame. Drayvex ignored them.

After a moment of relish, he pulled back, exposing its head. The creature gasped for air, jerking against him in a pointless attempt to pull free.

Tsk, tsk. Are you really so dense? His voice penetrated its weakened defences. *I suppose a half-breed like yourself wasn't created for its brains. I'll spell it out for you, then.* Drayvex squeezed. Bones creaked, taut.

Just then, another presence flickered against his heightened senses. Something else was nearby.

The creature screeched and thrashed in pitiful twitches, a fly in his web. He spoke again to his captive. *Give me a name, and I'll kill you. Make me dig for said name, and I'll destroy you, then kill what little is left of you.*

His captive fell still.

Drayvex tensed in anticipation. *It's a no brainer. Really.* The fire was spreading in rapid bursts, as though on a mission of its own. Flames climbed, surrounding them on all sides.

"He's *your* superior, demon."

Drayvex pulsed. A seething wave of raw power rippled through his being, hitting his captive from all sides. The creature juddered and stiffened, hissing as it absorbed the impact.

Superior. Fucking please. *A name.*

"And he will rise," it spat through garbled hisses.

Pathetic.

Drayvex pulled himself back all at once, reverting to his previous, more solid form. The second he settled, he grabbed the creature by the throat, whipping it in close. "What use is a soul-sucking half-breed without its eyes?" he snarled, his black flesh gleaming against the surrounding tongues of flame.

As the creature in his grip opened its maw, Drayvex brought up a single curved claw. The half-breed froze, becoming stone under the claw tip that twitched over the membrane of its dark eye.

A disturbance tugged at Drayvex's focus from behind the fragile walls of the sectioned barn. He stilled as a sound snagged his attention.

Screaming. It jarred him, ripping him out of his bloodlust.

Drayvex fell into a semi-human guise, almost as a knee jerk reaction. Ruby. The stain on his spotless control. Would this girl never quit plaguing him?

He slammed the creature down to the ground, hearing the fragile floorboards splinter from the impact. Ruby. It was all very convenient. Suspiciously *easy*. What the hell was she playing at?

Drayvex snatched at the hag with thick black tendrils. He couldn't have planned it any better had he tried. The stone's previous owner was going to die in the fire. Her remaining ties to the stone would die along with her and he, Drayvex, would become the stone's one true owner, all without lifting a finger.

All he had to do was do nothing.

He wound himself around his captive's neck, wrists, ankles, crushing the wiry throat in his grip with increasing pressure. He pulled the appendages, snapping them out taut in a star shape. Damn that foolish girl. His head wasn't in the game. How did she even know he was here?

Ruby's panicked voice carried through the panels of the neighbouring room.

The answer came to him almost immediately. He wanted to kick himself. "You picked the wrong side," he drawled to the demon, his interest waning, plunging his free hand into its stomach.

The siren call. He had advertised the stone's whereabouts. Of course, her lingering connection to it had allowed her to see.

He glowered, rummaging with clumsy movements inside the creature in his grasp. Unless it *wasn't* a lingering connection. As he'd previously suspected, the girl was hiding her own insidious power, and she was playing him. Again.

The derisive commentary in the back of his mind rebuked the thought. That girl is about as malevolent as an earthworm. Her power is **dying**.

Drayvex closed his eyes and drew on his own power, heightening his senses. They were all dying. From the moment they were born.

The screaming had stopped. He wondered whether she was losing consciousness. Or maybe, as a human and therefore slave to a slew of nasty emotions, she was far beyond fear.

He licked his lips. She should be. After all, he would soon be able to pick out the smell of her burning flesh amongst the mix. The flames that would lick away at her skin, stripping it from her bones as she melted like a human candle. Humans did always burn so well.

Drayvex wrapped his hand around something soft and tugged, ripping out glistening entrails. The hag creature screamed, springing to life once again. It stretched its mouth wide, revealing a dark chasm of tiny jagged points. Taking a great suck, it aimed, with effort, at Drayvex's face.

He sneered, grabbing it by the throat. "You think you can handle *my* soul? I hope you choke—"

The surrounding walls of the entire structure gave an almighty groan. Crackling flames engulfed them where they stood.

Drayvex watched the tongues roll harmlessly off his skin. It was deceptive in this form, having the appearance of human skin while maintaining the many perks of his tough demon flesh. Two beings, a demon and a mutated fire hag. Both immune to the blaze's power.

A crash sounded from the neighbouring room. The being that wasn't immune to fire remained silent.

Something inside him squirmed. Drayvex tried to enjoy the vivid mental images his mind was throwing at him, but the response was unsatisfying.

What the *Hell*?

Drayvex grabbed the creature's head and twisted with sharp crack. When he heard the wet crunch of a broken spine, he kept twisting, ripping the head from the shoulders and smashing it through the wall behind him. His entire being seethed.

You don't need to keep her sweet anymore, the voice in his mind offered, rough and impatient. You got what you wanted.

He had exactly what he wanted. His side-quest to eradicate the competition was a bonus prize and a way of dragging out his spontaneous and very much temporary abdication.

The girl brought this on herself. She took you on and lost. That's just tough shit.

Drayvex shot forward and smashed through the wall, breaking through the partition into the neighbouring room. He was more angry with himself than anything else. But that didn't stop him from blaming her.

He crossed the burning room and stood over his persistent bipedal headache, scanning her unconscious form. A steady trickle of blood flowed from a gash on her forehead, soaking into the wooden slats beneath her head. Her lips had a blue tinge, with her complexion a colour that would rival any corpse.

There was no doubt about it. Ruby was toast.

The question was, did he really want to help her? Drayvex studied the girl at his feet, deliberating. A better question: how would her existence better serve his needs? He considered this as the room burned. Her death would serve his needs.

Ruby's smiling face sprang to mind. He recalled how easy it had been to gain her trust. She had looked at him with wide green eyes, suspicious yet curious. And he had fed her exactly what he wanted her to believe. Hardly the challenge he'd anticipated.

He watched the blood beneath her head collect into a pool. She certainly wasn't the conniving witch in hiding he'd suspected her of being. Just the unsuspecting keeper of the key to life.

A support beam crashed through the wall he had decimated. The ceiling above them gave way.

Drayvex reached out as pieces of ceiling fell, catching them with mental reflexes. He suspended hunks of wood above them both with the power of his mind, putting his other muscles to work.

And yet, here she was. Lying at his mercy for the umpteenth time, *still* alive. He was a Demon Lord, feared and despised by all who knew his name. Those that didn't would one day know and wish they could forget. He'd wiped out entire worlds, entire races without blinking. He was death, darkness incarnate. And she was still alive. Not because she was powerful, but because he had spared her, for no real reason other than because he could.

She had come to him, knowing what he was—*knowing* that he could snap her like a twig without blinking. She was a curious creature. The pawn that insisted on being a queen.

Making up his mind, Drayvex bent down and scooped the unconscious Ruby up into his arms. The girl was a small, persistent itch at the back of his mind. One he had no idea how to scratch.

He took the slow exit, avoiding high speed and collisions with brittle walls. A human exit for the human girl in his arms.

Drayvex exited the over-sized bonfire and put some distance between them. When they were far away enough, he lay Ruby on the grass and stood, watching her chest rise and fall. There was something he was missing. Something that he hadn't yet taken from her.

That was why she was still alive.

He ran through several scenarios in his mind, debating what to do with her. Whichever way he looked at it, first she needed to be fixed.

A shadow moved in his peripheral vision. His head shot up.

Drayvex powered up, reacting. He combed the darkness with his senses, scanning the open space around them, looking for the thing that had moved. Ruby's blood, thick and heady, trickled towards the drain. A rodent dug in the soil five feet to the right. A mouth-breathing woman stared at them from ten feet to the left.

He turned to stare at the woman. Her vision would be limited, but she was watching them all the same. He smiled and then dropped it.

Problem solved.

Chapter 11

R uby opened her eyes and reeled.
   She blinked, trying to clear her smudged vision. She was
   surrounded by white.

Heaving herself upright, she squinted. Her head was heavy, and she ached.
Everywhere.

All at once, her vision snapped into focus. Ruby stiffened as her mother's
tormented face swam into view.

"Ruby?" The figure next to her grabbed a fistful of gown, wrapping her
other arm simultaneously around Ruby's neck. "Oh, hon, you're awake."

She felt her mother's tight embrace and froze.

"I thought I was going to lose you."

Ruby was stunned. She tried to remember what she'd been doing before
she ended up in this strange place, but her brain was stuck. She did a sweep
of the room.

The steady, monotonous beeping of machinery. Rows of beds with white
sheets, each with a clipboard and padded chair. With sluggish realisation,
it hit her: she was in a hospital.

Ruby's gaze shot down to her hands and arms. A wave of relief coursed
through her as she found no wiring. Not attached.

The relief quickly left her. "What's going ...?" She licked her lips. Her
throat was dry. Her head was *pounding*. "What happened? What's going

on?"

Without warning, her mother shoved her backwards. A bony hand gripped either one of Ruby's shoulders, holding her out at arms length. "You don't remember?"

Ruby met her fierce gaze, and any words she'd been forming died in her throat.

"You've been hurt. You're in Callien General. You don't remember?"

She stared at her mum, her limbs buzzing in a building restlessness. Yeah, she'd gathered that much. But she'd been walking. Through the village at night. Because …

Ruby sighed and ran her fingers through her untamed hair. "Because?"

The figure beside her narrowed her eyes, a familiar but forgotten gaze, as though she was about to interrogate a suspect. "Oh, Doctor. I think something's wrong."

"Mum, please—"

"Ruby, I have to know. Did someone hurt you?"

Ruby's breath suspended inside her as she processed her mother's words. What?

"Did *he* do this to you?"

A lump of ice settled in her stomach, cold and heavy.

"Hello, Ruby. How are we feeling today?"

Ruby jumped as the new voice addressed her. She hadn't heard him enter the room.

"Doctor." Her mother retracted a hand to place it on her forehead.

Ruby looked up at the good doctor. He was a tall, dark-skinned man with a warm smile.

"I feel fine," Ruby said. "What happened?" She glanced over towards the only window in the room. It was covered by a closed blind. "How *long* have I been here?"

Pause. "Doctor, is that normal?"

"No need to panic, Mrs Peyton. Your daughter is going to be just fine."

Ruby felt that restless energy pushing inside her again as the two people in the room that knew what was going on ignored her.

103

"This kind of behaviour is normal with patients who have suffered a bang to the head. We'd like to keep her here for a bit for observation, just to be safe, but she should be fine to go home in a few hours." He gave her mother's shoulder a brief squeeze, then turned back to face his patient.

Ruby folded her arms.

The doctor pulled a small torch out of his breast pocket and shined a light into each of her eyes. When he was satisfied, he gave her his best serious-but-concerned doctor look. "So, what do you remember from the incident, Ruby?"

At the word 'incident', memories she barely recognised flickered at the edges of her mind. She was walking towards the old abandoned barn. Ruby grabbed at the mental images, not willing to let them slip away.

She risked a sideways glance at her mum. Despite her obvious stress, she was doing okay. She chewed on her lower lip. Not only had her paranoid mother left Crichton for the first time since calling it their home two years ago, but she was acing it. Maybe there was hope for them both yet.

"The fire, honey."

Ruby met her mother's gaze. The fire. Her mind spluttered to life with vivid memories. The sound of crackling deafened her, the air growing thin as everything around her burned. Drayvex. She was looking for Drayvex.

"I don't—I don't know," she lied, breathless. How had the night gone so horribly wrong? How had the fire started? How had she got from there to here?

Her mum ran her hands through her frazzled hair. "Ruby?"

Ruby fixated on the odd marks on the ceiling. "I don't remember," she deadpanned. She didn't want to think about it. She didn't want to talk about it. Especially not about Drayvex and certainly not to her mother.

"It's okay, Mrs Peyton. Ruby will remember in her own time." The doctor stepped away from the bed and give a small cough—the signal that his consultation was over. "Until then, she just needs plenty of rest and quiet."

"Thank you, Doctor."

Ruby waited until she heard the click of the door before speaking. "Mum." She measured her words as she spoke. "You're a long way from home. So I know what this must be costing you."

The figure next to the bed exhaled, an audible sigh that made her shoulders sag. Then, she smiled. "Oh, my dear. I wouldn't be anywhere else but by your side."

Exhausted but wired, she reached out and took the hand closest to her bedside. "I'm fine now, Mum. *We're* going to be just fine." Trying not to think about the monsters that wanted her dead, she smiled back at her mum, trying to mirror that feeling inside.

Just fine.

It was out of control. A crazed beast.

Taptaptap.

Her lungs were bursting. She couldn't run anymore.

"Ruby?"

The dog lunged for her throat, fangs bared.

"Ruby, you have a visitor."

Ruby sat up with a start, scrabbling as she slipped sideways off the strange narrow bed. Gasping for air, she grabbed at the thin sheets, catching herself just in time.

The three soft taps sounded again. Ruby looked up towards the door.

A familiar blond head peeked around the frame. She stared at her best friend from across the room, unsure of how to respond. Sandra.

It was stupid. They'd spoken online since their spat, and it had been fine. Now, seeing her standing there, it felt new again.

Sandra's eyes flicked around the room before falling upon the wild-haired Ruby, sitting amongst the tangle of bed sheets.

Ruby wracked her brain, trying to find some way to break the ice. "Sand …"

The tall figure lingered in doorway, her whole demeanour guarded. Then, as if the world was ending, she shook her head and dashed across the room. Ruby froze as Sandra flung herself into her arms.

"Oh my God, Rube." Her voice quivered as she spoke, low and emotional. "We thought you were a goner for sure." Her loose hair splayed out across them both, curtaining her face and fanning over Ruby's shoulder.

She gripped her friend, neither one of them moving. It felt good to embrace Sandra again. She was soft and tangible and *real.*

At last, Ruby broke the lull. "I'm fine," she said, trying to sound reassuring. She pulled back and looked Sandra in the eyes. "Honestly."

Sandra did the same, narrowing her gaze with a playful intensity. She shuffled backwards, perching on the end of the bed. Then she sighed, her eyes glistening with fresh emotion. "Ruby, I'm—"

"It's okay, Sand."

"No, Rube. I need to say this." As she held a hand up for emphasis, Ruby couldn't help but notice her nails. Usually pristine, Sandra's well-manicured talons were now plain and cut short. The world clearly *was* ending.

Ruby focused on her friend, giving her a curt nod. "Okay. Go ahead."

Sandra took a moment to collect her thoughts and then continued. "I'm sorry I didn't tell you I was moving. I knew it was going to suck, and I thought it would be easier to say goodbye if we didn't have to talk about it."

Ruby took a breath to respond but stopped herself.

"I was wrong. Ignoring the problem didn't solve anything. So I guess that does make me a coward." She gave miserable shrug, a half-hearted smile pulling at her lips.

Ruby's hasty insult had come back to haunt her on many an occasion since that awful evening. But none more than now, as a fresh wave of regret battered her conscience once more. Taking a deep breath, she followed with her own confession. "You're not a coward, Sand. You're the bravest person I know. I should never have lashed out at you. I know how much you want a relationship with your dad. I was just being selfish."

Sandra's eyes brightened at her words, and Ruby felt a small weight lift from her chest. "This is nothing that we can't work through. Honestly, Rube, you have an excuse to come and visit me in the city now."

They laughed in unison, and for a moment, it was as though Sandra had never left. But Ruby's aching body was an unrelenting reminder of the night's events, and her pounding head and aching lungs were waiting in the wings to drag her back.

"So, what are you doing here?"

Sandra's eyes popped out of her head. "What am I—? Ruby. You've been unconscious for nearly forty-eight hours."

Her mind did a backflip. Forty. Eight. Hours. Two *whole* days.

"Your mum was frantic. When she called me to say you'd been rushed to hospital, everything was so vague. No one seemed to know what was going on. We were both so scared."

Ruby's gaze was glued to Sandra's as she listened to her story, a numbing horror spreading. "So, you …"

"So I dropped everything. Got here as fast as I could." She smiled a faraway smile. "How's the head? Are your memories back? Your mum said that you were pretty blank when you first came around."

Blank. Ruby laughed despite the seriousness of the conversation. "Sort of." Her mum did always have a way with words. "There was a fire in the old barn. It came out of nowhere and I just couldn't get out. I must have blacked out."

Sandra fidgeted on the edge of the bed. "Oh. Well, the doctor says you knocked your head." She paused, looking around the room, before continuing. "What were you *doing* there, Rube?"

Ruby hesitated. She wanted to tell her. She wanted to tell her everything. But was that really such a good idea?

Sandra raised an eyebrow. "Well?"

Ruby stared at her, her whole body stock-still. She needed this, someone she could confide in. A way to sort out her racing thoughts and feelings. "There was a light. A strange red beam and it was coming from that barn. It was like nothing I've ever seen before. So, naturally, I went to investigate."

"Did you find out what it was?"

No. That much was still a mystery. In fact, the entire night had turned out to be a pointless expedition. She shook her head.

"And then the fire started, while you were still inside." Sandra hummed under her breath. "Maybe it was that weird light that started it. You know, Rube, you really should stop 'investigating' things by yourself. Curiosity killed the cat."

Ruby held her breath, considering her next words carefully. She had been looking for a monster. Would Sandra believe her? "What I don't recall is how I got out by myself."

Sandra's eyes gleamed. A strange look crossed her face.

Ruby raised her eyebrows. Knowing her friend like she did, Ruby was certain that she had some juicy gossip, just waiting to burst out of her.

"Well, your mum said someone pulled you out of the fire."

That wasn't what she'd expected. "What?"

Sandra gave a cryptic smile. "Yeah. Old Mrs Whatsername from number twenty saw someone emerge from the burning shack with you in their arms. The silhouette of a man."

Ruby was speechless. Someone had saved her life?

"It was her who stayed with you. Someone pulled you out and just left you on the side of the road. She thought you were dead until she checked your pulse. That's weird, right? *Mysterious.*"

Someone had been there after all.

Sandra was staring at her, expectant. "Do you know anyone tall, dark and mysterious, Rube?"

Ruby knew what she was getting at. She had a strange feeling that there was only one person in this village that fitted a description like that. No one else around here was 'dark and mysterious', that was for sure.

"Are you still seeing that guy from the Tavern? You know, Mr *Mysterious?*"

And, there it was. Ruby's heart did a strange little lurch. "Say what you mean, Sand."

Sandra smiled, her eyes growing overly wide as she shrugged. "Don't know what you're on about."

Ruby sighed and looked down at her hands. She needed to talk to someone. "No," she said finally, picking at one of her fingernails. "I thought we were friends, but he turned out to be a bit of a bastard." She had been played. But she still couldn't bring herself to say it out loud.

Sandra didn't respond. After a long pause, Ruby stopped playing with her hands. Tension crept back into her shoulders as she waited for a response.

"Men are pigs. I would imagine that any stunt like last night, though, speaks volumes."

Ruby looked up.

Sandra's eyes were soft. *"Someone* cares."

Ruby stared. Did fire affect monsters in the same way as humans? "I'm not so sure he's one of the good guys, Sand. He's just ... not." This wasn't helping.

Sandra tilted her head to one side, studying her from the other end of the bed. "What do you mean?"

Ruby bit the inside of her cheek. "Forget it. I'm done with him, anyway." Bad idea. She couldn't talk about Drayvex. Not to anyone.

Sandra continued to eyeball her, and Ruby could almost hear the cogs turning inside her head. But to Ruby's relief, she smirked and looked away. "Well, I have something that'll make you smile."

Ruby looked up at Sandra, who suddenly seemed to be glowing. "Oh?"

"I have a secret." Her voice was barely more than a whisper. "Although, I'm not supposed to say anything."

Ruby raised her eyebrows in disbelief. Her best friend was the biggest gossip she knew. "Sandra, you can't keep a secret to save your life." She rested her hands on her lap and threaded her fingers together.

Sandra smiled. It was a secret smile that Ruby had never seen her use before. "This one's different. This one's worth keeping. Are you proud?"

"Well, yeah." Ruby leaned forward, curiosity getting the better of her. "What is it?"

Sandra tapped her nose with a finger. "Nice try. I can't tell you!"

Ruby baulked. She was serious.

"But one day, I'll show you." As she said those words, that same strange smile appeared on her face. "Oh, hey, that reminds me." She whipped a scrap piece of card out of her handbag and scribbled on it. She placed it on the bedside table. "This is my new number."

Ruby stared at her, gobsmacked and grudgingly impressed. She'd forgotten just how nice it was to have her best friend around. It was good to have her back.

Chapter 12

T he warm midday sun shone down upon Crichton, a great big 'screw you' in the sky. Drayvex cursed it, hating the hold it had over him. It wasn't the heat that bothered him; it was the light that burned. And he had been exposing himself to Earth's rays on a semi-regular basis for as long as he'd been on the throne. Partly because he was a masochist, but also because he didn't like to lose. Not even to his own physiology.

Drayvex lingered on the roof of the green house, listening to the girl in the room below. Despite himself, he had to admit, approaching a demon in the middle of the night took sizeable balls. What she'd hoped to achieve, though, was beyond him.

Making a reckless decision, Drayvex dropped and landed on the narrow window ledge below.

Ruby turned at the sound, her eyes flicking towards the window. He watched with satisfaction as those eyes grew wider, mouth opening to scream.

She didn't. Instead, she threw her hand up, catching herself.

Drayvex considered Ruby from behind the glass. Not screaming for dear old mother? But that gun would come in oh so handy.

Her heart put in overtime as she considered him back, pounding through the fragile shell of her chest

Drayvex narrowed his eyes. It it's rude to keep a demon waiting outside your window, Ruby, he thought silkily. His fangs inched down inside his mouth in anticipation.

You wanted to play with monsters. I'm *all* yours, dear.

After a moment, as if in slow motion, Ruby padded over to the window. She stopped short, her hands held behind her back. She met his gaze head-on and licked her lips. "What do you want from me?"

It wasn't a bad show, by any means. But the quiver in her voice betrayed her. The knife she concealed was more of a danger to her than to him. Still, it sent a message—the kind of message that kept things interesting.

She looked as though she'd just dragged herself out of her blanket-swaddled pit, her dark flame hair wild and unkempt. The shadows under her eyes revealed the toll of her most recent endeavour, along with her milky skin, paler than ever under the cheap bedroom lighting.

Drayvex stared back, unflinching. "Don't play games with me, Ruby." As he spoke, his breath clouded the flimsy piece of glass between them. "We both know what I'm doing here."

Her mask of calm slipped as she watched him talk, her eyes resting on the vicious fangs behind his lips. He wasn't messing around anymore. She would *know* who she was dealing with.

Ruby's eyes were locked on his.

"What do *you* want?" Drayvex waited for her to make her move.

She looked away, suddenly seeming unsure of herself. When she looked back, her hand inched towards the window latch.

Drayvex waited until the window was open wide before stepping into the room. He pulled the curtains closed behind him, shutting out the painful light.

He was standing in a small, neutral bedroom, walled with organised clutter. Every inch of space had been utilised, every available surface covered with items and trinkets.

As he idly scanned over the desk closest to him, his gaze snagged on one item in particular. It was a soul candle. Black and hungry. Drayvex regarded the dark object, tension creeping into his muscles. He took a closer look, skimming over the items he'd all but disregarded a moment ago. There were more. Dark artefacts, arcane objects—albeit low level—broken, dormant or neglected, sitting amongst her normal human junk.

Drayvex watched her through accusing eyes, picking her apart with fresh scrutiny. *What* was this infuriating creature?

"You're a monster."

Drayvex cocked his head and narrowed his eyes. "Your point?" he said, his voice cold and crisp. Are *you* a monster, Ruby Red?

"You're a mythical being. Y-you don't exist." Running her fingers through her hair, she took a half-step backwards and met the shelves behind her. "You can't exist."

"You're wasting my time."

Ruby gripped the shelving at her back. "I'm scared."

Drayvex felt his expression flicker, her bare confession catching him off guard. He didn't know what he'd expected, but these days, honesty was about as rare as the ancient power that throbbed in his pocket. It was a dangerous card to play against the likes of him. He, who could spot a liar from a mile off. Despite this, she wore it well.

Pushing away stray thoughts, he inched towards her, until their faces and bodies were almost touching. Ruby tensed as the proximity between them changed, her breaths coming sharper and quicker.

"You should be," he said, adding a touch of soft menace to his voice.

A strange expression crossed her face, and Drayvex couldn't read it. Her right hand snaked out from behind her back, the knife she gripped dropping to the floor in a gesture that was borderline suicidal.

"I'm scared of the monsters that want to kill me." She reached out towards him. "The monsters that you saved me from." She reached, stopped. Tried again.

As he felt her light touch brush against his arm, Drayvex braced himself for the overwhelming urge to rip her throat out—but it never came.

He looked down at her hand, and a violent frustration filled the empty space where his blood lust should be.

Drayvex sighed and whipped his arm away. He folded them and took a deliberate step back, maintaining control of the room. His eyes were drawn to the infernal trinkets dotting the shelves. What a maddening contradiction. It was obvious that this girl didn't have a clue what she'd got herself into. No human in their right mind would use a Lapis Vitae. And yet, this was *her* space. These were her possessions.

Drayvex plucked one from a nearby shelf and held it up in front of her, a hundred accusations buzzing through his mind. "What's this?" He waved it in her face, demanding.

It was a test that she would either pass or fail.

Ruby eyed the spindled weapon his hand, her face changing, giving him everything he needed to know.

Drayvex waited.

She eyed him with dubious surprise. "I, um—I'm not sure." He could see her every thought, playing across her face in minute detail. "But it's interesting. And I collect interesting things."

It was unsatisfying. He frowned, trying to read between the lines.

"You can't have it."

Drayvex focused on Ruby, who was giving him a look that may have been vaguely ominous had it belonged to anyone else on the planet.

Caught between mild amusement and maddening frustration, he closed his eyes, placing the dark object back on the shelf. The yawning chasm between her limited understanding and his own expanded.

Well, this was going to be interesting.

"I'm a Demon Lord. I'm not your average monster." He couldn't have made it any simpler. Yet, she had no damn idea what he was talking about.

"A Demon Lord?" Ruby laughed under her breath. Drayvex couldn't tell if it was genuine, or if she was losing her grip on her sanity.

He didn't know why he was telling her this. It was as though she'd flicked a switch inside him, could shut off the parts of him that craved violence and chaos at will. Before he met her, he'd have mocked the very idea.

He stalked back and forth as he spoke. "I rule over the demon planet, Vekrodus." Ruby followed his every movement, never taking her eyes off him. "It's a long way away." Drayvex grinned, flashing fangs "And all demons there answer to me."

Ruby twirled her hair in stunned silence. "Well, that's …" She paused, failing to string a sentence together. "Not what I was expecting."

He watched in amusement as she tucked one side of her hair behind an ear, and then the other.

"So then, you must know why those things wanted to kill me."

Drayvex knew that he'd walked into a trap. He did know. Of course he knew.

It wasn't her they wanted. They didn't *need* to keep coming at her in such a pointless manner. If she could rid herself of the stone's aura, then they would be forced to look elsewhere.

But there was nothing simple about that task. And he didn't trust her. Not one bit.

"I can't help you."

Ruby's face fell, before rearranging into a scowl. "Can't, or won't?"

Drayvex glared at her. "Alright. I *won't* help you." Mercy.

"Will you help me fight them, then?"

He stared. This girl had a deathwish. "Fight them?" he jabbed, standing up straight. "Don't make me laugh. A twig like you wouldn't last a second in a scrap. Not with your toothpick, and not with your stolen magic." Not even if you knew how to wield it.

Ruby opened her mouth in blatant protest, then stopped and frowned. She stepped forward, her body tensing as she all but squared up to him. "I don't have a choice. A 'Demon Lord' stole my necklace and now my village is overrun with his pets."

"If you go near her again … I will kill you."

Drayvex glared at the small girl but squirmed on the inside. Like mother, like daughter.

"Please, Drayvex."

He needed to finish what he'd started. He didn't give a damn about her village, and he certainly didn't do favours for glorified snacks.

"Please?"

"No, Ruby. Your welfare is not my problem. Your *village* is not my problem. So if you're done wasting my time, I'll be off."

114

Ruby stared at him with wounded eyes.

Drayvex folded his arms.

Unbelievable, that annoying voice in his head sneered. Drayvex ignored it.

"Right. Not your problem. Why would it be?"

Just say it.

Say what? He didn't save lives, he took them. He didn't protect humans, he ate them. Broke them. Hunted them for kicks. The girl was lucky to still be alive. In fact, no human had ever survived this long in his company.

Admit it,said the insolent voice. You want her problems.

Ruby turned away, hiding her face behind a curtain of hair.

She confounds you. She infuriates you. She's becoming a weakness.

Drayvex glared at her, burning a hole in the side of her head. Weakness. The very word made him want to laugh out loud. But ...

He ran his tongue along his sharpened teeth. If he was, hypothetically, developing a weakness for the girl, it would at the very least provide him with the challenge he still craved. Drayvex felt his curiosity burn in response.

It would be a bad thing for her.

He smirked, earning himself a strange look from Ruby. The stone would still be his when he was done with her. Besides, she had the attention of his inept rival for the stone. She was his best lead.

As Ruby witnessed his visible change in attitude, her heart audibly accelerated.

Drayvex motioned for her to approach, thoughts of predator and prey forgotten. When she didn't react, he stepped forward and closed the gap between them, demanding her full attention. "Maybe, we can make this work after all," he murmured, the corners of his mouth raising into the slightest of grins.

Ruby blinked. "You—really?" Her surprise was audible. "You'll help me?" Her hand reached for the place where her necklace had once hung. She pulled away sharply. "Oh, well thanks." Her voice said otherwise.

Drayvex tilted his head, expectant. He stepped around her, the sound of his boots muffled by the soft carpet underfoot. As he moved, he kept her in the corner of his vision. "Spit it out. I've not got all day."

Ruby blinked. "What?"

"Whatever's on your mind. Spit it out." He'd thought *he* was capricious.

She seemed to deliberate for a moment before answering. "You have my necklace. Can I have it back?"

"No."

The hope that had remained in her eyes choked and died.

"I have a question," Drayvex said as he stopped pacing. He turned his head to gaze sideways at her through predatory eyes. "Where did you get the stone?"

Ruby, who had been looking at him with all the fury of an angry, wet kitten, stopped breathing. A small crease appeared between her eyes, and Drayvex could almost hear the cogs grinding in her head. "The … what?"

Drayvex sighed. It was like talking to a child. He reached down and hooked a finger around the cord in his pocket. Pulling the Lapis Vitae out, he let it dangle in his grip. "They don't want you. They want this."

Ruby's eyes widened. She stared incredulously at the necklace. Then, her face hardened. "Are you taunting me?"

Drayvex watched the girl that had just taken Ruby's place with newly kindled interest. All fear and doubt banished, this version was out for blood.

"You're not playing fair." Her voice was soft but contained an undercurrent of something dark and delicious. And defiant.

"I'll make things simple for you." Drayvex moved around and stepped in front of her, invading her personal space. "Fair warning: I don't *do* fair. So, if this is going to be too difficult for you, you can find someone else to solve your damn life problems. Got it?" Defiant was something you squashed with intense prejudice.

Ruby glared at him with fresh, glistening eyes. She looked as though he'd just snatched her screaming baby sister and waved her around above a flaming pit. He might as well be a child snatcher, for the way she was looking at him.

"Fine." She folded her arms and closed her eyes. "Where do we start?"

Drayvex smiled, satisfied. "Close to home," he urged, lips close to her ear.

Her eyes flew open, his voice in her ear, or the mention of home, grabbing her attention.

"Where did dear old Grandma get such a weapon of ungodly proportions?" He watched her from the corner of his eye, silently judging her deceased gran. He'd bet anything that her precious gran knew a thing or two more about the world of demons than she'd let on.

"What weapon?"

Lordy. "The stone." He paused. "The *necklace*." Something silver flashed in the corner of his eye. Drayvex turned to find the culprit.

A silver coin, lost amongst the clutter, marked with some kind of Earth currency. Dull, but still gleaming in the stuffy bedroom light. As he studied it, a strange impulse overcame him. Before he'd thought about what he was doing, he'd swiped it with lightning reflexes.

Ruby was staring at him as though he had two heads. "My necklace. Right." She frowned, a far-away look on her face. "I don't know where she got it. Grandma travelled a lot, and um ..."

Drayvex began to pace. He smelled a rat.

"Huh." She padded over to the bed and sat at the end. "I loved Gran, but I guess I didn't really know her at all." Ruby traced her collar bone with a finger, making absent-minded strokes. "The day she gave it to me was the day she died. She told me to keep it close. That it would bring me luck, as it had brought her luck."

Drayvex stopped fiddling with the paper clip holder on her desk. He laughed once, short and hard, and saw her jump at the sound. "Luck?" He raised an eyebrow. "You mean the power to outlive your every bastard enemy? Or the ability to bend any living thing to your will?"

Ruby was staring at him with that same expression, the one she had used so many times these past few days. An expression of pure dumbfounded shock, mixed with a little fear and a dash of something that looked a lot like awe. He didn't know why it gave him a kick, but every time he'd seen it, his fangs had sharpened in response. "If that's what we're calling power these days, then sure. It's luck."

Her hand clenched against the bed, bunching the sheets beneath. "What makes you so sure that you know my family better than I do? Does it have to be a weapon? Has that even occurred to you?"

Challenged yet? mocked his sarcastic internal monologue. Drayvex rolled his eyes. So what if he'd accused her shady family of dabbling with malevolent powers? He was usually right. And the girl wasn't doing herself any favours.

Hungry yet?

He sighed and crossed the room in a second, appearing in front of a disgruntled Ruby.

Ruby flinched.

"Look," he said, soft but firm. "We know it's demonic. Whether or not your gran knew about its capabilities is beside the point." It wasn't. For all he knew, her whole family dabbled with the black arts. "We don't need to know the pesky details, of say, where the thing came from, or how the hell your family have managed to keep it under the radar for so long. No, they're not relevant at all."

Ruby's eyes widened with fresh understanding. "Kept it away from *them?*" she managed, ignoring his sarcasm or missing it completely.

"Ruby? Who are you talking to?"

As Ruby's demented mother called up from the floor below, Ruby froze. The colour drained from her face as she stared at him.

Drayvex folded his arms and smirked at her. "Why don't you introduce us?" Formally.

Something flashed across her face, reacting to his empty threat. His smile slipped. What was that?

"Ruby?"

Ruby glanced at the door. "Stay here," she managed, before stumbling out of the door backwards.

As she shut it behind her, Drayvex moved across the room. He flicked the switch down, taking out the light. His head hurt. Even the dim rays piercing through the curtains was more than he wanted. Standing in the darkness, he felt a dull throb inside his head.

Pacing over to the bed, Drayvex made himself comfortable. The sounds of Ruby pacifying her nosy mother floated up from the room below. That wasn't the reaction he'd expected. He wondered how much she already knew about their previous meeting.

Ruby was denying her mother answers. Deflecting suspicion. Her mother was pushing for explanations to far-out questions, ironically, not so far from the mark, but missing it all the same.

Drayvex scoffed, tuning them out. Lying to her daughter, covering her own dodgy secrets and yet demanding the truth. That woman would get nothing from either of them. Not if *he* had anything to do with it.

He closed his eyes. There wasn't much known about human-summon stone interaction. What he did know, though, was that for lower species, while the stone did indeed protect the wearer, the luck was reversed once removed. The longer the contact, the worse that luck when taken away.

Ruby had moved on. He could tell which footstep was hers without trying, and he trailed her from room to room, building a mental map. The girl couldn't do quiet if her life depended on it. It was as though she walked around in life with her eyes shut. Drayvex smirked to himself. How had she even made it this far?

The sound of cussing reached his ears, followed by the smell of fresh blood. Drayvex ignored the instinctive sharpening of his fangs, the moistening of his mouth with venom. The stone was slowly killing her. And it was only going to get worse from here.

The sounds of Ruby making her ascent snagged his attention. He sat up out of reflex. The door creaked, and the scent of blood sharpened, sticking in the back of his throat. Ruby shuffled through the darkened room, stopping a few feet away from him.

A harsh light snapped on at the bedside table. Drayvex cringed away, feeling his retinas protest at her ignorance.

"Oh, does the light bother you?"

Drayvex glared at her moodily from across the bed, trying to ignore the renewed throbbing at the back of his head. "What do *you* think?" he

119

snapped with unintended venom.

Ruby flashed him an apologetic look. She grabbed the bedside lamp and placed it on the floor behind the stack of drawers. "Better?" she asked, sounding small.

Drayvex nodded, feeling a slight prick of guilt. It wasn't her fault that she was clueless. She was a creature of the light, blind in the dark. He, Drayvex, was *born* in darkness.

"So. How long have you been … uh, here?"

The light was poison. And yet, he could never stop himself from trying to touch it. He glanced back at Ruby, who was perched on the edge of the chest, and raised an eyebrow. "You mean Earth?" The corners of his mouth twitched.

Ruby gave a soft laugh, a musical sound that filled the room. "Yeah, I suppose I do." Her eyes sparkled with curiosity as she studied him, her previous nerves melting away.

Drayvex found himself drawn to them. "Not long. But my planet will manage without me for as long as it needs to."

Her mouth opened in response, but the words that followed were delayed. "I thought you were the leader of your world."

"I am." He grinned, flashing a few fangs daringly. "What do you think happens when the ruler of a planet decides to take an open-ended vacation?"

"You didn't," Ruby exclaimed. "Why?"

Drayvex gave a reckless laugh. "Because," he said, "when you reach the top, life gets dull. I sought out a bigger challenge."

She chewed on her tongue while she mulled over his words. "And running a planet isn't challenge enough for you?"

He indulged in a stretch. "No," he said, his tone almost bragging.

Ruby's eyes grew wide. Drayvex tensed. Was it something he'd said? He followed her gaze to where his claws were stretched and gleaming under the dim bedroom light. He hadn't even thought about it.

Ruby gaped at them, her green eyes rising to his face, lingering there. "May I?" She made a timid gesture with an outstretched hand.

Drayvex was taken aback. Was she serious? Surely, any human in their right mind would want to put as much distance between themself and these lethal weapons as possible.

He reached out and offered her a claw, keeping his movements to a minimum. "Knock yourself out," he retorted, trying to sound indifferent. And just like that, things had jumped to a whole new level of weird.

Ruby reached out, and ever so slowly, placed a finger on his claw. When he didn't move, she ran it down its black, gleaming length, stopping when she got to the point. Drayvex found that he was suddenly hyper-sensitive to her touch. Where her skin brushed his claw, it tingled, like the aftermath of an electric shock.

"Jeez ... that's—that's mad." Her voice was barely a whisper, like she was talking to herself rather than to him. She traced back up again.

Drayvex looked up and met Ruby's gaze. She was focused on him.

In that moment, he was more aware of her presence than he had ever been. The soft heat radiating from her warm body, just inches away. Her shallow breaths, uneven, quick. As Ruby's finger travelled back along his outstretched claw, a tingle shot down his spine.

Something inside him snapped with violent force—that alien, parasitic thing that had been growing inside him since subjecting himself to the basal drone of humanity. Now, it threatened to become a part of him. For the first time in his long life, he felt vulnerable.

Seconds passed. Drayvex found himself drawn to the girl facing him. Wanting to *protect* her.

Ruby's hand stilled. Her eyes gleamed with wary curiosity.

The way the remaining sliver of light shone through the curtains, hitting the side of her face, made her seem almost angelic. His senses were completely focused on her and he didn't know how to stop them.

Drayvex's mind scrambled. He heard Ruby stand. A dull, throbbing horror seeped inside him. He had been spending too much time around humans, and now, he was in danger of joining them.

"This weather is pretty odd. It's not normally this nice."

But he wasn't human. He was a cold-blooded killer. A demon. He would never be human.

Drayvex stood, the strong urge to escape becoming his dominant need—to be as far away from *her* as he could get. "I have other things to do. You'll have to manage without me."

Ruby relinquished the curtains and span to look at him, a protest forming on her lips. "Wait, what? What about the demons?"

He bristled, her every word grating against the fragile remnants of his sanity. "I said I'm *busy*," he growled, striding over to the window. "Deal with it."

"Oh. O-okay." The fear was back in her eyes. She sucked in a breath, but Drayvex wasn't interested in anything she had to say.

In the blink of an eye, he was next to the window. He yanked back the curtains and jumped out, almost forgetting to push open the glass first.

Drayvex dropped to the ground, not bothering to break his fall, subjecting himself to sun once again which, in hindsight, was the preferable method of torture.

The screaming woman leapt to her feet.

Drayvex welcomed her with outstretched claws, slicing through her soft neck. Blood spurted from the open gash.

The woman choked, coughing as her lungs filled, spraying red droplets around her in spasms.

Flames crackled and seared, eating their way through the village and its saccharine houses. The surrounding landscape glistened with the blood of victim after victim, staining the gravel and surrounding greenery a deep, sinister red. The bodies that were splayed at his feet lay pale and empty; bags of meat waiting to be disposed of, or devoured.

Drayvex stood at the centre of the chaos, breathing in the heavy scent of death that hung in the air. Eyes as black as the night surveyed the surrounding scenes with a distant contempt. Remnants dripped down his fingers, running down the length of his claws to join the mess on the ground.

The last surviving villager stumbled towards him in a blind panic. Drayvex watched the man and felt his blood lust rise. With lightning reflexes he struck, lashing out with his mind.

The man stumbled. He moaned, hands flying to his ears.

Drayvex ramped up the pressure. The stone throbbed in his pocket.

The man gripped his head, screaming as trickles of blood ran from every orifice. As he fell to his knees, Drayvex pushed him harder, barely breaking a sweat.

Then, without warning, the man exploded, sending pieces flying in all directions.

Drayvex smiled, feeling nothing.

Chapter 13

Ruby perched on the edge of the bed, towel-drying her hair in methodical rubs. It was amazing what a hot shower and a good night's sleep could do for a person. Ease the aching muscles. Wash away that unclean feeling after a long hospital stay. Provide some perspective on a problem.

What no amount of sleep or showering could do, though, was make a problem go away.

She stared at the muted TV, her attention drifting. Her mind had long since reached its info-dump limit, but the familiarity of her morning routines were soothing. They made it easier to avoid the difficult questions buzzing in her mind. Questions that all revolved around Drayvex.

Ruby let her damp towel drop to the carpet. She reached for the bedside table and lifted a steaming mug of hot chocolate to her lips. Knowing the truth about him didn't make him any easier to understand.

Drayvex. She knew almost nothing about him. Yet, she wanted to, despite everything. Did that make her a bad person?

She slid her mug back onto the table. She didn't know. What she did know was that when he was in the room, every fibre of her being was on edge. And she didn't trust him.

As she stared vacantly at her mug, she focused on its base. The thing she was using as a coffee mat. It was Sandra's card.

Ruby smiled, slipping it out from underneath. The card was warm, but not wet. She studied the number scrawled on the front in black Biro. It was embellished with little hearts, which made her smile even wider. They hadn't needed to text much in the past. Now that they were miles apart, it was time to work those thumbs.

Ruby flipped the card over and felt her smile fade. There was picture on the back. She squinted at it. It was a symbol of sorts, treated with a gold, shiny foil. The card itself was black, with no clues about a corporation or its meaning.

Ruby chewed on her lower lip, trying to think back through the many conversations she'd had with Sandra about her dad. What was it that he did again?

Moments later, Ruby was sitting at her laptop, her fingers flying over the keyboard. She'd never met Sandra's dad, but she'd heard a lot about him over the previous decade. Mainly bad.

She landed on the search engine and stopped, her reluctant fingers hovering over the keys. Curiosity was a weakness of hers, but on this occasion, she felt justified in doing a little digging. After all, Sandra'd had many a complaint with her dear old absentee Pa, and Ruby had sat and listened to every single one.

She typed into the search bar: BENDY Y-SHAPED SYMBOL, and hit enter.

Millions of results were immediately listed, all as vague and far-reaching as her description. Yoga positions, the Greek alphabet, a kids' cartoon show …

A noise grabbed her attention. She slammed the lid down in shock and sprang to her feet

Ruby spotted the demon lurking at her window and froze. Drayvex. She wondered if he knew that windows weren't entryways, but in fact had many other, more practical uses. "Most people use the front door," she muttered, slipping the card into her back pocket. She moved to let him inside.

"That's nice," said Drayvex, making her jump. His tone was anything but nice. "Demons create doors in whatever happens to be in their way. Didn't think you'd go for that."

Ruby looked up and met his gaze. He'd heard her from across the room. He was glaring at her, and his eyes were a moody grey. His hair was dark and dishevelled.

Ruby was crippled by his abrupt tone. Did he really hate her? It seemed that way. He couldn't get away from her fast enough yesterday. What the hell was this jerk's problem?

Drayvex's impatient tapping at the glass made her realise that she'd stopped. Vaguely aware that she was staring, Ruby scrambled for something, anything, to say. Grey eyes.

When she'd first decided to seek out the demon in disguise, she'd assumed that she would have to tolerate him—the dirty thief who had taken her grandma's last gift to her—because she needed his help. Now Ruby knew that she'd been foolish to assume such a thing. It was *he* who was tolerating *her*, with his own hidden agenda and her necklace in his pocket.

Ruby bit down on her tongue, suppressing the restless ire building in her muscles. Be careful, she warned herself. You still need him. You can't do this alone.

Avoiding eye contact with the looming shape behind the glass, she lifted the catch.

She headed towards the mirror on the dresser. Showing Drayvex her back, she sat and turned to pick through an array of makeup on the tabletop. "So, what is it that you want?"

The silence that followed was long and tense.

Ruby looked up at her reflection, unable to concentrate on the makeup in front of her. Her gaze snagged on the mark on her neck, that unexplained trophy from her alleyway scuffle. It was bumpy and smooth, and like nothing she had seen before. It was strange, but it was more like an old scar than a new wound. She lifted her hand to touch it.

"What do *I* want?" Drayvex said with biting sarcasm, close behind.

Ruby started, her arms swinging in alarm. As they did, she collided with her mug, knocking it straight off the table.

In the small amount of time she had to process and react, she barely registered the blur that passed her. When her brain caught up with her eyes, she turned to assess the damage.

Drayvex was standing at the end of the table, a sloshing cup in his hand. "Will you watch what you're doing?" His voice was flat. He held the cup out at arm's length and stood, waiting for her to take it off from him.

Ruby didn't move.

When she didn't respond, he narrowed his eyes and slid the cup back onto the table with disdain.

Ruby closed her eyes. She ran a hand through her damp hair, pulling it back off her face. She felt stupid. Why did she let him do this to her? Breathing slowly, she stood and willed her heart to calm.

When she opened them again, she discovered that she was being watched. Drayvex was looking at her as though she were a bomb, primed to explode at any moment.

Ruby found herself tickled by this. Despite the plethora of amusing responses springing to mind, though, she decided not to provoke the demon standing in her bedroom. Not today.

"Thanks." She sniffed, letting her hair drop back around her in a curtain. She spun back to face the mirror. "And yes. I'm wondering what you're doing here, as you agreed to help yesterday and then disappeared."

Another pause. She dug her nails into the sides of the chair.

Suddenly, Ruby could feel him right behind her. That unnatural heat that seemed to radiate from his body, and only now did it make any kind of sense. She glanced into the mirror—and her stomach lurched.

There was only one reflection. Her necklace hovered in mid-air behind her head.

"As I said, it's not you they want."

Ruby swivelled on her seat, drawn to the bait.

"It's this."

Exasperated, Ruby stared at the necklace dangling from Drayvex's finger. This again. "You mean my necklace? It's a piece of jewellery that reminds me of my gran. Why would monsters want my jewellery?" It was ludicrous.

"Listen," Drayvex ordered, his serious tone cutting through her mental clutter. "This," he raised the dangling necklace, "is the Lapis Vitae. It has untold power, and its rarity gives it untold *value*. Those demons are the tip of the nightmares that will come for you because they all want its power."

Ruby looked up from her necklace. His eyes were cold. "But you have it now."

They lingered on her for a moment, before moving back to the charm. "I didn't say they were smart."

She laughed. She couldn't help it. Not because what he'd said was funny, but because she wanted to cry. "That's why you want it, isn't it?" It all made sense now.

As she watched the precious remaining part of her grandma sway below Drayvex's hand, she felt herself drawn to it—yearning, even. If she snatched it from his lax grip, would she get away in time?

"Yes, Ruby. Let it go."

Of course she wouldn't. Drayvex outmatched her in every possible way. Even if she could get away, he would find her again. She rolled her eyes upward and frowned as a trinket on the far shelf caught her eye. The little spindle-legged ball sat amongst the clutter, its dark metallic shine gleaming under the soft bedroom light. She squinted at it, a memory tugging at the edge of her mind.

"What's this?"

Ruby shook her head. "And I suppose that funny little trinket you grabbed off my shelf yesterday is the key to another realm?"

She was joking. But as the demon eyed her with fresh sullen regard, her face fell.

"It's a shadow lantern. A low-grade black magic armament and an odd choice of decoration for a small human girl." Drayvex pocketed the necklace, flicking a forked tongue at her.

Ruby blinked at him. A shadow lantern. Of course it was.

With her grandma's soft voice in her mind, she summoned up all her strength and committed to her cause. "The necklace belongs to *me*. Not to you, or them, or any other demon thrill-seeker looking for kicks. Me. I won't just roll over."

To her surprise, Drayvex laughed. "Stubborn, aren't you?"

She was staring again. It was awkward, but she couldn't help it. Every time they spoke, she saw a different shade of him. Feeling her face glow, she twisted back around in her chair.

Just then, Ruby felt warm lips brush against her ear. It was such a shock, her whole body tensed.

"Then, I have a plan," he whispered, voice smooth as silk.

Goosebumps spread down her arms unbidden. She spun back to face him, her mind reeling.

A mischievous grin was spreading on his face. There was something sinister about it. His eyes glowed orange-red, flickering and burning against the reflection of the silent TV. His eyes had changed, and she'd missed it again. As she stared, transfixed by the demon standing before her, it was impossible to tear her eyes away. She realised that Drayvex had never looked more stunning, or more deadly. She should be scared. She knew this, just as she knew that the grass was green. And she was scared, in a way. But it was the wrong sort of scared.

Ruby found herself smiling in response. "I'm listening."

Drayvex regarded her, his eyes gleaming with untold secrets. "I'll go one better," he said, taking a step back. "I'll show you."

Ruby gripped the sides of her chair, wondering why he had to distance himself to show her.

She didn't have to wait long. Right before her eyes, Drayvex was changing. It wasn't like the way he'd changed in the alleyway. This time, he was getting *smaller*.

Ruby watched him blur and remould himself, her sense of realism slipping through her fingers. She was glad she'd had the sense to stay seated. She doubted very much whether her legs would support her, for the foreseeable future.

Then the figure stilled.

As the thing in front of her stared back with all her features, Ruby's head reeled. Her perfect clone smiled at her in a way that Ruby herself had never smiled. It was a callous smile that sent chills down her spine.

At a total loss for words, Ruby took a deep, steadying breath. Then, she inched towards the demon with her face.

Drayvex folded his arms—her arms—and stood with an expectant still. The raise of an eyebrow invited her to take a closer look. The arrogant slope of that mouth, familiar in more ways than one, challenged her to pick a fault.

Ruby got as close she dared. She found herself face to face with her own green eyes, their wicked gleam unsettling. It was like looking in a mirror, only her reflection didn't copy her. She studied her twin closely, making sure to zone in on the tiniest of details.

After a while, Ruby had to hand it to him; he hadn't missed *anything*. He'd noticed the awkward way her hair parted, straight down the middle, right up to the point where it zigged off to the left at the front. A remnant of her fringe days. He'd got the tiny mark just under her nose that her Mum insisted was a beauty spot, and the little dent on her forehead, which was only visible if you knew where to look. It was only then that she saw her necklace. It was hanging around his neck.

"It's a fake," her evil twin said, reading her like a book. "It's all part of the illusion." Cold eyes gleamed at her, a sly look on her face. He was clearly enjoying himself *too* much.

"How ... how do you look like me?" Ruby honestly believed that her own mother would be fooled by this disguise. What was his true face?

Drayvex stared back, unconcerned by her question. "Ruby," he soothed in her voice, a slow smile spreading on his borrowed face. The teeth in his new mouth were elongating, pointing, and Ruby found herself checking her own teeth with her tongue in alarm. This was starting to feel like something from a childhood nightmare.

"It's time we found out exactly what we're dealing with." He ran a feminine finger along the edge of the false charm resting on her chest, looking thoughtful. "In other words," he said, a touch of soft menace coating his words, "end of the line."

*

Drayvex strolled around the edge of the empty square, tuning out the

130

distracting remnants of rain that splattered down from the surrounding rooftops. This was either going to be absurdly simple, or it would backfire spectacularly.

A clicking sound snagged his attention. He turned, his senses on high alert.

A withered human male stepped out of the grand building across the square. Fumbling with an over-sized bunch of keys, he locked the building and turned to leave, nodding in vague greeting from across the square.

Drayvex smiled his sweetest Ruby smile, flashing his small, blunt teeth. Humans were rarely amusing. But as he watched this one leave, he paid particular attention to the large medallions hanging around his neck. *Fancy yourself as someone important, old man?* He snorted. *Talk about delusions of grandeur.*

The cobbled square was large and open, with nowhere to hide. At the centre of the square was a fountain, isolated and exposed. It was *perfect.*

He moved towards it, taking care to exaggerate his footsteps. Based on the utter failure of the previous demons' attempts to snag the stone, his money was on simple.

He didn't smell like Ruby, but he wasn't going to need that level of detail. Not for the low-level bootlickers that would be lurking nearby. Eager to please, not much between the ears. And in their doltish enthusiasm, they would lead him right to their leader.

As Drayvex perched on the edge of the dry fountain, the majority of his attention settled on his surroundings. Every now and again, he probed the area with subtle tendrils of power, waiting for something to take the bait. He wasn't kept waiting for long.

As if to prove the point, a scrappy demon poked its nose around the corner of the far building and peered into the square. It surveyed the area with beady eyes, a creature no bigger than the height of Ruby's knee, and when it noticed the girl at the fountain, its eyes screamed 'jackpot'.

That was exactly what Drayvex planned on giving it.

The stragglers weren't far behind. A thick set demon with purulent lumps, a tall demon with red, glistening skin. As they closed in from all sides, Drayvex resisted the urge to sneer at their pathetic attempts at stealth.

A guttural rumble sounded to his left. Drayvex smiled to himself, ready to feed them what they were so anxious to receive.

Four small demons surrounded the fountain, one at each compass point. Whoever had decided that this would be enough to overpower a small human girl would, under normal circumstances, be right. Today, however, all four of them were at his mercy. Even if they didn't yet know it.

Aware that he was being watched, Drayvex widened his eyes. He took a calculated, faltering step back, kicking the rim of the fountain with his heel. Playing to the idiot crowd, he allowed his breath to hitch and quicken.

Overeager, they moved in, caught up in the show of fear and defeat playing out before them. Not one of them bothered to scratch below the surface.

"It's her. She's the one. Let's kill 'er."

"P-please," Drayvex begged, hearing his feminine voice quiver as he manipulated his captors. "What do you want with me?"

"You know we can't kill her, Fen, you turd."

The demon in his direct line of sight cackled, an array of jagged stumps glistening inside its mouth. Saliva dripped freely from its dank maw and dribbled down its shiny red face. "Oh, my dear," it sneered, leering at the girl. "It's *you* we want. The boss man is going to be so pleased."

The demon grabbed Ruby's wrist with stubby fingers. Drayvex went limp and unresponsive, allowing himself to be pulled into the face of the repulsive puke who clearly fancied himself as the alpha. It drank in Ruby's form with greedy eyes, pausing at an exposed section of throat. Well, my *dear*, he thought, I can hardly wait.

Drayvex studied his demon captors. They were dragging him down lesser travelled paths, which proved that they weren't complete morons. They would hit a snag if one of Ruby's do-gooding neighbours spotted him and decided to intervene. Every so often, they turned to leer in his direction. He stared at each of them in turn, unflinching and unamused. They laughed in response, clueless in their ignorance.

They approached the portal, the same one that he himself had arrived through on that first day.

The thick-set demon stepped forward, eager to be the one to activate it. But before it could take any action, the red demon lurched forward.

"Don't even think about it." It shoved the demon out of the way, sending it flying. "*I'm* the one with the key, idiot!" Producing the long, cylindrical key, the red demon pushed it against the crumbling wall and watched it sink into the bricks.

The portal rippled around the key in response.

Drayvex smiled. These idiots were going to walk him right to their boss. And whoever they were, today was the day they would die.

The red demon tugged the key out of the portal, before grabbing his wrist once again. Drayvex quelled the urge to decapitate him.

"Welcome to Hell, dead girl," it taunted, stealing another filthy glance at Ruby's form.

Your eyes will be the first to go, he bristled, before he was shoved through the portal.

Chapter 14

T he moment they emerged on the other side of the portal, Drayvex had known where he was. Even blind, the noxious gasses that hung in the air would have given it away. They were on Vekrodus, and that meant only one thing.

Underneath his disguise, Drayvex worked up a black rage. The very thought that some pathetic wannabe deemed itself worthy of ruling in his absence made his blood boil.

"Move," barked the materialising demon, jabbing him from behind.

He bristled. Fangs crept down, taking form inside Ruby's small mouth. He could think of only one demon ambitious enough to attempt something so stupid.

Drayvex was no longer in the mood to put up and shut up. He glared across the stretch of land into the far distance, contemplating his next move. He didn't need these unremarkable bootlickers any more. He didn't need Ruby's form, either. But the thought of being able to toy with Saydor was too good to resist.

Drayvex turned to face the scrappy red demon and flashed it a sweet smile, doing his best to look innocent. He didn't have much practice. "Of course. After you."

The demon's face fell blank. Confusion pooled in its protruding eyes.

"Is there something on my face?" asked Drayvex.

Its eyes narrowed. "Feeling feisty, are we?" A fat tongue came out and licked its lips. "We like that in a human. Makes things more interesting."

Oh, things are about to get very interesting, Drayvex mused, keeping his expression neutral.

The castle loomed on the approaching horizon, a large and imposing silhouette against an ashen backdrop. Its myriad pointing spires and turrets stretched high into the sky, piercing the lingering smog hanging in the lower atmosphere.

His castle was far older than he was. It was first built during his father's long and bloody reign centuries ago. It had been his now for almost two.

They moved north-west towards the impressive structure, navigating the arid red desert at a human pace. Drayvex allowed the goons to guide him to his own abode, using the time to analyse their movements.

They weren't his minions, although technically, all demons were his to claim if he so wished. No, more likely than not, they belonged to Saydor. If they weren't taking a faster option of travel, it meant that they couldn't, so they were level ones and twos with minimal power and privileges. The portal key they had lent weight to this train of thought, as only level three demons could request unrestricted travel. And they didn't need a key.

As they approached the lake that surrounded the castle, individual faces stood out on the walls, their eyeless stares forming the very aesthetic of the structure. His castle was built almost entirely from the bones of his family's enemies. Anything that had defied him became a part of his fortress. Of course, that meant that by now, he had more space than he could ever dream of filling.

The throne room was exactly the way he'd left it; with one exception.

As Drayvex was half guided, half dragged down the centre of the cavernous room, he stared dead ahead, a cold calm burning in the pit of his stomach. Their footsteps bounced and echoed off the smooth stone floor, jumping high into the immense heights of the ribbed ceiling above.

Drayvex fixed his gaze ahead to the far end of the room, where the large onyx throne sat on its raised platform. Golden veins in the stone gleamed in the dim light, catching at the corner of his vision.

Finally, he fixed on the demon who had planted himself on the throne. *His* throne. The one place of total, unquestionable power. The one demon he loathed more than any other on the planet.

Saydor peered down from the height of the steps, his beady eyes narrowed in silent triumph. He was smiling, an indolent grin that revealed the rows of pointed barbs in his mouth. It was a grin that got toothier the closer they got to the throne. His pudgy, clawed hands gripped the arms of the throne in anticipation, and as he leaned forward, his eyes followed them down the aisle. A mad gleam lingered in their oily depths, fixed on the girl he saw.

Saydor had always had a mildly comical appearance. His short, round frame gave him the look of something squashed and swollen, with eyes small enough to be out of proportion with the rest of his face. His skin was a deficient yellow and clusters of black veins stood out in various patches on his flesh. This was as close as he came to looking human.

Despite appearances, though, Saydor was not one to be taken lightly. Of all the demons crawling over this planet's surface, Saydor was the only one to come even remotely close to matching Drayvex's power. Drayvex had never had to fight the Demon Master, but he was sure that he'd have to flex *all* his muscles if he ever had to put this beast down.

Drayvex stopped at the base of the steps and glared up at the demon on his throne. Saydor'd had his eye on the position of Demon Lord from day one. He'd made no secret of his asinine ambitions, and Drayvex took no end of pleasure in repeatedly reminding him of his true place. He was, however, as much it pained Drayvex to admit, an asset.

His demon captors surrounded him possessively, creating a wonky semi-circle.

The red demon was the first to take charge. He bowed down low, the tip of his long nose brushing the floor, and waited for permission to rise. "Master."

Saydor stared down at the group. A long, black tongue snaked out and stroked the side of his mouth, a subconscious gesture that Drayvex assumed revealed the enormous strain that his tiny brain was under at this precise moment.

"Rise, Pock," Saydor commanded.

The red demon rose and smiled. "Your Greatness, we found the girl. I mean, the stone. But also the girl." He paused, a dim-witted smile frozen on his face as he waited for the praise he clearly thought he was due. "I did as you asked, Master."

Saydor examined his prize through slitted eyes, sweeping over Ruby as though looking for the rest of her. Drayvex fought the strange impulse to smile. Ruby was small. Even for a human.

"Leave us," Saydor barked at the room, giving each far corner and its guard a well-practised glare.

The guards were slow to respond.

"NOW!"

Jumping to attention, they gave a clumsy salute and filed towards the exit, leaving their dignity behind them.

Drayvex scoffed. They'd been taking their orders from him, their Demon Lord, for nearly two hundred years. This impostor had no idea how to give a real command.

Saydor heaved himself to his feet and fixed his attention on the sad group of minions at the base of the steps. "That includes you bunch of snivelling worms."

Pock's face fell. "B-but Master." He fell to his knees once again. "You promised th—"

"*Get* out of my *sight*, Pock!"

As his captors scattered, Drayvex stood and observed the atrocity that was manoeuvring down the steps towards him. He stared into those two black pits, now solely focused on him, and remembered to blink.

"Well, well, well," Saydor purred, slipping into a guise Drayvex could only assume was meant to be charming. "What do we have here?"

Drayvex made no attempt to respond as Saydor stopped in front of him, reaching out with a stubby finger that hovered inches away from his face.

"The little human girl with demonic powers. I have to say I was expecting something a touch more ... well, more." He grinned, exposing the rows of minuscule points in his mouth. "No matter, my dear. Your fate will have the same outcome, regardless of your durability." He sighed and retracted his hand. "I'm afraid you're going to die either way."

Drayvex smiled. Then, he broke character and laughed.

Saydor's sly expression flickered. Confusion leaked over his features as Drayvex broke the expected mould of typical human behaviour around a demon presence.

"Is there something amusing you, human?" His voice had a growling undercurrent as he struggled to smooth out his ruffled composure.

Aside from the obvious blunder on Saydor's part, that being if Drayvex were indeed Ruby, there would be no way in hell that he would simply hand over the one thing keeping him alive, having just been told that he would 'die either way', he realised that this moron needed a hint.

Drayvex gave him one.

His black aura emanated from within. It flowed around the edges of his form, bathing him, Saydor and the floor nearby in the darkness.

Saydor reacted as though he'd been slapped. His mouth fell slack, comprehension dawning on his face at Drayvex's signature haze.

"D-Drayvex," he wheezed, all thoughts of superiority forgotten.

"That's 'My Lord' to you," he retorted, hearing the dangerous edge to his voice. Shedding his disguise like a second skin, he glared down at the squat demon.

Saydor was paling, his yellowed skin turning a rather interesting shade. He forced a smile. "My *Lord*," he simpered, bowing low without waiting to be released.

Drayvex ran his tongue along his materialising fangs, now pushing down into his mouth. Despite his ignorance, he'd always taken no end of pleasure in watching the self-righteous Demon Master bow to him.

"My Lord, if only you had confided in me. What an honour it would have been to travel to Earth and retrieve the Lapis Vitae for you. These menial tasks are surely beneath Your Lordship?" His words dripped with false pleasantries.

Drayvex sneered down at him, his skin darkening and hardening as he

138

gradually reverted to his normal demon form. As usual, Saydor had put two and two together and come up with twenty-two. Then again, these little misunderstandings did have a habit of working themselves in Drayvex's favour. His actual reasons for taking off were far less complicated. Sheer crippling boredom for one.

"As it happens, I *have* managed to track down the girl and the stone." Saydor held his gaze for a defiant moment, his dark eyes glistening with hooded menace. "The same girl you appear to be tracking." Saydor stepped around him and fell into a slow pace at the foot of the throne. "My minions are in the process of extraction, and will bring me the right girl very soon."

Saydor stopped. He spun to face Drayvex, a small smile pulling at the corners of his mouth. "My Lord, just think of what we could do together. The things we could accomplish. Taking over the Earth, ruling over the human plague and doing with them as we see fit. There would be nothing to stop us. No one to stand in our way." He paused, carnal eyes narrowed as he lost himself in his musings.

Saydor paused. Waiting, Drayvex assumed, for his approval.

"Just leave it all to me, Your Greatness. The girl will soon be begging for death, I can promise you that."

Drayvex laughed, a cruel sound, sharp as the bite of a whip. He would rather jump into the molten flow beneath the Vekrodusian crust, let its contents strip him of everything he was with slow and painful precision, than make a deal with Saydor.

"My dear, deluded fiend," Drayvex drawled, hearing his voice deepen with his demon form. You may think that the stone is almost within your reach, but the truth is, you couldn't be further from it." His claws grew longer, his previously slight form bulking and heightening. "In fact, not only do I know where the stone is, but both the stone and the girl are in my possession as we speak."

He'd not been stupid enough to bring it with him but had hidden it safely with its previous owner before setting his plan into motion. Ruby would kick herself if she knew how close it really was at this moment.

Saydor's face was a careful mask of neutrality. Drayvex wondered how long the demon would be able to keep it up.

"So you see," he continued, his voice hardening, "I would either have to be utterly moronic or have a giant tumour pressing into the side of my brain to consider partnering with you. You, who by ruling for a brief period in my absence, think yourself worthy of my throne and title."

Drayvex pushed himself into the face of the scorned demon, demanding not only his own, but Saydor's personal space.

Saydor looked as though he'd been forced to swallow something unpleasant, his face twisting into something between loathing and a grimace.

"Tell me," Drayvex whispered. "I already have everything I want. Why in Hell's name would I share it with you?"

He'd predicted Saydor's next move before Saydor himself had thought of it. So when the short-tempered Demon Master reached the end of his short fuse, Drayvex was ready.

Saydor sprang to life in a blur of claws and teeth, a hateful snarl erupting from his chest like the rev of a chainsaw. He barrelled into Drayvex, who deflected the assault with relative ease, using the demon's momentum against him.

Saydor was on his feet as soon as he touched the floor. Unphased, he launched himself once more at Drayvex's form, an expression of pure loathing plastered on his face.

Drayvex stared him down with Demon Lord arrogance, holding his position until the last possible second. Then, he brought up his hands. Claws clashed with claws. The impact sent sparks flying, miniature fireworks leaping into the atmosphere.

Drayvex caught and held the furious Saydor with scythe-like blades, pushing back against him. "Tell me," he snarled, "are you even trying? I could fight you in my sleep and still be bored of your pathetic attempts at power play."

Saydor hissed. "You know I always get what I want, Drayvex." A thick, green liquid oozed from the tips of his claws and dripped down his fingers. His skin was dotted with the same substance, squeezing through his skin. "Sooner or later, that stone will belong to me. That, and whatever else I desire."

Drayvex laughed out loud. "How adorable." A line of sharp protrusions erupted down his spine with a crack, the sound echoing around the cavernous room. Twisting black horns pushed their way through his skull, taking their familiar place on his head. "Do you reward your underlings when they laugh at your jokes, or do they actually find you funny?"

He released the knotted ball of darkness he'd worked up inside.

The burning sphere of black flames blasted into Saydor, pushing them both back with the force as it hit the hastily erected barrier. Drayvex pushed harder, forcing the Demon Master back further.

"I am far older than you," Saydor spat, grunting against the force of the orb. "I possess infinitely more cunning than you. You, who were born into privilege. Handed your power on a pissing *plate*. I was born into nothing. I have clawed my way up through the festering pits you rule over to get where I am." A reflection of the dark flames flickered in the demon's crimson eyes, two crazily dancing orbs. "I always get what I want, and I am living proof of that."

No sooner had he spoken these words, than Saydor sprang to action. Despite his large proportions, he was fast. Drayvex had to give him that.

Saydor hissed, pushing two lethal shafts out from his body, straight through the barrier towards Drayvex's chest. They were coated in the same green substance as his claws. Drayvex was well aware of how much damage just a few drops of that poison could do. It seemed to be unique to the Demon Master, or at least, he had never found anyone else capable of producing the same substance.

As the shafts came shooting towards his torso, Drayvex tweaked his burning sphere. The sphere exploded against the invisible barrier. The force of the blast knocked Saydor off balance, sending the sticky shafts off course; one over Drayvex's right shoulder, one narrowly missing his side.

Saydor scrabbled, struggling to get to his feet, but Drayvex was not about to let him. Without pause, he pummelled Saydor's barrier with sheer, undiluted power, one blow after the other, in a destructive cascade. The barrier buckled under the force, becoming concave from the repeated impact. But it held fast.

Despite himself, Drayvex was impressed. It was rare—no, unheard of—for anyone to be able to withstand the type of attack he was throwing out.

He fell still. Echoes of the blasts bounced around the vast room, slipping away as the throne room fell into silence once more.

Drayvex chuckled, a low sound that vibrated deep in his chest. "Well, you certainly know how to put on a good show."

"My Lord, this is futile. We should be—"

"But no matter how hard you try, you will always be an overly polished turd." Drayvex stepped forward so that they were face to face, meeting Saydor head-on as he finally picked himself up off the ground. He was a fair bit taller than the squat demon, but the human phrase 'if looks could kill' sprang to mind. In Saydor's case, they probably could.

"You were born as nothing, and you will die as nothing," he continued with cruel nonchalance, watching as a dark shadow fell across Saydor's face. "You are merely another head to step on beneath my throne."

Drayvex pushed down on Saydor with mental muscle, forcing him back down to the floor to hammer his point home. Saydor buckled, falling to his knees. Drayvex leaned down, pushing himself into Saydor's face. "You will drop the search." He felt Saydor twitch, and he pushed down harder. "You will not stand in my way, and you will not touch the girl again under any circumstances. Do you understand?"

For a moment, Saydor neither moved nor spoke. Then, as he looked up, he spat caustic green mucous at Drayvex's face. It bounced harmlessly into the air, his barrier forming in the nick of time.

"I will make you pay for this, Demon Lord," Saydor growled.

Drayvex whipped Saydor backwards in a hot flash of temper. A crack reached his ears as the spine beneath him folded under the insane contortion. *"Do you understand?"* he blasted, hearing his voice moving around them.

"Yes, My Lord," croaked Saydor from the floor.

A door opened at the far side of the room. Neither one of them spoke. Small skittering footsteps weaved across the room. "Muh … My Lord?"

Drayvex finally looked up.

The interrupting demon stared at Saydor, eyes pinned on the unmoving lump on the floor.

Drayvex sneered, his claws twitching at his sides. "Clean this filth up," he ordered, his voice toneless.

The little demon saluted and scuttled away.

Drayvex turned to towards the grand throne, studying it through slitted eyes. He wasn't ready to come back. Not yet. He alone would be the judge of when that time would be and no one or nothing would force him to do otherwise. Not even Saydor.

Chapter 15

uby breathed in the city smog, absorbing Callien's delicious grime into her very being. The sun glinted off towering buildings, each window a tiny mirror in the sky. The roads shone like black rivers and the smell of fresh bread carried on the breeze, along with the soft, pulse beat of a nearby bar.

She was home. *Truly* home.

As life buzzed around her, Ruby took it all in, feeling happy and complete, if only for a moment. Then, squaring her shoulders, she headed in the direction of the library. If she stayed still for much longer, she would never leave again.

Callien's library was a spectacular building. It had once been a cathedral, and on the few occasions she had visited in the past, Ruby had always come away feeling small but empowered by its grandeur.

She approached the large, polished desk and smiled as a librarian clocked her presence. "Can I help?" asked the woman. She had a breezy voice that matched their hushed environment. Her eyebrow raised in a polite enquiry, and she smiled with warmth.

Ruby cleared her throat. Suddenly, being here seemed like a waste of time. "Um, yes. Hi there." It was a long shot, no doubt. She patted her pockets, rummaging through each one for Sandra's card.

When she found it, she pulled out the square and flipped it over in her hands. Taking a deep breath, she offered it to the waiting librarian. "I'm looking for information on this symbol. I was hoping you could point me in the right direction?"

The woman took the card from Ruby's outstretched hand and studied it. Her forehead creased. Her gaze rose to hover somewhere behind Ruby's head, before glancing back down to the card. "Hmm …"

Ruby played with her fingernails. At least this hadn't been a total waste of time. After all, she had got to see the city again.

"Follow me, please." The librarian left her desk and headed into the depths of the building. Hardly daring to believe her luck, Ruby gave a small smile and went after her.

They walked to the far side of the library, past the modern authors and the classics, past light reading and what she'd thought was the reference section, down into an area that Ruby hadn't even known existed.

When they stopped, the lady turned towards her. "Try the big book over here," she said, struggling to carry a tome with both hands. As she dropped the book onto the nearest table, it landed with a heavy thud. A cloud of dust rose into the air, swirling particles misting in the beam of light made by the tiny window above.

"Okay?" mumbled the librarian, pulling out a hankie and covering her nose. Then, she shuffled off, leaving Ruby alone with her thoughts.

Ruby watched the dust settle, questions swirling in her head like the motes. What was Sandra not telling her? Why did she suddenly feel as though she was intruding?

She shook her head in the gloom. No. Sandra had given her the card herself. Ruby was just looking out for her, guarding her blind spots, so to speak.

Sandra's card had been left on top of the book. The book was a large, leather-bound thing with worn gold lettering, the shine long faded. Ruby pocketed her card and read the title. 'DEMONOLOGY'.

A wave of shock reverberated through her. Demonology. She snatched at the book, forgetting how heavy the librarian had made it look. She stumbled backwards as her grip slipped. Demons.

She grabbed at the book again, and this time wrenched open the cover. The smell of old pages wafted up her nostrils. She leafed through, scanning chunks of text and pictures. Scales, teeth and claws. Jagged lumps and mutated flesh. And black, black eyes. The stuff of nightmares.

Ruby's skin prickled. How much of this was true? A few days ago, she would have dismissed it all as fiction. Now, she knew better. She wondered why she'd been given this, of all the books in this section. Was it obvious that she'd allied herself with a demon? It wasn't as though she had a big 'D' on her forehead.

Then again, her grandma's necklace had turned out to be a demon stone. Her favourite weird car-boot find was actually a black magic shadow-thing, and she had been none the wiser about either.

She kept going, unable to stop; unable to look away from the encyclopedia of monsters. Horned Pirexees, large and proud. The Scaly Ympus, small and mischievous. Some, she had to admit, seemed *too* far-fetched, even for her wild imagination. Others jumped out at her from the pages, poisoning her mind with an instinctual fear.

Something on a page caught her eye. It was the symbol.

Ruby had almost forgotten about her original mission. But there it was; the wonky Y-shaped logo. Big and bold amongst the creatures from the pits of hell. She ran her finger over the picture, pausing as her eyes found the small block of text underneath. Her breath caught in her throat. 'The symbol commonly associated with the *vânători de demoni*.'

Ruby read it again. *Vânători de demoni*.

Barely pausing for breath, she whipped out her phone. Search and translate. Ruby bit her lip. Bad wifi.

Abandoning the book, Ruby turned and made for the exit. As she moved through the narrow aisles, her head threatened to explode. Sandra, she mithered. What have you got yourself into?

She paced into the big open reception area, avoiding eye contact with the helpful librarian. Come to think of it, what had *she* got herself into?

Ruby pushed through the double doors and back out into the street. She ran her hands through her hair, unable to think clearly with so much going on in her mind. Her browser sprang to life.

She froze as she read the translation. Demon hunters. It was clear as day on the screen.

"Ruby? Is that you?"

A familiar voice plucked at her concentration. She spun towards the sound, only half present.

As soon as Ruby saw her face, old memories swam to the surface. Her mother as a policewoman, standing amongst her colleagues. Laughing and joking, ushering Ruby into the room as the chief hovered just a few paces away. *"I'd like you to meet my daughter, Ruby."*

Ruby had been much younger then.

"Oh, God. You look so grown up!"

Ruby was slow to respond. But at that typical adult statement, she felt her cheeks grow warm. "Heh—oh, wow. Carol. I didn't see you there." She looked up at the tall woman, dreading the obvious question that was bound to follow. "It has been a good while."

"How's your mother? Is she with you?"

Ruby cringed, her insides twisting. "No, she's back at home." Home … "But I'll get her to check in with you real soon." Would that help? Would hearing her old boss's voice help to pull her mother out of this rut they now lived in?

"Oh, good. That'd be nice." She beamed, her hard eyes glowing with genuine warmth.

Ruby relaxed a touch, relieved that she'd bought them a little more time.

"Did you hear about Lorenfield? Nasty business. I've been thinking of you both."

Ruby's thoughts did a one-eighty degree flip at the mention of their neighbouring village. Lorenfield? "Sorry, no. What's going on with Lorenfield?"

The chief of police put her hard face back into play, before continuing in a lower tone. "Some sick bastard wiped it off the map a couple of days ago. It was a total blood bath. No survivors."

Ruby stared up at the chief, at a total loss for words. A bloodbath? At

Lorenfield? A tiny village on the outskirts of nowhere. Mass murder, just a short drive away from Crichton. Ruby's blood ran cold.

"Your mum must be tearing her hair out. Don't worry, though. You can tell her that we're not going to rest until we get the son of a bitch."

What were the chances that this was totally unrelated to Drayvex? Surely, the odds of this happening in such a remote place were a thousand to one. Ruby couldn't breathe. Her chest tightened.

The chief cleared her throat. "Ruby, are okay?"

No, she was jumping to conclusions. Drayvex wasn't the only demon in Crichton. Ruby made herself focus on Carol's face. She had to get home, now.

"Uh, yes. Fine. I—gosh, that's so awful. I didn't know. I don't watch the news much these days." Ruby pulled a smile onto her face, holding it there long enough to seem convincing. "I'm sorry, I've just remembered that I've got to dash. But it was nice to see you again."

With an, "I'll pass on your best," she was pacing back down the street towards the train station. What the hell was going on? How was she—?

The bus came out of nowhere. One minute she was power walking down the street, the next a double-decker bus was skidding towards her, moving as if drawn to her presence.

Ruby's mind went blank. Her body thinking for her, she scrabbled to the left. The people just ahead of her scattered.

Tyres squealed as the bus swung round in a perfect arc, following her. She felt the front corner of the hood as it collided with her hip, but the pain never came.

She grabbed out as the impact bounced her forward, sending her flailing. When she met the concrete, she didn't feel it; didn't hear the crunch of metal as the side of the bus kissed the barber shop's low, overhanging roof. She didn't hear the sounds coming out of the mouths of those rushing towards her.

Ruby's vision slid sideways. Car horns, shouting. All sounds muffled into one droning buzz. And then, finally, the pain. A burst of sharpness, a burning sensation flaring up her side.

Her train. There was no time for this.

She pulled herself to her knees, ignoring the angry throb radiating from her hip. A blurry figure was rushing towards her, moving in to block her route of escape. Her mum's boss would have probably heard the smash. She would be here any moment now.

Ruby heaved herself to her feet. She was fine. Everything was going to be fine.

*

Ruby was back.

Drayvex's eyes narrowed as he probed at the girl's aura through the walls of the green house. Unlike previously, it was a skewed mess, a tangled array of black, white and angry red, a festering wound in the fabric of the space around her.

He'd been right after all. She *had* had more to offer him. And as he'd fed her lies about a golden future, she'd swallowed every word without question. Despite having used Ruby for a second time, though, he'd kept up his end of the deal. Her demon problems were now history. It was a pity the stone's absence would kill her regardless.

He stood at the front door, hovering beside the fragile panel of wood. The gesture felt unnatural, needless. He stepped back and tensed, jumping up and scaling the wall to the top floor.

Drayvex perched on the windowsill, peering briefly into the empty room, before taking the liberty of letting himself inside. Focusing on the window latch, he used a burst of telekinesis to lift it from its seated position.

No sooner had his boots met the carpet, than he heard Ruby's footsteps on the staircase.

Ruby came bursting into the room, dropping her bags in a trail behind her, oblivious to his presence as she crossed towards him.

Drayvex cleared his throat as she approached.

Ruby jumped. She swore at him, manoeuvring to a sudden stop, just about avoiding a collision of bodies.

"You really should invest in a lock that, ah, actually locks," he gibed, the corners of his mouth lifting.

Ruby eyed him warily, a flicker of something—what, fear?—crossing her features. Drayvex faltered, sensing a change in atmosphere. Something was different.

"*Is* there such a thing? As a demon-proof lock?" Her eyes raked over his form, looking him up and down.

Drayvex did the same. God, she looked like hell. Her bloodless complexion was paler than he'd ever seen it. Now that he bothered to look, she was clearly in pain. The way she held herself, her stiff movements, her discomfort showing as creases in the corners of her eyes and mouth. She looked like a strong gust of wind would take her out. Despite that, her bags and attire suggested that she'd been for more than a stroll around the block. But frankly, he'd seen healthier looking corpses.

They stared at each other for a long moment until Ruby broke the silence. "Did the plan work?"

Drayvex fought back a grin, picturing that bloated sack of bile breaking under his will. "Yes." It was oh so satisfying. "You won't be bothered by those idiots again."

She breathed out, but the tension remained in her shoulders. "Thank you, that's ..." She breathed in. "... good to know."

Ruby watched him. Her eyes were fixed on his hands.

Drayvex considered her in return, scrutinising her movements. He raised an eyebrow at her, impatient. "But?"

"Did ... you kill my neighbours?"

Drayvex stared at the girl in front of him, taken aback. She looked surprised too, as though her tongue were a separate entity with a mind of its own. Her wide eyes were fixed on him as she waited for his answer. Her neighbours. She must mean the sweet little village he'd taken out his frustrations on not so long ago. Huh. *Where* did she say she'd been today?

He waited a moment before inching closer. As he did so, she flinched and made to step backwards, before changing her mind and holding her ground. She pouted, an expression that almost passed for nonchalance. Almost.

Drayvex looked down on Ruby and smiled, his teeth lengthening as he did. This defiant streak was both a temptation and an irritant. Her hands were clenched into fists at her sides and her heart worked overtime. *What are you going to do about it, little girl?*

He considered his next words, then spoke. "That's an odd thing to ask," he murmured, running his tongue along the tops of his fangs. "Should I have?"

Ruby frowned, a small crease appearing between her eyes. This time, she allowed herself to step back. "I ... no. What?"

"Is that what's expected of a Demon Lord? Should I have ripped off their heads and squeezed their insides all over my chips? Scooped out their middles and decorated my domain with their entrails?" He began to circle her in a predatory manner. As he passed the desk he snagged the stone from amongst the clutter, taking advantage of her confusion. *How far could he push her? Which way would she snap?*

She opened her mouth, one hand fumbling behind her for something to grip. "Are you being funny? I'm not laughing."

Drayvex started to respond, but stopped, distracted by the number of empty cups cluttering every available free surface behind her. Was this normal human behaviour? He looked back at her. "Are you opening a coffee shop?"

Much to his amusement, a burst of colour spread across her pasty complexion. Her eyes wandered across the array of cups collecting around the room, and then flicked back up to him. "Aha, I, um, no." She ran her fingers through her unkempt hair, her eyes losing their focus. "I don't sleep much these days. And when I'm awake at stupid o'clock, I drink tea."

Drayvex watched her as she shuffled towards the nearest desk. "Tea," he said, hearing the scepticism in his own voice.

Ruby reached out and ran a finger around the rim of a cup. Her eyes were suddenly far away, and somehow, their previous conversation already seemed to be history, lost within the recesses of her tiny human mind. Drayvex made a mental note, filing 'distraction' away for future use.

"Tea is soothing. Lately, I've had nothing but nightmares. The same ones, over and over, and it's getting worse."

Drayvex tensed. "You get these every night?"

"More or less." She shrugged, then winced.

Outside, Drayvex was cool and detached. Inside, he seethed. Kaelor. That rat. How *dare* he go against a direct order.

"I mean, that's clearly not your problem. But …"

Her nightmares no longer served a purpose. Yet, her dreams were still being stolen to satisfy the appetite of an insolent speck who had forgotten its true place. Drayvex sneered, lost in thoughts of punishments that fitted the crime. *I hope you enjoyed your last meal, Kaelor,* he projected, knowing that the demon would be somewhere close by. His sneer turned into a smile.

"Right." His mind stilled as he brought himself back to the present, to the room and its owner, the human-shaped conundrum named Ruby.

She was watching him with a sideways glance, one hand with fingers resting on the rim of a mug. As she glanced down at the carpet, she looked vulnerable, and Drayvex had the sense that he'd done something villainous. Or not done something.

"Excuse me," said Ruby, taking a deliberate step backwards. "I should start on tea. I mean, dinner. You know, food. Not tea-tea."

Drayvex watched as she walked over to the bed and smoothed down her hair. She began to gingerly tug at the sleeve of her jumper, inching her arm out.

This is the part where you eat her, voiced his unchecked nature, almost a detached entity of late. *It would almost be a mercy at this point. Poor broken thing.*

Fangs inched down further still as he watched Ruby fuss with her clothes. Mutually beneficial. He took a step forward, noiseless.

Ruby pulled her arm free, lifting both to do so. Her top rode up, exposing bare skin at her waist.

Drayvex stilled. A mass of blueish-purple covered her lower waist, staining her skin. Fresh bruising. Her top slipped back down and Ruby discarded the jumper in her hand.

How much punishment could a human body withstand? The answer was a surprising amount, although human strength varied a hell of a lot, and some could take far less than others.

"I don't have anything else to offer you," Ruby said, her voice soft and flat.

Drayvex found himself scanning the small room, seeing it in a new light. The shelving above her head, glass figures with pointed edges lined up in a row. Candles on a bookshelf. Shoes with ridiculous heels. A tangle of wiring by an open window.

"I'm fresh out of demon gadgets." Ruby looked at him from across the room. She was staring at him with wounded eyes. "Unless ... you want the shadow ball?"

The stone pulsed at him through the jacket material as his finger dragged over the pocket. He had won. He knew it, she knew it.

"Drayvex?"

It should be simple. Eat her, walk away. Slice her open, walk away. Leave her at the mercy of an ancient curse, walk away. Varying options, one common outcome.

Before he thought about what he was doing, his hand was slipping into his pocket, fingers curling around the leather cord.

Eat her, walk away.

As he produced the necklace, Ruby's eyes were drawn to it from across the room. She stared at the swinging stone as if it were encrusted with diamonds.

Slice her open, walk away.

Drayvex sliced through the room. As he came to a hard stop in front of Ruby, she stumbled backwards, sending objects tumbling off the shelf at her back.

He dangled the stone between them, holding it at eye level. This was madness. "You owe me. Big time."

Ruby looked up at him with guarded eyes, as though expecting him to deliver the punchline to a cruel joke.

Drayvex growled softly into her ear. This time, she didn't flinch. "And I *will* collect." Counterproductive. As he stepped back, he held the pulsing object out towards her, once again feeling the tug of it in his veins as power reached for power through the air.

Leave her at the mercy of an ancient curse, walk away.

"I...can have it?" She gazed at the necklace for a few seconds more. Then, without warning, she threw herself against him.

Drayvex froze beneath her, her slender body pressed against his. He felt the pressure of her arms, the soft heat of her small form. Torn between the natural instinct to rip out her throat and returning the embrace, he decided it was best to do neither and continued with his lack of response.

After a beat, Ruby pulled away, withdrawing all at once. She coughed and stepped back, remembering the art of personal space. Or maybe she'd remembered what he was, *who* he was. That they weren't friends. They were enemies.

Regardless, she glanced at him and smiled. It was hesitant at first, and then steady, sure. "You don't know what this means to me," she said, the smile now audible in her voice.

Drayvex was stunned by the wave of satisfaction that rose up in response, lapping at the edges of his consciousness. He stabbed down, not wanting anything to do with it. What use to him was this poison? Would it make him powerful? Destroy his opponents?

The stone still dangled from the claw that he held out between them, dark and throbbing. The girl was a snake in the grass. Had he really won, or had she, in fact, played him at his own game? "Take it," he barked, his tone carrying the venom of his thoughts.

Seemingly oblivious to his annoyance, Ruby took the necklace from his outstretched hand and slipped it over her head. As the stone settled around her neck, Ruby looked up at him. Her expression was serene and he couldn't help but be taken in by it. The change was almost instantaneous. He watched the pain in her face vanish, her eyes grow bright and alert. He saw her face flush with colour.

A look of confusion flitted across her features. She blinked hard.

"What?" he pressed, racking his brain as to what, at this point, would make her look at him that way.

"Your eyes. They just changed colour."

Drayvex studied her face. "Yes, they do that," he said. "I'm a demon."

"I know they do," she said. "But I've never seen it happen."

He folded his arms. She didn't look scared, as surely she would be if they were red. "What colour?" Black. Pissed off black.

Ruby squinted at him, leaning in closer. Drayvex let her. "They're blue, but mingled with purpley splashes."

Blue and purple? Now *he* was confused. He had no idea what the hell that was supposed to reflect.

"They're incredible," she whispered.

Drayvex watched her, feeling stifled. His true demon form bristled just below the surface of his skin, barely contained within the confines of his current form. He needed to kill something.

Without another word, he turned and slipped out of the window unnoticed. Drayvex knew just where to start.

Day gave way to night. Night dredged up the vermin.

Drayvex stood on the edge of the rooftop, looking down. The demon presence was directly below his feet, hidden from the untrained eye, but not from him. Never from him.

The talents of a dream eater were slim but potent. They could make themselves invisible on command, and when threatened, their limited shape-shifting abilities would usually save their skin. Their choice of diet was unique to their kind. Feeding on dreams, daydreams, hallucinations, delusions, they took what they wanted and left nightmares in their place. These talents made the demon a worthy tool in any ruler's arsenal. Worthy, but nonetheless *dispensable*.

"Here, kitty kitty," he jeered, his voice carrying down to the passage below.

Drayvex moved a touch to the left, then stepped off and dropped. The second he hit the ground he spun and grabbed at the space where the presence was strongest. Straight off, he struck gold.

As his fingers snagged on matted fur and flesh, the demon yelped. The sound resounded through the confines of the passage and Drayvex wrenched him in close by the throat.

155

"Augh, My Lord! Wait!" Kaelor materialised all at once, a twisting tangle of bony limbs. "I can explain myself!"

"Oh, thank fuck for that," Drayvex spat, squeezing the throat in his hand. His claws penetrated the surface, and within seconds, his hand was damp. "You betray my trust, disobey a direct order from your Demon Lord to get fat against my will, stealing that which does not belong to you, but at least you can *explain* yourself."

Kaelor made a choking sound. "No. I mean, yes. Buh—but My Lord, you understand not. I tasted her. Then I needed more." As the creature struggled feebly in his grip, his form began to blur at the edges.

Oh, no you don't, he blasted, pumping red hot power down his arm to the squirming lump he held. He wasn't going to let Kaelor slip away from him that easily. He wasn't going to kill him, either. No, he had something far better planned.

"Like no other taste!"

As the demon let out a yowl, Drayvex shook his head, glaring into the fearful eyes of his minion.

"Please, Your Greatness. I'll not touch the human. I can do better. You'll see."

"You overestimate your worth to me, Kaelor."

Drayvex thrust his hand over the demon's face, gripping his mouth with tendrils of power, forcing the strands down his throat. Then, he ripped.

As Kaelor dropped to the ground, Drayvex absorbed the excess power. A dream eater without the ability to feed was about as useful as the dirt at his feet.

You should never have come here, Kaelor, he said as he shot up the wall. *You overstepped.*

Chapter 16

The sun streamed in through the large cafe window, bathing the table in warmth and light.

Ruby watched Sandra with her head propped on one elbow, the comforting weight of a familiar leather thong pulling at her neck. Sandra was talking at her in an animated fashion, waving her hands around for added emphasis, and Ruby found it easy to pretend, for the moment, that life had resumed some kind of normalcy, if only for one day.

"You should come and stay with us sometime." Sandra took a swig from a lipstick-smeared coffee cup and beamed. "You'd love our apartment. It's chic and stylish, but also quite minimalist. You know, so the room doesn't clutter your mind or seem too OTT."

Sandra looked good. City life suited her, almost as much as it suited Ruby herself. Her short blonde hair had been professionally styled into a shock of tousled locks, ending at the base of her jaw in a trendy windswept look. She'd lost that innocent, almost child-like visage she once carried and now seemed focused and alert, ready for anything.

"Ruby?"

She wondered how much of that she could attribute to her dad's dark lifestyle. As his apprentice, how much did she know about demons? Was she kept in the dark and given chores? Did she even know what that symbol meant?"

"Hey. Earth to Ruby."

"Hmm. What?" Ruby sat up straight, jarring her back. "Yes," she said, realising that she hadn't said anything for a good while. "Yeah, I'd love to."

Sandra frowned, then licked her lips. This was a Sandra special, a look she knew all too well. It was a look that said 'I'm on to you'.

"You seem distracted," she said, pushing her cup to one side. "Something on your mind? A problem shared is a problem halved, you know."

Ruby smiled. Sandra and her proverbs. Her fingers moved to the charm resting against her chest, instinctively clutching it within her hand. Distracted. That was one way to put it.

Before she could stop it, her mind drifted again. Drayvex was never what she expected. Ruby didn't know anything about real demons, that much was clear. But every time Ruby thought that she was getting his measure, he'd throw her off in a different direction. Last night had been one of those nights.

When he'd given her necklace back, Ruby had almost lost her mind. It was only now that she'd come back down to Earth with a bump. She hadn't considered his *why*. Had he had a change of heart or had he somehow gotten what he wanted from it? Did he even have a heart? Or was he planning something far worse?

"That's an odd thing to ask. Should I have?"

Ruby closed her eyes. When she'd asked Drayvex about Lorenfield, his eyes had remained those of a winter's sky. But then later, out the blue, she'd seen them change. It was strange, yet beautiful. The colours had mingled and then separated, fanning out in splashes not unlike the way paint hits water. Or blood.

"Are you thinking of tall, dark and handsome?"

Ruby looked up, feeling caught in some terrible act. "What? No."

"Oh, Rube. Don't tell me you let that one go. I won't believe you."

Exasperated, Ruby rubbed a hand over her hair. Maybe Sandra would be more willing to talk about her *own* secret. "So, how is life with your dad?" At the very least, it would distract Sandra from matchmaking her with a demon.

"Y'know, Rube, I think I came along at just the right time. The apartment was in dire need of a woman's touch. But now, it looks utterly fab." She leaned forward, resting her weight on the table. "He's a workaholic, you see."

Ruby gazed at her friend, the cogs in her mind whirring. Did demon hunters ever get a day off? "Oh, well I'm sure you've put him in his place."

Sandra laughed and gave a cheeky wink. "Of course, Rube. Who do you think I am?"

She had to be more direct. Ask a question that she couldn't skirt around too easily. Ruby gave a small smile. "You're Sandra Serling, queen of organisation. I'm sure he had a bit of a shock." Resisting the urge to look down at her half-full cup, she continued, "What does he do for a living? I don't think you ever told me."

Sandra's eyes hovered for a moment on Ruby's face, before she broke into a sunny smile. "He dabbles in lots of things. Bit o' this, bit o' that. Got loads of plates spinning at the same time. I've told him, Rube, one day he'll wear himself into the ground. But for now, he's got me, and I'm helping out where I can." She sighed, a playful, drawn-out sound.

Ruby watched her friend, feeling torn. On the one hand, she didn't want to push her and jeopardise their relationship. Again. On the other hand, she *needed* to know what was going on. The symbol could have just been a terrible marketing choice. In which case, there was nothing to fear. But the chances were, something was amiss.

Making a decision, she slipped her hand into her back pocket and pulled out the card. "What's this?" she said, pointing at the shining symbol.

Sandra's gaze fell upon the card and lingered there. Then, after what felt like a lifetime, she looked up and stared into Ruby's eyes. "It's what we stand for."

Ruby was taken aback by her serious tone. Her hand didn't move, fixed in place holding the card above the table. *We.*

After a moment, Sandra broke into a grin. "Maybe one day, Dad will let me give you the tour." She rolled up her sleeve, placed her elbow on the table and rested her hand on her head. A silver bracelet slid free from the material of her jacket. Charms dangled from the chain, brushing her skin.

The gesture was so subtle that Ruby almost dismissed it as an attempt to cool down. But as she looked more closely at the bracelet, one charm in particular caught her eye. It was the symbol from the card, dangling at her wrist. She couldn't take her eyes off it.

"Well, look who it is." Sandra beamed.

Ruby spun on her seat and froze.

Drayvex was standing just inside the entrance. He was leaning on the door frame, dark and dangerous, and out of place in such a modest room. He was looking her way.

Her stomach did a familiar squirm as their eyes met across the room. He was watching her with that soft, calculating look that she often saw when he was deep in thought. His eyes were that pale shade of blue, the same as when they'd first met. Dammit, it wasn't fair.

Ruby turned back to the table, a fresh protest on her lips—then stopped. She was about to say that she didn't plan this, that he wasn't here for her, until she realised that he would probably hear her. Instead, she pulled a face.

Sandra's responding face said that she did not believe her feeble excuses. Ruby glowered at her from across the table, resisting the urge to turn and see if he was still there.

"Rube, please don't treat me like a simpleton. You clearly have a thing going on."

Oh, Sandra. If only you knew the truth, she thought, looking out of the window for help. 'Hi Sandra, this is Drayvex and he's a demon. You're familiar with them, right? The monsters that your daddy hunts? We do have a "thing", but I'm not sure what it is. He may be saving me for a rainy day snack.'

She glanced back towards the far entrance. It was empty.

"Go," Sandra urged, all of a sudden lacking her usual drama. "Go do whatever it is you need to do. I'll be around for a bit." She smiled.

Ruby paused for a moment, then found herself smiling back. "Okay." She rose to her feet. "Okay, I will. Thanks, Sand." What was Drayvex up to now?

"You owe me. Big time."

Bracing herself, she headed for the exit.

Ruby stepped out into the brisk morning and squinted against the brilliant sunshine. She folded her arms over her chest, lingering just beyond the door. She didn't know why she was nervous. She supposed that she never knew what to expect when it came to Drayvex, and now was no different.

A cough to her right pierced her thoughts. Reflexively, Ruby spun towards the sound.

Drayvex was standing a few feet away. His posture was relaxed, his expression neutral, and she felt herself relax in turn.

Ruby approached the demon by the side of the road and stopped, leaving plenty of room between them. "Hey."

He looked up as she spoke and nodded infinitesimally, his eyes carrying out their usual assault of her body and mind. She wondered if he ever felt the need to blink.

"I wasn't sure I'd see you again." Despite the show of sunshine, it was deceptively cold. Seeking warmth, she wrestled with her dodgy jacket zip, making a meal of the simple task.

After what felt like forever, she gave up. "What are you doing here?" she asked, abandoning the zip and shoving her hands in her pockets.

Drayvex's gaze rose to the sky. He stepped forward, closing the gap she'd left between them. Ruby felt the difference immediately. It was like standing in front of a crackling log fire. It must be nice to never get cold, she thought, inwardly resenting his strange ability.

She waited for him to speak, unsure that he ever would. Did he want something, or was this time truly the last she would see of him?

Finally, Drayvex broke his silence. "I want to show you something." He tilted his head in a curious gesture, the tips of his pointed teeth showing as he spoke. "Will you come?"

"Come?" Ruby hadn't known what to expect when she'd abandoned her best friend and stepped out after Drayvex. She was no better off now. But his cryptic question tugged at the deepest, wildest parts of herself. The parts that craved adventure and danger and wonder. "Come where?"

The corners of his mouth lifted. "Will you come, or not?"

Ruby frowned at him and pursed her lips. The smart thing to do would be to tell him where to go. Would she really follow a demon to God knows where for God knows why without so much as a backward glance? A demon that could well have slaughtered an entire village of innocent people not so long ago?

When she'd asked him outright, he hadn't reacted the way she feared he would. In fact, he almost seemed offended by her question—except, he hadn't *actually* denied it. This had only occurred to her after he left.

"Well?"

Ruby looked up and met his gaze. "Okay," she whispered, cursing her weakness.

Drayvex grinned at her, a mischievous smile she had only seen once before. "Keep up," he quipped. Then, he turned and headed off down the street towards the unknown.

Drayvex led her to the abandoned grounds on the outskirts of the village.

Before they'd moved to Crichton, there were plans to build a cinema on this large, open stretch of land. It was an awful idea. Still, the project went ahead, and the ground was dug up, only to discover that they didn't have all the permissions they needed after all. The site had been this way ever since.

As they walked across the hard earth, Ruby realised that they weren't going around it, but through it. If they were about to leave Crichton behind, why were they taking the long route to the main road?

"We're here."

She reacted to the sound of his voice, startling after the quiet they'd maintained since the cafe, then understood his words. Here? She scanned the area.

Drayvex had stopped next to the sad remains of a brick wall. It had once marked the boundary of the village, but now it was the only piece that was left. It jutted out of the ground in a jagged lump, standing solitary at the edge of the site, out of place.

Ruby stared nonplussed at the ruined wall; at Drayvex, lounging against the bricks, a grin spreading across his face as he measured her reactions. He was messing with her. Surely.

She moved in close, eyes raking over the damaged wall. She couldn't help but feel as though she were missing something obvious. At least, that was the way it felt.

"It's a wall," Ruby deadpanned. But then, he had a knack for making her feel stupid wherever they were.

Drayvex's smile grew bigger, revealing the unnatural points that resided in his mouth. "Shh," He whispered in her ear, his voice beside her. A tingle skittered down her spine.

Something grazed her throat, a sharp tickle moving down *behind* her. "Trust," he purred, his hot breath searing her skin.

Ruby blinked, and Drayvex was leaning against the wall in front of her. She hadn't seen him move, but she'd felt it. His pale eyes were fixed on her like a cat on a mouse. *Did* she trust him? Was he sizing her up, or was she doing him an injustice? "I don't know—"

Without warning, he began to disappear. Ruby watched in horror as Drayvex sank into the brick. Within seconds, it had swallowed him whole. As the last of him vanished, the brickwork rippled and pulsed where he had been, like liquid, before falling still.

Ruby's heart jackhammered in her chest. What the hell just happened? She stepped back and stood, gaping at the wall, struck stupid by the impossibility of what she'd seen.

There was no one around her, and after a moment, she stumbled over to where the wall had claimed him. When she poked it, it was hard. It felt like a real wall. She licked her lips, torn between sense and recklessness. This was wrong, this was wrong, this was—

Taking a deep breath, she put her palm flat on the bricks and then pushed. The wall was solid. Her breath puffed out. She didn't know what she had expected. It was almost as though she'd imagined the whole thing, *except* the brickwork was strangely clammy, radiating a faint heat.

Just then, the wall began to ripple and pulse underneath her hand.

Ruby stumbled backwards in alarm, almost tripping over her own feet in the process.

Curved, black claws, then a hand, pushed its way through the centre of the wall, followed by the arm it was attached to. Drayvex. He stopped at the arm, holding it out in an unmistakable invitation.

Ruby glanced back at Crichton one last time. Then, throwing caution to the wind, she stepped forward and took his hand.

He held it loosely for a few seconds, caressing her skin with his fingers. Then he gripped tight and tugged her forward.

She screamed as the wall came lurching towards her at high speed and prepared herself for the smash.

But it never came.

Chapter 17

Ruby stumbled forward, flailing within the space around her. Even with her eyes screwed shut and no real sense of what was happening, she knew she should have collided with the wall by now.

Her feet slowed to a stop. Her legs gave out beneath her. She didn't hit the ground. Ruby opened her eyes—and regretted it immediately.

The world was doing sickening loops around her. Dizzy, clammy. Her coordination was shot. It was only then that she realised that he had never let her go.

Her upper arms were clamped in Drayvex's firm grip, a clammy warmth spreading out from where he touched her. Her head was resting against his burning chest. She closed her eyes, wondering if she had collided with the wall after all.

Somewhere between fighting for her dignity and simple comfort, her need for solid things claimed a victory. Breathing in through her nose, Ruby used the demon that gripped her as a prop. He was the one solid thing around her, and as she waited for the world to stop spinning, Drayvex kept her steady.

After a moment, Ruby risked another peek. "What the hell did you …" She wet her lips and peeled herself from his chest. This was his fault. He'd quite literally taken her out with a wall. That was what you got for trusting the king of the demons.

Drayvex released one of her arms. He pushed her chin up with a finger, forcing her head up and studying her, as though he was looking for something.

Ruby blinked, snared by his serious gaze. "Am I dead?"

He laughed once, a hard sound. Dropping her all at once, he took a step back. "I should be so lucky."

She scowled, opening her mouth to protest at his casual dismissal, until she noticed her surroundings for the first time.

It was night time. Not only that, but the building site they had stood in was gone. "Um ... it was midday just two minutes ago?" Her head was spinning. "Now it's the middle of the night." Perhaps she was concussed.

Drayvex's gaze flicked up, then back. He raised an eyebrow, looking at her as though she were a simpleton.

Ruby looked up and gasped. The sky was filled with stars. Billions of them dominated the night sky, gleaming and blinking like diamonds. She'd never seen so many in one place. They were big, they were small. Some were no more than little specks. The result was a paint splatter effect, speckling the night sky. The most striking thing of all, though, was that they were *red*.

Ruby tried to form words. Instead, laughter bubbled from her lips.

Tearing her eyes from the sky, she took in her surroundings. They were standing on a grassy plain, except it wasn't quite grass. Each blueish-green leaf looked more like a small tentacle than a blade. The tentacle grass stretched as far as she could see in every direction, swaying to a breeze that she couldn't feel. The movement was almost hypnotic.

Drayvex's scoffing voice interrupted her thoughts. "The crystal mountains are far more deserving of your awe. *This* is nothing."

Questions popped into her head in response to his words. He was making no sense. Where was Crichton? How did they get here? Why did the grass appear to be alive?

Ruby started with the obvious. "Where are we?" She took deep lungfuls of air and found that it was strangely pleasant. It had a rough quality, like petrol.

Drayvex tugged on her arm, spinning her as he moved away. "Keep up," he quipped, striding off through the grass.

Numb, she watched him get smaller and smaller. A moment later, it occurred to her that she was being left behind. Panic rose up in her chest. Ruby ran to catch up to a disappearing Drayvex.

Ruby was drawn to the strange grass as she walked. They appeared to be in a meadow. A meadow of swaying tentacles. "Drayvex?" No response. She stopped abruptly, her head snapping up. "Drayvex, where *are* we?"

He stopped and turned his head a fraction towards her. "This is Vekrodus, planet of shadows and darkness. My domain."

By his nonchalant tone, he could have been talking about the weather. But Ruby's mind was going into meltdown. "This ... we're on another planet?" Ruby tried to wrap her mind around this plain and simple fact. Drayvex was a demon, and this was his planet. She scanned the surrounding land, absorbing it with all her senses. That explained why everything felt so foreign. It made so much sense, and yet, it made no sense at all.

As they crested a gentle incline, Ruby could see a huge forest just ahead. It was unlike any forest she'd ever seen. For one, it was glowing. She frowned, tempted to ask him where they were headed, before snubbing it. She would soon find out.

It didn't take them long, and a short walk later, Ruby was stood at the mouth of the glowing forest, surrounded by alien foliage. The trees all twisted like corkscrews, knotting as they reached for the sky in a bid for freedom. The lurid purple vines that snaked around the branches were dotted with oozing droplets that spilt over and dripping down onto the grass. Pulsing black lines ran up the length of each trunk, reminding her eerily of veins. Everything about the forest was surreal.

Drayvex kept moving. Ruby followed him, her breath coming in rapid drags. Venturing inside felt like stepping into a whole other world within a world.

There were no leaves on the trees, just round, blob-like flowers that lined the branches. These were the source of the glow she'd seen from a way off. They lit up the expanse of forest in all directions and, like the flaming stars, they too were a brilliant red.

A little way in, Drayvex stopped.

Ruby stopped too, her curiosity piquing. They had reached a copse, a small circle of sparser ground, surrounded by thick forest. He was stood in the middle, and he was watching her.

In that moment, she felt like a bug under a microscope, her every movement studied for science. Analysed. She lingered on his face, analysing him back. Maybe he was waiting for her to collapse in shock? If so, he was in for a long wait. She couldn't remember the last time she'd felt this alive.

Ruby wandered over to where Drayvex waited. A laugh bubbled to the surface, and she threw her head back to the star-speckled sky. "You abandoned this place for Earth?" She followed a small shooting star for a bit, before losing track of it. "What the Hell possessed you?"

The forest was silent, and Ruby realised that this was one of the many things that had felt off since arriving. No birdsong or rustle of leaves or obscure-sounding animals. Just silence.

"Don't be fooled by the scenic views, Ruby." His voice had dropped, becoming low and captivating within the warm darkness. "This is a cruel planet."

Ruby tore her eyes from the sky. One second he was there in front of her, the next he was gone.

"And I'm its cruel leader."

His voice came from behind. Hot breath brushed the back of her neck, and the warmth at her back was accompanied by several pinpricks at the base of her throat.

Ruby forgot how to breathe. Her heart thudded in her chest. "Tell me," she whispered, hyper-aware of the points resting against her bare skin. Points that she knew could slice through her like butter. "Tell me about your world."

Ruby felt Drayvex pull back. She breathed out. He was toying with her. Well, he wasn't going to get the reaction he wanted. Steeling herself, and her voice, she turned to face him.

As she turned, words failed her. The slick response she had hastily prepared scattered like autumn leaves to the breeze. In that moment, standing before him in an alien world, it was easy to believe that this creature was the deadliest thing she would come across for miles around. Her intuition was smarter than her, and it was telling her to run; that every move he made was a calculated step. Every word he spoke a strand of glistening lies, weaving a sticky web around her.

Her eyes wandered over his form as her mind continued its downward spiral. No doubt even the tiniest sounds registered somewhere in his mind. Every breath she took, every beat of her heart. Small and ignorant as she must be in his eyes, she knew this to be true, and Ruby was scared.

She was scared, yet she'd never been so terrified and thrilled at the same time. The two emotions warred for dominance, keeping her prisoner in her own body while she struggled, holding the gaze of the demon that had featured so heavily in her life this past week. Had it only been a week? It felt much longer.

The corners of his mouth turned. Then, with a nod, he gestured behind her.

Ruby broke the stare. She turned to look, following his gaze. She had trusted him blindly when they'd first met. And where had it got her?

It had got her burnt, that's where. So why was she trusting him now?

"A leopard never changes its spots, Rube." One of Sandra's old proverbs echoed inside her subconscious, ever the angel on her shoulder. As someone so perpetually optimistic, that one had never sounded right coming out of her friend's mouth.

Just then, she saw where he had gestured. There was a fallen tree lying on the ground near the circle's edge. Ruby headed over, grateful for the chance to sit.

As she sat, her palms brushed against the strange tree. It wasn't rough like she'd expected, and her hands sprung back in surprise. The surface was like velvet to the touch. Perched on her makeshift tree bench, she began to trace the smooth twists and knots of the trunk, exploring with her fingers.

The air here was warm, and she'd long stopped being cold. It wasn't warm like a hot summer's day back at home, but the kind of warm where the air itself hung in curtains, hot and heavy on her skin.

Drayvex lingered by the tree's splayed roots, unmoving. His attention seemed to be elsewhere, but as he watched something in the distance, his eyes flickered in the red light. They were changing colour more frequently now than Ruby had ever seen. She wondered what it meant.

"What are the crystal mountains?" she probed, stroking the velveteen bark with a finger.

His gaze slid back over to where she sat. Drayvex seemed unwilling to talk. Ruby wasn't going to let him off that easily, though. Not now she was here.

"Where are they?

After a few long, drawn-out seconds, he threw her a bone. "Mountains of naturally forming crystal," he said. "Black and translucent. When light pierces through them, they gleam in hundreds of varying shades of black, from shadow grey to purest darkness."

He paused, presumably for effect, as extravagant images flooded her mind. She could see it *all.*

"When they're struck," he hummed, lowering his voice, slipping towards her, "you can hear them ring from miles away."

Ruby revelled in the picture he'd painted. "They must look truly beautiful first thing in the morning and in the last light of day." She could only imagine how stunning they must look against the backdrop of a rising sun.

"Vekrodus doesn't have a sun," he deadpanned from her immediate right.

Ruby jumped out of her skin. No longer in front of her, he was sitting on the log beside her, staring at her as though she was mentally challenged. No sun. Surely not. She found it hard to believe that anything could live in a permanent state of darkness, even someone like Drayvex. "Never?"

His face was blank, but as he peered down at her, his blue-grey eyes narrowed the smallest amount. "No."

Ruby thought about it. If his aversion to bright light was anything to go by, then dealing with the sun would no doubt be a major inconvenience.

"I see," she said, a memory from earlier that week popping into her mind. Drayvex, reacting like a cat thrown into water after she'd switched on her bedside lamp. A laugh bubbled up and escaped as this memory resurfaced. She could see the funny side now, being a bit more in the know. It felt good to laugh, therapeutic. She laughed again, louder, enjoying the giddy feeling that came with it.

When she looked back at the demon beside her, he was giving her an odd look. She couldn't read it. But then, if he was half as confused as she felt at this point, then she wouldn't need to.

Ruby studied the bizarre creature next to her, taking advantage of the temporary veil of peace that had descended between them. Drayvex truly was glorious to behold, in a terrifying, unearthly kind of way. When they'd first met, he had charmed her, acting as though butter wouldn't melt in his mouth. In hindsight, it was an impressive feat for someone so naturally skewed. Still, he hadn't always been nice to her by any stretch, but Drayvex had kept her safe, even when he had no real obligation to do so.

Could she *trust* him, though?

"Why did you give it back?" The words tumbled out before Ruby could stop them.

Drayvex didn't move. He didn't speak. He simply sat, his gaze boring into her. He didn't feign ignorance, and as she watched him, his eyes filled with understanding. A knowing, almost as though he'd expected this. "Does that bother you, Ruby Red?" he probed, her name lingering on his tongue.

Bother her? She supposed it did. She frowned, irked by his stupid questions. It also bothered her that he clearly had no intention of answering.

Drayvex slid closer. Ruby's instincts screamed at her. She fought against them, torn between two conflicting feelings. He was only an inch away from her, yet they had been this close before. Somehow, though, here on this planet, he seemed closer now than he had ever been.

She took a breath, forcing her lungs to keep doing their job. That same deep-rooted instinct was pushing at her to run. It was telling her that she was in danger.

Yet, another instinct wanted to be closer still. It was reckless and wild. It was what defined her, what she had lost when she left the city life behind her.

Ruby stared into the depths of those piercing eyes, watching strands of sleek black hair fall around them. They were soft but veiled. With … with what? She wet her lips.

She wondered what his lips would feel like against hers. They looked soft too, and she found herself tracing their curves with her eyes. One slip was all it would take.

Drayvex pulled away in a jarring motion. One moment he was there in front of her, the next, back in the tree-strewn forest, engulfed by red and black.

Ruby sat rooted to the spot. It felt as though a door had been slammed in her face. Had she misread him? She ran a hand through her hair. A sensation close to disappointment seeped into her muscles, making her feel heavy. Of course, she'd gotten carried away. What did she honestly expect? She had no right to feel disappointed.

Squinting through the trees, Ruby saw Drayvex moving back towards her. That was quick, she thought, folding her arms across her chest. Looking down, she chastised herself. Drayvex was a demon. He had never been a romantic option, and he *never* would be, for good reasons.

Ruby felt rather than heard him. She looked up, expecting him to be there in front of her. A flash of red filled her vision. It was a round, glowing flower, one of the blobs that lit the trees, resting on his outstretched palm. It was astonishingly pretty.

"Dealing with the degenerate that made you public enemy number one was only half of the job."

Degenerate? No love lost there, then. Ruby mirrored his businesslike tone. "It was?"

Ignoring her question, Drayvex retook his place beside her and held the flower out towards her. Ruby hesitated, before taking it from him. It was shaped like a teardrop, fatter at the bottom. The petals—she assumed they were petals—had the same velvety texture as the trees on which they grew.

"Listen to me," he said, softer this time.

Ruby looked up at Drayvex. His teeth were pointed but small. They didn't look as threatening as they had back in that alleyway. Were they smaller, or had she just got used to them?

"The Lapis Vitae has been shrouding you in its demonic energy since you acquired it. As long as you wear it, you cannot be touched. Within reason, of course. There are always loopholes in these situations. *Ah*-ah, don't speak. Not yet."

Ruby closed her mouth and frowned at him. Why was she only finding this out now?

"But humans are not made to sustain such power. And so, in return for every year you have worn the stone around that fragile neck, your luck became that bit more sour without it. It's called 'death luck'. Are you with me?"

She didn't respond.

"Ruby." Drayvex threw her a hard look.

Ruby nodded, words failing her.

Reaching for the flower in her hand, he ran a finger along its bottom curve. "The sap from this particular plant will heal the damage to your aura, and separate it from the stone. You can then be without it *without* taking yourself out."

No sooner had Drayvex finished, than Ruby felt everything click into place. When they'd first met, he'd charmed her with a hidden agenda. He'd been nice to her, listened to her prattle on about her boring country problems. She'd been stupid enough to believe that they were friends then. But Drayvex had tricked her and treated her like a job. He'd even bragged about it afterwards, before threatening to kill her.

"Fool me once, shame on you," sang Sandra's voice inside her head. *"Fool me twice ..."* Well, shame on me, she thought. I really must be desperate.

"Ruby," Drayvex snapped. "Do. You. Understand?" He was glaring at her now.

Oh yeah, she seethed, glaring back. I get you. She'd honestly thought that there was a part of him that had simply wanted to see her again. Of course, this was about the necklace. "Yes."

Ruby shut him out. She squeezed her free hand closed and felt her nails bite into her palm. Her heart was heavy, and angry tears had begun to well up in the corners of her eyes. It was in that reactive moment that she decided that Drayvex was not going to get to her again. She blinked and relaxed her stiff fingers, laying her hand on her lap. He was simply not worth a reaction.

"The sap is inside," he said, continuing in a calmer voice. "You can consume it or soak in it. There's no difference."

"Right."

The silence that followed was deafening. It stretched beyond what was comfortable.

Drayvex watched her, unconcealed suspicion radiating from him, becoming more prominent with each passing second. "Right?" He raised his eyebrows.

As Ruby met his gaze head-on, she fought against her natural response, against the urge to wilt under his penetrating eyes. Nothing wrong with your hearing then, she thought, a touch of scathing creeping into her thoughts—then she thought better. No, it was best not to bait a demon when he was your ride home.

"Yes. Fine." Ruby turned away and glared into the depths of the forest. If Sandra was the angel on her shoulder, then Drayvex was the devil.

When she glanced back at him out of the corner of her eyes, he hadn't moved. Drayvex's eyes had become suspicious slits. He looked as though he was about to say something. The silence was beginning to drive her mad. What she wouldn't give for a little birdsong. "Take me home, please," she said with as much indifference as she could muster.

Ruby watched his eyes darken in the gloom.. It was then that she realised, rather remotely, that this was not a coincidence, but a reflection of his darkening mood. Those eyes regarded her anew with equally glacial courtesy. Then, without a word, Drayvex turned and stalked off into the forest.

He didn't bother to set a pace she could match, and soon, she was trailing behind in the red darkness. Ruby, she thought, look at the mess you've got yourself into.

Ruby pushed her way through the undergrowth, feet springy on the tentacle grass as she jogged to keep up. She'd been this way once already. Now, though, travelling at a fair pace through a demonic forest, she discovered how truly clumsy she was. Even with her so-called wonder necklace, she'd tripped several times, tumbling towards the floor with her hands outstretched in the vain hope of snagging something solid.

Drayvex neither slowed nor bothered to look behind him. Clearly, he felt that the pretence of giving a rat's arse was no longer necessary, and in a way, Ruby was glad that he was finally being honest. After all, she'd often wondered if he hated her. Now, she knew.

By the time they made it back to Crichton, Ruby was both relieved and sick to her stomach.

She shivered in the Earthly evening cold, trying to regain her bearings. They were back in the old construction site. Almost home. She looked down, and her vision slid, the effect of jumping between worlds making her head spin. This time, she'd had to tough it out alone. She'd met the floor soon after arriving.

The otherworldly flower was still cupped in her hand. It was no longer glowing, just red, and she wondered with vague interest if it had something to do with the different atmospheres.

Drayvex was lurking somewhere near the portal behind her. Don't look back, Ruby willed herself. Don't give him the satisfaction. Her inner voice sounded stronger than she felt. "I can find my own way from here," she said to the shadows behind her, barely recognising her own voice.

"Suit yourself." The voice was uninterested.

Ruby took a few steps, then stopped, looking dead ahead into the night. "Oh, by the way. You can take it when I'm done. I don't want it anymore." And she didn't. All the good memories of her and her gran, once associated with her necklace, had now been replaced by darkness and deceit.

Taking one step after the other, Ruby left Drayvex and the portal behind her.

Ruby barely heard the local nightlife as she dragged herself through the village. The sound of nighttime birds, the rasping of grasshoppers in the grass, both she realised should be a comfort to her after where she'd been.

But they didn't penetrate her bubble of misery. Tonight, she knew that nothing would.

She stopped walking and stood, shivering in the night air. Squinting into the darkness around her, she tried to shake the gnawing agitation that was creeping inside her. Was Drayvex following her?

Ruby squeezed her eyes shut. Silly Ruby. She was already giving him what he wanted. He had no more reason to—

Something hit her from behind. Her vision tunnelled, and then all she knew was black.

Ruby was roused by the buzzing in her ears. She swallowed and felt her throat grate together with a painful dryness.

Wincing, she gave her brain a moment to come to. Had she had a bad night? She couldn't recall going to—

Her eyes snapped open. It was pitch black. Ruby baulked.

She did remember.

Her eyes widened redundantly in the dark. Not one spec of light was visible, not the thin strip of light under a door, or the fuzzy greyness of an obscured window. Nothing.

Ruby lifted her hand to her face—no, she didn't. Panic.

She twisted her arms, straining, and a short, sharp shock flashed across her wrists. Ruby blinked, her sluggish brain lost without her sight. She twisted her pinned arms again and felt the cold bite of metal against her wrists. Her arms were bound behind her back.

Panic squeezed her insides. Her heart pounded in her ears. The last thing she remembered was leaving Drayvex behind her. She'd been on her way home, and something had come at her from behind.

Where the hell was she now?

Ruby wrestled with fear as her lungs wrestled with their basic function. Something had grabbed her. Now she was their hostage. Holy *Hell*. She shook her head, unwilling to simply fall into the role of the victim. Think, Ruby, think. What can you hear?

Straining her ears, she listened for telltale sounds, for anything other than pressing silence. Her breathing, ragged and shallow. She could hear that, and nothing else.

Ruby struggled against her bonds. She didn't know how to fight, or defend herself from attackers, or—

She stopped and held her breath, listening for the sound she'd just caught. She held her breath. There *was* a sound. It was unmistakable now; slow, laboured. She could hear breathing that wasn't hers.

It was coming from behind her.

A crippling fear seeped into her muscles, a realisation hitting her. Her captor may have been standing in the room with her this whole time.

"H-hello?" Ruby's voice crackled, hoarse from disuse. How long had she been here?

Someone grabbed her from behind. The force of the action pulled her backwards, yanking her to her feet.

Her captor breathed out, a sick-sounding rattle that made her skin crawl. They sounded small and frail, except— their hand was huge. Ruby felt it smother her small arm, an icy cold embrace that kicked her imagination into frenzied overdrive.

Then, it squeezed.

Ruby screamed as pain shot up her arm and into her chest. Her voice sounded alien as the grip tightened like a vice, crushing her with an over-sized palm. she struggled in her captor's grip, the pain in her arm overwhelming her senses.

Suddenly, an animalistic hissing sliced through the dark. Her captor jerked, a violent spasm that jerked her in turn, before releasing her arm. Ruby's knees buckled. She dropped to the floor.

Silence rang out once again.

Arms unable to support her, she curled inward, forehead resting against the smooth ground.

Get up off the floor, Ruby, she pushed. You have to get up. And then she did, awkwardly. Because no one was going to save her this time. She had to save herself.

The room started to glow. It was a red swell, building, as though the darkness itself was on fire. Ruby blinked, afraid her eyes were playing tricks on her. They weren't.

She turned, stomach churning, to face her captor, and felt her jaw drop. The glow was coming *from* them. A ball of red sat in the centre of a large stomach, lighting up the hulking outline of a misshapen person. A person with its ginormous fist raised right above her head.

Ruby fought to stay conscious, to stay on her feet. "W-wait. Please." She thought of her mum, of Sandra, of—

"*Yjúos.*"

A word reached her ears, but she didn't understand. She spun on the spot, less careful, more hopeful, and saw a burst of light.

The monster in the doorway stepped into the room, shutting the door behind it. The door disappeared into the wall. All her hope died.

Chapter 18

*S*he could see. There was real light in the room, and she could see. And now she wished she couldn't.

The monster who had entered was black all over. It walked upright like a person, but that was where the similarities ended. It was tall and wide with hulking muscles and black skin that gleamed against the flickering torch in its clawed hand. On the top of its head sat two horns, flat and curved, like the blade of a scimitar.

Ruby stared with a spreading horror, unable to tear her eyes away from the monstrosity—the demon—she was trapped with. She found herself studying its face out of morbid curiosity, a curiosity that was out of control. As if she needed any more fuel for her nightmares. Its mouth was a gaping maw of needle-like fangs. Its eyes …

She sucked in a ragged breath. It had none that she could see. Just two black sockets.

"Now now, friend. The stone still protects it."

Ruby's blood ran cold. The stone. She registered its weight against her chest. It felt heavier, somehow. She didn't know if it was a symbolic weight, or if it truly had changed since being in Drayvex's possession, but she was more aware of it now, hanging around her neck, than she had ever been. This was never going to end.

The black demon placed the torch into a socket in the wall, then moved towards her.

Ruby's racing heart kicked into overdrive. "S-stay away," she hissed, breathless. She stumbled, her body reacting of its own accord, and backed straight into her captor.

A scream rose up her throat. She spun on the spot, swaying, and stared open-mouthed at the creature she was trapped with. Not a person, but an it. A thing that made the black demon look like a dream in comparison.

Ruby froze, unable to look away; unable to finish the scream that was caught in her throat. She was in Hell.

A deep, bass laugh sounded from behind her. It didn't sound amused, just as though it was making the noise. "Look at me."

A hand landed on her shoulder, its weight pushing down on her with unexpected force. It turned her roughly, yanking her forward until she faced the black demon—the lesser of the two evils she was trapped with.

Ruby looked at its hand. It covered her shoulder. She could feel the points of each claw poking through her jacket, resting uncomfortably against her skin. An itchy prickle. The fingers, though, were not still. They twitched, as though dying to dig all five claws deep into her flesh.

A shudder ran through her.

"Yes. You are right to be afraid, little human."

She looked up at the demon, unsure of how to look at a creature with no real eyes. It wanted to hurt her. So, why hadn't it?

"You are in far more danger than your simple mind is capable of comprehending. But, fear not." Its head tilted to the side, black sockets trained on her. "By the time we are through with you, you *will* know true suffering."

Drayvex's voice penetrated her thoughts. *"As long as you wear it, you cannot be touched."*

Was that it? The one thing everyone wanted was the one thing keeping her alive?

"Within reason, of course. There are always loopholes in these situations."

What were the loopholes?

The demon made an impatient guttural sound and whipped back its hand.

Ruby flinched as a point grazed her shoulder. She should have asked more questions, put her personal feelings aside, taken advantage of Drayvex's rare willingness to provide her with answers. She closed her eyes and tried to control her breathing. But she hadn't wanted to talk to him. And how on Earth was she to know that she'd be kidnapped by demons on her way home, anyway?

"Where did you find the Lapis Vitae?" barked the demon, making her jump.

Ruby kept her eyes screwed shut as fear spiked in her veins, holding her captive.

"How long have you possessed it? What else are you hiding from us?"

She had to be brave. But she didn't know how. Sandra knew how to fight them, the monsters in the dark. That was what her dad was teaching her, wasn't it? Her special secret. Maybe Sandra could teach her how to be brave, too.

"SPEAK!"

Her eyes flew open, a reaction that she couldn't control fast enough, and a soft scream escaped her lips. The demon was right in her face. She could feel its hot, moist breath on her cheek, count every single fang in its dripping mouth.

Don'tlookdon'tlookdon'tlook.

Queasy and desperate, Ruby looked around her for the first time. She was in a small, circular room with no windows and no visible door. The walls looked as though they were made from a black stone, the floor a black marbled surface. The room was bare, but certainly not plain. She'd never seen anything like it and she wondered what kind of person would keep their victims in such a room.

The demon grabbed her face, twisting her head back around. "No!" she screamed, trying to pull away. "Let me *go!*" She would never tell them anything. Never give them what they wanted.

"Now, now, Malsurg. Temper."

Ruby stopped struggling. The black demon stiffened.

The third presence had barely spoken loud enough for her to hear, but

181

at the sound of his voice, the demon in her face stood to attention. It was suddenly very clear that this black demon was not the one in charge.

Ruby's stomach twisted. Was she back on Vekrodus?

"Master."

A third demon stepped into the room. He had a large, round frame and also walked upright. From a distance, he could almost pass for a person, and Ruby almost cried out in hope. As he moved closer, though, she saw how mistaken she truly was.

"You're scaring the girl. Let me handle this one."

Without question, the black demon let go of her face. It stepped back and lingered by the torch with unnerving still.

Ruby stared at the new demon moving towards her, unable to decide which monster she'd rather be trapped with: the one by the torch, the one in front of her, or the thing behind her. She honestly didn't know.

It wasn't any one thing in particular. Not the small claws that tipped the end of each of his webbed fingers, or the unhinged madness that gleamed in the pits of his eyes, which were now focused on her. It wasn't even his skin, with its unnatural bruised yellow hue, or the prominent black veins that bulged on parts of the flesh. No, Ruby was sure that it was the overwhelming feeling of menace that oozed out of his every pore that shook her to her core.

He stopped in front of her, studying her with beady eyes. Then, he grinned. As his mouth widened, Ruby went cold. If a shark could smile, she thought it would look a lot like that.

"You must be the little human child that's causing all this ruckus." His tongue slipped out and back, tasting the air like a snake.

"Ruby," she said, before she could bite her tongue. "My name is Ruby." And I'm not a child.

The demon's eyes narrowed, grin slipping into a malicious smile. "Of course, it would have a name."

Unlike Drayvex, this demon had as much charm as a pit viper. She could smell blood on its breath, a salty metallic waft that turned her already weak stomach, and as she stared into the eyes of the demon only inches away, she fought back the bile that was rising up her throat. *She* was the 'it'? Not likely.

"I must apologise for my general, my dear. You see, Malsurg enjoys taking his temper out on sweet little girls. Beating them into submission, if you will. I would imagine that he feels *cheated* that he can't get his hands on you. Yet."

He reached up and ran a thick finger down the side of her face. Ruby jerked away, removing herself from his cool, clammy touch. Why was this one cold? she mused, unable to switch off her curious nature.

"You're quite the tempting package. All wrapped up in a delicious black bow of … power."

She followed his eyes down to her chest, where her necklace sat under her clothing. It wasn't on show, but he knew it was there all the same. Her breathing hitched. No.

"You have something I want, dear," he purred, reaching for her face once again. This time, a green, gunky liquid oozed from the tip of his claw and flowed down his finger. "I'm going to ask you once, and you will give me what I want. Is that clear?"

Ruby watched the green liquid out of the corner of her eye. What was that? Nothing good, she suspected. Her heart hammered in her chest. He couldn't hurt her, though, could he?

"Give me the stone, Ruby."

She took a shaky breath. "Bite me." Her heart was going to explode. "You can't hurt me."

The demon's eyes widened briefly, as though surprised by her words. Then they narrowed to cold slits. "What is he playing at, Malsurg?" he growled, all the previous smoothness in his voice gone. "What is his *fucking* game?"

Ruby closed her eyes as she waited for what came next. She couldn't take much more of this.

"Oh, my dear. You thought this was for you?" Ruby's eyes flew open. His voice had resumed its previous oily smoothness. His shark grin was back. "No, no, no. This is for your dear old mother. Courtesy of her selfish spawn,

Ruby." Then, he turned and walked towards the door.

Ruby couldn't breathe. Little black specks danced in front of her eyes. No, not her mother. Anything but that. "No … no, wait."

The demon didn't wait. He kept walking.

"WAIT!"

He paused.

Angry tears welled up in the corners of her eyes. Ruby looked down at the cord around her neck.

*

Twenty-four hours. That was how long the tharelum sap needed to work its way through her entire system and repair all damage in its path. Provided Ruby had done as he'd instructed, not only would her aura be spotless, but her fragile human body would be in better condition than it had ever been.

Ruby. Her name lingered on his tongue like the taste of rancid flesh.

Drayvex prowled through the stunted village of Crichton, unconcerned by his gleaming tail, or the curved hooks at his fingers, or any other visible appendage that didn't belong on a human being. Ironically, the place was devoid of life, human or otherwise.

Lashings of rain pounded the pavements, transforming the road into a shallow river as water fell from the sky in infinite amounts. It soaked him, before quickly evaporating on his hot flesh and turning to steam, rising into the atmosphere in an endless cycle. He barely felt it.

"You can take it when I'm done. I don't want it anymore."

Her last words echoed in his mind. They made about as much sense as this whole ridiculous obsession she had with the stone. No. Not the stone, the 'necklace'.

His first thought had been *Halle*-bloody-*lujah*. It was about damn time she showed him some gratitude for sparing her poxy human life. His second thought questioned everything.

Why, after insisting this whole time that it was rightfully hers, would Ruby give up now and hand it over without so much as a whimper? It made no sense.

Drayvex stretched his neck, working the tension from his muscles. He had to admit the girl had been a frequent occurrence in his thoughts over the past twenty-four hours. In fact, she seemed to have set up camp in his cortex, anchoring herself to a nearby brain stem.

Ruby had gone from vampire in a blood bank to ice queen in a single moment. It was erratic, even for her. Even considering the strange circumstances. And the more he'd thought about it, the more suspicious he became. What was she hiding? Why now, *after* he'd brought her to Vekrodus, and not before?

After cycling through several infuriating theories, Drayvex had decided that he didn't give a damn. If she screwed him over, he would make her wish she was dead. Besides, in a few moments, she would be a means to an end and no more. By rights, he should leave her waste of space village in the same state as its neighbour.

It would certainly send a message.

A flash of red in his peripheral vision stopped him in his tracks. It was wrong, out of place. A splash of colour on a sepia backdrop. Drayvex sharpened his senses, focusing on the culprit.

His first thought *almost* caused him to doubt himself. Wrong, it said. Not possible. But no, he was never wrong, and as he reached through the shrivelled thorns of the bush, he plucked the red thing out from within the tangle and sat it on his palm.

It was Ruby's flower.

The tharelum bud in his hand was untouched and unravaged, a perfect shape. Drayvex considered the idea that she had simply abandoned it, tossing it into the bushes in a show of defiance. He quickly dismissed this. No, he didn't think Ruby would be so reckless. Putting her own welfare at risk? To what, piss him off? No childish rebellion necessary there.

Then there was only one way to find out.

Drayvex approached the lurid green house with focused intent. He tensed to spring, to enter the place that he had been coming to for far too long, when a voice caught his attention through the walls. It was coming from the lower floor.

"Carol, I'm sorry to put on you like this. I'm just beside myself."

Drayvex slipped around the side of the building, stopping outside a large window.

Ruby's mother was pacing in a tight line, her path restricted by the corded phone pressed to her ear. She held it as though her life depended on keeping it close, her hands white from the pressure of her vice grip.

He watched the woman pace through narrowed eyes.

"She didn't come home last night. Her bed hasn't been slept in and I ..."

The voice on the other end of the line was attempting to comfort.

"Yes. Well, she's normally good at letting me know where she is. She knows I worry."

The brusque female voice was making assurances now, spitting her words out in angry snatches.

"Yes. Thank you."

Drayvex tuned her out. Ruby hadn't made it back. The impact of that simple statement hit him with unexpected force. She had insisted on walking herself home, could barely bring herself to acknowledge his presence; and he had been spiteful in return, only too happy to oblige. To be rid of her. Rid of the stain that she left on his perfect control.

He had turned his back on her without a second thought. The girl on every demon's mind. Now, she was gone.

Drayvex stood beside the window, rooted, as something uncoiled inside him. That parasitic thing that had dug its way into him, burrowing deeper each time they met. Growing inside him. Suffocating him this entire time.

Now, he felt it burst with violent force.

He placed a hand on the side of the house, digging his claws into the bricks. For three hundred years, Drayvex had been all but dead inside. It was an essential quality for any demon with an ounce of ambition, let alone the Demon Lord of Vekrodus. Now, all kinds of strange things were surfacing. A gnawing nagged at the back of his mind. A restless writhing in the pit of his stomach pushed him dangerously close to the edge. But most of all, he felt pure, undiluted rage.

He watched the wall, the little cracks spreading out from where he penetrated. Drayvex had assumed that demons were immune to insanity. They were naturally warped, a side effect of living in darkness for hundreds of years. However, he was open to the possibility that he may have been wrong on this one occasion.

As he stood and wrestled with the turmoil that raged inside him, it was easy to accept that he may indeed be completely and undeniably insane. Anger, hot and fresh, seared through him as he considered Ruby's kidnappers. An anger, he was surprised to discover, that was partly directed at himself. He thought about what he would do to them when he found them, the varying ways in which he could make them suffer.

And they *would* suffer.

Ripping his hand out of Ruby's house, Drayvex took off in a blur, wasting no more time. He knew *exactly* who was responsible for this. He would bet his throne.

He reached the hidden portal at the rubble site and pushed straight through, barely leaving enough time to control the destination.

When he stepped through on the other side, he was a long way from the light-touched planet called Earth.

Chapter 19

The atmosphere on Vekrodus matched his darkening mood. The air around him crackled, sparks of friction flaring at the smallest of disturbances. Angry masses of swirling gasses converged in the upper atmosphere, heating and thickening in unusual ways. It was as though the whole planet was on edge.

The Tower was Saydor's personal stronghold in the crimson waste. Made up of a single jagged spire that thinned at the top into a sharp point, it was where the Demon Master disappeared to whenever he wasn't kowtowing with transparent motive or plotting Drayvex's demise. His own filthy, fetid recess.

Drayvex approached the heavy ornate gates at the base of the Tower and regarded its burly guard with contempt. This one he knew.

The self-indulgent killer writhing under Drayvex's skin wanted blood to flow and bones to shatter. But it was important to exercise patience, to not only know when to slash and rip, but when to apply a gentle pressure instead. Aside from being born into status, it was one of the many things that separated him from the mindless masses on this godforsaken rock.

Summoning forth his aura, he allowed it to tumble from him in black wisps, sending a clear message to any who would question his face. Things that looked human did not fare well here. Still, this face was familiar to Ruby, and maybe, it would give the remaining shreds of her sanity something to cling to as he plucked her from the bowels of the underworld. He'd have to work harder to make an appropriate impact in such a form. But impact was a strength of his.

The guard inspected him as he advanced. It was unconcerned, its lazy, slitted gaze sliding to the stretch of crimson sands behind, before snapping back in alarm. He sprung to life, panic flashing across his features as he failed to compose himself in time. "My Lord?"

Drayvex knew that look well. It was a look of torn loyalties and hidden agendas.

The guard's weapon hovered as he held it out in an uncertain gesture.

Drayvex stopped in front of the scaled creature and stared into its yellow, slitted eyes. They were alert, measuring. He smiled at the demon, slow and savage. "Thera," he purred, hearing the dangerous edge to his voice. "Are you going to attack me?"

The demon lowered its weapon, too fast. "Uh—no. Of course not, My Lord. That's funny." The words tumbled off its pronged tongue with an urgent undercurrent. It fell into a bow, bending as low as its armour would allow. "My apologies. Is there something I can help you with?"

Drayvex glared down at the demon, not bothering to release him from his bow. "Oh, I hope so. I'm looking for a girl."

Thera, who had been craning in a futile attempt to look up, froze. The demon looked down at the floor, eyes dancing in their sockets as they flicked from one black boot to the other. "A ... girl?"

"Yes. A human girl. Have you seen one?"

"Have I ... seen a human girl?" Its voice lilted, rising to a strained squeak.

"Lately," Drayvex clarified, flexing his claws.

Thera flinched, shuffling backwards in a subconscious act of self-preservation.

Drayvex shot forward, reacting to the simple action like a match to sandpaper. "WELL?" He grabbed him by the throat and yanked him in close. "You have five seconds," he snarled. "*Five.*"

"Wait," it cried. "I remember. I've seen one. I've seen one!"

Drayvex fell silent, maintaining his tight grip on the writhing demon's throat. Then, he punched out with mental power, penetrating its mind with unnecessary force. He didn't need to hear whatever garbled half-truth would come out of its mouth. He would just take it.

Not bothering to be careful, Drayvex dug around inside the guard's head. This mind would be left in useless tatters, without a doubt. Impatient, he scanned through its most recent memories, stopping within seconds when a particular image caught his attention: Ruby.

In the memory, she was unconscious, slumped over the shoulders of a large, black demon twice her size. This demon, he knew to be Saydor's most trusted minion.

He ripped himself out of Thera's mind and dropped the demon in a crumpled heap at his feet. Its glassy gaze and blank expression gave him no real satisfaction. As a fresh wave of anger and frustration washed over him, he brought his boot down hard onto its head.

The demon's head exploded like rotten fruit. And as Drayvex watched the paltry carnage, one single obsessive thought circled in his mind. Saydor would pay for his disobedience. He would pay in blood.

Drayvex smashed through the entrance doors with a concentrated blast of power. It seemed to take the demons inside a single skewed moment to realise what they were dealing with before the circular hall erupted into chaos.

He let them scatter. Let them dare to hope that maybe, just *maybe,* they were going to make it out of this alive. Gave them a head start. And then he killed them all, one by one.

One. Two. Three. Four.

He sliced through the room like a knife through butter.

Five. Six. Seven.

He inhaled their fear, dismissed their feeble pleas as he picked them off.

Eight. Ten. Twelve.

They screeched and begged. Level one demons with no purpose, barely fit to clean the floor with their tongues, let alone guard an entrance hall.

The large room was silent and still as Drayvex slipped through its centrum. Demon corpses littered the dark stone floor, their lifeblood splattered across the walls, the floor. The smell of blood was thick in the air, a sour stench far inferior the human variant. Nineteen.

The first floor was ready for him. Despite this, the anxious shuffles of the first-floor hordes promised the same uninspired show of cowardice. Blood dripped down the length of his claws as he scanned the dim room and its dubious specimens. He gave them a sinister smile. The last thing that they would ever see.

Then, a single demon sunk into a crouch, baring its teeth in a final, resolute gesture. Drayvex killed that one first. He made it quick, but not entirely painless.

The others followed suit, were no better than the floor below in most aspects, except they no longer fled. Smart enough to know that they never stood a chance.

Another caught his eye for a different reason.

Striding through the carnage, he moved towards the last remaining demon in his sight. This one was familiar. It had been in the memory, part of the entourage that had taken Ruby from her world.

The creature scrabbled against the stone floor in a panic, attempting to find its feet on a floor slick with blood. Drayvex watched it squirm. Soon, it would have no use for feet.

"Tell me," said Drayvex as he approached. He leaned in towards the pustule-ridden demon, crouching at its level.

Its black eyes flared with wild panic. "My Lord, wait."

"What do you think happens to lowlife scum that steals from their superiors?"

The demon on the floor stumbled backwards, losing what was left of its nerve. "Please, I—I was just following orders. I didn't know the stone belonged to you."

"A liar and a thief. Predictable." *Was* this about the stone? He no longer knew.

Drayvex rose upright to stand over the demon. Then, he punched out with viscous black tendrils. As they burst from his form, they pierced the sad creature on the floor, plunging through muscle and organ, curling around and around in constricting loops.

The demon writhed and hissed as the tendrils bled inside it. Unlike Saydor, *his* personal brand of poison was in no hurry to end things at all. It was a corrosive substance that destroyed every living thing that it touched, killing them slowly.

He allowed this to continue for one drawn-out moment, filling its body with enough poison to take down an entire floor of minions. Then, he slid the tendrils out and turned his back on the dying, hole-riddled demon that had backed the wrong monster.

The next few floors housed competent fighters. Demons loyal to Saydor and fully aware of the situation. They exchanged grim glances at his arrival and fell into a mixture of attack and defence stances. Some even tried to reason with him.

Their reasoning fell on deaf ears. Drayvex killed them all with ruthless indifference, a driving anger pushing him on with relentless appetite.

By the time he reached the top floor, the trail of devastation stretched from ground to tip in a long-overdue purge. But most of all, it was a message for his dear friend.

The top floor of the Tower was empty.

Drayvex scanned the spherical space. Torches burned in brackets that lined the walls, throwing their flickering light around an elaborate, ageing room. The two lines of pillars that ran down the centre laid a ready path to welcome him through. Each one was a pale marble, with thin red trails that ran down their length, trickling to the base in wounded patterns. Every other had the same design at the bottom. A group of carved humans at the height of his knee, all being crushed under the weight of the pillar in their attempt to hold it up. Above that were little demons, looking down on the humans and mocking them. It was the chain.

Drayvex scoffed. Saydor's tastes had always been exorbitant. This was likely because, unlike himself, Saydor wasn't memorable. He had to remind others of his status on Vekrodus on a frequent basis. He was doing it wrong.

He spat at the base of the nearest pillar, loathing the Demon Master with intense prejudice. He would show that worm what a true show of power *really* looked like.

At the end of the room was another room. A portable room within a room, sectioned off and complete with hidden door. Guarding this room was Saydor's pet, the same demon that had taken personal charge of Ruby's kidnap.

Not worth it, said his waning voice of reason. Malsurg is a cornerstone. He glared at the demon from across the space and felt his claws lengthen. And you're already screwing the rules sideways, bub.

Some rules just begged to be broken.

Drayvex was in no mood to be messed with. He was pissed off. Far more pissed off than he logically should be, which made things worse. And made himself harder to contain within the flimsy human skin that he wore.

The burly demon at the door seemed all too aware of this. As Drayvex approached, he held up his hands in a feeble gesture of peace. "Lord Drayvex." He bowed low, managing to keep his hands out while he did so. "I apologise for this unfortunate oversight."

Drayvex sneered down at the two-faced demon, quelling the impulse to rip his tongue from his head. "Rise."

The demon rose, and glared, looking him up and down with suppressed ire. Drayvex knew what he was staring at. It was the grisly mosaic of Saydor's familiars, little pieces of them splattered all over him, dripping down to stain the pale floor.

Saydor's pet narrowed his eyes. "My Lord, I must apologise on behalf of Master Saydor for this misunderstanding, and for the sheer incompetence of his minions. They know not what they meddle with."

Malsurg's voice was fluid. He was a silver-tongued fiend. There was a clear reason why this demon was Saydor's favourite.

"Please." He reached into the folds of his cloak and pulled out the stone, holding it in front of him. It swayed under his fist. "Allow me to fix this."

For the second time that evening, Drayvex felt something twist in his stomach. Had he not explained to Ruby with total clarity the many reasons *not* to remove the one thing protecting her from this world? Clearly, he had not.

You can't take her back, drawled the self-serving voice in his head. *You've known this all along.*

Drayvex snatched the stone from the demon's outstretched hand. He dangled it from a curved claw and bored into him, glaring with a semi-composed conniption. "This is half of what you took from me."

Some rules just beg to be broken. Others, will decimate you on contact.

"Is this really the extent of Saydor's attempt to save his worthless hide? Or, wait—don't tell me. Are you part of the bargain as well? I accept."

The demon shifted, the muscles in his arms flexing. "My Lord, the human is not worth your time," he said, raising his deep voice to a considerable volume. "Besides, it is spoken for."

Drayvex felt what little calm and composure he had maintained up to this point shatter. His aura poured off him in a black vapour, tumbling down to collect in pools on the floor. "Are my words not penetrating your thick skull?" he snarled, pushing himself right up to the demon general. His voice echoed and bounced around the circular room, lingering and repeating. "You will return *exactly* what was stolen from me. You will not keep me waiting. You will not tell me what *is* and is *not* worth my time, and you will not open your mouth again unless I command it. Or I will make sure that when I dispose of that impotent puke, his most loyal subordinate is rewarded *in kind!* Am I making myself clear?"

The demon shifted, his muscles bulging with stress. He glared back, his face contorting in evident resentment. "As you wish," he muttered, bowing his head in defeat. Spinning, he strode over to the hidden door and placed his hand on a panel.

The door opened. He snapped his thick fingers at something in the darkness. "Bring her!"

Drayvex's fangs lengthened in response to his sudden agitation. He stared into the dark room, the bad angle blocking his view of what lay inside. His claws twitched at his sides, moving of their own accord. What really bothered him was his current state of mind. He, Drayvex, was always in control, had spent his entire life being five steps ahead. Yet he had no idea how he was going to react when Ruby walked through that door. And if she had been messed with ...

He cut the thought dead. He would have smelled her blood the second he entered the room. If they had touched her, they'd taken a more heavy-handed approach.

Ruby was led into the room by a skeletal demon twice her size. Translucent skin stretched tight over a large, gaunt frame, its corpse-like appearance typical of its kind. A keeper. She was bound at the wrists and attached to a thick chain that would have sufficed for something five times her size.

Drayvex critically scanned her over. Her face was blank, her eyes glassy, as though she'd gone into shock and decided that she would rather stay where she couldn't be reached. Despite her obvious lack of mental presence, though, he found himself somewhat pacified.

A small amount of tension slipped away, which only allowed more space for his unquenchable rage. "I don't have all day," he snapped, a restlessness building inside him once again.

At the sound of his voice, Ruby's eyes flicked up. She found his gaze and stared across the space. Holding him with big green eyes. Better the devil you know, Ruby Red, he thought, tearing himself from her.

The keeper stopped as it reached the spot where Drayvex stood. It tilted its head, emaciated face twisting as it studied his form.

"Release it," said Malsurg, still at the hidden door.

After a reluctant pause, the keeper reached for the chains at Ruby's wrists.

Drayvex glared at the depraved creature, the many things he'd like to inflict on it playing out in his mind. If she'd been 'spoken for', it would no doubt have been for this demon.

The keeper stared back through its shrivelled sockets, frozen in the act of pulling open the unlocked chains.

Drayvex felt Ruby take her place at his left. With effort, he broke the stare.

"I hope that My Lord is satisfied and that you can find it within your greatness to overlook this misunderstanding."

Drayvex stared at the two-faced general, a loathing squirming in the pit of his being. Satisfied.

As he sliced out in a flash of temper, the silver-tongued demon finally lost his cool head.

Lines, rules. Who the fuck needs those? The voice was unimpressed. Clearly, not you.

It hit the marble and bounced.

In truth, Drayvex had known that Saydor wasn't in the building as soon as he'd entered. Of course, he was all too aware of the human in the Tower, who was highly vulnerable at this moment. Saydor would wait.

"Stay out of my way," he growled to the statuesque keeper, before grabbing Ruby by the wrist and dragging her away. He *was* the rules. And they would do well to remember it.

Chapter 20

*R*uby chewed on a fingernail, tearing it to pieces with her teeth. Drayvex had barely said two words since rescuing her from her demon kidnappers. The silence only added to the mounting tension between them. She risked another sideways glance.

He was draped in shadow, looking straight ahead.

She stressed in silence, feeling herself unravel. Was he still angry about their last meeting? Was *she* still angry? Were they even on speaking terms?

Maybe he was simply sick of saving her life. But whatever it was, something was brewing inside him. She could feel it like an invisible force, pushing out into the air around them, making it harder to breathe.

Crichton's waterlogged roads were a welcome sight. The drizzles of rain that wafted like a fine mist around them clung to her clammy skin, cooling her. With that, came a renewed sense of feeling.

Her brain was the opposite. Half-formed thoughts twitched, limping to the forefront of her mind in a semi-paralysed effort. She dragged her aching body through the village, fatigue weighing her down.

It had been a long day. But Ruby doubted that she would ever sleep again.

The sensation of cold, dead flesh against her own was still fresh in her mind; nauseatingly so. Black staring sockets haunted her, the beast they belonged to just itching to crush her skull between two hulking hands. Most of all, she saw *him*. Him with the smile of a hungry piranha, and eyes that danced with evil.

"Are you okay?" Drayvex's voice interrupted her spiral. His voice was soft but had an edge that sent a shiver running down her spine.

Ruby looked up. She'd fallen behind.

Her pulse throbbed a steady rhythm in her wrists, in her neck, as she stared at her hellish saviour. Was she okay? The answer wasn't a simple one. On the one hand, she was surely only a short moment away from a white padded cell. On the other, she was alive and breathing. She was alive.

Drayvex tilted his head towards her, the details of his face draped in the shadows of the dying day. She didn't need to see him to know what would be there. His eyes would be a sinister crimson, the streaks and splashes across his person a different hue of violence, and a remnant of his well-timed rescue.

He hadn't offered an explanation, and Ruby hadn't asked. She had just been so grateful that he was there. She hadn't questioned his authority when he'd 'suggested' she keep her eyes closed, allowing herself to be led blind through the building. She didn't need to know any more to put two and two together. There had been resistance. Drayvex had pushed on regardless.

Ruby wet her lips and ran a hand through her damp hair. "I'll live," was her delayed response. Her voice barely worked.

When she pulled up beside him, she realised that Drayvex had stopped. As she drew level, he started walking again. She followed in silence, finding it easy to keep pace as she trudged beside him in a stupor.

Suddenly, a sharp pain shot up her arm. Ruby looked down at her hands. She'd been squeezing them into fists, hard, and her nails had pierced the skin of her palm. Ruby relaxed her right hand and saw three crescent nail marks. Blood oozed from the slices in her flesh. 'Stressed' was not the word, she thought, shoving her hands into her jacket pockets.

She glanced up at Drayvex. He was giving her an odd look. His eyes weren't red, but smoky grey. They were narrowed, but not in the cold, calculating way that she had come to expect, and as their eyes remained locked, she felt herself becoming self-conscious. A repeat of countless times gone by. Yet this time, something was different. For one, Ruby was positive this was the quietest he had ever been in her presence.

Drayvex's gaze dropped to the region of her right pocket. They lingered there for a moment, before flicking up and ahead. If he could smell her blood, he'd decided to ignore it.

"Tell me," he said, his voice low. "The stone. You took it off. Why?"

Ruby's breath hitched, the triggered memories fresh and vivid in her mind. She hesitated, unsure if going down this path was a good idea.

Watching Drayvex's mood change was often like flicking a switch. Only you never knew you'd actually touched it until the lights went out.

"Ruby."

But then, she thought, gritting her teeth, there was no real reason for him to care about the why. Not in the same way that *she* did, anyway. Just that, after giving it back to her, she'd given it away—and almost lost it.

"Why? You played right into their hands, you know."

Ruby breathed out. How could she explain this to a demon who only cared about his next power fix? "Yes," she replied, her voice surprisingly steady in comparison to how she felt. "But that yellow bastard threatened my mother. He would have killed her had I kept it. It was a no-brainer for me."

The demon on her left didn't respond, and Ruby began to feel lighter; almost as though a weight had been lifted.

Her relief didn't last long. It shattered as a darkness descended over Drayvex's features. His smoky eyes dropped to jet black, pupil and iris merging into one. "Yellow?" he spat.

Ruby couldn't tear her eyes away. It was fascinating and frightening. "Uh, yes. Large, round. Repulsive." Right. Of course, he was still angry. She tore her eyes away and fixed them straight ahead.

This side of him scared her more than anything else. More than the hot flashes of temper. More than the cold, scheming mind that saw her as a small cog in a large machine, a means to an end. There was more darkness in those eyes than she had seen in her lifetime on Earth.

As the little green house she'd reluctantly come to think of as home moved into view, Ruby realised that she must have zoned out. Home, she reflected, feeling somewhat giddy. She had thought that she'd never make it back. The green chipped paint that she had so despised when they had first moved in. The sorry, shrivelled attempts at growing any kind of green thing in the front garden. The grinning gnomes that smiled almost maniacally at her from beneath their red floppy hats. Right at this moment, she loved it all.

Ruby approached the front door, eager to get inside and shut out the world, before remembering Drayvex. She spun to face him, a polite 'thank you' forming on her lips. They vanished as she found him.

Drayvex was under the sensor light, leaning against the fence at the garden's perimeter—and he was staring at her.

Ruby stared back. His eyes were that same mingling blueish-purple they'd turned when she had first watched them change. Mesmerised, she found herself unable to look away. Not because they were beautiful in an exotic way that was out of this world, or because the setting sun was dull in comparison to the swirls of colour in his eyes. No, it was the *way* he was staring.

Drayvex watched her from across the small garden. His eyes burned with an intensity that seemed to pervade her very soul. Those piercing eyes tore through her defences, leaving her mind stunned and defenceless.

She stood, half turned towards him, half facing the door, her outstretched hand floating above the handle. Her pulse quickened, reacting with a mixture of thrill and fear.

Drayvex crossed the space between them in one fluid movement, closing the gap. Ruby started but caught herself. He stopped a foot away, and that fierce heat that radiated from him bathed her in warmth. It sent a pleasant shiver down her spine.

Her heart hammered against her ribcage, threatening to break free. This close, Drayvex was always a shock to the senses. But right now, her senses were out of control, something that she doubted she would ever get used to.

Ruby studied him, taking him in as she had done many times since their first meeting. Cold, handsome face. Dark hair that was chaotic and untamed, falling around his eyes in an effortless way that had her stomach doing backflips. Drayvex is a demon, she asserted to herself, trying to get a grip. Demon, demon, demon.

Drayvex didn't speak. He simply watched her, looking down on her, her hand still hovering over the door handle. But there was a fierceness to that stare, and to Ruby, it was almost as though he was trying to communicate something vital.

As she held his gaze, all the fear and hurt and anger she had been feeling, almost constantly of late, melted away to nothing. That reckless gleam said, 'I will kill anyone who tries to hurt you,' and she believed it. How could she not?

He stepped forward, and more out of instinct than alarm, Ruby stepped backwards. Her back hit the door with a soft thud.

Giving no ground, Drayvex slipped forward again, pinning her between himself and the door. He brought up an arm and placed his hand against the door next to her head. "Fuck that lowlife," he proposed, a sincere expression on his face.

Ruby blinked.

"He won't escape. Not from me." He smirked, a wicked grin spreading across his face as he spoke. The points of his teeth emerged from behind his lips. He was looking down on her now, his face so close that his breath warmed her neck.

The way he was looking at her made her feel invincible. She raised both her hands and placed them flat against his chest, marvelling at the heat searing against her palms through the material. "Fuck him?"

"Fuck them all."

Ruby's mind raced. She didn't know what she was doing. But somehow, her previous fatigue had almost vanished entirely. She didn't want to say goodbye.

Drayvex leaned in, and warm lips brushed over her right ear. He lifted his other hand, and his finger found the strap of the necklace, tucking itself under. He trailed its length down her chest, brushing her skin as he did. Every nerve ending she'd never been aware of came alive. Every part of her skin that he touched tingled in his wake.

Suddenly, Drayvex froze. His finger was curled around the strap of her necklace, and he was staring at it as though it were a poisonous snake coiled around her neck. Ruby was jarred back to some semblance of reality, the cold light of day penetrating her bubble of bliss.

His lips lifted into an animal-like snarl, and an impatient hiss hit her ears.

The hair on her body stood to attention, the sound ripping straight through her. "W-what is it?" She stood stock-still, wishing at this point that she had the room to shuffle backwards.

"Give it here." His voice was hard and short.

Ruby lifted the cord over her head, trying to process his sudden change in temperament. With great reluctance, she handed over her necklace, dreading what his response would be, but needing it all the same.

Drayvex moved back and held the necklace at eye level, watching it sway, a disgusted look on his face. "It's a fake," he growled, spitting on the ground at his feet.

Ruby's stomach dropped. She tried to respond, but words failed her. Of course, it had changed hands several times in these past few hours. From her to her demon kidnappers to Drayvex, who had then given it back to her. But where had they got such an accurate-looking copy?

She glanced at Drayvex, who looked as though he was ready to break something. Or someone. His face was hard and cold, his eyes dark once again. " Stay here," he said, tossing something red her way. "I will deal with this."

And then he was gone.

Ruby looked down at her hands. It was the red flower, looking as smooth and healthy as it had when freshly picked. She rolled it from hand to hand, studying it with new interest. It was soft like velvet. Just like rose petals, except as far as she was aware, it had no scent. Ruby sighed, feeling her arm throb and ache. She supposed she'd better do as she was told.

As she crossed the threshold and stepped into the lamp-lit hallway, she was hit by something hard. It grabbed her, wrapping itself around her, and pulled her in tight. Her mother.

Ruby froze within the wiry embrace. Something was wrong. The way she was gripping her was wrong.

The silence inside the house was eerie. She couldn't remember the last time the house had been so quiet. There was no music playing in the kitchen, no wailing sirens or gunfights blaring from the TV. Just the heavy tick of the old grandfather clock in the hall.

Ruby wrapped her arms around her mother, responding to the rib-crushing embrace. "It's okay, Mum," she soothed, hoping that her voice wasn't as rough as it sounded to her. "It's okay. What's wrong? Tell me."

No sooner had the words left her lips, than she was yanked backwards. "What's *wrong*?"

Ruby stared into red, swollen eyes, in the face that she knew like the back of her hand, and knew that she was in trouble.

"What's wrong?" Half whispered, half screeched, her mother's voice was on the verge of breaking. "I thought I'd lost you. Again. That's what's wrong!"

Ruby flinched. What?

Her mother released her, pulling back to glare at her. "Where the hell have you been? You look like Hell."

Ruby fingered her bedraggled hair and took a deep breath. She felt like it. "Did we have plans?"

As her mother's eyes almost popped out of her head, Ruby became alarmed herself.

"What? Mum, just tell me."

"You can't just … you—where have you been for the last twenty-four hours? I've been worried sick. I even called my old boss!"

Ruby felt the blood drain from her cheeks. No, that couldn't be right. "What day is it?" It was a ridiculous question, and Ruby prepared for another round of motherly wrath.

Instead, she just blinked. "You're forgetting again. I knew they should have kept you in that ward for—"

"Mum. Please."

Silence.

"Humour me."

Her mother placed a hand on her forehead and closed her eyes. "It's Wednesday."

Ruby stifled a gasp. Wednesday. She really had been gone for a whole damn day. If her Mum had called Carol ... well, things had just got complicated. But it only felt like a few hours. Her head span as she struggled to process the gap. How she could explain this to her mum without using the words 'demon' or 'Drayvex'?

"I ..." She couldn't. There was simply no way to sweep this under the carpet. "Mum." Ruby cringed as she fished around in her head, looking for a believable excuse for her mother's suffering.

"Ruby Peyton. You tell me what is going on. *Now.*"

Ruby met her mother's unblinking gaze. Well, here goes nothing, she supposed. "Right. Wednesday. Well, I was on my way home this time yesterday."

She groped for the telephone table behind her with one hand. What she really wanted was to take the weight off her aching feet.

"Before I got here, I bumped into some ... old friends. They wanted my help." How could she twist this without lying through her teeth? Her mother had always been good at spotting lies.

"They lead me to the old building site at the edge of the village." So far so good, she thought, resisting the urge to fidget. "But when we got there, we started messing around. We managed to lock ourselves inside one of the metal containers left behind. Stupid." Okay. Now she was lying. But what could she say? That she was kidnapped by demons and held hostage in a far off world, only to be rescued by the king of the demons, who's inclination towards her was about as changeable as the weather? Oh, and all for Grandma's old necklace!

Her mum didn't respond. As Ruby waited for some sort of reaction, a familiar stab of worry crept in.

Eventually, she spoke. "Are you in trouble?"

Ruby stared. That wasn't what she'd expected.

"Ruby, you're lying." Her voice had dropped and become low, quiet.

"These friends of yours. Are they new friends?"

She didn't like it. It wasn't mother-like. She stared at her mum, unsure of how to respond.

"I warned you to stay away from him. You know what? I forbid you from seeing him any more. Do you understand me?"

Ruby's stomach dropped. She meant Drayvex. "Who're you—?"

"Ruby, you know who I'm talking about. I don't want you seeing that lowlife any more. If I still had my badge, he'd be behind bars before he knew what'd hit him."

She chewed on her bottom lip and felt the skin break. Ruby doubted very much that Drayvex would let anyone put him behind bars. Her heart hammered in her chest. What the actual Hell did he think he was playing at?

"If you care about this prick at all, you'll walk away. Because when he inevitably puts his hands on you, I'll have to kill him."

Ruby swiped out in alarm, grabbing at her mum either side of her shoulders. "Woah, I ... Okay. Okay, you caught me. I was with a guy." Drayvex wouldn't have hurt her Mum. Would he? She mithered, squeezing the shoulders. What possible reason would he have to do this behind her back? "But it's not what you think."

"Not anymore."

Whatever his reasons were, they wouldn't have been pure. "Okay, Mum," she conceded, hating herself. "I won't." Except, she would. If only to confront him about his less-than-pure intentions.

At her words, her mother seemed to visibly relax. She blew out a breath, deflating like a balloon, before grabbing Ruby's face between her hands. "Are you okay?" This time, she sounded more like her mother and less like an officer of the law. Worry creased in her features, touching her eyes.

Ruby lifted a hand and touched her mother's cheek. "I'm fine." She gazed into her eyes for emphasis. "Promise." This time, she wasn't lying. "I'm sorry."

Her mother laughed once, a tired, humourless sound. "Why didn't you call me?"

Ruby pulled her phone out of her trouser pocket and waved it in front of her. "Dead." This earned her a disapproving look. "Are you going to be okay?"

She smiled, this time with warmth. "Yes. Yes, of course I will. Why don't you have a nice hot bath?"

Ruby took a shaky breath, able to breathe freely at last. A bath sounded like an amazing idea. Tomorrow, she would be covered in bruises. But there was something on her mind. Something that had been niggling at her for some time.

Taking a moment to think about her question, she looked back towards her mother, now leaning against the bannister. "Question."

Her mum straightened, standing to attention at the sound of her voice. "Yes, dear?" She looked so pale and tired.

Ruby frowned, distracted. "Did Grandma ever tell you where she went on her 'adventures'?"

She blinked. "Uh, no. No, not really. She was very private. Why?"

"Is there other family that she spoke to?" Ruby dug her fingernails into her arm. She needed to know. Had her grandma been aware of the stone's power? Or had she been as oblivious as Ruby herself?

The thin figure stiffened and then folded her arms. "No. There's no one." She almost sounded offended.

Ruby was taken aback.

"He's not interested, Ruby. If he was, you'd know."

"What are you talking about? I was—"

"Your Dad. That's what you're getting at, isn't it?"

After a beat, Ruby sucked in a breath. Where had that come from? "God, no. I'm talking about *Grandma*." She hadn't even thought about him in years.

Her mother sighed out, her shoulders sagging. Then, finally, a weary smile pulled at her mouth. "Try the box in my wardrobe. Your grandma wrote everything down."

Ruby returned the smile.

The soft carpet of her mother's bedroom claimed her bare feet as she stepped into the room. She approached the wardrobe with a curious trepidation, acutely aware of the fluffy white robe enveloping her in its fleecy embrace. She was hyper-sensitive to its touch.

She had been this way ever since her last encounter with Drayvex. It was as if his touch had fully awakened her senses, leaving her flesh tingling and exposed in its wake. If she closed her eyes and concentrated, she could still feel the burning trail his finger had traced down her chest, his lips against her ear.

Ruby curled her hand around the wooden knob and yanked back the door, revealing the contents of her mum's wardrobe. A bath had been exactly what she'd needed.

The cardboard box was at the very back. Reaching past the clothes dangling over her head, she tugged at its edges, distracted.

At the glowing forest, Drayvex had made it clear that he was taking her necklace, with or without her permission. His own selfish agenda was all he cared about, and she was only getting in his way—except he didn't *have* to cure her before he took it back. This appeared to be purely for her benefit.

Dragging the heavy box over the wardrobe's edge, she pulled it out into the room and stood, staring at it.

He'd made no real indication that he gave a damn about her before. Everything that had happened since that day in the tavern was a calculated lie. The moment she had stopped feeding his ego in the forest, he had treated her with contempt. A burden to be rid of. It was something she was used to, and yet, it was always a shock to be on the receiving end.

So, if he hated her, as she had convinced herself he did, then what had happened earlier?

Ruby squeezed her eyes shut, and took a deep breath. The box.

She dropped to the floor and folded her legs beneath her. Her hand skimmed over the top of the unopened box, and her heart fluttered. What was left of her grandma's life was in this box. Pulling at the tape with anxious fingers, she worked to free the lip of the box, a strange, curious ache making her clumsy.

She didn't know what was going on with Drayvex. What she was certain of, though, was that there was a part of him, somewhere within the tangled recesses of his dark soul, that wanted her. And, rightly or wrongly, she supposed that there was a wild, reckless part of her that wanted him too.

Chapter 21

*T*he counterfeit stone crumbled to powder within his fist. He stormed through the twisting bowels of the castle, taking a sharp left at the doorway of the Magus Nox. How could he have been so blind?

Drayvex pushed into the room, assaulting the door on his way in. Like his imitation of Ruby, no illusion was truly accurate. He couldn't make himself smell human. There was *always* a tell.

The large glass sphere sat on its plinth in the centre of the room, colours swirling with sluggish serenity inside the orb as strands of liquid gold. The room was empty.

He scanned the vast space from the doorway, sweeping over the myriad bound tomes and grimoires nestled on the endless rows of stacked shelves. A worthless trinket wouldn't produce the aura of the legendary Lapis Vitae. The *real* stone was hard to miss. He should know; he'd spent a good portion of his time courting said power.

So, how in screaming Hell had this simple switch escaped his notice?

Drayvex exited the room and moved on, stalking down the dim corridor. He'd been distracted. That was how. If he was being honest with himself, which was becoming somewhat of a nasty habit of late, his single-minded focus at the Tower had been Ruby. He'd been so preoccupied with the girl that he'd barely even looked at the stone.

"You know I always get what I want, Drayvex."

He lashed out, sending the large, elongated skull on the wall exploding into shards of bone. *Pissing* Hell. That smug bastard knew how to get under his skin. He should have squashed the cretin while he had him thrashing on his back.

He'd *had* the stone. He'd let her distract him, and now, neither of them had it.

As he reached the end of the passage, Drayvex burst through the black lacquered doors and into the central chamber. Saydor's lackeys had assumed that he was there to reclaim the stone. It was the logical assumption. But, defying logic, Drayvex had seen only her.

Ruby was his blind spot. That made her dangerous.

The large central chamber was lacking its usual clamour, with a few low-level lackeys milling around like rejects from the party of the century. On a normal night, his entrance would see demons collapsing at his feet, falling over themselves in a desperate attempt to gain his favour, to rise above the sprawling masses. Not today.

Drayvex stood in the centre of the room, a knowledge spreading in his thoughts. It was compete or die on Vekrodus. Today, Saydor would die.

The lack of activity in the castle told him everything he needed to know. Saydor had taken his quest for world domination to the next level. Clearly, he wasn't fussy about which world he forced himself upon. Drayvex could work out the main aspects of his half-baked plan without breaking a mental sweat. Acquire a large amount of power: check. Advertise a free-for-all buffet on Earth—and it had to be Earth, as no other planet in existence would get demons so excited en masse—in exchange for fickle loyalty: check. Open a portal strong enough to withstand a good portion of his underlings pushing through for said chow down…

Well. That was a different matter entirely.

A scarlet blur passed by his feet. Drayvex slammed his foot down, snagging the tail of the scurrying demon for kicks. The demon squealed as its wiry tail stretched taut, protruding forehead smashing into the floor.

"Quiet," he warned the squirming lump beneath his foot. "I'm thinking."

Drayvex ignored it as it twitched in silence. Watching that bloated fool put his plan into action piece by piece had told him far more about the ex-Demon Master than he could ever have extracted by force. His plans were simple, his methods even more so. Saydor went straight for the jugular.

Two could play at that game. He, Drayvex, could have used Ruby's mother as leverage a long time ago. It would have been child's play to take the stone this way. But *he* wasn't interested in a quick and easy kill. He preferred the chase. The longer and the harder the struggle, the more satisfying the reward.

He lifted his foot, and the small demon scrabbled off across the wide chamber. Saydor was going to need a vast amount of power to open the portal. A catalyst to charge his stolen power to its full potential. There was one place he could go to achieve those results in record time. A stone-charging short cut, so to speak.

Drayvex smiled, shedding what little remained of his human visage as he crossed the room. There was about to be a very public execution at the Sea of Blood.

Almost as old as the planet itself, the Sea of Blood lay east of Vekrodus. A prevailing legend told of a long and bloody war that took place in that very spot a millennium ago, the aftermath of which, supposedly, resulted in the Sea of Blood. A violent conglomerate of the thousands that bled onto the hungry earth that day.

Legend or not, the sea's mystical properties could not be denied. Within every longstanding myth lay a shred of truth. And blood was a powerful weapon.

Drayvex heard them long before he saw them. Clamouring shrieks and howls carried on the warm, stagnant air, rising as he approached the unruly swarm. He crested the mound and looked down on the mass of frenzied beasts below. One hundred. Five hundred—no. A thousand. He scoffed, dismissing them, scanning for one head in particular.

He found it almost immediately. A small, angry pustule in an entire sea of ugly.

Saydor was stood at the edge of the red sea. Suspended above him was a large portal. It flickered at the edges, almost fully formed, but not yet ready to support large numbers. Despite this, every now and again, a single demon would get through.

Drayvex narrowed his eyes in distaste. No prizes for where that led to. Earth. The human planet, his primary choice of sustenance, and source of reckless escapism from his tedious existence.

Portal: check. Dominate the Earth, raining blood and hellfire down on its clueless inhabitants—Saydor was almost there. That would not do at all.

As he sliced through the riotous masses, they fell silent, sinking down to the red, cracked earth as he neared. His presence had always carried a considerable amount of weight amongst demonkind, and as he effortlessly carved a path through the crowd, those he passed fell mute.

Fear was a powerful device.

By the time he reached the edge of the bloody sea, a potent silence dominated the barren stretch of land.

The figure by the shore didn't acknowledge his approach. His back was exposed, his bloated body facing out towards the far horizon, where the inky sky met the sanguine red sea, but Drayvex knew that he would be ready.

"Enjoying the view?"

Saydor didn't respond. He continued to stare out ahead, as though alone, and not head of a stolen army.

Drayvex fiddled with the spherical ball of darkness in his hand, a mingling of resentment and building power burning in his veins.

"Sooner or later, that stone will inevitably belong to me. That, and whatever else I desire."

He glared at a spot in the centre of Saydor's back. Death would not be enough, would not satisfy his ravenous appetite. Drayvex would have to make an example of him. He would settle for nothing less than barbaric.

Drayvex launched the throbbing ball of darkness at his unprotected back with a flick of the wrist.

Proving his theory, the Demon Master twisted, ready with his own built-up blast.

The two orbs clashed in mid-air, green flame and all-consuming darkness meshing against their will. Drayvex held the darkness, pushing it harder against the crackling flames. *You desire power, you worthless ingrate?* he pushed, raw fury at recent events coiling as pent up rage inside him. Power thrummed down his arm, rebounding and returning as Saydor pushed back. *I'll make you choke on it. All you can fucking eat!*

Emerald tongues spat with angry sputters, the edges swallowed by the hungry darkness he controlled. A savage smile spread across Saydor's face as he wrestled against the force, green flickers dancing in his crimson eyes. "Drayvex," he hissed through his teeth. "A pleasure, as always."

Stray wisps of power crackled in the air around them, escaping into the atmosphere. Drayvex held the pulsing orb for a moment longer, and then, with great reluctance, dropped it.

It fell apart as it hit the ground, dissipating as small, black wisps that scuttled away across the cracked earth.

At almost the exact same moment, the green flames fizzled out. Saydor glared, a defiant sneer that stretched his over-sized mouth and contorted the yellowing flesh of his face. "Now, what could I have done to deserve the *honour* of this personal appearance from Your Lordship?"

The sarcasm that bled into every word grated against the remains of Drayvex's last nerve.

Just take his head off and be done with it, drawled the impatient voice in the back of his mind.

Drayvex sighed, dramatising for his captive audience. "Don't worry. This won't take long." He began to pace in a slow circle around the ex-Demon Master, keeping him in his sights, restricting his movements. "You see, it's one thing to be a delusional has-been that screws with his own poisoned mind ..."

Saydor's eyes were fixed on his, piercing with unbridled contempt. They followed Drayvex as he moved, his whole body turning in sync, facing him always. A tell that he wasn't playing games any more.

"... It's another matter entirely to enlist these weak-willed parasites you call an army and suck them into your deranged fantasy. Do you think that they would be here without the feast you promised them on the other side?

"You know nothing of loyalty, Demon Lord," he spat. "I—"

"Your insolence," Drayvex blasted, talking over him, "you pathetic creature, knows no bounds. I turn my back and soon after catch you sitting on *my* throne, commanding *my* people, pawing with greedy claws at *my* position of power. Still, I granted you a mercy that day. And what do you do? You piss it away."

"Mercy?" Saydor laughed, short and sharp. "You don't know the meaning of the word, you arrogant f—"

"You're right. Mercy was the wrong word. I *pitied* you."

Drayvex watched his features darken as he uttered the magic word. The veins on the demon's arms bulged. A thick green substance bled from the tips of his still claws, sliding down his fingers unchecked.

It was simple to bait the proud Demon Master. It served no purpose, other than the vindictive pleasure Drayvex got from watching him boil, but Drayvex didn't stop. He was no longer cool and detached, eliminating a traitor, as was his right as ruler of Vekrodus. This time, it was personal.

"Poor pathetic Saydor." He stopped pacing and stood, facing his deluded rival. He lowered his voice. "Pretender."

An expectant anticipation rippled through the demons around them, ruffling the tentative silence that hung on the knife-edge of chaos. The horde had enclosed them, surrounding them in a wide semi-circle in the waste. On the other side lay the sea; and the large flickering portal, suspended just above the shallows.

Drayvex paused, and for the first time since arriving, he grinned. "Did you like my gift?"

The mask of calm and sophistication Saydor had worn so well until now slipped, revealing the beast he bated underneath. No, he had not liked it. Not one bit.

Drayvex was under no illusions that the demon gave any sort of regard for those who served under him; to the pathetic creatures that clung to his empty promises like leeches. But Malsurg had been different. And Drayvex

214

would bet anything that the general's death had hit him where it didn't often hurt.

"You fool," Saydor growled. "You think there aren't legions more where they came from?" Green drops splashed down onto the dry earth, the poison hissing where it made contact. "I have an endless supply of willing underlings, courtesy of Your Lordship. Where do you think your waifs and strays end up when you cast them aside, hmm? Who do you think plucks them from the waste and gives them purpose again?"

Saydor strode towards him, leaving a hissing, smoking trail in his wake. "They're all here. Willing to serve. All pissed as hell, and loyal to *me*."

As the restless masses rumbled in approval, Drayvex laughed, a cruel bark that caused the demons closest to him to flinch. "Please. There are no end of worthless saps that consider my disposal of them a grave injustice. This is not news, but a sad fact of life. Your standards are simply far lower than mine."

His extended claws twitched in anticipation. Despite what he would allow the squat demon to believe, Drayvex had never been foolish enough to underestimate him. Ambition and desperation were a dangerous mix. If he said there were more, chances were he'd built himself a small following of devoted underlings, willing to die for his misguided cause.

With what looked like a large amount of effort, Saydor grimaced. His face contorted, as though he'd swallowed something unpleasant.

Then, his face relaxed all at once. Saydor smiled.

Drayvex narrowed his eyes.

"You didn't come all the way out here to discuss my sub-par standards of subordinate, I'm sure. And I'm sensing that you're not here for pleasure, My Lord."

Oh, I wouldn't say that at all, he mused. Drayvex was a firm believer in mixing business with pleasure. Why choose when you could have everything? "Business, then," Drayvex said, running a long, black tongue along rows of teeth. "I'm here to execute you, of course." He flashed a grin, showing plenty of teeth.

Saydor watched him with an arrogant stare. It wasn't the look of a demon expecting to die at any given moment, but of one with a trick up its nasty sleeve.

Drayvex folded his arms. He stared back, equally arrogant. He was far superior, in every way that counted. Did Saydor think he was born yesterday? Whatever stay of execution the Demon Master thought he had would have to be on a world-crippling scale to slake Drayvex's thirst for traitor blood.

The demon before him smiled. "You could do. But then, you'd never find her." His voice was low and oily, barely above a murmur. "You know, the last survivor of those tree-hugging savages you so despise?" Saydor licked his lips in a flickering motion and met his gaze head-on. "That secret would, of course, die with me."

Drayvex surged forward. He grabbed the Demon Master by the throat, a black fury ripping through his being, the mention of the Fae competing with Saydor's sheer gall. As Drayvex whipped Saydor off the floor, he squeezed the throat in his hand, wringing the neck of the demon that came a close second.

The warrior fae and their world should have been his biggest conquest to date. Wiping them out of existence had almost cost him his title, but it had been oh so worth it just to watch them scream and burn, mourning their homeworld and comrades while they themselves waited to suffer the same fate. Their suffering was self-inflicted. Their end, however, had been inflicted by him.

Most went down with the planet. One escaped. One.

The demons around them were giving him a wide berth. The space around him had increased.

"I—can—explain—My—hu—"

Drayvex dropped the snake in his grip, letting him fall to the ground. A stay of execution on a world-crippling scale. He sneered, his earlier hatred for the traitorous demon paling in comparison to the old wound he'd reopened. That moment should have been glorious. Instead, it remained his greatest personal failure.

Saydor massaged his throat, a sly look on his unsmiling face.

"Speak. You have one shot. Convince me of your *worth*."

His mouth split into a small grin. The demon stood, his blade-like hands relaxing. "I knew you'd see things my way, Drayvex. After all, we're not so different from each other."

"*Speak*, worm. Or hold your tongue." They were nothing alike.

"I have the location of the last fae in existence. It wasn't easy to come by, as she's hidden herself rather well. But, clever as she is, I am cleverer." His tongue shot out, tasting the air around them. "I, and only I, can direct you to their door. And I will gladly do so, in exchange for immunity, and, oh … free reign over the planet Earth."

Drayvex watched him through slitted eyes, an age-old hunger warping his thoughts. Give Saydor the Earth? That halfwit would destroy it. He could think of nothing worse. Except …

"I will even round her up for you, and throw her at your feet to do with as you see fit." His eyes gleamed with a fervour that Drayvex wanted to squash. Oh, how he wanted to squash it. But as he glared at the demon, a knowing excitement spreading across his sick face, he knew Saydor's words were just adding to the congealing pool of loathing stagnating in his shrivelled black heart, stirring up the venom that was already there.

"Drayvex. Demon Lord. Notorious hell-raiser and destroyer of rebel worlds—or rather, almost-destroyer of worlds," he purred, like a cat with eight more lives to spare. "Right, My Lord?"

Drayvex didn't want to give up Earth. His guilty pleasures. But as he glared into the eyes of the expectant Saydor, he knew that he would. Because he just couldn't let that she-devil live.

He grinned outwardly, showing Saydor teeth. So be it. Saydor could have his very own speck to rule over, and one day, when he had squeezed every last drop of worth from his bloated hide, then Drayvex would take him out. Without mercy, and without giving him the chance to blink.

And the girl?

His smile slipped.

"Do we have a deal?" The Demon Master returned the fleeting smile.

A year of immunity. An exacted revenge. Then that fool and everything he had built in that time would be his to claim. Drayvex smiled once again. "I'm sure we can come to an *arrangement*," he said, feeling the extensive portal pulse in close proximity.

The demons surrounding them burst into a raucous chorus.

He would throw Ruby a lifeline. And if she had any sense, she would grab it with both hands.

Chapter 22

"Over there." Ruby competed with the pounding rain and gale force winds snatching at her breath. As a strong gust hurled into her, muting her voice, she resorted to tapping and pointing. They had to get out of this storm.

Sandra nodded, assuming the role of storm guide. She grabbed Ruby by the wrist and led them, step by step, towards the nearest sanctuary, the Golden Spoke.

The doors slammed back on their hinges as they burst inside. Ruby flew to catch the door. Sandra went for the other, sliding on the wind-sprayed floor as the weather chased them into the room.

All heads span to watch them do battle. The doors refused to go down without a fight, but as the commotion died, the curious gazes of the taverners returned to their business.

Side by side, the two of them stood dripping from head to toe. Ruby peeled off her jacket, a second skin by this point, scanning for a table near a radiator.

Sandra snorted. "Holy hell, Rube. What's up with this crazy weather? It was sunny this morning."

Ruby sniffed, wincing as her sinuses protested. Great. She was catching a cold. She frowned, turning to her friend. "This is *Crichton*, city-girl. In case you'd forgotten, sunshine here is a myth."

Sandra rewarded her with an elbow to the ribs. "She has a sense of humour. Give the girl a medal!"

Swatting her away, Ruby smirked and grabbed Sandra's arm, leading them over to a window table.

Their soggy jackets drip-dried on the back of their chairs, rainwater soaking into the carpet. Ruby studied the menu. "Do you think they sell hot chocolate?" She could barely feel her fingers.

Sandra's eyes slid towards the bar. "This is a pub, Rube. I'm sure they'd rather sell you alcohol."

Ruby raised an eyebrow at Sandra's logic. Well, chocolate or not, there was no way she was going back out there any time soon. Her mind wandered, and as her gaze drifted across the tavern, she found it falling upon a familiar table. Memories of meeting a dark, handsome stranger popped to the forefront of her mind. It felt like a lifetime ago.

"Besides, after what we've just battled through, we need a stiff one."

She had no idea what Drayvex was up to. Now she'd been 'cleansed', would he even have a reason to find her again?

Ruby fidgeted in her seat. She didn't know how that made her feel. Had he retrieved the stone? Was he giving someone hell, or had he moved onto his next project? She was in the dark, and she hated it. The fact that she was now referring to her grandma's necklace as 'the stone' proved just how insane her life had become.

A bright flash in her peripheral vision pulled her back to the present. Ruby turned and peered out of the window.

An almighty rumbling echoed around the tavern. A thunderstorm. She dug her fingernails into the padded seat. She was ten years old all over again.

She peeked up at the sky. Sandra was right. Ruby couldn't remember the last time she'd experienced weather this intense. It was midday, but a blanket of black storm clouds had filled the sky, cloaking them in darkness. With the thunder, lightning and driving rain, it was almost biblical. What was next, a plague of locusts?

She gazed out into the gloom, staring at her reflection. The first thing she'd found in Grandma's box was her diary. An exhaustive list of names, of relatives Ruby had never even heard of, filled the book. Next to each were dates of birth and death. This had spurred more questions than it had answered. Like, why were there only female names in the book? And why had no one in the book made it past forty-five?

As she gazed at her reflection in the glass, she realised that she was sitting by herself.

Ruby pulled herself away from the window. No doubt, Sandra was flirting with the barman for free shots. Which was all well and good, but you couldn't warm your hands on a shot glass.

She turned away, lingering just long enough to see a large object smash to the ground just beyond the window.

Ruby scrabbled backwards, falling out of her seat and landing on her feet. Her heart pounded like a jackhammer. Her rapid breaths were louder than the wind. Was that ... a snowball? But it wasn't even snowing.

Another white ball crashed down into the street, further away. Then another. Another, faster and harder; falling from the sky. Muffled bangs and thuds sounded above their heads.

Ruby felt a numbness spread throughout her body, rooting her to the spot. It wasn't snow; it was gigantic balls of ice. A hailstorm.

Now, she was scared. Was this some kind of freak storm sweeping in, or was this linked to the demons in Crichton? She couldn't tell if she was being paranoid or logical.

A news outlet would tell her. If this storm was rolling in from somewhere, the news would be all over it.

The inhabitants of the Golden Spoke were rising to their feet. Crowds were forming at the windows, their soft murmuring a palpable agitation.

Ruby scanned the bar for Sandra. She couldn't shake the feeling that something bad was going down. She didn't want either of them to be around when it did.

But Sandra wasn't at the bar.

She scanned the large room, stomach churning, and spotted Sandra at its far end, peering outside along with a small crowd of taverners.

"Sandra," Ruby half whispered, half hissed. Another flash and rumble. She dug her nails into wood of the chair back.

Sandra turned towards her. She pulled a playful look of surprise, a small smile dimpling her cheeks. "Ruby, d'ya think—?"

Her words were drowned out by the lump of ice that smashed through the far window. Shards of glass exploded inward, showering the closest group with the lethal fragments. No one could react fast enough.

A hailstone, easily the size of a man's fist, hit the barman standing at the front of the crowd. It collided with the side of his head. The barman dropped to the floor.

Ruby's legs wouldn't work. She tried to think through the rising commotion. Her fingers threaded through her hair, paralysing panic freezing her muscles. She was a spectator, disembodied from the chaos.

People around her were screaming, crying, bleeding. The lady she recognised as the owner of the Cosy Corner was holding her arm, staring at the shards of glass embedded within it as though the limb belonged to someone else.

Sandra's distressed voice snagged her from within the discord. "Ruby?"

"Sandra."

"Rube, over here!"

Ruby's body knew what to do, where to go, as her friend's voice called to her. She sprung into action, moving in the opposite direction to the panicking crowd.

Sandra was on the floor with the barman. Ruby dropped to her knees below the broken window, doing her best to block out the loud smashing from outside. It wasn't safe here.

"Rube. We need to go. This place has a basement. The door is behind the bar and—Rube, he's fine. I just checked."

She pulled her hand back, satisfied that the man had a pulse. He was bleeding from a head wound.

It was then, with horror, that she realised that her knees were wet. Lurching to her feet, she grabbed for the nearest table. "Help me with this," she called.

Sandra flew to the other side, and between them, they dragged it over the barman, creating a makeshift barrier from the lethal weather.

As they ducked under the table in sync, visions of her mother, alone in the house, haunted her. If she were injured by a stray lump of ice, who would help her? Who would think to check?

Ruby got to her feet, the sudden need to get home driving her. "I need to get to my mother."

She stood. Then, leaving her best friend with the bleeding barman, she made for the exit. A wave of guilt washed over her, powerful and immediate. It was hard to ignore.

"But you can't go out there." The panicked voice followed behind. "It's dangerous."

Sandra wouldn't even be in Crichton if she hadn't been visiting *her*. Ruby couldn't ask her to risk any more, and she knew that she wouldn't rest until her mother was safe.

When she got to the doors, it suddenly hit her how exposed she was. She scanned the clutter around her and spotted a tray of glasses abandoned on a nearby tabletop. Ruby jogged over to the tray. Was she mad? Probably. Did she have any sort of plan? Grabbing at empty glasses with clumsy hands, she cleared the tray and held up her makeshift shield. She did not have a plan. But that wasn't going to stop her from trying.

Wired, she paced over to the nearest window and peered out into the storm. The hail was falling thick and fast, the clouds—

Ruby did a double-take as everything stopped at once. It was as though someone had reached into the sky and switched off the storm. The angry clouds were parting right down the middle, pulling back to reveal an unnatural strip of grey, washed-out sky.

As quick as the clouds had parted, the grey trail was fading, pulling back once again. What was left in its place was red.

Ruby watched the heavens unzip with wide eyes. No, not unzipping; wounding. It was a great bleeding gash in the fabric of the sky.

"Rube, I can't allow you to do this." Sandra's soft voice spoke from right behind her. "Look, I know you're worried. But going out in that would be madness."

The gash was getting wider, bleeding down onto the streets below in a crimson haze. She was beginning to regret making jokes about biblical plagues.

"Come on. You know it's my job to look after you, Ruby Peyton! You certainly don't … what's that?"

Ruby shivered in her soggy clothes. "I don't know," she answered, feeling small. The red slice of sky was calm, but around it, the weather had resumed its tantrum—minus the hail, she was relieved to see.

Tearing her eyes away from the window, she found her dear friend, who had taken up a place beside her. But Sandra wasn't looking at the sky.

Ruby followed her gaze, squinting through the rain to the buildings opposite. There were two men standing outside in the chaos. One of them was her boss; the other a man she didn't recognise. But even odder than two men standing out in the battering elements, was that they seemed to be wrestling.

"Is that … your boss?"

Without warning, the stranger produced a large knife and plunged it straight into his stomach.

A scream escaped Ruby's lips. She stumbled away from the window, pulling Sandra with her in a knee-jerk reaction.

Her boss dropped to his knees. His whole body jerked as the knife was ripped free.

"What's going on?" Sandra cried. "Who is that maniac?"

The man's head snapped round to face them. Ruby could see an angry snarl twisting his lips. Shock coursed through her body. He couldn't possibly have heard them, could he? Through the thick glass windows, roaring wind and pelting rain? There was a look of intense hatred on his face that she had only ever seen in Drayvex.

"Rube, the basement."

Ruby's hand flew to her head as realisation hit her. She was being thick. What she had mistaken for a knife was probably something else entirely. Something monstrous.

One moment he was still, the next he was careening towards them. He moved faster than any normal human, hurtling forward in a series of jerky movements. He looked as though he was teleporting, but Ruby was sure that he was simply that fast.

She blinked, and suddenly he was right there, leering at them through the glass as though they were animals in a zoo. The disgust on his face was unmistakable.

"Oh no," Sandra moaned. Her eyes were wide with understanding.

"Sand ..." Ruby whispered, wondering if she knew what Ruby herself knew.

Ruby stared, frozen, at the thing on the other side of the glass. The thing stared back, its human features contorted, barely recognisable, as the monster within surfaced. Its eyes were red, its irises becoming indistinguishable from its eyeball as that too turned red.

"Sand, run. The basement."

Just then, the world erupted around them for the second time as the monster hurled itself through the window.

Shards of glass flew in all directions. Ruby grabbed Sandra and threw the drinks tray up in front of them, just in time, as glass pelted the plastic.

The demon landed in the room with a heavy thud.

As Ruby peeked over the tray, she recoiled. A deformed thing stood on all fours in the tavern, its visage no longer resembling a human, but a leathery, insect-like creature. It opened its dripping, toothy maw and the room filled with an ear-splitting screech.

Ruby threw her hands over her ears, dropping the tray. Nearby glasses and bottles shattered. One hand covering an ear, she reached out and tugged at Sandra's arm with the other, pulling her with all she had. They had to run.

Sandra was rooted to the spot. She stood staring at the nightmarish creature, an odd look passing over her face.

"Sandra!" Ruby screamed at her, trying to get through. It was just then she realised that Sandra did not look scared. The look on her face was not shock, but acceptance. The grim sort you would see in a film or TV show, when the hero was about to step up and sacrifice everything to save the day.

"Stay back, Rube," she warned, putting her arm across her. "Hide—"

A rattling hiss drowned out her words.

Sandra threw herself against Ruby as a glob of black gunk came shooting towards them, straight from the monster's mouth. She slammed into Ruby, knocking the wind from her sails. The shove pushed her clear of the black gunk —or not quite clear. Her arm was on fire. It stung like nothing Ruby had ever experienced, and as the black substance ate through her clothes, it seeped into her flesh.

Ruby screamed through her teeth as the pain threatened to overwhelm her. Her basic senses flickered, dying and reviving at an alarming rate.

Muffled darkness. Bursts of full-volume uproar. Surely soon, she would have no skin left on her arm. Just a raw, exposed mess of muscle and bone. All she knew was pain.

Ruby's fingers raked the carpet. She was on the floor. She blinked through her blurry vision as the volume returned. The first thing she heard was Sandra's screams.

The sound pierced her heart and drove her to the brink of madness. Ruby squeezed her eyes shut then opened them wide, trying to focus. Her body squeezing, she followed the sound.

Sandra was huddled against the bar. She was writhing and screaming, one hand clutching at the right side of her face. Sitting on her left, Ruby didn't need to see to understand. Sandra had put herself between her and the demon. She had taken most of the hit.

As the creature towered over Sandra's writhing form, Ruby's stomach lurched. Its revolting mouth was stretched open wide, head thrown back in a way that almost looked like it was gloating. Drawing out the moment, before …

Ruby jumped up from the floor, springing to action. *She* was now the protector. Fighting through her pain, she grabbed for a broken beer bottle lying on the floor. She held her makeshift weapon out in front of her. Now, she thought. It has to be now.

Ignoring her instincts that screamed flight over fight, she charged across the room at the beast. She swung out and smashed the jagged glass up into the demon's mouth.

As the shards connected, it screeched in a sharp blast. It stumbled backwards, losing its footing.

Seizing her chance, Ruby dropped to her knees at the bar, grabbing at any part of Sandra she could get hold of. "Come on, Sand," she soothed. "It's okay." Her gaze dropped to the right side of her face and body, the side that had taken the hit. The skin was red raw, layer upon layer having been stripped away. It was bubbled and blackened in places, with slimy yellowing patches.

Ruby tore her eyes away as her stomach squeezed. Was that what her arm looked like? "We're getting out of here," she said, fighting the urge to check.

Silence cut through her fumbling like a knife. That was not a good sign.

Ruby heaved Sandra to her feet, dragging them both with adrenaline-fuelled energy to the tavern exit, and flung them blindly through the doors. She hoped to hell it was better outside than where they were now.

The sky was an angry, blistering wound, not unlike the arm that rested gingerly against her abdomen.

Readjusting her grip around Sandra's waist, Ruby pushed on in the rain through the drenched streets of Crichton. She dared not stop. There were eyes everywhere. Vicious, black eyes that saw them as nothing more than bugs to be squashed.

Ruby had no idea how she was going to get them through this.

She pulled them under the shelter of a corner shop's awning, jarring Sandra with the sudden motion. Demon.

Sandra moaned, her lolling head rising as she fought through the jolt of pain.

Ruby's skin prickled in fear. "Shh, Sand." If they could hear spoken words through glass, Sandra's groans of pain would draw them all out. "Please, we're almost there." They were both going to die.

The demon passed them without pause, making Ruby wonder if there was a god after all. Tall, black and lean, it looked like it had armour for days. Her breath left her all at once. She had to keep them moving.

Dragging an injured Sandra by herself, with her own wounds, through a demon-infested village in brutal weather was a little like hanging off the side of a mountain by her fingernails. It was only a matter of time before she met the floor.

Since they'd witnessed her boss's murder, more demons had taken to the streets. None of them looked remotely human, and as they limped across an exposed section of road, she found herself wondering where they had all come from. She no longer had the stone. They wouldn't find it here.

Suddenly, Sandra dropped like dead weight. Ruby lost her grip.

As her best friend crumpled to the wet ground, Ruby panicked. "Oh, crap. Sand ... no, hold on." Crap.

She dropped to the floor with her, gripping her shoulders like a vice. "Stay with me, Sand. A bit further." Ruby needed her conscious and walking.

Sandra mumbled something incoherent and took a laboured breath. "I just ... need a moment," she mumbled.

Ruby's eyes darted around them, searching the open stretch of road they were stranded on. She gritted her teeth, fighting a fresh wave of nausea as her arm keened in pain. She couldn't do this by herself. Where the hell was Drayvex when she needed him?

She looked around her for a makeshift weapon—and froze.

The thing blocking the road ahead was big. Big enough that, even a little way away, size of it shook her to the core. Standing on all fours at what looked to be at least six foot tall was the hulking silhouette of a bear-like beast.

Ruby felt the blood drain from her face. Don't panic, she willed herself, slowly lowering to Sandra's level. Don't freak out. You need to stay calm.

Sandra wasn't moving, but her body quivered. Eyes closed, her head rested on the ground, the damaged side of her face turned towards the sky.

"Don't panic," she whispered, barely moving her lips. "But twelve o'clock. Monster."

Sandra's eyes sprung open, as though the word 'monster' had flicked a switch somewhere inside her. As she raised her face to fully meet the sky, those eyes found hers. "Rube." She took an unsteady breath. "On the count of three, we run."

Ruby baulked. Run? Sandra could barely walk.

"One."

Ruby slipped her arm behind Sandra's back, inch by inch between them, pulling her into a sitting position.

"Two."

Ruby ignored the fresh wave of agony as she used the muscles of her damaged arm, taking a portion of Sandra's weight. Swapping to her right would only waste precious seconds. Besides, she thought, keening just a little. Ruby's good side was Sandra's bad. Their eyes locked once again, and this time, they were in perfect sync. This was going to hurt.

Sandra nodded.

Resisting the urge to look for the demon, Ruby braced herself and pulled.

The world slipped. Her vision swayed and blurred as Sandra's weight shifted against her. Ruby squeezed her eyes shut, then opened them, her vision snapping back into focus.

It was coming straight for them. A monstrous ball of muscle and teeth.

"Three!" Ruby screamed. "THREE!"

Sandra was already screaming. Her fingers gripped the material of Ruby's jacket, holding on with what remained of her strength.

Ruby tore off back the way they'd come. It felt like they were running against the flow of water. "Hurry." They weren't going fast enough. "The buildings."

Feet pounded the ground behind them. It was close.

"Rube!"

She could hear its breathing, fast and heavy. Sandra wasn't up to this. They weren't going to make it. Oh god …

With a rip-roaring snarl, the beast leapt right over their heads. Ruby recoiled as it landed in the road just in front of them, skidding them to a sudden halt.

Sandra moaned into her jacket. "Rube," she panted, gripping her with both hands now. "I can't ..."

"Shhh," she hushed, a helpless feeling of terror washing through her, overriding all the pain. "We're going to be okay." Her eyes were drawn to the deliverer of their demise, not wanting to see, but looking all the same.

It was a demon dog. Raw, flesh-coloured scales covered every inch of its muscle and sinew, with paws the size of dinner plates, and a double layer of claws on each foot. *Eight*.

The dog demon bared its fangs and snarled, a guttural, never-ending sound. This was it. The end of the line.

"Rube, please. Just *go*."

A chill ran through Ruby that had nothing to do with the rain. "What?"

Sandra lifted her lolling head, pulling herself upright with the collar of Ruby's jacket. "Save yourself. Just leave me here. There's no point ... in us both dying ... here."

Ruby gazed at Sandra, her best friend in the whole world, and a laugh bubbled up from inside her. It came out as a sob. "You're mad," she hissed. "I would never leave you."

"Ruby. Please—"

The dog sunk down on its haunches, done playing games. It growled, a bass-like rumble.

"I don't know what kind of crap your dad is teaching you—"

"Ruby Peyton. It has always been *my* job to protect *you*."

No. This wasn't happening. It was all some terrible nightmare.

"Now, go. It might ... chase you." She tugged up her sleeve with a shaking hand and fumbled at the clasp of her bracelet, tugging it from her wrist. "But if you're lucky, it will just ... go for me."

Any minute now, Ruby would wake up screaming in her bed.

Sandra dropped her bracelet into Ruby's half-open palm. "Wear it, always."

As the dog demon leapt, Sandra pushed her backwards. "Now go."

Ruby toppled, losing her balance. She scrabbled to right herself, scrambling away from the beast. Her instincts screamed at her to run. Her heart fractured. No.

She turned to find Sandra, and froze. The demon was right on top of her, standing over her in a possessive way, paying Ruby no heed.

Ruby stared at her brave friend until grief blurred her vision. Then, as that grief turned to a maddening fuel in her veins, she turned and stormed off down the street towards the shelter of the nearest building.

Someone was going to pay.

Chapter 23

R uby pounded the pavements, her feet smacking against the wet ground as the remaining drizzle of rain flurried around her. Her chest heaved. She couldn't breathe.

She dove into a narrow passageway and flung herself at the wall. Her palm bounced off the brick, and a shockwave shot up her left arm. Ruby screamed out, punching the wall with her good hand. She panted, sucking air into her closing lungs, grief and frustration consuming her. This wasn't happening.

Something shifted in her peripheral vision. It was fast, barely a blur; but she didn't miss it.

Ruby froze, her muscles tensing. Stupid. Losing herself here was stupid.

Her eyes swivelled in their sockets, her neck stiff as she tried to see without turning her head. Something was hunting her.

A soft scuffle sounded from behind her. Balling her fists, Ruby spun on the spot. She wasn't going down without a fight. She turned and almost collided with her pursuer.

For a moment, she stared without seeing. A scream rose up from her chest, the sound sticking in her throat as her brain caught up with her eyes. It was Drayvex.

Ruby slumped and breathed out, her body bowing. Relief and exasperation hit her in a wave, the combination making her weak. She'd never been so happy or so infuriated to see anyone in her life. If he had found them just a little sooner, then Sandra might not be …

Ruby flinched as the words got stuck in her head.

Drayvex stood opposite her in the alleyway, unmoving, his eyes soft but veiled. She couldn't deny that he was a sight for sore eyes.

"Drayvex." She put her hand to her forehead, taking him in. She wanted to scream and shout and weep; to throw at him the one hundred different questions rushing through her mind. Instead, she took a breath.

The timing was tragic. But she couldn't blame him for that. "Where have you been?" she whispered, her voice breaking. Would Sandra have accepted the help of a demon?

She watched him scan over her bedraggled form, take in her dripping hair and clothes. "Did you fall in a pond?"

Ruby opened her mouth to tell him where he could stick his charming concern. But as his eyes fell upon her injured arm, she bit her tongue. What little colour lay in Drayvex's eyes disappeared, dropping through to black. Feeling vulnerable, Ruby waited for the demon in front of her to either explode or disappear.

He did neither, and within seconds, the black was replaced by a steely grey. Drayvex stepped forward, moving towards her at a human pace. When they were close, he stopped. Ruby looked up at him, panting with the effort of staying still and composed. A horrible sharpness grated in her veins, like nails in her blood. This pain was unreal.

Drayvex lifted a clawed finger, grazing the tip down the length of her jaw in a preoccupied way. It was a strange tickle, and the surrounding skin on her cheek tingled. When he reached her chin, he paused and tilted it up with a finger.

Her traitorous stomach jittered as she met his gaze, two pools of liquid ash. In that moment, she found herself wondering what he was thinking. Did her pain really register with him, even now?

"Save yourself. Just leave me here."

A jolt of entirely different pain flashed through her chest. How many people had he killed with those claws?

"Don't move."

Ruby didn't, even as a thick, black vapour poured from his mouth and headed towards her face. But she was unprepared for what happened next.

The vapour didn't stop. It slipped into her open mouth, and when she closed her lips, it went for her nose. Ruby gagged as she felt the vapour slipping down her throat. Panic throbbed in her bloodstream. It was choking her.

She lashed out in a knee-jerk reaction, or tried to. Her limbs were suddenly made of lead.

Shh, soothed a velveteen voice in her head. *Don't fight me.*

She stopped struggling for control, and instead looked for Drayvex, who had disappeared. Was he inside her?

Trust.

Ruby tried to relax as the demon took over her body. He had asked for her trust. She gave it to him.

Her arm tingled. It tickled and hurt at the same time, a sensation that grew, until the need to scratch it was insane. Could he hear her thoughts?

Her fingers twitched, an involuntary movement. And gradually, she came to realise that Drayvex was standing in front of her again. She had lost track of time.

Ruby moved her fingers, wriggling them, before clenching her hands into tight fists. She relished the feeling. She looked down at her arm, and a gasp escaped her lips. Her sleeve was still missing, but it was the only remaining evidence of the mess that had once been her right arm. Her skin was smooth and pale, woundless. Not a single blemish or mark remained.

"How did you …?" She looked back at him in shock.

Ruby was overcome with emotion. She'd made the wrong choice. She should have fought harder to keep Sandra alive. She waited for the tears to come, but they didn't. She couldn't.

Drayvex smiled, a fleeting smile that disappeared as fast as it had appeared. "You can thank me later." Under normal circumstances, the implications in his voice would have made her blush.

He must have seen something in her eyes because his expression faltered, then hardened. The change was unnerving, like the flick of a switch. "Come. We're done here."

Ruby stared, transfixed, as he threw one last look her way, before striding off through the demon-infested village.

Ruby followed Drayvex through the chaos. Each small step she took demanded resolve she didn't possess.

The place that she'd grudgingly called home only hours ago was well on its way to being unrecognisable. Black smoke spewed into the atmosphere as the Cosy Corner burned to the ground, taking livelihoods and warm memories with it. Someone was screaming a ways behind her. A young child cried for their mother close by.

As they passed the pretty little church near the park, Ruby was transported back in time, to when they had first arrived in Crichton. It was the only time they'd ever attended a service. Now, the steeple lay discarded, a severed limb, at the mouth of the church. A lump rose in her throat.

When she and Sandra had been fighting for their lives, she hadn't seen anyone else. Now, she saw them. The odd neighbour dashing past them, a co-worker, a familiar stranger. Some spared them a glance, but most were like her: focused on survival.

They never got far, these scattered people. The demons were smart. They lay in wait, ambushing strays, ripping them limb from limb. Ruby had to look away. The sounds were unbearable. Sandra's face was on every victim, dying again and again.

She should help them. In the midst of her stupor, she knew this. She was no different to them, no more deserving of life than them. But she didn't.

Her body shook with every step. She was trying so hard to keep it together, but inside she was falling apart. Why did she get to live, and Sandra …? She took a deep breath and held it, counting to five.

Ruby forced her gaze forward, putting her focus on Drayvex. It was like they were in their own little bubble, strolling through the chaos as if it were a hologram, not a demon massacre. As long as she was with Drayvex, it seemed that nothing would touch her.

Ruby clenched her jaw. Of course, he was one of *them.* It wasn't hard to see, and yet, she had to remind herself all the same. Not only was he one of them, but their ungodly leader. And he had let this happen on his watch.

She rubbed her palms together, dragging her nails across the skin. It was because he didn't care.

She sucked in breath after breath, her chest rising and falling. Of course he didn't care. Earth was one stupid little planet to him. He could jump between worlds in the blink of an eye. How small would the human race appear to someone like that?

Ruby ran her fingers through her hair, her mind wavering like the two sides of a spinning coin. Drayvex was a demon. But that didn't make him guilty by default. After all, he had come back for her, and now he was going to help her fix this.

"Almost there, Mum," she mumbled, trying to soothe herself.

Drayvex stopped without warning, lurching to a halt. Ruby stepped straight into his back. She froze, anticipating the worst. When he didn't move, concern crept into her thoughts. "Drayvex?"

She didn't get an immediate reaction. But when Drayvex spun to face her, there was an air of grim determination about him. His eyes were hard, and Ruby found herself pulling away in anticipation of something unpleasant.

Drayvex grabbed her by the wrist. His dark eyes flicked up and hovered on a point somewhere behind her, reacting to something that she couldn't hear. They resettled on her. "Let it go." His voice was low and toneless. "Don't look back. It won't help." He gave her arm a tug.

Ruby didn't move. Her nerves wound tighter by the minute. Her mind raced as she tried to figure out how the hell they were going to get out of this mess. "Let what go?" Her head was pounding.

"Don't ask stupid questions." Drayvex gave her arm another impatient tug. He sounded distracted, his tone lacking its usual snap. He started walking again, and Ruby had no choice but to be pulled along with him. Clearly, the first tug was just a courtesy.

For the first time, Ruby realised that they were going the wrong way. They had already passed the house. She stopped dead, then regretted it. Her top half continued its momentum, and she lost her balance. Ruby groped the air with her free hand, reaching out for something solid, and fell into Drayvex.

Drayvex appeared to be on the verge of losing what little patience he possessed. "What?" he snapped, throwing her an exasperated look. There it was.

The emptiness in her chest widened, engulfing her where she stood. "Sandra." She took a deep, shaking breath and felt fear seeping out of the cavernous hole. Say it out loud. "She's …" Say it. "She's—dead."

The demon before her didn't move. His dark eyes gave nothing away, no indication that he'd even heard her heartfelt confession, and his face remained stony. He dropped her wrist and folded his arms.

Ruby felt the sanity she was clinging to slipping through her fingers. She blinked. "Didn't you hear me? I said she's *dead.*" The last word burst from her in a violent blast.

Drayvex sighed. "Ruby." He stepped forward, closing the gap between them, and paused, waiting for her to look into his eyes. "The Earth is screwed." His voice was devoid of emotion, delaying the impact of his words. "This planet will soon belong to Saydor, and when the portal is ready, demons will descend like a plague. The humans here will die." He paused, then added, as if an afterthought, "There's nothing you can do."

Ruby was stunned. They were abandoning ship. "You …" She was lost for words.

"You expect me to—what? Just accept that?" She pulled away from him, taking a step backwards. "To abandon everyone I've ever cared about and save my own skin?" Her voice was rising by the second, but she didn't give a damn. A bubble of panic and fury was growing in the pit of her stomach. "My mother," she said, her voice breathless despite the volume. "She needs me. She's waiting for me right now. I can't just leave her behind!"

Fury flickered across his features. "What I *expect,*" Drayvex hissed, stepping back into her personal space, "is for you to have some sort of regard for your own life." His eyes were both black and red, the colours flowing and intermingling in an angry vortex.

Ruby flinched. Drayvex was different. Harder, maybe. She didn't know what, but something had seemed off from the moment he'd found her. "What the hell is wrong with you? This *is* my life!" She met him head-on and held her ground, fighting the overriding impulse to slap the confrontational jerk across the face.

A gunshot rang out. The sound was almost on top of them. They both turned towards it. But before she could locate it, Drayvex was in front of her.

A man in a crumpled business suit trembled a few feet away. Ruby could see the sweat pouring from him as he pointed the handgun. The barrel was aimed straight at Drayvex's head.

Ruby peeked out from behind him, trying to get a better look. The gun wielder seemed to be having some kind of internal struggle as his fear-rimmed eyes flicked back and forth between her and Drayvex. Despite his terror, his aim was steady.

Drayvex snarled, and even from a side view, the disgust was plain on his face.

Ruby tensed. It reminded her of the demon in the cafe. Were they really all the same? Demons. Monsters. It seemed so.

"Demon." The gun clicked. "L-let her go."

Ruby's stomach twisted. He thought she was a captive. She opened her mouth, taking a breath to call out to him, to straighten things out, but stopped. Was she really here, now, of her own free will?

Drayvex was unphased. He smiled in a mocking way, making a gesture that dared the stranger to take his best shot.

Ruby's heart stopped. "Wait!" Her body sprung into action. She didn't know which of them she was more scared for.

Before she could properly react, three deafening blasts rang out through the air. One. After. Another.

She screwed her eyes shut in a reflexive action, covering her face with her hands.

Ruby squirmed in the silence that followed. When nothing happened, she peeked through her fingers, sick to her stomach, and—her hands dropped.

The three bullets were hovering in mid-air, inches away from Drayvex's face. The man with the gun was staring, incredulous, at the floating pieces of metal. Drayvex was smiling again. It was a smile that turned her stomach.

As the man's stare turned to utter horror, Ruby had the urge to shout out to him, to warn him of his impending demise. She should have known better than to worry about Drayvex.

The bullets turned, one by one in mid-air, spinning back to face their owner. Ruby wasn't breathing. "Don't," she pleaded, feeling helpless. No more death.

The man was rooted to the spot. The gun in his hand clattered to the floor.

She grabbed the demon's arm with both hands, digging her nails into his warm, hard flesh. "Drayvex."

To her surprise, Drayvex recoiled, stilling almost immediately. A reaction so small, it was almost a flinch. Ruby let go of his arm, her hands springing back in a nervous twitch.

The bullets pierced the man in three different places. His left eye socket, and both cheeks. He collapsed to the ground, body convulsing, before stilling with an eerie suddenness. She stared at the body, mind stuck. Dead. Killed him. The blood drained from her face, leaving her skin cold and clammy. A human, just like her.

"Why?" she screamed, turning on Drayvex. "How did he deserve that?" She gave him a shove, which seemed to do nothing. "He was trying to save me."

Drayvex spun to face her, a murderous look on his face. He disappeared in a blur of colour.

Ruby froze, stopping dead. She searched the surrounding area, eyes spinning in the emptiness.

"*Save* you?" he bit from behind her, making her jump.

She gasped, her shot nerves keeping her on permanent edge. She squeezed her hands into fists and spun towards him. "Yes. To save me from you." Drayvex was a murderer. She'd seen it firsthand. Her faith in him had been misplaced all along.

He sneered, showing fangs. Her eyes were drawn to them. "And what in Hell's name do you think I'm doing? Going on a tour of Earth's most pointless sinkholes? I came back to this shithole for *you*." Clearly no longer in any mood to be told 'no', he grabbed her wrist and resumed pulling her through the village.

But Ruby was in no mind to be messed with either. And despite the vague sentiment in his petty jabs, she would not let him sway her. She wondered if anyone *had* ever said 'no' to him before.

She pulled against Drayvex, twisting in his iron grip. "It was you who killed all those people at Lorenfield, wasn't it?" How naive of her to think otherwise.

Drayvex gave her arm a sharp tug, ignoring her accusation. Ruby stopped fighting and fell into step. Her struggles were getting her nowhere. "And that man? He probably has a family somewhere, waiting for him to find them." She would make him regret taking her along for any length of time. She would become an ever-present ache, throbbing at the back of his head. "Why would I want to leave with someone who kills innocent people? Who kills *my* people?"

Drayvex stopped and let go of her wrist. He whipped around to face her. Her soggy hair stirred as he turned, and to her utter disbelief, he rolled his eyes at her. "He had a gun," he said, sounding caught between annoyance and mild amusement. "Or have you forgotten that part? How convenient."

Ruby glared at him with everything she had, which at this point felt like a waste of precious sanity. She did it anyway. She couldn't believe they were having this conversation. "You're a Demon Lord. I'm sure you could have sucked it up."

Drayvex smiled, the corners of his mouth turning up in the briefest of movements. "Without a doubt. You, however, not so much." He tilted his head to the side, looking lost in thought. Ruby noted the way his eyes softened, changing to a milky red. "You snap like a twig."

Like bright, fresh blood.

"Do you want to die, Ruby?" His voice was soft and strange. It made her feel odd and weightless.

240

He leaned in closer still, and Ruby's body tensed in anticipation; an anticipation that was both right and very wrong.

As she glared back, somewhere amongst the horror and the heartache, she found herself getting lost in eyes of endless depth. She screwed her own shut, clinging on to her crumbling willpower with everything she had. Drayvex was a murderer. A killer with no morals. She repeated these words to herself like a mantra, over and over. Drayvex was a demon. Demons killed her best friend.

A jolt of pain lanced through Ruby's chest. Sandra. A sob rose up and escaped from her lips.

Something sharp grazed her lower lip, and with it came a heat comparable to having her face next to a furnace. Her eyes sprung open, her body reacting before she had time to think. Drayvex was right there, just inches away. "Tell me," he muttered, meeting her gaze, "what mindless half-breed took your friend's life, and I will even the score."

Ruby's heart stopped. What?

"An eye for an eye. A life for a life."

The heated look in his eyes caught her off guard, as did his words.

His breath enveloped her skin in warmth. Ruby couldn't tear her eyes away from the captivating creature before her. "Say it, and I will make it so."

Despite the pain and the fear and the anguish settled deep within her bones, in that moment, Ruby felt alive. She gazed into the endless depths of his eyes, allowing herself to be consumed by something she couldn't begin to understand.

Ruby licked her lips and tasted her own blood. Stunned, she lifted her hand to her lips.

Drayvex blocked her path with a hand. "Don't."

Obedient, Ruby kept still. As he traced her lower lip with the tip of his warm tongue, she closed her eyes, trying to ignore the renewing sensations he was awakening inside her. He was manipulating her; trying to sway her resolve. It was working.

Forgive me, Sand, she pleaded. I can't avenge you.

Ruby opened her eyes and looked straight into his. She was also a human. "I'm not going with you," she sighed. Despite the monster he was, everything he wasn't and would never be, she wanted him to understand. She willed it, pouring everything she had into her imploring gaze. "My place is here. If you won't help me save them, then I'm going do it alone."

Drayvex made a frustrated noise, a sound close to a growl that came from deep within his chest. In one fluid motion, he pushed her backwards until he was lightly pinning her against a wall.

She gasped in surprise as her back touched the concrete.

"Listen," he ordered, his tone sincere. "It's going to go a little something like this. Most of your people will die down here. A good majority of those people will be eaten while they're alive and wriggling. Some will be hunted for sport. Some will be tortured, simply to pass the time, and the lucky few that get to live will be kept as a food source for those with status." He held her with a relentless gaze as he spoke, gauging her reaction to his words. "Am I making myself clear?"

Ruby took a good long look at the demon before her. She had known that they were from different worlds for a long time. Hearing him speak now, she truly believed it.

"You don't have a hope in hell of saving anything."

She chewed on her lower lip. What he was saying, without tact or grace, was that if she stayed, she would almost certainly die. But if she left with him now, she would be abandoning not only her mother, or the memory of her best friend and her home, but her humanity. She still had a lot to lose, and those things were worth fighting impossible battles for.

"Maybe so." Her eyes blurred as painful memories rose to the surface in her mind. Sandra's sacrifice would not be in vain. "But if the human race is damned, as you say," Ruby looked down at the floor, her stomach twisting. "Then I will go down fighting for it. I don't expect you to understand what it's like to care for someone beyond the border of your own selfish existence." Ruby paused, looking back up at him. "But I do."

Drayvex's features were visibly darkening, as though a black storm cloud was descending upon him. As she looked down at his arms, Ruby realised that he was *physically* darkening, patches of his skin black and smooth. Nightmarish memories of being held hostage by a large black monster jolted through her, shocking her. Was Drayvex really no different? She had hoped with all her heart that he was. Without a doubt, she'd been fooling herself.

His eyes smouldered, lips curling into a snarl as the fangs behind continued to lengthen. "Is that so?" His voice was mocking, its tone dual pitches, with a growling undercurrent. "If the righteous Ruby says it, then it must be so."

As he laughed at her, Ruby realised that Drayvex looked more like a demon now than he ever had. She would have to be truly stupid not to be scared. Looking at him now was not unlike staring into a yawning black abyss.

"I could just take you, you know." His words were loaded, a calm threat. As he spoke, he grazed a curved claw along her neckline. "I don't need your permission."

Ruby swallowed, a sense of calm finality washing over her. "But you want it." Taking a deep breath, she sealed her fate. "And you're not going to get it."

She watched his eyes drop from red through to pitch black, and with the change went anything close to resembling humanity. A jolt of something lanced through her. This wasn't the way she wanted to leave things between them.

Drayvex stepped back and folded his arms, leaning against the wall beside her. "Fine. But don't expect me to come and save your ungrateful skin when something twice your height fancies you as a pint-sized scratching post."

A chill ran down her spine. Could he really dismiss her so easily, after everything they'd been through?

Drayvex didn't wait for a response. He surged forward, disappearing in a blink. One second he was there, the next there was only a cloud of disturbed dust, whirling in the air. Ruby stared, numb, at the spot where Drayvex had been. She looked up at the angry sky, and the cold, hard reality of her situation hit home.

She was alone. She was vulnerable. And soon, the demons nearby would realise that she was no longer untouchable.

She shivered, curling in on herself as the emptiness in her chest expanded. She couldn't remember ever feeling so alone.

Pressing herself flat against the wall, she tried to contemplate her next move. He hadn't even spared her a final glance. She supposed she was easily dismissed after all.

Chapter 24

Ruby's nostrils burned as she breathed in the acrid, smoky air, the taste of it sticking at the back of her throat and on her tongue. She crouched against the metal body of the car, her back nestled against the meagre cover. Crichton was the epicentre of unholy chaos, but how far beyond the village had the demons spread? Had they made the news yet?

A distant crash echoed on the breeze. Ruby jumped, her body on high alert. She had to keep moving. No matter what, she had to make it home.

Closing her eyes, she said a silent prayer, scraping the barrel for her remaining courage, and then pushed off the car.

The houses she stumbled past were silent and empty-looking. Her heart thumped in her chest, nerves unravelling like a runaway ball of string. Had they made it out?

As she crept through the village, Ruby mithered over her slipshod plan. She would get to the house and find her mum, who was hopefully packing heat, and together, they would get as far away from Crichton as physically possible. It was a far from watertight plan. For one, neither of them knew how to drive. But it was a plan all the same.

Ruby blinked back angry tears. The short trip up the hill towards the park was yet one more mountain to climb. It was exposed, beyond the enclosed shelter of the village terraces. But Sandra had never given up on anything, and neither should Ruby. It was one of those things about her that had really tested Ruby's patience; her inability to know when to quit.

Once, they had played an old board game they'd salvaged from a car boot sale. Ruby had beaten Sandra four times in a row, before letting Sandra win on the fifth. She was sure that they'd still be there now if she hadn't. Ruby smiled, her heart aching at the already painful memories. Each time, Sandra had accepted the loss with grace and reset the board for another round. She took a sharp intake of breath, making a vow to herself then and there, that she, Ruby, would *never* give up on anything that was important to her. Never again.

Without warning, something fell into her path. It happened so fast that Ruby had no time to process it. She ran smack into the obstacle, bouncing off it, tumbling to the floor.

Ruby twisted as she fell, using her hands to catch her as she hit the rough ground. The impact jarred her wrists. They buckled inward, and her head hit the floor. Pain exploded. She lay on the floor face down, head throbbing.

Even through the haze, Ruby knew she was in trouble. Her blood ran cold, body quivering as she strained her ears in the silence. The tension in her frozen muscles made the smallest movements painful. Hoping to hell that whatever had found her didn't resemble a childhood nightmare, Ruby turned her head to look behind her.

She was out of luck. A large, fleshy spider about the size of a hippo stared back at her. It had six legs instead of eight, the front two much smaller than the others, and a gaunt, fleshy face that had an almost haunted look. As she took in the creature between her and her mother, she lost her mind.

It dropped to the ground in a silent crouch, movements jerky.

It was in that moment that Ruby realised something vital: she wanted to live. She wanted to live so badly it hurt.

With one graceless shove, she pushed herself to her feet and ran. She ran, tearing back the way she'd come.

She heard it before she saw it, a scratchy hiss that signalled its charge.

Her muscles screamed, sending sharp electric spasms running through her legs. She ignored the pain.

The spider demon landed in front of her, leaping straight over her head.

Ruby scrambled to a stop, gasping for breath. It was toying with her, and she was giving all she had. Her best wasn't good enough.

Realising that she was next to the park, she flung open the gates, throwing herself through. She couldn't save herself, and she certainly couldn't save her mother. She was going to die after all.

Desperate, she shoved at the swinging metal, hoping to buy herself a few more precious seconds. The gate bounced back, rebounding off the charging creature. Ruby screamed, her hands flying to her face, and—

Nothing.

Ruby peered out from between her fingers. The demon was still there. It hissed and threw itself at the gates, and she flinched, before it was thrown backwards. Bouncing off thin air. It tried again and again.

An invisible barrier?

The spider demon took off around the edge of the park, hissing and spitting. An invisible barrier. Maybe she would get to live after all.

*

Drayvex crashed through the entrance of his fortress, creating shockwaves from the force of his movement. They throbbed across the room in a destructive ripple, sending small mingling demons dropping to the stone floor in throes of anguish. A hellish rage surged at the core of his being. It was powerful, all-consuming.

His fangs extended, responding to his riled up state. Horns broke through his skin, thickening and twisting as they grew to resume their once familiar weight on his head. He stalked towards the stairway, each demon in his path just managing to scrabble out of harm's way before he went through them.

Drayvex paced along the network of corridors, moving towards the heart of its vast network. Vekrodus had become aimless and docile in his absence—two qualities that he would not tolerate now he was back in his rightful place.

Something hot and tumultuous was building inside of him. He could feel it like a maddening itch underneath his skin, giving him an overwhelming need to spill some blood. He knew exactly what to do with it.

The demons he passed regarded him with eager tenacity, falling to the ground in a familiar ritual. Ruby had denied him. He had slaughtered entire races for far less. The girl had no idea who she was dealing with.

As Drayvex strode through his domain, ruling in person for the first time since his spontaneous departure, he garnered an expectant entourage.

"M-my Lord—"

Drayvex lashed out at the loitering demon as he passed, opening its throat into the passage. Blood hit the walls, the floor, the clamouring familiars trailing in his wake.

He embraced the seething anger coursing within him, welcomed the reminder it presented: that he was still the vicious, hateful bastard he had always been, and that no self-righteous human speck was going to change that.

When he crashed through the doors into the atrium, the room fell silent, as if plunged into a vacuum. The group that had been trailing him through the castle dispersed, mingling with the demons already present. News travelled fast. They were waiting for him.

Their whispers bounced and echoed throughout the vast room, filling his head with their meaningless tripe. Drayvex stood, watching them all as he inwardly burned. Demons of all shapes and sizes, staring, waiting for his word, his will. How many of these insolent pukes upheld Saydor's best interests, he wondered, sizing up the room with a sweeping look.

As the growing masses edged closer, he allowed the itch to build, the waves of molten fury to consume him. A rising pressure mounted inside him as the remaining physical aspects of his demonic form pushed towards the surface.

Until he met her, he had never *felt* much of anything. As a Demon Lord, he was cold and dead. Logic and strategy governed his every action; ungodly ambition dominated his every thought. But it would seem that something uncorked could not be re-corked. This would prove unfortunate for anything standing in his way.

The air of anticipation drenching the atmosphere began to peak. Drayvex tasted it with a forked tongue. Demons were savage creatures. The girl would soon get her wish. She would die for her weak little planet, and on the brink of death, she would remember the moment that she refused him. Dying in agony, screaming his name in a wasted cry for help.

Thanks to you, nudged that ever present virulence in his head.

A stabbing sensation surged through his core. Drayvex ignored it.

He glared at the demons filling every space, taking his violent musings further. When the Earth was nothing more than a charred, blood-soaked rock littered with human remains—and with Saydor in control, it would not take too long to happen—he would seek her out and pick his teeth with her ungrateful bones.

A creeping mania licked at the edges of his mind, loosening his precarious foothold on sanity. He couldn't enjoy her death the way he wanted. He gained no satisfaction from her pain. The bitch had poisoned him with her toxic human emotions. He may have branded her skin with his mark, hung a death sentence over her head and handed her kind to Saydor on a plate, but she had made sure that she would get the last laugh. She had left her own mark on him. And now, there was no doubt in the matter—he was undeniably insane.

"Your Greatness. I had heard you were back. I had to see you for myself." The demon in front of him stepped forward.

Drayvex bristled at the direct address. They all wanted a piece of him. Every single mangy cur wanted something from him. And every single one was undeserving of the breath they took, let alone his favour.

"My Lord. My Lord, down here."

He looked down with disdain at the demon pawing at his feet. Three words was all it would take. One command, and a basic strategy. Then, Vekrodus would sit in the palm of his hand once more. "Light the beacons."

At his words, excitement flitted across the small familiar's features. As it darted for the far doors, so did two others. Within a single second, the demons were moving across the room in a snarling, nipping brawl, fighting for a little piece of his attention.

Drayvex watched the flurry of teeth and claws head into the stairwell, like starving dogs fighting for scraps of meat. His tail coiled around direct addresser's leg, the skin of it black and gleaming under the dull light of the room.

The demon screeched as its legs were ripped out from under it, cut short as its head smashed against the stone.

"You wanted to see me? How's the view?" Drayvex placed his foot against its skull. They were all dogs, really, he mused, watching his captive audience lap it up. Every single one of them. And they would all heel at his command.

The jet black flames of the beacon roared to life. They blasted, reaching for the sky, filling the immediate space with their sheer size, before falling still in the stagnant air. Of the six strategically placed beacons across Vekrodus, this was most important.

Drayvex narrowed his eyes, surveying the arid, red desert from the highest peak of the fort. Now that this one had been lit, the rest would follow suit. They were the colour of his signature aura, sending a clear message to all throughout the planet: that he, Drayvex, was Demon Lord and was back where he belonged.

*

Ruby wore a line in the grass as she paced. She was safe. Nothing could reach her in here.

She stopped, making an immediate one-eighty for the umpteenth time, and walked another length of the lake. Safe. Her heart squeezed in her chest, snatching her breath. What was the point of safe when those you loved were not?

As she reached the park gates, she made an impulsive turn, veering towards the exit. Pushing the bars open wide, she threw herself back into the danger zone and took off. No point whatsoever.

Street lights streaked past her as she ran. It would be getting dark soon. Ruby mithered, torn between her careless, full-pelt sprint, and the slow, careful sneaking that had got her this far. Would the darkness make the demons stronger?

Suddenly, a large creature stepped into her path, appearing from around the corner just ahead. Ruby skidded to a halt. She threw a hand over her mouth, stifling a scream. Diving behind a nearby metal waste bin, she held her breath, her throat pulsing.

The demon wasn't alone.

Mrs Groben-Smith, the pie baking queen. Three cats, a granddaughter who visited often. As she was dragged through the village by her bun, her hoarse wails barely reached Ruby's ears from her crude hiding place.

Ruby swallowed, fighting the hot squeezing in her stomach. These were real people, with real lives. How many more would die while she watched from the sidelines? How many more lives would be snuffed before the day was out? She didn't know. But as she crouched, frozen in place, she couldn't help but feel like a terrible person.

Pressing herself flat against the metal, she closed her eyes and concentrated on the cold against her forehead, her squeezing stomach. She couldn't watch. It was too much.

Then Ruby paused. Listened.

Silence. Steeling herself, she took a breath and peeked around the bin.

The demon was gone, and so was her neighbour. She ran her fingers through her matted hair and breathed out. Hope you escape, Mrs G. Sorry I'm not stronger.

Ruby broke into a sprint. Her feet pounded the ground, the solid slaps echoing louder than her shot nerves could take. No, if Mrs Groben-Smith was still alive, it was because the monsters wanted her alive.

She turned onto her street and reverted to a stealthy sneak, crossing through neighbouring gardens as she kept to the sides. Were the demons taking hostages? She shuddered at the thought; at the vision of being stuck in a small dark room for any length of time. Being taken alive would be worse, she thought, her breaths coming in ragged pants.

As her house came into view, Ruby felt a longing that was almost too painful to bear. Almost home. She approached the garden fence, her nerves wound so taut that they could snap at any point.

Suddenly, she noticed her pocket. There was weight to it, bumping against her thigh, moving in time to her steps. Ruby vaulted the low fence, ducking behind the slats. Reaching into her pocket, her hand curled around something cold—and her heart squeezed.

The charm bracelet dangled from her fingers, its worn silver gleaming in the dull light. Her eyes welled as a wave of emotion rose up from nowhere, threatening to drown her where she crouched. Sand ... how will I ever do this without you?

Her breathing heavy, she slipped the chain around her wrist and hooked the clasp. She had never been the strong one.

"Ruby! Get in!"

Ruby's head shot up, darting to the doorway. Mum.

"Quick, before they come back!"

Her mum was okay. Pushing her grief to one side, she sprung away from the fence and scrabbled for the door. Ruby would have to learn fast. Unless she became strong, they were both going to die.

As she crossed the threshold and kicked the door closed behind her, she threw herself straight into her mum's arms. "Are you okay?" she sobbed, squeezing the wiry frame in her arms.

Her mum squeezed back. Her breathing was sharp and shallow in Ruby's ear. "I—I'm fine." She gasped, digging her nails into Ruby's shoulders. "I knew you'd come. Quick, lock the door. There are things out there that are eating people."

Her mother pulled away and made for the hall table.

Ruby froze. No. They had to leave. Now. "Mum, we can't stay at the house. It's not safe, we—Mum! Stop!"

Her mum didn't stop, but continued to rummage through the little table drawer for the key to the second lock. "We need to secure the door. Help me find this key."

Ruby grabbed a handful of her own hair, threading her fingers through as a wild urgency thrummed within her. How was she going to get someone who had been practically housebound for the past two years to leave now, during the demon apocalypse?

Stepping forward, she grabbed her mother from behind, squeezing, as though she could instil urgency into her through direct contact. "Stop. Stop, we're not staying. We have to get out."

"In that? We can't."

"Mum, we have to leave Crichton."

"Ruby, it's not—"

The startled shriek that escaped her mother's lips mid-sentence made Ruby's blood freeze in her veins. Ruby's snapped around, and stifled a scream of her own.

It was a demon. Large and beefy, upright like a man, but twice the size. And it was standing in the kitchen.

Chapter 25

R uby gaped at the large silhouette framed by the kitchen door. They'd been found.

"Ru—Whuh … what the hell is that?"

She gasped for air. This nightmare was never going to end. Drayvex had told her so in no uncertain terms. Told her that they couldn't win. Now, for the first time, she believed it.

"Kill it. We need—we … Ruby, wake up! We need to kill it!"

Her mother's urgent words penetrated her self-pity, grounding her in the moment. It was moving down the hallway towards them.

Ruby sprung to life. "Mum, stay back," she yelled, grabbing her mum's arm and yanking her backwards with her. Weapon, she needed a weapon. Her mind drifted to the object in her room. He'd called it a shadow lantern. It was a weapon, wasn't it?

Fear squeezed her heart. Visions of Sandra lying on the floor, helpless, tore at her soul. It was happening all over again.

A thunderous roar ripped through the hallway. The hair all over her body stood erect. They were out of time. Her breath caught in her throat. *Time.*

No sooner had this thought entered her head, than Ruby threw herself at the old grandfather clock and ripped open its lower door. What she found inside was hope.

She tugged at the shotgun, ripping it free of its bonds. She hadn't used one in a while, but with any luck, it was like riding a bike. Once you knew, you knew.

"Honey, watch out!"

As she brought the gun around, she tried to pull it up and choked. The demon was right on top of her. A meaty hand came ploughing down towards her, grabbing for her throat.

"*No!* Get away from my daughter!"

Unable to bring the gun up in such close proximity, Ruby screamed, throwing her free arm across her face. She wasn't ready to die. But then, neither had Sandra been, or her neighbours, or anyone else who had died today. She couldn't imagine ever being ready.

The demon's large hand crashed into her arm. But before it could get its hand on her throat, it let out a painful screech, recoiling from her in a clumsy jerk. Its retracting claw snagged her bracelet as it pulled back. She felt it spring free from her arm. Ruby flinched, too stunned to move. The bracelet fell to the floor with a tinkle. Could it have …?

The shotgun was ripped from her hand.

Panic. Ruby whirled around, arms outstretched, and saw her mother, standing beside her with the gun, looking fiercer than the beast. Wasting no time, she brought up the shotgun, tucked it into her shoulder and aimed for the head. "Go to Hell."

The gunshot blasted their eardrums and jerked her mum backwards. The impact blasted their target. Ruby's ears rang. She'd forgotten how vicious a weapon it was. Muscles aching from tension, she looked for the creature, frantic—and her body buzzed with relief.

The demon was sprawled on the floor, the contents of its head spilling out onto the hallway carpet. It looked dead.

"Ruby …"

Ruby spun to face her mum—the woman who was once a local hero, who once took down corruption and evil every single day with a smile—and smiled herself. She was dizzy with adrenaline and fear and gratitude. Her mum was a bad-ass. "I knew you'd never truly left the force. Not where it counted."

Her mum sucked in a shaking breath. Her eyes fell to the beast sprawled on the carpet, then rose to meet Ruby's dead on. "Honey. I ..." She licked her lips. "I'm sorry for being such a selfish mother."

Pain lanced through Ruby's chest. Was this really the time for a heart to heart? And honestly, her mum had done nothing wrong. Not really. It was her, Ruby, that was the selfish one.

Ruby reached out and took her mother's hand, holding it between her palms. "When we get through this," she said, squeezing the cold hand in her grasp, "we'll sit down with a bottle of Jack and talk about where we want to go from here." She hated lying to her mother, but it was preferable to telling her the truth: that they had no future. Not one they were going to like, that was for sure. "But right now, we'll barricade the house. Make it safe and hope for the best."

Her mother stared at her, taking in her words. Then her expression hardened, and the bad-ass was back. "Okay. Okay, let's do this."

Ruby scooped up Sandra's bracelet, but almost dropped it. It was warm. "Why were you covered in blood that day?"

Ruby stopped breathing. The alleyway incident. Drayvex's big reveal. Her heart pounded, the breath she held swirling inside her lungs. She slipped the bracelet into her pocket. "I ... made a poor judgement call," she muttered, stepping over the dead demon and heading into the lounge. "And no, I don't want to talk about it."

*

Time raced and idled. It was irrelevant on Vekrodus, planet of eternal night. Hours, minutes, seconds. Meaningless.

Drayvex had sealed off all portals between Earth and Vekrodus. He had cut off an entire line of powerful dark mages, and then taken them back, brokering a deal that left a lazy species with far less than they had before. Statistically, the girl was long dead.

But the more he tried to erase her lingering presence in his mind, the harder it became to smother the flames that licked at the edges of his thoughts. Was she dead, or was she surviving somehow by herself? Did she still possess that size-defying spunk, the almost arrogant optimism of the light-dwelling heroine? Or was she ready to embrace her demise? They picked away at him, subtly at first. Drayvex found that he could ignore the thoughts, put them down to misplaced curiosity. But as the initial turbulence subsided, reducing to a persistent simmer, they began to gain weight and substance.

He ran a claw along the length of the ledge, looking down the drop. He was restless, on edge, like a user overdue on their next sweet fix of poison. The nagging that tugged at the edges of his consciousness became harder to ignore.

He frowned. His thoughts would always circle back to her. One stubborn, vertically challenged human. One human within a sea of mindless, identical, dispensable cattle standing on a small spit of rock—a rock that he had allowed Saydor to bring into ruin, not only because it gave him something he'd wanted for quite some time, but because it made his life that little bit easier.

And the human in question? She had spat on her one chance of survival. So why, in Hell's name, why did she continue to plague him, to the point where even maintaining his fury at her was exhausting?

Drayvex stood at the highest point of the fortress, paying little attention to its view. Life on Vekrodus had swiftly returned to its normal droll, with a helping fist that pounded anything insubordinate into paste. He sneered, his lip curling as he thought of his rogue underlings. When the humans on Earth had thinned out and food became scarce, his fatheaded familiars would attempt to come crawling back with their tails between their legs, and fail.

Cutting them off sent a message. Playing the long game was often far more rewarding than instant gratification. Ultimately, they would die either way. What he needed now, though, was a distraction. He needed to kill the spineless, festering maggots that had lived in his shadow and got fat off his leftovers, only to move on to what they thought was the better option, and destroy them in ways beyond their darkest musings. But summoning up any kind of blood lust was a far more arduous process than it should be. And since most of his efforts were put into snubbing the endless spew of neurotic nonsense in his head, he didn't have much to spare.

'Why would I want to leave with someone who kills innocent people? Who kills my people?'

Drayvex glared out over the stretching sands, skimming the vicinity out of habit alone. She was a virus, infecting his system with foreign rubbish that his defences would eventually kill. All he had to do was shut it out until it was dead.

He tensed. Something shiny caught on the edge of his vision, a small chink of light on the floor. Reluctant, he bent down and picked up the object, laying it flat on his palm.

It was a silver coin, marked with one of Earth's currencies. Its faces were smooth and worn, showing some age as it gleamed dully in the limited light. It was *her* coin. The impulsive swipe he'd made on one house visit while chasing the stone.

Drayvex stared at the object, held in place by an invisible force. The last time he was up here, he'd disposed of everything related to his human facade. Somehow, this had escaped that fate. He glared at the coin that he held between two fingers, treating it as though it was the sole source of his misery. It was unwanted.

Reaching over the ledge's edge, he dangled it above the lake of acid that surrounded the fortress. He watched it dangle, ignoring the restlessness that was still so alien to him.

You're letting her win, mocked that self-righteous voice, calling him out. She's dead, and she still has you on your back.

Touche, he thought.

As Drayvex watched the silver coin plunge towards the lake's surface, he found his release, and for one blissful moment, he felt nothing. Then, as the gleaming disk gained a reflection in the surface of the clear liquid, an irrational urgency throbbed through his being.

Leaning over the edge of the sharp drop, he argued with gravity, testing his mental reflexes as he grabbed at the plummeting coin with his mind.

The throne room was beyond its capacity, yet silent enough that the most incompetent dunderhead would hear a pin drop. Or a coin.

Drayvex glowered across the vast room from his powerful perch, scanning the sea of demons as he spun the coin within a half-closed hand. His impenetrable exterior was the most valuable weapon in his arsenal of deception. Outside, he was a steel mask of indifference. Inside, he seethed, berating himself for his weakness. Attachment was a human affliction. A base emotion that favoured the more devolved of mind.

The curved claws of his other hand rested on the black onyx armrest, tapping in a steady rhythm. For the hundredth time within the space of Hell knew how long, he cursed *her*. But blaming a human for his problems wasn't going to get results. It had also long stopped getting the desired effect.

"Ahem."

Drayvex rolled his gaze down to the foot of the throne, where a guard knelt on the marble floor. It was time. "Proceed."

Moments later, the scent of blood reached his sensitive nose. Human blood. His fangs reacted to the scent, lubricating his mouth with a slick layer of venom. Drayvex welcomed the blood lust, the clarity it brought. He ran his tongue along his teeth, appreciating the simple reaction. He was going to make their life a living hell.

"Your Eminence, we beg your pardon."

Drayvex narrowed his eyes as he watched the two gnarled demons move down the centre aisle towards the throne. The human was between the two, a struggling form being half dragged, half carried towards him. Living humans were a rarity on Vekrodus. It wasn't possible to stumble onto the planet by accident, and plucking yourself a ripe, juicy human only to set it free on the Hell planet of your origin was counterproductive.

As the latest pair of numbskulls approached the base of the throne, they glared at each other, pulling their catch from one to the other in an escalating tug of war, before throwing her to the floor.

Drayvex scanned over the human in his midst and tensed. His mind did a painful one-eighty degree flip as he took in the girl that had been tossed at his feet. She was petite, with pale skin and a curtain of burgundy hair that glowed under the flickering overhead torches. As she knelt on all fours on the marble, her hair covered what he wanted to see. What he needed to see.

It's not her.

He held his frozen position, aware of the room of demons awaiting his response, unable to take his eyes off the girl.

You know it's not.

He did know. He would have smelled her the moment she entered the vicinity. This obvious fact refused to pacify that volatile, alien thing inside him, a thing that defied all logic as it spread through him in ripples of agitation.

The girl peeked up at him from behind her hair.

Drayvex clenched his jaw. A sensation close to relief swept through him. He thought he had known insanity well before this whole debacle. He was mistaken.

"Speak," he ordered, unable to muster his usual vitriol. His gaze fell back to the human on the ground. It wasn't her.

You did this.

She looked back, not only with fear, but with a mournful presence in her eyes. The resemblance to *her* was vague at best. She was just another human.

You sold the Earth behind her back and left her to die.

And yet, when he looked at her, he saw the girl with the demon stone necklace.

A girl whose name seems to have escaped your perfect memory.

"My Lord, I found and claimed this human," boomed the demon on the right. "But this idiot also claims to have ownership. How can this be?"

"I have. You stole it from me!" whined the second demon.

"Silence," Drayvex barked, on edge. Worse than a headache, he was arguing with himself. Well, it was simple. He had a job to do; a reputation to uphold. "I couldn't give a flying fuck which of you claimed her first. But the last maggot standing here, now, before the room, gets the human in full." His withering gaze dared them to defy him, and as he trained it on each of them in turn, their eyes fell to the floor. "Am I making myself clear?"

The girl was still watching him. Her eyes pleaded with him, wide and brown and clueless. *She* had once looked at him that way. Pleading for his help, just before he'd abandoned her on a dying planet. Because destroying the last of the fae was more important than the lives of a billion, billion humans.

As the two demons launched themselves at each other at the foot of the throne, much to the delight of the hordes gathered to witness, Drayvex stood and strode down the gold veined steps. Attachment was a human affliction. A base emotion that favoured the weak.

The guard at the foot of the throne reached out, opening his mouth to utter a protest. Drayvex brought his hand up and, using his mind, whipped back the guard's protruding arm in its socket with a sharp snap. What about the life of one human girl? What was that worth?

As he slipped out through the back exit of the throne room, heading toward a portal, he studied the coin in his hand. He needed Ruby safe. The impact of these words penetrated him with a subtle realisation. He wanted her safe, and damn it, there was no reason on this ungodly planet and beyond that he couldn't have everything he wanted.

One day, she would thank him.

Drayvex strode through the gutted carcass of Crichton, observing the lack of human life with increasing unease. He was wasting his time.

Smatterings of glass and other debris crunched underfoot. The scent of blood hung thick in the air, along with the lingering remnants of fear, and death. Something burned in the vicinity, filling the atmosphere as the jumble of smells infused together into one intoxicating tangle.

The chances of Ruby surviving when the majority of her people had perished were slim. Her instincts were backwards. She had no sense of self-preservation and trouble went for her like a magnet.

The chaos inside him had fallen still. But his forcibly expanded palate continued to throw an imaginative array of undesirables his way, and Drayvex found himself unable to see her as anything short of alive. Denial. Once again, logic was speaking to an empty room.

He stalked on at a human pace, heading for the green hunk of brickwork that had served as her self-imposed cage during his time here. If she had an iota of sense in that oddly wired brain, she'd be long gone. But in the spirit of being thorough, if only to rule it out, he'd start there.

Before he arrived, he found one survivor. Drayvex turned a corner and regarded the living human with vague detachment. A dumpy woman struggled in meek spasms in the grip of a rogue demon. Feet dangling, her face was turning a steady shade of purple as she struggled to breathe. The horned brute toying with her was absorbed in its prey, holding her by the throat.

Drayvex tutted with exaggerated slowness, injecting himself into the scene. "Are you going to eat that?" he drawled. "Or do all lowborn halfwits play with their food first?"

The demon let the human drop to the ground. It span around and flexed its muscles, stepping forward in an alpha display, before stopping short. "My Lord?" it rumbled, realising its mistake too late. "What are you—?"

"You dare to question me, you pathetic sack of puke?" he hissed, feeling his fragile temper snap. He whipped forward, grabbing the larger demon by the throat and slamming it against a nearby wall with unnecessary force. Cracks spread through the bricks, fanning out around the demon's bulk. Drayvex heard bones snap and squeezed the throat in his hand tighter. He'd grown morbidly accustomed to this halfway form. It wasn't human, nor was it demon, and it was a skin that Ruby had come to accept. The planet he ruled over was only familiar with his true form.

"No, My Lord. Forgive me. I-I forget my place."

Drayvex was driven by an intense need to kill. To engorge himself with violence and blood. Death. Yet he had an inkling that it was a bottomless pit—a pit that all the bodies left on this planet couldn't fill. A bleeding, Ruby-shaped maw.

As his subject begged for forgiveness, Drayvex plunged his other hand into its chest cavity and closed his fingers around its beating heart. The demon jerked as he squeezed. Drayvex increased the pressure until the organ was a warm, gooey pulp in his fist. He would kill anyway. He had made his decision, and there was no going back.

As Drayvex approached the house, his senses reeled. The windows were boarded, and an array of smells seeped through the pores of its crude defences, the dominant scent being blood. He tried the door and met resistance.

Drayvex lifted his boot and smashed it through the feeble door, launching the contents piled behind it.

It wouldn't have kept out much. But as the strong mix of bloods rushed through the hole and stuck in the back of his throat, he discovered that keeping the monsters *out* was the least of Ruby's problems.

The blood was of three separate entities. He could smell her in two. One was sour.

Three entities, two heartbeats.

Her scent was on everything around him, including the red streaks smeared along the walls. As he walked with slow, purposeful steps through the wrecked house, he doubted that he would ever be able to purge her scent from his mind.

Drayvex stepped over the large black stain on the carpet and into the lounge. His relief was immediate and levelling. Ruby was alive. Alive, and facing down a demon.

The demon was worse for wear. Even so, it wasn't a match a pint-sized human could win, and as it towered over her in triumph, there was an air of calm finality around her that seemed to mirror his thoughts. Its claws were within slashing distance of her delicate throat, one move off making her just another body.

Drayvex struck out with ruthless precision.

The demon's head hit the floor. The head rolled past her feet. Ruby didn't react. As the headless body collapsed to the floor, she stood, pale, still. *Alive.*

Drayvex shook his head, laughing under his breath. Her injuries were superficial. He scanned her once, twice. As Demon Lord, he was naturally deserving of anything he set his sights upon. Right at this moment, her condition seemed more to do with luck than worth.

He moved towards the frozen girl—then stopped as her expression cut through his mental clutter. She was focused on the ground.

Reluctant, Drayvex followed her gaze down to the broken thing at his feet, considering the situation as it all clicked into place. The mother.

He had dragged his feet in coming back, and now that pest of a woman was dead.

A new demon presence registered somewhere within his split focus, drawn to the blood. Of course, Ruby would blame him for her mother's demise. He frowned, and his fangs responded in kind. He'd been right all along. That woman really was more trouble to him dead than alive.

Drayvex shifted as he watched the object of his delirium fall into shock, caught between wanting to pacify her and protect her. If he took her now, it would no doubt push her over the edge of whatever precipice she was standing on. Then again, she smelled like a walking buffet.

Stepping over the corpse, he approached Ruby from behind. He looped his arm around her waist, and when she didn't resist, he placed his other hand against the side of her head. As his influence slipped without effort into the recesses of her mind, her body sagged, becoming dead weight at his command. Her mother had been a dead woman walking if he ever saw one. His only mistake had been in trusting Ruby to know what was best for herself. And that was a mistake he wouldn't be making again in a hurry.

Chapter 26

*T*he milky substance inside the globe moved in sluggish swirls, pushing out in disks that fanned at the edges. Drayvex skimmed over the thin membrane with a finger, caressing the skin of the sphere as he controlled the liquid within. It reacted to his touch, deepening into inky ribbons that spread faster, forming a network of linking trails across its surface. The seldom-used west wing was the perfect place to harbour a human inside a fortress of demons. Still, Ruby's presence required a certain amount of finesse. Forward-thinking.

The Magus Nox room was the control tower of the entire fortress. The globe itself contained the power of his direct ancestors, with each Demon Lord that had reigned before him having contributed to it during their time on the throne. As current Demon Lord, its deep well of potency was something that he alone could access.

These days it was more surplus than quietus, but during his first decade in power, it had tipped the balance in his favour on more than one occasion.

His finger glanced over the spherical face, guiding the spreading strands within. A selection of unrivalled guards were positioned at the wing's entry points. Their orders were to eviscerate anything that strayed too close. As for the guards themselves, he'd made their fate crystal clear; that any fool willing to disobey his orders would beg for death by the time he was done.

And death was a mercy he would not be granting any time soon.

Drayvex gave the great globe one final stroke, activating the spell. It pulsed in flashes of cobalt blue, lapping in waves that pushed out from its centre, bathing the room in blue light and pockets of darkness with each swell.

As a last resort, the dark magic he was erecting throughout the wing would ensure that no demon but he would survive inside the area for more than a moment.

The pulsing stopped, plunging the room into darkness. Done and done.

Drayvex left the room. He slipped down the dark passage, heading for the outer bridge that linked one section of castle to the next. There was no such thing as overkill when it came to getting his own way. There was only success or failure.

Now Ruby's fragile life had been added to the mix, failure was not an option. He couldn't let her go, and he couldn't watch her die. This was something that continued to vex him. Not that he would admit that to her.

As he entered on the other side, he paused, noting two scrawny demons scrapping in the corner. Don't mind if I do, he thought, approaching them from behind.

The demons ceased as he neared, hastening to disentangle themselves from each other.

Drayvex jabbed out, grabbing one by the throat.

The second bolted as he pulled the first towards him. The familiar thrashed in his iron grip, abandoning all respect for its Lord and ruler in favour of a basal need to survive.

Ignoring the choked pleas of the rat squirming in his grip, he headed towards the west wing. Ruby would hate his guts when she awoke, but it made no difference to him. He could comfortably bask in her hate from now until Vekrodus froze over. She could join the long waiting list for Drayvex Haters Anonymous, along with anyone else he'd ever pissed on during his short time on the throne. Ruby had the freedom to hate him *because* she was alive.

The demon guarding the left section of the wing bowed as he approached.

Drayvex signalled vaguely to the guard, studying the barrier that he'd set in motion. There were no obvious signs, no tells that gave it away, unless, you knew what to look for.

If one turned one's head in a particular way, it was possible to catch a subtle glimmer in the atmosphere, a sheen that flashed within the corner of the perceptive eye. Perfect. There was just one thing left to do.

"Make yourself useful," he drawled, before hurling the scrawny demon headfirst into the wing.

It squealed as it hit the floor, once, twice. Then it rolled along the corridor and stilled in a sprawling heap. The demon got to its feet and stared back at him from the gloom. Confusion was plastered all over its thin face.

Drayvex folded his arms.

The minion dropped to the floor. It began to scream and claw at its face, and a moment later, blood was trickling out of every orifice.

The escalation was swift and brutal. It stumbled towards him, blood spurting, pushing out in jets with the building pressure. Its eyes bulged out from its skull with the force.

Finally, as if possessed, the demon's head span of its own accord. It twisted around at breakneck speed, until a wet crack echoed within the enclosed space and the magic claimed its first victim.

Drayvex smirked, satisfied.

He continued on, his lightless flesh melding with the darkness as he proceeded through the wing's twisting network. He could easily keep her up here for the next seventy or so years, confident that nothing would ever find her. At least, nothing that would survive to tell the tale. Somehow, though, he doubted that would go down well with the human.

You've lost your mind, jabbed the scathing voice of reason in his head, if you think you can keep that here indefinitely.

Drayvex approached the door to the small room and hovered at its threshold.

That creature will be your undoing.

He allowed his form to slip, his body to mould into something less threatening. As his tongue glided along a significantly smaller canine, he listened to the steady heartbeat on the other side. Like Hell. A blip like

Ruby didn't have a vicious bone in her body. He, however ...

He placed his hand on the handle and turned it. She would be dealt with in whichever way he saw fit, and she would swallow it or die. Because at this point, he was all she had in this dark and twisted world. And if she fought it, she would learn fast.

As he stepped into the dimly lit room, his eyes were drawn to the small figure kneeling on the rug. She didn't immediately respond. But as his presence affected the atmosphere, slowly, she raised her head.

Ruby peered at him from behind a dark curtain of hair. "Take me back." Her voice was no more than a hollow whisper. But there was something about the simple utterance that suggested something was brewing. "Now."

Drayvex didn't respond. *To what, my dear?* he thought, watching her fingers weave into the rug's depth. *That wreckage you insist on clinging to with suicidal obstinance?*

"You can't keep me here." Her body didn't move, but a touch of conviction bled into her quiet, monotone voice, strengthening the last word.

Without speaking, he turned and shut the door. The magic lock echoed with a final resounding clunk. *Watch me.*

When he turned back around, Ruby had looked up. She was staring at him, her face a mask of calm. Her eyes, however, were burning a hole in his head.

Drayvex folded his arms, and matched her accusing stare. If she thought that she could beat him at his own game, she was wrong. He was the master of the mask, and she would not win. "No."

She rose to her feet, her slender body straightening, expanding like a crumpled piece of paper being flattened out. Her dark flame hair tumbled over her shoulders. "Take. Me. *Back.*" Each word was forced out through her teeth, spat between audible breaths that agitated her rising and falling chest. She glared at him with swollen eyes, her posture stiff, fingers curling and uncurling at her sides.

Drayvex didn't move. He held his position, his entire form still and composed. "Okay then. How about this?" If she was beyond all reason, then he would hammer it home. "When hell freezes over—no," he said, matching her previous deadpan tone, "when *Vekrodus* freezes over. When the sun penetrates the darkest corners of this planet. When the scum on the festering pool of humanity is nothing more than a distant memory, I will drop you on what's left of your planet in the same spot I found you and send you on your way."

He opened his mouth and flashed her a smile as his responding fangs competed for space, no doubt making an entirely unplanned point of their own. "Do we have a deal?"

Ruby openly gaped at him, speechless, as she processed his words. Silence pressed against his senses. It didn't last long.

"You *bastard.*" She stepped forward once, a single hostile stride, telling him more about her mindset than if he'd had direct access to her inner thoughts. "You're insane. You know that?"

Drayvex bristled. "Says Earth's weakest ray of hope. We tried things your way, remember? You *failed.*" He knew he was being cold. He knew he should show some patience. The girl was completely out of her depth. But he just couldn't stop himself. "Bad life decisions are clearly your forte, so do try to remember that the next time you open your mouth to spit out asinine demands." The last person to speak to him in this way had lost more than their tongue.

"What the hell did you just say?"

He watched her hands balling. He was fairly certain that was a rhetorical question.

Without waiting for a reply, Ruby lunged across the space between them, throwing herself at him. She barrelled straight into his chest.

Drayvex dropped his guard. He didn't fight the momentum that pushed them both backwards through the small room. Nor did he did he make any attempt to restrain her fists as they struck out at him in blind stabs, and as his back hit the door, he congratulated himself on not shredding the girl he'd abducted on sheer impulse.

"My life went to hell the day I met *you*," Ruby screamed, her voice hitting his eardrums with more impact than her punches.

Her futile attempts to hurt him were just sapping at her energy. He let her vent, her already slowing punches bouncing off his chest in harmless stabs. If she got through this shitstorm in one piece, he'd show her how to throw a *real* punch.

"I hate you!"

As he witnessed this onslaught of his senses, it suddenly occurred to him that Ruby was making a lot of noise. Sound travelled in large buildings, and that was without factoring in the enhanced hearing of its demonic inhabitants. Not to mention that the barrier he'd erected would not block out sound.

Drayvex reached out and grabbed her by the shoulders, jerking her with the sudden movement. "Wonderful," he snarled. "Speak up, will you? There's a group of small mudsuckers on the far side of the planet that *didn't* hear you!"

"You forced yourself into my life, took what you wanted and left a goddamn wreckage in your wake. My home is gone. My future is in pieces. M-my best friend in the world, guess what? She's dead. My mother?" She sucked in a breath, fast and sharp, her eyes shining with emotion. "She's … dead. *Dead*. And that's all on you."

He stared at her, and for once in his life, he had no idea of how to respond.

Ruby stilled, her arm stopping mid swing to hover near his chest. Her body slumped, arms falling to her sides, having exhausted herself of all that was driving her. "No. Maybe this is on me after all." Her voice dropped, becoming a casual murmur. "Even after finding out what you truly were, what you'd done … I allowed myself to trust you."

Drayvex watched a single tear run down her cheek. Her pain was a tangible thing, bleeding into the space around them.

"A demon. How stupid does that make me?" She sounded more like she was talking to herself than to him.

Suddenly, she laughed. It was a soft, high-pitched sound that made him wonder about her sanity. "You know, the day I met you, I should have run in the opposite direction. I wanted to, you know. But I didn't." She paused, considering her words. "Why do you hate me, Drayvex?"

Without giving any thought to his actions, Drayvex reached out to her and lifted her chin with a finger, forcing their eyes to meet. There was a time when he'd thought that he hated her, not so long ago. It shouldn't be news that he'd made her feel this way. But as she stared up at him, anguish swimming in those two green pools, he found himself growing restless. He wanted to protect her, but not just her physical body. Her mind, her soul. To take away her suffering by any means necessary.

He was coming up blank. The whole thing was a mess of contradictions. In aggressively protecting one, two other aspects were vulnerable and open. There was no way to serve her needs without screwing his own in the process. There was insanity, and then there was sheer bloody *lunacy*.

His presence here was counterproductive—for both of them.

Ruby's eyes drifted down. Drayvex let his hand drop from her face. He followed her gaze and watched as she produced an object from out of nowhere. It was the shadow lantern. She held it out towards him, her gaze fixed on its small spindles. "Show me how to use it. I need to know."

Her voice was as dead as her eyes. Drayvex stared at the dark object and shifted. It didn't work that way. She was human.

"I should know how to protect myself. From, you know. Demons." She idly fiddled with the weapon in her hands, any sense of self-preservation she may have once had, gone.

He sighed, exasperated. "Not if you do as you're told." Even if he could show a human how to access the lantern's power, he wouldn't. Giving a volatile Ruby access to black magic would be the last mistake either of them made.

"Ouch!"

As the scent of fresh blood confirmed his last thought, he looked down at the shadow lantern. His fangs throbbed.

Blood welled from the slice in her finger, seeping into the mechanisms of the pointed object she held.

Unbelievable. Drayvex closed his eyes, shaking his head in a minuscule gesture. The girl needed protecting from herself, never mind the hordes in the castle. "Give it here," he said, the scent of her blood testing his worn impulse control.

But as he reached out towards it, the lantern sprung to life. Ruby gasped, dropping it to the floor.

Drayvex watched the small spindles as they spewed out jets of darkness into the room, his mind reeling in a hundred different directions. How hell did she do that?

"You could have warned me!"

He stared at her, frozen in place. Ruby wasn't human. But she was. She was as weak and soft as any of them. He knew this.

Ruby stared back. Her expression faltered. "What?"

Her blood. He'd tasted it, and dismissed it. But her blood had been charged.

Drayvex forced himself to move, to work through the tension that gripped his entire being. Ruby's blood was charged because it was *cursed*. He was sure of it. And Ruby herself was none the wiser.

Slipping into what he hoped was a calmer manner, he reached down and plucked the twitching artefact from the floor. It fell still at his touch. "Stay here," he warned, allowing some ice to creep into his voice. "Unless, of course, you want to join your mother in the afterlife."

He repositioned a somewhat yielding Ruby a few paces back with one hand and slipped out of the room.

As he closed the door behind him, he paused at its threshold, held in place by an invisible force. Something prickled at the back of his mind.

'*My life went to hell the day I met you.*'

A muffled thud rattled the door as Ruby threw something against it from the other side.

Drayvex rolled his eyes. If she only knew how right she was, she would soon wish she had the knowledge and skill required to kill a demon of his calibre. His deal with the yellow devil had not only sent her precious Earth into its pre-death spiral, and in turn, the demons released as a result had taken from her the two people on the planet that she deemed an unacceptable loss.

He shifted, stretching his muscles as he headed on through the winding passageways of the wing. He could still feel it, the echo of her pain. Dragging at him.

As he rounded the corner, Drayvex pushed outward, allowing his true form to explode into being all at once. What she didn't know wouldn't hurt her. What she thought she knew couldn't be proved. And that was just how life worked around here.

Chapter 27

*T*ime passed in a lethargic crawl. Minutes dragged with excruciating slowness, stretching beyond logic. Beyond all reason. She had no sense of time or the passing hour. No sense of the world moving around her. Just her, and her thoughts.

Ruby grabbed handfuls of the fur-like material beneath her. Her wounded finger pulsed in protest. She didn't know how long she'd been curled up on her side, but as she unfolded her legs from her body, her knees screamed.

She wriggled her toes and then, propping herself with an arm, she gazed across the room.

Her shoe was on its side near the door, where she'd thrown it. She pulled her eyes away, the memory tugging her niggling discomfort into a physical ache. It spread out from her chest, an invisible bruise that throbbed when she thought or moved. Or breathed.

Ruby sat upright, pushing with her palms. Too fast. She gripped her head, little black specks dancing in front of her eyes. Letting her head droop her, she clung to the long fur and waited for her vision to clear. When was the last time she'd had a meal? Probably the sandwich her mum had made her, just before …

Her heart lurched. She couldn't deal with this right now. She couldn't even begin to know how. The irony was that her demon saviour, despite having protected her against her will, didn't seem to give a damn about her wellbeing. So why was she here?

As she thought about Drayvex, Ruby became hyper-aware of her breathing. It was laboured, weighty. She had no idea that it was possible to be so angry with someone without physically combusting. Go about your normal life, Ruby. Forget about the stone, Ruby. Oh, and what I'm not telling you is that, in twenty-four hours, everyone you know and love will be dead.

She breathed in through her nose and out through her mouth, glaring at the fur fibres. If he'd actually said that, it would have been more useful. The obvious question though, aside from how long had he known this would happen, was: had he lifted a finger to stop it, would it still be happening?

The answer was obvious. Of course, it wouldn't. But even now, a single, hopeful shred of doubt refused to be quenched. Maybe, just *maybe*, he had tried to stop this. Maybe, he would prove her wrong.

Feeling like she'd aged by twenty years overnight, Ruby pulled herself to her feet and took in the unfamiliar room.

It was small, but somehow still spacious, with minimal contents that added to the illusion. The floor was strangely clammy, and it warmed her foot through the fabric of her sock.

Ruby took in her dim surroundings, her eyes well adjusted to the gloom by this point, and was drawn to the one source of light in the room. It was a large rectangle of grey light, spanning almost from floor to ceiling. As she studied the shape, she noticed the thin, translucent veil that covered it. She held her breath, hoping to see it ripple or sway. A window?

Ruby shuffled towards it, drawn to the answers that it might provide. As she approached the grey light, the hair on her arms and legs prickled in warning. She ignored the sensation.

Reaching for the veil, she brushed the fabric aside with tentative fingers—and gasped. Her jaw fell slack. It *was* a window. And she was a long way from home.

An exotic red terrain stretched out in front of her, its blood red sand carpeting the ground as far as she could see. The sky was thick with turbulent black clouds, their wild spumes dominating the atmosphere as their flaming edges reflected off the sands. The occasional breeze whipped up the grains and created tiny tornadoes that swirled for a short distance, before collapsing back to the ground.

Ruby tore her eyes from the view and looked down. She lost her stomach. Jerking away from the beautiful, alien terrain, she let the veil fall, stumbling back from the window.

Her mind screamed as she tried to process everything that had happened over the past week or two. Sandra had been mauled by a beast. Her mother was lying broken in the house. Earth was being taken over by demons. And she was back on Vekrodus, this time against her will.

Her thoughts swirled like a maelstrom, battering her with more than she could take. She ran her fingers through her hair, tugging the strands at the roots. The walls taunted her, closing in. The floor hummed beneath her feet, alive. Was she safe here?

'Stay here.'

Her gaze flicked up towards the door.

'Unless, of course, you want to join your mother in the afterlife.'

Ruby didn't plan on dying today. She did, however, need to get out of this room.

She started for the door, her mind made up, but stopped as something tugged at the corner of her vision. Eyes flicking around the room, she noticed a small nook in the wall. Her curiosity prickled.

Ruby moved towards the tiny square nook and eyed the glistening object within. It was a palm-sized pyramid, and it was beautiful. Black and translucent, it looked like it was made of glass. It captured what little light was in the room, and at the right angle, it gleamed in a rainbow hue, like the membrane of a bubble.

Entranced, her hand slipped out towards it. Drayvex had taken her shadow ball. He had taken what was hers, again, because that was what he always did.

As her hand closed around the cool object, Ruby took a small pleasure in her petty act. Now, she was in his house. And she would help herself to what was his.

When she reached the door, she studied the handle. It didn't have a keyhole. Ruby grabbed for it, before stopping herself mid lunge. What if Drayvex had locked it from the outside? If that was the case, she'd never get free.

She slid her fingers over the cold metal, forming a loose grip. Then, without further hesitation, she turned her wrist, sharp and precise.

The handle met no resistance. As she let it go, it made a metallic clunk, and the door inched inward. Apparently, he was leaving those life and death decisions up to her, then. She took a deep breath, and then stepped out into the dark world on the other side of the doorway.

Ruby wandered down the endless corridor without direction or purpose, her stomach churning in a mounting unease. She skimmed over the walls, taking in what little detail she could see. There was a definite air of prestige to the decor, with a simple style that exuded power, status. The walls were bare but layered, and carved in intricate ways that almost seemed to pop outward. They stretched up to a ceiling that was so high, the flames in their brackets couldn't touch it. Without a doubt, this was the domain of the Demon Lord.

The passage stretched out before her, and the more she ignored the subtle nagging of her subconscious, the stronger it became. It took her a moment to realise why. This place was utterly deserted.

It wasn't that she wanted to run into anything nasty, but the abandonment of it felt wrong somehow. It felt too good to be true.

Ruby turned her first corner, then skidded to a halt. Her hand flew to her mouth, stifling the scream rising up her throat. She *wasn't* alone.

More out of fear than natural instinct, she ducked behind a large chest against the wall.

Even with its back to her, even at a distance, despite every horrid creature she had beheld thus far, she'd seen nothing like it. As if the demon's sheer size wasn't enough to wipe out any balance between them, held in one hand was an immense sword, its sharp tip resting against the floor in a casual display of strength.

Ruby gaped at the immense weapon, willing her pounding heart to steady.

In a battle of sizes between herself and the sword, the sword would come out on top. Steeling herself, she filled her lungs with a slow, calming breath. This was a bad idea.

She clutched at the object she was just small enough to hide behind, sliding one leg out behind her. And now, she couldn't possibly get away without being heard.

As this morbid thought occurred to her, the demon's head twisted.

Ruby froze mid-slide. She teetered on the spot, trying to keep her balance.

Large nostrils twitched, sucking at the space between them.

Ruby missed *simple*. She missed her simple life, her simple routines. The oh so simple decision of what to have for lunch. How simple it was to stay alive and not be eaten by demons. She'd had it *all*, and she hadn't taken the time to appreciate it. Not once.

As the demon at the mouth of the passage turned to fully face her, Ruby relived her most recent nightmare.

The creature was bony but not thin, with a bulk that suggested its skeleton was on the outside rather than inside. It was covered with a fleshy substance, red raw and moist, like exposed muscle. Its face was the one exception. Deathly white.

Pure, undiluted fear seized Ruby. Forcing down a hysterical scream, she held her breath and prayed that she didn't smell like lunch.

Ruby's grip on the chest slipped. As her ankle gave out, she flailed, teetering. The floor came up to meet her, and she threw a palm out to catch herself. It hit the floor with a slap.

The sound echoed in the space around her, making her cringe. She couldn't see it. The chest was blocking her view. But the sound of heavy footfalls was unmistakable.

Her tongue stuck to the roof of her mouth. She could smell *it* now. An overpowering scent not unlike that of rotting meat. Her lungs ached, begging her for more than the shallow gasps that were barely worth taking.

In the distorted moments leading up to her inevitable death, Ruby pictured the many ways it was possible to die by sword. She closed her eyes, holding her semi-sprawl. She hoped it would be quick.

Just then, a gurgling reached her ears. It was so unexpected that her eyes sprung open. She strained her ears, listening to the sound, before realising with a jolt that the footsteps had stopped.

Against her better judgement, she stretched across, peeking around the chest. The demon was a few feet away. It glowered at her, as though she was a spider that had crawled out of a small dark space.

Ruby scrabbled to right herself as panic pulsed through her. The demon's hand shot out towards her, and she flinched, despite the space between them. But instead of grabbing for her, it flew to its own throat. Grabbing at its stocky neck with two hands, it abandoned its weapon, clawing at the skin in frantic gestures. The sword fell to the floor. It clanged against the hard material, thrumming from the impact.

Ruby deeply wanted to run. This was her chance to escape, to turn back while she had the chance. Yet she continued to watch, rooted to the spot, listening to the wet gurgle of its chest.

It dragged itself forward, murder in its black eyes. But almost immediately, its body slumped. The gargantuan creature fell into a coughing fit, spraying the ground between them with a sticky black substance with each hack. Retching gooey black chunks, the origins of which were blissfully unknown.

Eyes wide, Ruby took a step back, reaching behind her for the solid wall. Fear gripped her mind, her stomach.

The large demon collapsed onto all fours, the tips of its recumbent horns scraping against the floor. It continued to retch until the floor was slick and black. Finally, it hissed out a rasping wheeze, before collapsing into the black puddle.

Ruby eyeballed the demon. Something had killed it. Something she couldn't see that had spared her of the same fate. She should go back. Quit while she was ahead. Ruby tiptoed around the horrific mound leaking ominous fluids onto the corridor floor. She *should* go back.

Suddenly, the demon's fingers twitched.

Ruby stumbled, scrabbling out of grabbing range. Not dead. Her mother's screams echoed inside her head. Ruby never learned.

A clammy warmth rose up and enveloped her face. Her stomach squeezed. It had taken a shotgun to the head at point-blank range. By all rights, the creature should have been dead. It had *looked* dead. That assumption had cost her her mum.

It wasn't long before Ruby reached her first crossroads. Glancing left and right didn't help. The passageways all looked the same. More likely than not, she was looking at the entrance of a maze she would die in. The fact that this didn't bother her, bothered her more than the thought of dying itself.

Ruby froze. There was something moving up ahead.

It was like a walking twig. A creature no bigger than her knee, it had a thin body that took up most of its overall length and a tiny face with tiny features. Its skinny arms were the same length as its body; two limp limbs that flapped about it as it ran.

As it scurried across the junction and took the path to her left, curiosity got the better of her. She licked her lips. Come here, little twig.

The creature was hard to follow. They took a left, then a right and soon after that, Ruby had lost track.

The phrase 'curiosity killed the cat' was based on girls like her; girls that knew better than to follow a funny looking creature into the bowels of the underworld, but did so anyway, despite their better judgement. By the time they descended a twisting flight of stairs, Ruby was starting to regret her decision.

At the bottom, the creature pushed its way through a pair of double doors and disappeared from view.

Checking the coast was clear, she clenched her fists and darted through after it. The doors flapped closed behind her, and Ruby came to an abrupt standstill. It was a different world.

Long metal counters gleamed with a cold, surgical feel, spanning the length of the large room. Shelves were stacked high against every wall, holding jar upon jar of brightly coloured liquids and strange paraphernalia. An array of utensils hung from the smaller counters, all pristine and gleaming.

Ruby wandered further inside, blinking as her eyes adjusted. Stranger than it feeling out of place was that this room was brightly lit by a glow that seemed to come from nowhere and everywhere, all at the same time. As she scanned the large room, she noticed for the first time the alien amongst the somewhat familiar, ominous in their simple shapes.

A shrill sound pierced the silence.

Ruby yanked her gaze away and tensed, caught between fight and flight. She'd all but forgotten about the twig creature. But as she followed the noise to the nearest counter, she realised that it had screamed at her.

Its tiny features were moulded into pure, dumbfounded shock. If she wasn't so terrified, it would have been comical.

"Who are you?" it said, taking her in with a twitchy gaze. Its arm slid into a compartment in the counter wall behind. "W-well?"

Ruby was mesmerised by the bizarre little creature. Was it a demon?

"A human. A live human, here?" Its eyes never left her, but it continued to blind-rummage, one arm moving about within the wall compartment behind it. "What devilry is—?"

"Uhm." She scoured her mind for demon etiquette. "My name is Ruby. And yes, I'm human."

The creature moved quicker than she could react. It whipped its arm out from inside the counter and brandished a long metal spike. Ruby threw up her palms. "No! Please, wait."

"Stay back, creature! I will kill you." The little demon gripped the spike like a lance, pushing it out in minuscule jabs.

She studied it. Its arm was shaking, eyes darting about her person. It was almost as though this monster was scared of *her*.

She kept her palms raised in front of her. "I don't want to hurt you."

The demon continued to eyeball her with a dubious expression.

"I swear it." Ruby kept her eyes fixed on the tip of the spike. It was pointing at her stomach. Even with the smallest amount of force behind a jab, she would be in trouble. Ruby stood under the little demon's scrutiny, hardly daring to breathe.

Eventually, mercifully, it lowered the spike, and her stomach muscles ached in relief. "Thanks," she sighed. She lowered her hands.

The demon continued to stare. She blinked, becoming self-conscious, and watched as a pained look flitted across its face. Despite the threat of a skewered stomach, Ruby felt guilty as she watched the creature squirm. "Do you have a name?"

At the friendly question, it seemed to relax a small amount. "Yes."

Ruby bit down on her lower lip as the silence stretched. It was either being literal, or deliberately evasive.

"Krick."

"Oh," she said. "Right."

Its face fell. Panic flared in its eyes as it stared at a spot on her neck. "How did you get here?" Its voice dropped to a whisper. It glanced behind it to the door, before falling back on her. "Did you escape from a level one? You need to leave!"

Ruby frowned. "I …" Her hand rose to touch her neck. Her fingers found the smooth scar and faltered. "What are you talking about?"

"You have the mark. You're claimed."

She blinked, her mind reeling. It had appeared out of nowhere that day. On that first day the monsters had come for her.

Krick shuffled on the spot. "I've never seen a human before." Its big eyes hovered, watching her every move. "In one piece, I mean."

Ruby studied the imp-like creature, trying not to think about the meaning behind its words. Drayvex had saved her. But what else did he do that day? "Well, I've never seen a … a you before."

The little demon puffed out its chest in response. "I'm a greebo. I'm a server for our infernal Lord."

She frowned. "A server?"

"I make use of what I'm given and prepare it for consumption. By the time the bodies get to me, the species is often unrecognisable. More of a pulpy mishmash than whole pieces of meat. But Krick can identify anything, you know." It spoke fast, enthusiasm colouring its voice. "Sometimes, I get whole bits of human. A finger, an eye, a foot." It tilted its head to the side, as though studying her. "You're really not what I thought you'd be."

Ruby was sorry that she'd asked. Visions of dismembered body parts, piled up on a countertop, forced their way to the forefront of her mind. "So, um, you're a chef?"

Krick frowned. "No, a server." It hung the spike from the nearest counter hook. "What's a chef?"

She smiled despite herself.

After a moment of hesitation, Krick crossed the space between them, until she was looking down on the creature. "I could make something for you, if you'd like."

Ruby was taken aback. Eat the culinary abomination of a small demon chef? She knelt down on the floor, lowering herself to a similar height. Its eyes were pleading with her.

"Please say yes. You won't regret it."

Ruby pulled a face. "I don't know." She *was* hungry. Exactly how hungry, though, was a question that she didn't know how to answer.

She sighed. "What have you got?"

It didn't take her long to befriend the strange little greebo. Putting herself at the mercy of something that cooked humans for a living didn't seem like a good way to stay alive. But by the time she'd finished her portion of dodgy grey goop, she had to hand it to the creature; it *knew* what it was doing.

"The flesh of the mellorb is perfectly safe for human consumption. In fact, all it eats is dirt."

Ruby thought it tasted a little like sloppy minced beef. "It's good," she admitted, although it had looked far from it.

As the greebo beamed at Ruby, an impulsive idea came over her. She reached into her pocket and grasped the cool object inside. Krick's eyes bulged as she produced the beautiful black pyramid and held it up for him to see. "What's this?" she asked, keeping her tone light.

It flailed at her from behind the counter. "Where did you get that? Oh, good gracious. My Lord will remove your head!"

Ruby twitched her hand, impatient. "Krick. Tell me what this is. Please."

Its chest fluttered as it stared at her. "It absorbs power. Put it back! He might not noti—"

A crash from behind jolted her from her idle musing. She spun on the spot, jerking the pyramid back towards her. Shoving it into her pocket, she turned to face the double doors. They were moving back and forth on their hinges. Drayvex was leaning against the frame, his arms folded. His expression was black. "Poor foolish greebo," he purred, looking straight through her. "It's really not going to be your day."

Chapter 28

*T*he ice in his voice caused the hair on her arms to stand on end. She heard the veiled threat that dripped off every word, and suddenly, Ruby was worried about the consequences of her actions. Chances were, it wouldn't be her that paid them. "Drayvex, wait."

Krick's gaze shot from to her to Drayvex, and his eyes widened with fresh understanding. "L-Lord Drayvex. Oh, I can explain, My Lord."

Ruby baulked. How did he not recognise his own ruler?

He fell into a low bow, the tip of his nose brushing against the floor as he tried to make himself as small as possible.

Drayvex strode towards them, his booted steps heavy and slow. It was nothing like his usual gait, the silent way he moved when around her. He wanted them to hear him. "No, not your day at all."

The little demon jumped to his feet, stumbling backwards with wild eyes. "My Lord, please. The human—I-I had no idea it was yours. It came to *me.* I told it to go away!"

Drayvex moved past her without breaking his stride. Ruby tensed, her body reacting to his intense heat as it briefly washed over her.

"I don't know how it got here. I would never dare cross Your Greatness."

As Drayvex reached the counter, he dragged a single claw against the cool metal. Sparks erupted where the tip made contact, and a high squeal pierced the air, setting her teeth on edge. That was when she noticed that the fingers on that hand were splattered black.

Ruby gripped the counter she leaned against. There was something about the way he moved, the overbearing awareness in each step, that reminded her of a panther closing in on a wounded prey. He was going for the kill.

"Where would I hide a human in here? W-wait. Don't kill me. I'm useful!"

The small creature was lifted off its feet. He dangled in mid-air, limbs flailing as though grabbed by an invisible pair of hands.

Drayvex made an impatient sound in his throat, a cross between a hiss and a snarl. "I know how she got here, worm. What did you *feed* her?"

Krick, who had been wrestling with the invisible force constricting his throat, stopped dead. "Feed, My Lord?" A look of confusion flitted across his features, as though he'd been asked a trick question and didn't know how to answer.

"And *don't* even *think* about *lying* to me," he growled, the helpless gurgles of the dangling demon becoming smaller with each intonation. "I *always* know. What. Did. You. Feed. Her?"

Krick's eyes rolled over to the counter, where the remainder of the creature she'd been fed still sat. Drayvex followed his gaze.

Ruby could stand by no longer. "Wait!" Her body reacted before she'd made a conscious decision. He couldn't make her the subject of his third-degree grilling *and* pretend that she wasn't in the room. It was one or the other.

She shot forward and slid between the pair, then realised that her presence was about as effective as a chocolate teapot. She brought her hands up, waving her palms in a gesture that said 'stop'.

Drayvex's eyes left the counter, and Ruby fought to hold fast as his withering gaze trained on her. The black pits that were his irises became streaked with ribbons of silver.

"Just stop. He was doing what I asked him to." She lowered her hands. "I was hungry, and he fed me, so leave him be." She was lying through her teeth. But surely, Drayvex would see reason. After all, the only part of him that would be affected by this was his ego. And there was plenty of that to go around.

He glared at her through narrowing eyes. She could almost see him picking her words apart, measuring their worth. Ruby glared back, her gaze locked on his, and tried to ignore the sound of Krick being choked in mid-air behind her. It made her think of the demon she'd crossed in the passage further back, the invisible force that had taken it out with such ease. Had that been Drayvex as well?

Drayvex's eyes were now more grey than black, struggling to hold on to the wisps of darkness that lingered at the edges.There was a thud from behind her, followed by gasping and coughing. "Fine," he said in a clipped tone. "On your head be it, then."

Ruby scowled. She wondered whether any of the demons here spoke to him in the same way that she did.

"Move." His arm jabbed out towards the door.

She considered telling him where to go. And as if he'd read her mind, his eyes darkened, daring her to try it. She decided not to push her luck.

The moment they left the room, Ruby was shoved straight through a different door. When it clicked behind them, she turned to face Drayvex. Tall and imposing in the restricted light, he was far too close for comfort. But then, there was nowhere else to go within the confines of what seemed to be a storage cupboard.

"Let me get this straight," Drayvex spat, his face inches from hers. "I don't care if you feel hard done by. I don't give a damn about your moral code, and I'm well aware that you'd rather be anywhere else but here."

As he brought up his hand, the speed with which he moved whipped loose strands of her hair around her face. He placed it on the wall behind her, making her feel even more pinned than before.

"I don't need your gratitude, and you're welcome to hate my guts in whatever form that may take." His eyes were a brilliant blood orange-red. The colour, her stunned mind threw at her, of a tropical sunset from a childhood holiday. He paused, taking a breath for the first time since they'd entered the cupboard. "But my point," he said, continuing in a calmer tone that looked like it required a great deal of effort, "is that you cannot just wander off as you please. Not here."

Ruby heard a grinding sound at her right ear and wondered if the wall was suffering. He was going to kill her. This time, surely, if only by accident.

"If I don't know where you are, then I can't protect you."

His words caught her off guard. They didn't match the aggressive verbal battering he was dealing. It almost sounded as though he'd been worried about her.

"Understand?"

Ruby met his gaze. "Right," she mumbled. "Sorry." She had no one to be worried about anymore. Her family was dead. She breathed in through her nose, sucking air into her lungs.

An overwhelming sadness rose up and engulfed her out of nowhere. She clenched her teeth, struggling to keep herself in check. Not here, she willed herself, blinking back tears. Not now. She pouted at him, deflecting her pain. Not in front of *him.*

She needn't have bothered. As he watched her, his red eyes paled, slipping towards that soft blue she'd seen most often in the first week they met. His expression was wary. For a heartless tyrant, he was oddly attuned to her emotions. If she didn't know better, Ruby would have mistaken his attitude problem for concern. But she wouldn't allow herself to fall for his tricks again. No, he wanted something from her. She just didn't know what yet.

"Ruby. I'm trying to keep you alive, for pity's sake."

He sounded sincere. Then again, he'd also sounded sincere as he'd pretended to be her friend and then went on to steal her necklace. "Why? What difference does it make?" It didn't make any sense. What more could she have that he wanted?

Drayvex didn't respond. He hesitated, a host of conflicting responses flickering across his face, before disappearing. It happened so fast that if she hadn't already been focused on him, she'd have blinked and missed it all. It was replaced by something unreadable. It wasn't like previous times, where she'd asked him a question and he'd refused her the answer out of spite. This time, his silence was vulnerable and guarded.

"Why?" He glared at her as though she was some kind of demon-killing snake. "Because I'm impulsive. And I always get what I want, even when it makes no damn sense!"

Ruby stared at him, lost for words. His tone was accusatory, and despite her earlier resolution not to let Drayvex get to her, his words prickled. How dare he hate her for *anything*? He was the one who'd ruined *her* life. She didn't asked to be saved, and yet, here she was, once again at his mercy.

"Well, if it's any consolation," she seethed, hearing the quiver in her voice, "I wish you hadn't bothered. In fact, if I'm such a burden to Your Lordship, maybe you should just mind your own damn business and stop saving me. At least I'd be with my family, and not stuck here with you, waiting for you to get bored and eat me." Drayvex was pulling no punches. Neither would she.

They glared at each other for what felt like a full minute, a staring contest between two equally stubborn players, until finally, Drayvex broke the silence.

"Okay," he snapped, making her jump. "Fine. You want to die?" He turned to the door and wrenched the handle down, shoving it open with one hand. It swung outward and hit the wall outside with a crack. *"There's* the door." He jabbed at the air, motioning towards the open doorway. "No one is stopping you."

Ruby stared at Drayvex, mesmerised, as the space around him seemed to ripple and distort. Wow, she thought, feeling oddly detached. Anger issues really didn't cover it.

"You wouldn't last five minutes out there without me, girl."

She looked up at him, gazing straight into his eyes. That sounded like a threat. Well, he didn't scare her. And two could play these games. She looked away, and without a second thought, headed towards the door.

She got there unhindered. Pausing for a moment at the threshold, she filled her lungs and then stepped out into the darkness beyond.

Eerie silence pressed at her from all sides. It reminded her of the room she'd woken in as a prisoner, captured by the demons who had wanted her dead. She hadn't known where she was. Now she knew better, and it didn't help one bit.

Ruby focused on her dim surroundings. A large flame was seated against the wall at the far end of the corridor, bright and unflickering. She would aim for that.

"Where the fuck are you going?"

She ignored him and fixed on the flame in the distance. She didn't want to live in the dark. The dark was cold and lonely.

"You're playing a dangerous game, you know." His velveteen voice echoed down the passageway, coming at her from several directions. "And puerile isn't your best look."

His tone was composed and aloof. He'd switched off on her, just like that. Now that she'd mentioned it, she *was* cold. And lonely.

"Neither is dead-girl."

Still taking shots. Did he honestly think that he could just snap his fingers and she'd jump on command? Well, he was in for a big disappointment. She would not bow to him. Not ever.

"Ruby."

Something in his voice made her falter, but it was the skittering sound to her immediate left that stopped her in her tracks.

She hadn't planned to die. But as she suddenly found herself faced with the very real possibility, she realised with a dull pang that she didn't care either way.

Ruby kept going, forcing her feet forward, one step after another. She couldn't stop here; she hadn't reached the light. Her heart hammered in her chest, pounded in her ears. Drayvex had given up on her, and now she was all alone.

She stopped. Not quite alone.

She strained her ears in the gloom. Animalistic movements sounded from the walls around her. Scratching, like claws on a hard surface. They came and went, circling her in disorienting movements. Coming from the right. Behind her. The left. Something was closing in.

Then a strange sensation overwhelmed her. Her head became heavy, weighted, and a soft warmth travelled up her spine. Ruby allowed her head to loll as her neck became weak. Her eyes rolled to the back of her head in a lazy motion. What had she just been doing? She couldn't remember. All she wanted now was to sleep.

Why, Ruby?

Ruby stopped fighting the warmth and gave in to sweet nothing.

Ruby woke with a start and shivered. She was cold. Yet, just moments ago, she had been warm.

She clenched her fist. Her palm filled with the soft material beneath her, and she wound her fingertips into it. Her eyes sprung open.

The corridor was gone. Blinking, she scanned the dim room and sucked in a breath of recognition. She was back where she had started.

Something moved in the corner of her eye. Ruby turned her head towards it, just in time to catch it again. A twitching bump under a sheet of material in the far corner. Something was in here with her.

The logical action would be to put some distance between her and the unknown bump. Instead, she moved towards it. She was sick of being the protected. The victim. Safe and sound, while everyone around her fought and died. Ruby Peyton was not a pushover, and she would take demon crap no longer.

Ruby reached for the thin sheet and ripped it back.

There was nothing there.

There was nothing there, but then, there suddenly was. Appearing out of nowhere with a tiny *pop*, it was none other than the mangled cat from Crichton.

Ruby dropped the sheet. She hadn't made the connection between the cat-thing and the demon world before. It had grinned at her on that first day, and later, she'd seen it around Drayvex. Not a cat, but a demon all along. It looked worse for wear. More so, she thought, than it had before.

The cat-demon stared up at her through large, yellow eyes, frozen in place. It was bigger up close than she remembered.

"What are you?" she mumbled, equally frozen in her defensive stance.

The creature bared its teeth and hissed, a wet rattle that dug under her skin, like nails on a chalkboard. Its fangs were splattered with a black, oily substance. "What am I?"

Ruby jumped as it answered her back, its voice no more than a loud, rasping whisper.

"What are *you*, tiny human? What is your purpose?" As it spoke to her in a bitter tone, it fell into a crouch, its bones jutting out and stretching the skin over them. "What makes you more worthy to serve our infernal Lord than Kaelor? Why should I starve while you get fat?" Then, to her dismay, it sprang for her.

It landed on her chest in a tangle of wiry fur and limbs. Ruby braced herself against the impact. "No." She grabbed the cat-demon around the middle with both hands. "More." The weight of it hitting her pushed her backwards, sending them both crashing to the ground. "Demon crap." Her back hit the floor and she lost her breath.

The creature thrashed in her grip, swiping out at her face with razor-sharp claws. Ruby brought up her arm in a reflex, protecting her eyes. Claws raked down her bare arm, drawing fresh blood.

Abandoning defence, she grabbed for its small throat with both hands. As they closed around it, she rolled over. "And I serve no one, demon."

As its back hit the floor, Ruby landed on top of it, pinning it under her weight. What was this creature's problem?

"Okay, okay. I give!" the demon mewled, stilling beneath her. "I'll talk." She stilled in turn. Talk?

"A deal they made, one Lord and one Master, no?"

Ruby stared at it. "What are you talking about?"

"The deal. Power for power. One little planet for a terrible treasure, long lost to the claws of the great one. An easy price paid right over your head. And now you're a castaway. A tickless clock with no place to called home. We're two of a kind, no?"

Her grip on the mangled creature beneath her slipped as its cryptic words span round and round in her head. A deal between a Lord and a Master. A planet for an unknown treasure.

"He sold your precious planet, human witch."

Ruby didn't move. Surely, it didn't mean Drayvex.

"You are nothing to him, just like I. And in time, he will cast you away,

292

just like I."

But he wouldn't. He couldn't.

The demon threw itself at her once again. But this time, as it hit her, it disintegrated into a cloud of black smoke—and swallowed her whole.

As the smoke filled her lungs, she choked. Panic lanced through her veins. Coughing, she ripped the silver lighter from her pocket and fumbled with the button, She couldn't breathe.

The lighter went pop. From within the angry, swirling maelstrom, a blue flame sprang to life. And then, as if possessed, the smoke was ripped from her and sucked into lighter.

Ruby's vision swam. Her face met the floor.

She woke with a start, with the sensation of something having been ripped away from her. She was cold, yet moments ago, she'd been warm. Wait—

Ruby stirred. She was lying on a rug of thick fur. She scanned the small room with bleary eyes, overcome by deja vu. Hadn't she just been through this? Maybe she was still dreaming, stuck in a recurring nightmare.

A sharp sting lanced along the top of her arm. She looked down and blinked. Three fresh scratch marks lay on the soft skin of her underarm. Not a dream.

Ruby pulled her arm close and studied the marks. They flashed, a single pulse of thin red light. She frowned, scrubbing her eyes, and studied them again. What was that?

Ruby looked up and searched for the cat, ready to give it a piece of her mind. Instead, she found Drayvex.

As her eyes fell upon the demon across the room, everything clicked into place. Memories, and the loaded revelation they carried, returned with a vengeance. It couldn't be true. Please, god, don't let it be true.

Drayvex was on the far side of the small room. His moody grey eyes were fixed on the view from the window, the veil having been pulled back, and as she approached him with soft steps, they slid over to her.

"Why did you do it?" Her voice was calm, the polar opposite of how she felt inside. He could still deny it. And she would still believe him. Even now.

Ruby watched him lean beside the window, his arms folded, unmoving. A tangled surge of emotions rose up within her. She bit the inside of her cheek, stifling the screams that wanted to burst out of her.

Drayvex watched her in return, his lack of response and perfect still infuriating her further. When he finally raised an eyebrow in a silent question, there was an uncharacteristic weariness to his inscrutable gaze.

She couldn't take anymore. "Why?" she moaned, feeling something inside her fracture. Deny it.

Annoyance flashed across his features, breaking the stony set of his face. "Why what?" he snapped, unfolding his arms and straightening himself in one blurry movement. "I don't read minds, so you'll have to be a touch more specific."

Ruby's heart pounded in double time. She sucked in breath after breath, a horrible sense of overwhelm creeping in through the cracks in her mind.

"Unless, of course, you mean why did I pluck you from the claws of death, *again,* when you're so determined to become a demon's lunch?" Always smug. "In which case, let me get back to you!"

She felt out of control. "Sell." Breath. "My." Breath. "World."

Drayvex tensed, stopping short of whatever he had been about to say. His features smoothed, ashen eyes holding her in a look that would have, under different circumstances, made her blood run cold in fear of what was coming next.

It was his fault. She had caught him off guard, and she could see it in his eyes. He had traded the Earth to a monster. He was the devil in her midst.

Suddenly, time skipped.

Ruby didn't know how it had happened. She had no recollection of moving, and yet, she was at the window, nose to nose with Drayvex.

He was holding her in a firm grip, his hands on either side just below her shoulders. His lips were moving, but she couldn't hear his voice.

She had taught herself how to lip read, but her brain wouldn't work. And she couldn't breathe. Her lungs were full. She couldn't breathe out. Was she dying?

"—*uby!*" A strong, commanding voice. A bossy voice. "Hey. Focus."

On what?

"Stop it, Ruby. You need to calm down."

This wasn't happening.

"Just take it easy. *Breathe.* Come back to me."

God, she was dying. With great effort, Ruby dragged in breath after breath, getting precious little of its goodness.

"Trust me. You don't want me to come in there."

What? Her chest ached as it started to relax. She couldn't remember the last time she'd had an attack like this.

Drayvex was watching her, his eyes pale and narrowed. He had the air of someone who was watching cracks spreading across a broken glass, waiting for the moment when the whole thing would shatter and surrender.

Ruby glared at him with tear-rimmed eyes. If she was a broken glass, it was because he himself had broken her.

"Welcome back," he muttered, his tone dry. He loosened his warm clamp around her arms, allowing normal blood flow to resume.

She shrugged him off, breaking his remaining hold in a rough motion. "Don't touch me!" she spat, panting from the emotional turmoil raging inside her. Traitor. Backstabber.

Drayvex stilled, neither giving space nor taking it. The points of his teeth extended in the stillness, the only part of him that moved as the two of them faced off.

She was angry with him, and she knew that was a dangerous place for her to be. Just looking at him made her want to punch his stupid face. She would probably lose her hand trying. But she was also angry with herself. After all, she should have realised that his loyalties lay with his own kind. She just hadn't wanted to see it.

"Where did you hear that?" Drayvex's voice was low, careful.

He really was a piece of work. "That's none of your business. You'd have to torture me to make me talk. That's what you lot do, isn't it?"

Drayvex rolled his eyes in an impatient gesture. "You're being ridiculous," he said, his voice rising to match her volume. "Why would I pluck you from one hellhole just to torture you on another?"

"Oh, I'm being ridiculous? You sell my home, my planet, like it's demon currency in your pocket. You wait until everyone I love is dead, then take me against my will and hold me captive on a planet that wants to eat me, under the dubious guise of keeping me safe. But *I'm* being ridiculous?"

An exasperated sound erupted from his throat, a mingle between a growl and a snarl. He darted forward, appearing in front of her in a blink.

Ruby stumbled backwards, attempting to maintain the distance between them. His touch caused more problems than it solved.

"In case you hadn't noticed," Drayvex remarked, sarcasm creeping into his voice, "I'm a demon." He placed a clawed hand against the wall beside him, and their black curves were longer than she'd seen them in a while. Almost as long as the night he'd taken her back from the tower where she had been held captive.

"Selfish is our default setting. So I apologise if I haven't lived up to your unrealistic, and frankly, naive expectations."

'Save yourself. Just leave me here.'

'Quick, lock the doors. There are things out there that are eating people.'

'There's no point ... in us both dying ... here.'

'Ruby, wake up. We need to kill it!'

'It might ... chase you. But if you're lucky, it will just ... go for me.'

Her knees buckled. She began to sink to the floor, and instinctively, she grabbed for Drayvex in a hopeless attempt to keep herself upright. She missed.

Drayvex crossed the small gap between them, a space that a moment ago had felt barely sufficient, but was now more of a gaping chasm, grabbing her as she descended.

Ruby had expected, if anything, an arm. But as she met the floor, she realised that he had, in fact, caught and dropped down with her. As she felt the hard floor beneath them, a vague symbolism nagged her in her broken state of mind. Rock bottom.

As these words threw themselves at her like a lingering echo, she did something that she'd never allowed herself to do around another living being. She fell apart.

She didn't know that it was possible to cry for so long and still feel unsatisfied. What was the point then, if not to purge the pain? She didn't know.

Ruby understood that in reality, she was alone. But as she worked through the ghosts that haunted her, the losses that had made her bleed, Drayvex held her; not attempting to comfort or console, just being, in a way that made her feel like she was far from alone.

As time passed and her mind began to clear, she came to a startling conclusion. If she didn't put herself back together, they were going to be here for a very long time.

With effort, Ruby scraped together what was left of her strength, and tested her weight with it. She shifted, changing her position. Then, inch by inch, she peeled herself away from Drayvex.

Drayvex hadn't moved or spoken for some time, which bothered her more than she thought it should. After all, the pretence was gone. She could no longer doubt the cold hard facts that she'd somehow ignored up until now. They were enemies. Predator and prey. Killer and the mark. She could see that now. And the fact that she'd allowed herself to fall apart on him of all people was mortifying. Yet despite that, he hadn't pulled away. Drayvex had embraced her, as though it was the most normal thing in the world.

"Why did I do it?"

Ruby started, the sound of his voice unfamiliar after the lengthy period of silence. As his warm breath stirred the fine hairs on the top of her head, his exhale almost sounded like a laugh. Bewildered, she looked up.

Drayvex's eyes were that beautiful, infrequent shade, a mingled merging of purple and blue. He almost looked like a different person, and she found herself marvelling at this. A long way from the sinister, crimson-eyed demon that had so callously condemned an entire species to death at the hands of a maniac.

She squirmed, shaking her head as she realised that she was once again letting him get under her skin, inside her head. She hated him. Both versions of him. Didn't she?

He watched her with a soft, almost curious gaze. Then he raised his hand and brought it up towards her face.

Ruby tensed, unsure of his intentions.

He held back just short of touching her, a now modest claw hovering just out of contact. "I went there to kill him, you know. To make him pay for daring to lay his fat fingers on you. I wanted to make him *suffer*."

His conversational tone caught her off guard. But despite the casual mention of murder, there was a weight to his words that held her in place.

Drayvex brushed a few strands of hair from her cheek, damp and stuck to her skin where her tears had dried, before continuing down the side of her face to her chin. His touch was light, the wings of a butterfly. But still, it left a burning trail in its wake, and despite herself, she found herself in equal parts horror-struck and mesmerised by his bare confession.

"But Saydor bargained for his worthless life, and his offer was worth far more than I could have imagined. The end that justifies any imaginable means."

Drayvex dropped his hand. As he made a move to rise, Ruby pulled away. She could take a hint. She shuffled backwards, her head spinning.

Instead, though, she was secured with a strong pair of hands, pulling her up onto her feet. She glanced at him sideways, swaying on her feet as she reeled at the simple act of compassion amid this emotional chaos. What was going on?

"When I first took the throne, I also acquired my father's flaming shit heaps." She hadn't heard him move, but Drayvex was stood at the window. As he spoke, he gazed out across the red desert, a faraway look in eyes.

Ruby's mind faltered. The word father sounded odd coming from Drayvex's mouth. She hadn't even considered that Drayvex would have a family.

"I offered a truce to his enemies—*my* enemies. A fragile accord between two species needlessly at war with demons. The Nagur accepted the deal." He paused, his claws inching down, curving in slow motion as he spoke.

298

"The Fae spat on such an offer, and in turn, sealed their fate with blood."

She stood rooted to the spot, her mind reeling.

"Selling the Earth to that fool was easy. Watching you suffer the consequences of that deal …" His eyes slid from the view outside to where she stood a few feet away. "It should have been child's play."

Ruby stared at the demon who had stolen her necklace, then given it back. Who had abandoned her on a demon-infested planet, then removed her against her will. Did she blame him for her mother's death? For Sandra's?

She licked her lips. He hadn't killed them with his own hands, but at the very least, he was indirectly responsible for their death. Her feelings towards Drayvex were far from simple.

"But the fact is," he concluded, his face compelling in its serious composure, "it's not." It was a confession. A grudging admission, not unlike that of an addict with a crippling habit. But it tugged at her all the same.

Breathing out, she crept over towards the window where he stood.

"I'll make you a deal," he said.

Back to business. Ruby stared at him, distracted by his ever-changing demeanour. "What deal?"

"I can't raise the dead." Drayvex turned towards her as she approached, his form dark and imposing against the minimal light at his back. "But I *can* recall the demons on Earth, destroy Saydor and reclaim your planet."

His black tongue slid down the length of a fang and rested on its point. "And I'll make it look easy."

She was stunned. "And what will that cost me?"

A small smile pulled at the corners of his mouth. "Stay alive," he said, a reckless gleam in his eyes. "At all costs."

Chapter 29

*I*t had been so subtle that he hadn't felt the change.

Drayvex studied the girl propped against the wall on the other side of the room, watching as she fiddled with her wrist in absent gestures. One moment he had been curbing Ruby's hysterics—and he had been sure that in his previous interest of seeing how far a small human girl could bend before snapping in two, that he had bent her too far—the next, he was bending alongside her.

He flexed his muscles, working out the restlessness that lingered in his blood. It was almost like being under attack from the inside. It shouldn't have bothered him, but it did. And her pain latched onto the to the black rotten heart he knew he possessed, but aside from providing a convenient bullseye for his enemies, had never actually served a purpose. It was dozens of aggravating splinters lodged in his mind, and he didn't like it.

He couldn't ignore it. He couldn't control it.

Ruby wasn't paying him any attention. Her fingers wandered in aimless spirals, her eyes softly glazed with a faraway look that was both calm and wild at the same time.

This is the calm before the storm.

Drayvex ignored the rational voice in his head. Rational wasn't his forte these days.

A maelstrom entirely of your own making. And you were so close. Almost close enough to crush the fae bitch's throat in your bare hand from where you stand.

He ran his tongue along the tops of his fangs, his agitation and blackening mood sharpening their tips. Maelstrom or not, he could list a hundred different tortures that were all preferable to watching Ruby break in two.

He would do whatever it took to make this right. And if that involved taking on Saydor, slaughtering a third of his kind and becoming saviour of a people he regularly dined on, then so be it. That was what he would do.

Ruby looked up, her green eyes finding him from across the room.

Drayvex gazed back, his mouth set in sullen acceptance. Pity that meant stepping down from the deal of the century.

As he approached, she rose to her feet and folded her arms. The stubborn set to her jaw did not escape his notice, and as she stared at him, her eyes were guarded. Almost as though she was bracing herself for something unpleasant.

Drayvex folded his own arms, flicking out a serpentine tongue with an impatient snap. How long would she feel this way towards him? Did she think he was bluffing? "What is it now?" he asked.

Steeling himself in turn, he put the mithering thoughts to the back of his mind. Her opinions of him were of no relevance to anything. Letting such pointless things fill his head would only slow him down.

"I want to help," she said.

He should have seen it coming. After all, it made sense that she of all people would want to stick her nose right in the thick of it. "Absolutely not. Have you lost your bloody mind?"

"This is *my* home. Surely, I should help you save it."

Ruby was by no means stupid. She was, however, driven by impulse, and blinded by her single-minded focus. Her late tangles with demons had taught her nothing. *Nothing.*

"You owe me that much," she added.

Drayvex paused, the retort he had ready skittering away. He unfolded his arms, marvelling at the word that had rolled so easily off her tongue. Even if he did *owe* her—and he still wasn't unduly convinced that he could admit such a thing to himself, let alone to her—agreeing to take her with him to fight Saydor would be the strategic equivalent of sticking his head in a large blender. It would do neither of them any good.

A multitude of responses flashed through his mind, each progressively less restrained. He sighed. "I don't need, or want your help," is what he settled for. "You'll just get in my way." Allowing her to make him soft was not going to get things done. Feeding that rebellious streak that governed her thoughts was only going to get her killed.

Ruby's face fell. Then she composed herself and flashed him a disapproving look. "You don't know that."

Drayvex scowled at her. *Oh, I do,* he demurred, the urge to knock some sense into her testing what was left of his self-control. *You're doing it right now.*

He reached out to grab her wrist, more out of habit than anything else, and recoiled as a sharp current lanced up his arm.

Ruby turned back to face him, an uneasiness reflected in her widening eyes.

Drayvex bore into her, motionless, his demon form bristling just under the surface of a skin that no longer wanted to contain him. His fangs extended, inching down.

"What's wrong?"

Her voice was the blade of a knife. As it sliced through his darkening disposition, it called to what was left of reason.

"Drayvex?" Ruby didn't move, her posture unchanging. Her eyes told a different story. They told him that putting an entire army between them wouldn't be enough.

"Show me your hand," he muttered, his voice possessing a soft, growling undercurrent. His gaze fell to that arm. His fingers twitched, mouth slick with the venom that oozed from the points of his teeth. *Who have you been making friends with, Ruby Red?*

Ruby sucked in a breath and looked down at her closed fist. After a pause, she brought it up and opened it. "It's this."

It wasn't a question. The silver chain sitting on her palm was no ordinary piece of jewellery. Bearing both the mark of the biggest demon-hunting guild in existence *and* traces of molten core in the metal, there was no doubt about it: it was a ward. And one that only membership could buy.

"Where did you get it?" he asked, managing to keep the stress his body was under out of his voice. Throwing accusations would get them nowhere. Besides, if she chose to lie to him, he would know.

Or maybe she's about to screw you from behind. Revenge is the best form of therapy. You would know.

Drayvex ignored the voice. He wanted to give her the benefit of the doubt.

Ruby didn't look surprised. In fact, a new level of understanding was filling her gaze. She fiddled with the charms, suddenly far away. "This belonged to my best friend, Sandra. She gave it to me before she was killed." Her voice was soft as a whisper. "She told me to wear it, always." Ruby's fingers froze as she looked up at him.

Drayvex tilted his head, studying her as she spoke. Her posture was loose, her face relaxed and unchanging. He straightened, folding his arms once more and finally, allowed some of the tension to ebb from his charged body. Far be it for him to blow things out of proportion. Her acquisition of it, at the very least, was pure. And really, would the vânători give a girl who could activate demonic weaponry with her blood the key to their kingdom? It was unlikely.

"Does it hurt?"

So, she knew what it was then. Ruby wasn't a total space cadet. He stared down at her, reprocessing her words. "Hurt?"

Ruby licked her lips, her mouth opening long before the words came out. "I had a run-in with a demon. I couldn't be sure at the time, but now I know. It was the bracelet that protected me."

Drayvex listened to her steady human heartbeat.

"Does it hurt much?" she asked, echoing her previous question. "I was trying to fix it, but I can hold off."

He stared at Ruby for a moment, caught in some form of trance. She was standing on a demon planet, with no defences and no choices, hostage of a

Demon Lord with a long history of violence, and she was worried about *him?*

Ruby dropped her gaze to the ward wrapped loosely around her hand and closed her fingers around it.

Drayvex reached out and grabbed Ruby by her upper arm. She jumped as his hand curled around her and stared up into his eyes. "No, Ruby," he said, speaking with slow, uneasy precision. "Fix it." For pity's sake, did she not consider that she may need protection from him? And surely, if she blamed him for the death of her people, then she would *want* to hurt him.

He sighed, and reached into his pocket, plucking out the battered object he'd taken from her. Holding it flat on his palm, he held out towards her. "The key is blood." Your blood, to be precise. But such details would be little more than a burden. "You have to feed it."

Ruby blinked up at him, her green eyes clouded with something that looked a lot like doubt. "I—really?"

It caught him off guard. Again with the doubt. At what, his intentions? He scowled, and as she took the shadow lantern from his outstretched hand, he turned away from her.

"Okay. I can work with that," she mumbled. She wasn't talking to him.

Ruby paused, the bracelet tinkling in her hand, before adding, "I found a safe haven in Crichton. A demon-free zone that I can hide in."

Drayvex rolled his eyes. Knowing he was taking the bait, he turned back to face her. "What the Hell are you talking about now?"

Her posture had changed. She almost seemed to be pleading with him. "The park in Crichton has an anti-demon barrier. You could check it out if you don't believe me."

He narrowed his eyes at the girl. Magic? In that dump?

"Please, Drayvex, just humour me. You'll see."

Humour her? That was a good one.

"Please?"

Drayvex closed his eyes. Unbelievable.

*

Drayvex slipped through the shell of Crichton village, passing a number of lowlife demons in its backstreets. If Saydor didn't want to be found, then one thousand minions equipped with one thousand fine-toothed combs would not drag him out of hiding.

The Demon Master's talent for disappearing was, as far as Drayvex was concerned, the way he had managed to survive these past couple of centuries without being squashed. Despite this, Drayvex wasn't concerned. He didn't plan on wasting his time and resources on hunting the swine down. This time, Saydor was going to come to him.

The demons he passed were scavengers, parasites with no real abilities of their own. They relied on the rejects of better predators in order to stay alive.

A pack looked up as he passed. They dropped their findings and scattered, his footsteps sending them scuttling to the safety of the shadows. Vermin. He spat at them in disgust. He had thought about wiping out such creatures many times before. A quick and brutal cull for the sake of demonkind. Except they made good cannon fodder and were at his disposal in large quantities. This, he grudgingly had to admit, was useful.

The sky raged in a battle of its own as excess power bled out from the portal, rising to create vivid displays of marbled colour. The closer he got to the portal, the more he felt its pull. It was strong, there was no doubt about that. Ready to bear the brunt of a bloodthirsty horde.

Drayvex flexed his claws, ignoring the pull. Here he was, not only about to take them all on at the same time, but about to dismantle his highly fortuitous deal and save the Earth from a plague of his own making. He had to admit, he hadn't seen that one coming.

The plan was simple, but by no means perfect. For one, it left room for variables in a way that under normal circumstances, he would never allow. It also relied heavily on Saydor's blind spot: his inability to ignore a challenge. Regardless, Drayvex would keep killing until he got his own way.

As Drayvex approached the unnatural splattering of green, smack in the middle of the decimated village, he decided that it had to be Ruby's 'magical park.' He stood at the gates, regarding the stubborn glut of plant life inside with a healthy side of scepticism. It wasn't that he didn't believe her. After all, she would have nothing to gain by making such drivel up. But he couldn't just take her word for it either. He also preferred to do his own dirty work. Question everything.

Drayvex surveyed its edges, doing a full circle of the grounds, before returning to the gates. Why, he supposed, was the greenery *inside* the park unscathed, when the outside had been reduced to rubble and ash? Intuition on fire, he lifted the gate's latch and gave the metal a shove. It swung open wide. He lifted a heavy boot and kicked out at the space, testing for resistance. His foot hit a barrier.

The moment he connected, he felt its sheer power; a power that pulsed through him with an angry tenacity. It was power in its rawest form, but not one that he could utilise. He took a step back, putting some distance between himself and the barrier.

As he brought up his hands, Drayvex had already formed a flaming sphere in each of his palms. "Let's see what you're made of, then," he murmured, speaking to the strange power. How much of a battering could it take?

Without delay, he pelted the barrier with one fireball after another, driving a barrage between the open gates. The flaming orbs exploded against nothing, darkening in gradient with his increasing power level.

Not one broke through.

Drayvex stopped. He picked up a small stone from the ground and flicked it into the air, catching it in a fist as it fell. Then he tossed it through the gates.

The stone sailed straight through. He'd known it would. He laughed out loud, struck by the sheer stupidity of the situation. It was an anti-demon barrier, and it was created by none other than the Warrior Fae.

Saydor's bargaining chip had been right under his nose this entire time.

His grin widened, the teeth in his mouth lengthening as his form started to slip. Here he was, against his own best interests, about to sacrifice his one lead on a job he'd been trying to finish for a century, for the sake of one human girl. This for no other reason than serving *her* best interests over his was apparently the 'right' thing to do. And in return for this seemingly selfless act, Ruby had come up trumps for him.

Turning away from the park and its secrets, he started back for the portal, using an unnecessarily slow pace to think.

He didn't need Saydor. He didn't have to choose between Ruby and his own personal vendetta. And the Earth could continue to thrive in all its depraved glory. He *could* have it all. Ironically, just not in the way he had conspired to take it.

Suddenly impatient, he broke into a burst of speed. Ruby was right. She would be safer in that park than anywhere. It was the demon apocalypse that she needed protecting from, and if he couldn't break through, then nothing would.

As for Saydor, he would make that treacherous fool wish he'd never existed.

"This is how it's going go."

Ruby gasped as Drayvex spoke from behind her, snapping her out of her daydream. Breathless, she let go of the park gate and span to face him. His eyes were hard. She watched them as he spoke. They remained a charcoal black.

"You are going to stay where I put you. You will not leave this area under any circumstances. You will not defy me, and this time, you will do as you're bloody well told, or so help me, you will regret ever asking me for *anything*."

She hadn't realised that she was leaning away from him until Drayvex tugged her back upright, reacting with edgy impatience to the subconscious gesture.

"I will deal with Saydor," he continued, "and then I will come back for you. Are we clear?"

As Ruby tugged against him with the jerk of a shoulder, he retracted his grip. She rubbed the top of her arm. "I get it," she flared, feeling testy. "Stay put. Believe it or not, I do have a brain in my head."

Her gripe earned her not just a black look, but a Demon Lord special.

Ruby threaded her fingers through her hair, her body wired and restless.

There was nothing simple about what she felt for Drayvex at this point. She was angry with him, and that wasn't going to go away any time soon. Directly or indirectly, he'd taken from her the two people she loved most on this Earth, and she didn't know how to forgive him for that. But—

"A brain. Debatable."

—never in her wildest imaginings had she expected him to take his actions *back*. The lengths he was prepared to go to in order to make things right were, well … staggering.

As Ruby's focus lingered on the demon before her, he caught her gaze. His eyes narrowed the smallest amount, picking her apart with unconcealed suspicion. Drayvex was hard and soft; both selfish and highly perceptive of her every movement. A ruthless, despicable killer, about to wage war on his own kind to take back the Earth in her name.

As he sneered at her lack of response, he flashed his teeth. "Are we done here? Good. Go."

If Drayvex's reaction to the bracelet had taught her anything, it was that not even he was invincible. There was every chance that he would walk away and not return for her. Outnumbered, out-powered. She shouldn't care either way. She'd already lost her mum and her best friend. They'd put her first and died for their troubles.

Now, Drayvex was doing the same. And what shocked her most of all was that the thought of losing him on top of everything else was almost as difficult to contemplate as losing them all over again. She had no idea how to deal with that.

"Something on your mind?" It was an impatient drawl that didn't sound interested in the slightest. But Ruby had learnt to watch his eyes. For the first time since he'd come back from the park, they sparked with blue steel.

Ruby tore her eyes away from him. "No. Nothing." She couldn't. She was unravelling, and she had no idea how to keep it together. "I'm ready now." Her voice was hollow. Holding her breath, she turned and marched through the park gates.

She counted to five in her head before she turned back to face him. She was being irrational. And rude. Sighing, she spun back towards him.

"Drayvex, I ..."
Gone.

Chapter 30

*D*rayvex arrived at the vast, muddy expanse, once a big, useless hole on the edge of a village, now the churned up pit that would serve as planet Earth's smallest battleground. He stood at its edge, taking in the fledgeling chaos attempting to get to its feet. It was like watching a newborn carver trying to gain control of its limbs. Sure, it was pathetic now. But soon, it would grow to be a big, strong killer, a force to be reckoned with. It would not get that chance.

The sky hung in the perfect balance of darkness and light, with the portal's blood red glow competing with the dusk in a battle for space. That battle would be short-lived. Soon, light would give way to darkness, as it always did, and then the real fun would begin.

Drayvex slipped through the throng of his fickle subjects, preparing himself for their mass slaughter. Drawing Saydor out of his cosy little pit was the only thing that mattered at this point; a high body count would be merely a bonus. These demons were all dispensable. *All* on borrowed time.

The hordes weren't immediately aware of his presence. But as the first to notice him lingered on his form, Drayvex tasted the change in the atmosphere and waited with an expectant still. It was slow at first; a turning of heads, picking up speed in a domino effect.

He saw the familiar set of reactions play out across hundreds of faces, years of ingrained fear kicking in. Next was the hatred and animosity he inspired in their weak, festering hearts, the bitter resentment as they paid the grudging respect his presence demanded of them.

Drayvex had always had an extreme effect on those around him. It was as though no one could decide if their fear or their hatred took precedence. Those that chose the first would, under normal circumstances, live to serve another day. Those that challenged him lived only to see their heads rolling away from their bodies. It was that simple.

He stopped in the centre of the stretching horde, overseeing the sea of demons who bowed in a wavelike ripple en masse. Today, they seemed to have decided, was a bad day to die. Ironically, not one of them would live to see another.

The brute to his immediate right chose the latter. It glared at him in a witless display of defiance, the self-satisfied smirk on its face saying that it was beyond such trivial matters.

Drayvex felt his fangs lengthen and point within the confines of his dual form, and with that, a welcome pressure building inside him. Throughout his reign, there had been many a fool deeming themselves on his level. They were all dead.

His claws extended and curved in a passive-aggressive display. They were yet to figure it out. Alone, they were weak. United by their petty desires, they were ... well. Less weak.

Then again, they'd had no obvious reason to all fight for the same cause, until now. He was about to give them one. He was about to put his foot through the hornets nest.

When the demon strode towards him, Drayvex was more than ready. Thank fuck for you, he thought with vicious anticipation. Scumstains like you make excellent examples.

"My Lord. What is your—?"

He slashed out at the demon's exposed throat, meeting the flesh in a blur of darkness. He sliced straight through to bone with a crack. A jet of dark liquid spurted from the gash, erupting like an angry volcano. Drayvex artfully dodged the stream.

The impacted bone fractured, spine splintering like wood. As his claws sliced through on the other side, he snatched the head from the air, grabbing it before it could hit the ground.

Drayvex held it, dripping at his side. The flailing carcass crumpled at his feet, falling into an expanding pool. "Those of you who wish to keep their heads," he snarled, eyeballing the agitated walls of converging demons, "leave. Now."

Commanding the entire space around him, he grew, shedding the remnants of his human attributes as a snake would discard an old skin. Flesh, black and gleaming. A pair of twisting horns in their familiar place on his head. Tail growing in sync.

Raising the severed head, Drayvex sneered with dripping fangs. He wondered what Ruby would think of him now, when the outside matched the inside. She would be unable to deny it. Unable to pin him down with her selfless ideas and false expectations, because he wasn't remotely human. He was pure darkness, a devouring abyss. And her light would never reach the bottom.

Darkness and light never truly touched. They created shadows when they tried, and this shadow-stained world was proof of their efforts. Such a byproduct was neither darkness nor light, but both. Was that what had happened when his goals had aligned with hers?

The loudest sound in the vicinity was the splatter of blood on the soft ground, dripping from the gaping O of the neck. A clear space of five feet had formed in a circle around him, a space that he knew was about to implode. These demons had *all* screwed him over. They didn't need more than a handful of brain cells to know that they were doomed, and now, they had nothing to lose.

"Those of you who remain loyal to Saydor," Drayvex said as he dropped the head. The moment it hit the floor, he brought his foot down hard and fast. The head exploded with considerable force, propelling chunks of brain matter and shards of skull in all directions. "Will be dealt with accordingly."

It took five seconds for the crowds of demons that outnumbered him in ludicrous proportions to respond. As the sixth second passed, the stunned silence crescendoed, and the demons around him descended into a riotous frenzy.

The four demons that were first to step up to die lunged for him in unison, teeth and claws extended in a blind attempt to pierce something vital.

Drayvex released the pent up power he'd worked up throughout his violent display. The blast hit them in the chest. Their screams lingered on the breeze, barely outliving them as their forms disintegrated from the force. It continued beyond the four in a ripple effect, hitting the first two rows. Demons dropped like flies.

"Saydor is responsible for your pathetic deaths," he thundered, taking advantage of the uneasy hush. "That mongrel is watching you die, concealing his worthless hide with your corpses."

Drayvex spat at the ground, a black hissing glob that sank through the mud and left a small crater at his feet. *"Hiding."* The Demon Master would be close to the portal. He was sure of it. If Saydor had no interest in proving his worth, however—which if he thought with his brain and not his ego would be an obvious decision—then there really was no winning this.

The beasts he bated charged en masse, and as the solid wall of demons came within striking distance, Drayvex span. He extended his claws outwards, creating a lethal twister. It caught them off guard. The sheer number of eager bodies rushing inward worked in his favour.

The demons collided with each other, and having nowhere to go but forward in such a small space, the momentum of those behind pushed them into his blades. Drayvex sent pieces flying, hacking off large chunks in a semi-solid spray. Bodies, both whole and holey, lay sprawled across the vicinity, piling up in an already less than modest display.

Those closest, now looking worse for wear, struggled to disentangle themselves and take another shot.

Taking advantage of the reprieve, he stopped and focused. Then he proceeded to split his soul into two.

Filenos, and its many variations, was a tricky process that required a certain amount of skill. For those who could, the process of splitting one's 'soul' provided countless advantages. For most, the risks outweighed the rewards. But for Drayvex, it merely took concentration.

Moments later, one half of his black, shimmering consciousness rose to his call. The vapour slipped through the air, zoning in on the demon he'd marked for weaponised chaos.

The beast towered over the rioting masses, but as Drayvex slipped in through its mouth, it surrendered to his power. Drayvex took the reigns.

The annihilation that followed was swift and brutal. Despite this, there were always more to replace the dead. Soon, they would all be standing on bodies.

As he controlled the two separate halves of himself with adept concentration, he wondered what was going through Saydor's mind. They both knew that Drayvex could do this for weeks. Saydor wouldn't know what had changed, or why. What he would know, however, was that the deal between them was null and void. At worst, Drayvex would be a large and annoying thorn in his side. At best—

"My Lord." A slick voice oozed like a purulent sore. "I'm truly flattered that you would go to all this trouble to find me."

*

The ember sky burned above her head, despite the growing darkness. Its glow threw a marbled effect over the grass and plant life, giving them a coppery hue that was almost exotic.

As Ruby stood within the softly burning landscape, it was easy to imagine that she was back on Vekrodus. Except this was Earth, *her* home; and it was the end of the world.

She gazed out across the lake, lost in her own maddening thoughts. Once again, she was trapped in solitude. The more she allowed her thoughts to wander, the wider the yawning pit in her chest grew. Her mother would have known what to do.

Ruby checked her watch and wove her fingers through her hair. Forty-five minutes had passed since Drayvex had left. Five since she'd last checked. She clenched her fist against her scalp. Another lap of the lake might help.

She made it to the far side of the park and sunk down to the water's edge. Ruby had genuinely not known what she would do once she'd convinced him to bring her back. Maybe that was how she had gotten away with it.

Now that she was here, she was no better off. She couldn't remember ever feeling so useless.

Her hand stroked the soft grass, powdering the lake's surface with the disturbed grains of earth. Drayvex was fighting to reclaim the Earth, while she moped in the park. He'd ordered her to stay put because she was a liability. Anything she could do to help him would probably result in her death. In that instance, Drayvex would almost certainly abandon Earth for good, leaving the rest of humanity to die along with her. He certainly wasn't doing this out of the goodness of his heart.

Ruby dragged her fingers through the water, creating little trails that disappeared almost immediately. The girl in the water was barely recognisable. She stared back from behind the dark circles under her eyes and the corpse-like pallor of her skin. She brushed her face, smoothing one finger underneath a puffy eye. She looked ill. And although this came as no surprise, it did nothing to assuage that useless feeling eating away at her.

Punching out at the water, she left the rippling girl behind her and kept moving.

She'd taken but a few steps from the lake, when she stopped in her tracks. Ruby strained her ears. A soft whispering floated around her on the gentle breeze, warm and lyrical. Beautiful. The language was like nothing she'd ever heard.

It was coming from the lake.

Barely aware of what she was doing, she shuffled back over to the water's edge. She looked left and right, scanning across the vast surface to the far side; but there was no one else in sight.

The whispering repeated, insistent. Ruby looked down. The surface of the water rippled and stilled.

The sky flared in the water, bright and then dim, the orange haze flickering like a dying light bulb. Ruby jumped, her gaze shooting to the sky. What was that?

She looked behind her towards the tall metal gates and shook her head. The park was her own personal, impenetrable haven. Nothing could get inside. She knew this. But thinking these things made her sick to her stomach.

Sandra had gone out of her way to protect her, gaining debilitating wounds that had got her killed. Her mother had died the same way. She had tried to protect her daughter and paid with her life.

Ruby's face glowed. A clammy heat, both hot and cold, spread across her face. The backs of her eyes prickled, causing little dots to swim at the edges of her vision. She dropped her head and sucked in lungfuls of air, trying clear her head. They were dead because she was too slow. Too weak. Her knees buckled, and she dropped down onto the grass. Drayvex was out there, putting himself between her and the demons hellbent on destroying humanity. It was happening all over again.

She hadn't even spared him a final glance.

Ruby's gaze slid towards the gates. She should think of herself. Be content in that she, at least, would survive this nightmare. It would be what her mum would want. She certainly hadn't had anything good to say about Drayvex.

Heaving herself to her feet, she dragged herself towards the park entrance and rested her head against the cool metal. She wrapped her hands around the bars, cherishing her last moment of safety. Sorry, Mum, she prayed. Forgive me.

Drayvex was many things. A liar, a thief. Killer. *Demon*. He probably didn't even need her help. After all, there was a reason that he commanded the entire demon race. But she would not let him die for her today.

As she stepped out of the park, Ruby knew that she was taking her life in her hands. She had no plan, and no idea where Drayvex had gone after they parted ways. What she did have was a gut feeling. That yellow bastard had taken the stone and its power for himself. And he would be all the stronger for it.

As she wandered further from the safety of the park, she realised that she needn't have worried about the demons in Crichton. The streets were deserted, and bad omen or not, Ruby was grateful.

The red beam was back in the sky. It was coming from the old construction site, the place where Drayvex had first introduced her to his world. Her mixed memories of that long night came seeping back as the red beam got bigger and stronger. What would she find waiting there tonight? She'd never been so unprepared for anything in her life.

Ruby fingered the small charms in her hand, taking comfort from the bracelet's weight on her palm. She'd tried to fix it, and failed. It was a shame, because she couldn't have really used it.

Maybe Sandra's dad would come to her aid. Having experienced demon hunters to back you up in a fight would surely swing any battle in your favour. She chewed on her lip, breaking the skin. But then, the demon hunters would almost certainly refuse to discriminate. They would want both Saydor *and* Drayvex.

Ruby crested the last hill, becoming increasingly aware of her stinging arm. Curse that demon cat. She tried not to scratch at it.

As she reaching the edge of the muddy site, she looked down from the top of the peak, and paled. It was a sobering sight.

There was a sea of demons. So many creatures, hundreds, maybe thousands congregated below. So many bodies. Ruby had been wrong, so wrong to think that she could make a difference here. She was a drop in an ocean of monsters.

Ruby followed the direction of their gazes to the centre of the crowd. That was when she saw them. Two figures, standing out against the hordes for many reasons, one of which being the wide berth that the other demons afforded them.

One of them was Saydor. The chill than ran down her spine was part memory induced. But her memories couldn't possibly do a thing like that justice, even from a distance.

It took her a moment longer to realise that the other demon had to be Drayvex. Ruby couldn't tear her eyes away. She'd often wondered what the demon in her life *truly* looked like. Now she knew.

A searing pain shot up her arm. Ruby threw her hand over her mouth, stifling the answering scream. She ripped her sleeve back to the elbow. It was the cat scratch, and it was glowing bright red.

She stumbled backwards and stopped, her mind falling blank. Panicking, she tried to form a coherent thought. But her thoughts slipped through her fingers like water through a sieve.

An urgent need pushed at the edges of her consciousness. It was a persistent swell that dominated her entire being. A basal need, impossible to ignore.

Ruby looked towards the ginormous portal on the other side of the crater and felt a tug. A yearning. Somehow, she knew exactly where she needed to go.

Chapter 31

*D*rayvex halted both parts of himself with synchronised precision. The conceited voice carried an unmistakable smugness, despite the climbing body count. The kind of smug that was convinced it was still about to win.

Drayvex smothered a grin, keeping the deluded Demon Master staring at his back. So, Saydor was incapable of refusing a challenge after all. This was just too easy.

The rioting hordes were falling apart. Their palpable confusion split them into groups of easy pickings, the limited unison they had built shattering as they took in the scene before them. Drayvex was no longer interested in the small fry. He wouldn't need to kill any more to get what he wanted. He had that right here and now, a Saydor-shaped lump of clay, just waiting to be moulded to his will.

He watched the demon hordes as they struggled with what to do and who to follow. They needed to know who was in charge. He would clear up all confusion, right now.

"Saydor," Drayvex drawled, sharpening all of his senses, embracing the heady rush of sounds and scents and tastes that came at him as one. "I have to say, your presence is as much of an affliction as ever."

The demon chuckled, a low, drawn-out sound that grated against what little patience Drayvex possessed. "My Lord. *Your* presence confounds me.

Have I offended your greatness?"

Drayvex paused, letting his head settle, before whipping around to face him.

Saydor was a few feet away. The demon that had been a constant thorn in his side, from the moment he took the throne, to the present steaming mess. A look of mock surprise tweaked at his features.

Saydor had infested the castle even longer than Drayvex. He'd been his father's right hand at the time of his *nasty* fall from grace. Having served the previous Demon Lord, it had made sense to keep him around, if only for his wealth of knowledge and experience.

That experience had come at the cost of Drayvex's sanity.

"Tell me," Drayvex said, his voice soft and sly, "do I look like I was born yesterday? Take your time, have a good look. I'll wait." He looked down, proceeding to study the drying lifeblood that caked his claws, making a meal of it.

Saydor smiled, revealing the stunted barbs behind his lips, teeth that, as far as Drayvex was concerned, barely classed as fangs. "You never cease to amuse me, Your Highness. I know that you would never pass up on such a tantalising opportunity to crush that tree-hugging coward that calls herself a warrior. And yet, it almost *sounds* as though you've changed your mind." His smile slipped, his eyes dropping to two black pits. "Hilarious."

Drayvex sneered down at him, giving a lesson on what a real set of fangs looked like. "I'm afraid your value to me has expired." He lowered his voice, speaking with soft menace. "The only real use I have for you now is the exquisite example you'll set to your followers when I show them what happens to traitors to the throne." He addressed the surrounding underlings, "Find a good spot, bring a snack. It will be a night to remember."

The brief pause that followed was golden and complete. Bating the Demon Master wasn't part of the plan. But Saydor had a way of rubbing even the calmest entity up in the wrong way. Drayvex was not calm.

"My Lord." Saydor backpedalled, his poor attempt at civility marred by the expression of pure loathing on his face. "We may not have always seen eye to eye, but surely, we should not fight over trivial matters, such as which of us rules over where?"

Drayvex laughed, a sound that caused those closest to him to flinch on cue. He couldn't help it. For a lowlife worm, Saydor had the biggest balls he'd ever come across. It wouldn't save him.

Saydor's beady eyes narrowed, the clusters of black veins on the sides of his neck growing thicker and darker. A moment more, and that smile was back, rebounding with, undoubtedly, another change in tack. "My Lord, if you won't consider a deal, then I propose a truce. Do you not agree that we such mighty beings should be a united front? Working not against each other, but together, just imagine what the two of us could accomplish." His voice was slick, almost gleeful as he contemplated his own words. "Nothing would dare stand in our way."

Drayvex watched Saydor's eyes glisten as he spoke, noted their greedy gleam. His hands were rubbing together.

"Saydor." Stepping forward, Drayvex let him have it. "Your proposition is, at best, ludicrous. At worst, it's offensive to my fucking ears."

The demon's smile slipped once more, face becoming a stiff mask. His eyes flickered between crimson and black, his modest yellowing claws extending in slow motion.

Drayvex continued, sensing that the demon was approaching the end of his short fuse. "Let me put this in a way that even you will understand." He lifted the tip of a claw to eye level, looking past its lethal point to where the Demon Master stood. "I tire of your repeated disobedience. I've destroyed demons for much less. Why would you think yourself an exception to my rule?"

Saydor's expression was that of someone who had been forced to swallow his own poisonous bile. His usual yellow pallor was disappearing behind an angry shade of puce, the claws on his webbed hands becoming larger with each passing second. "What is it to you," Saydor spat, his eyes blazing, "if I rule over one little planet? You yourself have conquered countless worlds, taking them by force. Bending them to your will, just because you can."

Reacting to the hostile display, Drayvex shot forward, closing the remaining gap between them.

"Why do you care if I take this one? You didn't seem to give a toss when you made that deal with me, not so long ago. What has *changed*?"

Drayvex pushed himself into Saydor's personal space, cutting off the fierce whispers that had been flowing around them. The atmosphere thickened in the silence. The truth was, he wanted Ruby to have the Earth. He wanted the planet that had provided furtive relief from the relentless droll of Vekrodus to keep on turning, to thrive and spread like a beautiful plague.

Admitting this to Saydor, however, made jumping into the lake of acid surrounding his fortress, and then drinking its contents seem appealing. Outside of Ruby and his own selfish desire, Drayvex had been thinking about the 'why' at great length. He was well-armed.

"Let's say, hypothetically, that I did allow you to keep this godforsaken rock. Would you have the devastating leadership skills it would take to keep these degenerates in their rightful place?"

As Saydor opened his mouth to respond, Drayvex blocked his attempt. "I'm speaking," he growled, holding a claw up to Saydor's mouth.

Saydor's face grew dark, features contorting. Drayvex had no idea that the Demon Master possessed so much self-control. It was like watching a kettle boil. Soon, he mused, steam would be coming out of his ears.

"You may think you do, but I assure you, you do not." As he spoke, Drayvex paced around him, circling him like a predator. "Let me tell you why." He didn't wait for a response. "The demons will wipe out half of humanity in one fell swoop. From then onward, the human population will decline at a rapid pace and soon after, become an endangered species. Now, we have a problem. A rich and abundant hunting ground has been bled dry, with no quick way to repopulate. This, in turn, will commit us all to a couple of centuries' worth of slim and foul-tasting pickings until something better comes up."

Drayvex stopped pacing, coming full circle to face the Demon Master once more. The ruffle that his moving presence had caused among the masses fell still along with him. "This alone is reason enough to crush you and your paltry ambitions into dust. The fact that I can't stand to look at you makes it all the more satisfying."

Saydor's face was a mask of demonic outrage. "What about that mangy rat that you stole from *me*," he snarled, leaning forward as he spoke. "Unlike Vekrodus, there are no laws of human possession on this planet. I found her here on Earth, and yet you slaughtered my entire guard, killed my second, then took her from my Tower. The human girl, My *Lord*, is still mine."

Drayvex froze. Yes, he had broken his own rules in taking Ruby back. It hadn't seemed important at the time. Now, though, he would have to answer for his actions. Or she would.

"If you are taking back what is yours," Saydor hissed, his poison-coated claws flexing by his sides, "then I want what is mine."

He studied the smoking demon with trepidation. Handing Ruby over to that monstrosity would defeat the whole point of everything he was doing. It would also be the last time he ever saw her, of that he was certain. The thought was enough to turn his usually iron stomach.

Lie, demanded a voice in his head.

"You're welcome to what's left," he deadpanned. "I tire of humans quickly. Yours was no exception." The word 'yours' stuck in his throat like a barb. Laws or not, Ruby would never belong to that sadistic swine. He would make sure of it. "Regardless, I'm sure I can track down the scraps, if that's what you're into." Drayvex fixed on Saydor, holding fast. Daring him to question it. He didn't.

What he did do was narrow his eyes. A cold, calculating stare that revealed the cogs that were turning at speed in his small, skewed mind.

Distract him.

It was time to settle this once and for all. "In the spirit of keeping things interesting, I propose a challenge. Winner takes all."

Saydor's eyes widened.

Yes, he had his attention, all right. "If you can beat me," Drayvex growled, dangling the bait, "you can have the Earth *and* Vekrodus."

It took Saydor a moment to respond. After a pause, his usual warped grin returned. He ran a black tongue along the tops of his teeth. "You must be confident, Your Highness."

"Well?" Drayvex thundered. "Do you accept?" The Lapis Vitae was not on Saydor's person, but one with the portal. This meant that in theory, the demon should be no more of a challenge than when they last fought.

The Demon Master chuckled and sank into a crouch. "I accept your terms," he hissed, lunging without hesitation.

Drayvex flattened his hand and drove the claws towards Saydor's abdomen.

Saydor kicked out at the last second, knocking his arm clear, and avoiding being skewered by a narrow margin. He continued his momentum, barrelling into Drayvex, who had a welcome gift ready and waiting.

The pulsing ball of dark matter burst from his form. It connected with the Demon Master, pushing him back with the force of the blast. Ebony flames exploded around them.

As he hit the mud, Saydor screamed with primal fury. Dark flames licked at his flesh, stripping away patches of skin. Drayvex pummelled him with blast after blast, not above hitting his foe while he was down. All the while, Saydor hissed and writhed on the ground, body contorting from the effort of fighting the pain.

Then, form still aflame, the demon struggled to his feet.

Drayvex stopped. He frowned, annoyance prickling as he watched Saydor emerge, a headless cockroach that refused to die. It was then that it hit him. The bastard was amping.

Saydor's arms were spread out to either side of him, ignoring the flames lapping at his form. The demon's eyes rolled to the back of his head, noticeable for a fleeting moment, before a pitch black spread across and concealed them.

Drayvex took this as a warning.

An explosion of power burst from Saydor's core in destructive waves. They hit his barrier, a shield he'd erected not a moment too soon, and were absorbed upon impact. Slivers seeped through the barrier, stinging like flecks of molten lava as they made contact with his flesh. Drayvex held fast, already two steps ahead.

He'd never fought Saydor in such a way before. He had, however, made it his business to study his fighting pattern. And every time that worthless wretch had broken those below him, Drayvex had watched him win. He may have found a way to syphon from the stone of life inside the portal, but the Demon Master was predictable.

Demons scattered left and right, making their exits in a blind panic. A few disappeared further into the village. Others dived for the portal. Those who stayed remained a cautious distance from the ever-widening battleground, enthusiasm inciting blood lust in even the smallest of minions.

At the first opening he saw, Drayvex darted forward, dodging green appendages as they lunged at him again and again. He wanted to cut them off. Maybe he would. Cut the bloated fool down to size piece by piece.

Teeth and claws clashed, limbs moving in a blurry maelstrom. Maybe, he'd track down his beating heart and offer it to Ruby. After all, demon heart was rumoured to extend the life of a mortal by twenty years.

Saydor was fast, but Drayvex was faster, and for every hit that got past his guard, he would give two back. He distanced himself, slipping out of range of the close proximity attacks. Saydor couldn't go on like this forever. In a test of endurance, there was no competition.

Suddenly, Drayvex froze. His mind hung in limbo. Saydor was wearing a hungry smile. His eyes gleamed with wicked delight, but Drayvex needed to know. Needed confirmation that, yes, he was still in control of his senses.

His gaze slid to the far side of the portal grounds, to the place where his senses had intuitively pinpointed her location. He had always been very much aware of her. His entire being was on high alert when in her presence. His fangs reminded him of his true nature as they throbbed in protest, craving her in numerous ways. Ruby.

Drayvex hissed, a hard sound, which seemed angry to him. But he couldn't be sure. His mind had short-circuited. On what planet did she—?

Pain exploded in his right shoulder as something punched straight through, quickly retracting. An unpleasant creeping sensation burned in its place, seeping downward. *Vuiar nhfreto!*

Chapter 32

A string of profanities streamed from between his teeth as the cocktail of venom bled into his system. His muscles stiffened in response to the fast-acting poison, the viscous gunk burning through the network of his blood vessels.

Drayvex cursed Ruby in a plethora of tongues, rebuking her senseless human need to meddle. What gave her the gall to repeatedly defy him? Did she get her kicks out of making his life difficult? No, clearly the girl was mentally inept. He should have spoken slower.

With disdain, he studied the gaping hole in his shoulder, waiting for his body to fight back. It did, and as he watched, the skin around the perfectly spherical wound proceeded to pull itself back together.

The wound that remained was about the size of a bullet, his accelerated healing already stunted by the garbage in his system. Well, he hoped she was happy with herself. When it came down to a choice between her and protecting himself, he would always choose himself. She would only have herself to blame for this one.

Drayvex ignored the Demon Master and glanced back towards Ruby. She was strolling through the sea of bloodthirsty hordes, moving forward as though they were flowers in a meadow. His volatile state subdued somewhat as he watched her, and doubt set in. He knew how to pick them.

The demons parted as she passed, their hunger only overshadowed by the desire to toy with their prey and drag out the moment. Bad news for her—it only took one jackass to spark a chain reaction. But there was something about the way she moved that pushed with urgency at the back of his mind. Drayvex looked closer. Her eyes were glassy, her body stiff, almost robotic in its movements. Fear would do that to a human. As an inspirer of terror, he knew this well. But there was something more. Something almost somnambular about her, as though she were sleepwalking, or in a trance.

The answer hit him square in the face as he finished that thought. Almost as though she was being *controlled*.

Reluctantly, he turned back to his expectant rival—a rival who had been silent for far too long. Staring back at him were not one, but three pairs of eyes, with three canine heads attached. Saydor had abandoned his demon form and instead had chosen the hulking great beast known as Cerberus.

Even with this current guise, forced to look into the eyes of an overgrown dog, Drayvex knew that Saydor understood. The sly gleam was back in his eyes, all six of them, reflecting a look of triumph. And if the Demon Master had been in his previous form, he would have seen that revolting grin and the self-righteous look he detested.

Drayvex made a conscious effort to sharpen his focus, and the world slid sideways. Three heads became six. The cacophony of sounds around him intensified, pressing upon him like a physical force.

Do you like my gift? came that oozing voice, forcing its presence upon him despite the current lack of functioning vocal cords.

Get out of my head, Drayvex blasted at the demon, feeling the invasion of the lethal secretion sapping at his strength. A lesser demon than he would have dropped within minutes. For him, it was undoubtedly a handicap. But once he'd slipped away and bled himself dry, he would quickly recover; a luxury he did not have, that Ruby did not have.

He couldn't let Saydor win this. Would not let him take from him as he saw fit.

Tell me, Saydor simpered. *I'm simply dying of curiosity. Of all the humans on this wretched planet, why this one?*

Drayvex stilled. As he put two and two together, a fresh surge of heat coursed through him. Saydor's 'gift' had not been the poisonous blow he'd dealt. It was Ruby.

What are you thinking, Drayvex? What are you hiding?

The soggy ground steamed beneath his claws, heating from his contact. How dare Saydor involve her in this way. He was going to tear the demon limb from limb.

And the girl?

He ignored the stray thought. He had no idea.

You made it easy, you know, intruded Saydor. *It was almost too easy. That poor, pathetic dreameater you cast out with no way to feed. He was more than eager to help. He seemed to think that a human rat had taken his place. So I lent him my power, and he did not disappoint.*

Drayvex had heard enough. Without warning, he relinquished his form, feeling power burst to the surface in a pent up blast. He expanded at a rapid pace, muscles bulking and hardening, his smooth skin growing scaled, and hard as black crystal. His spine curved, a row of pointed shafts shooting down his back with a crack as he became quadruped. They continued down, erupting along his tail in uneven, razor-like shafts.

He met eye level with the smug Cerberus and continued to grow, snout extending, his claws thickening. Then, wasting no more time, he sprang at the hound.

*

She was in trouble. She shouldn't be here, and yet, she couldn't stop. Ruby's eyes swivelled as she crossed the battleground, somewhere far beyond terror in an almost numbing frenzy. She was surrounded by demons. But all she could think about was the large, rippling portal on the other side of the grounds. And the thrumming strands of red that were stretched across the entire site like string, linking it to the demon with three heads.

She couldn't think.

Couldn't move.

Her arm burned.

Ruby trained her eyes across the grounds, to the other monstrous presence. Drayvex. Her stomach squeezed. She had to fix this. Now.

*

Drayvex lunged for Saydor, aiming for the middle throat. Saydor swiped out with a large paw, three snarling heads reaching for him at the same time. He sunk his teeth deep into the soft neck, clamping down just as the Demon Master knocked him off balance. Rolling to the left, Drayvex held firm with his fanged grip as the three heads bit at him, targeting the parts Saydor knew he stood most chance of penetrating. Drayvex's tail snaked around the hound's middle, gaining purchase.

It's not nice to lie to old friends, dripped a voice inside his head. A voice unlike his own, even telepathically grating on his last nerve.

Drayvex ignored him. Something stirred in the pit of his stomach. There was no way out of this for her. She should have stayed on Vekrodus. He knew this. Why did he let her screw with his resolve?

If I didn't know you better, Drayvex, it continued, *know you to be the ruthless, power-hungry devil you are, I'd say that this creature is of value to you.*

Drayvex whipped his head to the side, ripping the flesh between his fangs. A spurt of warm, wet liquid hit his snout, the sour stench of demon blood attacking his senses.

Saydor snarled, whining and shaking his heads as he lunged once more in a relentless attack.

You really should learn to make your own life choices, Drayvex pushed, *instead of taking mine. Though, I suppose, that would require a significantly larger brain.*

As he clamped his teeth down on a neck once again, Drayvex squeezed his tail around Saydor's waist, his barbs piercing into the torso as he constricted. He waited for the satisfying sound of snapping bones that would be music to his ears.

Suddenly, something passed through him, an electric jolt that caused him to shudder. Fatigue lapped over him in a wave, spreading outward in a crippling spasm of weakness. When it reached his extremities, he lost his grip.

Drayvex sent a coma-inducing blast towards the Demon Master in a desperate attempt to maintain control. He heard a sound signalling that he'd hit something solid, but didn't bother to check what. Instead, he glanced at the suspended portal.

He ignored the ringing in his ears and waited for his vision to refocus. Kaelor must have got to Ruby, reconnected her to the stone.

But *when?*

Drayvex fumed. That was what he got for showing that ingrate mercy. He should have killed him on the spot.

His head pounded, throbbing with the tenacity of a herd of angry trolls. His nerves screamed, blood burning with an acidity that bled into his organs, causing them to falter and stutter.

"I care not what your plans for that feeble creature are. I'm still going to pick her apart, piece by piece." Saydor whispered from behind, the malice in his voice tainted with an edge of vicious glee. "And if I don't find your nasty little secret, I'm going to keep going until I do."

Drayvex dug his claws deep into the wet gravel, his breathing laboured. Turning, he rose and shed his skin in one fluid movement, reverting back to a simpler form. Saydor wouldn't find it.

Drayvex had no hidden agenda. No nefarious plan for the girl with the demon stone necklace. The secret was that there was no secret. And that alone would be enough to destroy him.

Saydor also reverted to a semi-human guise. He grinned from ear to ear as he dragged his battered form across the site. He was looking worse for wear. His flesh was torn away in several places, his sizable chest cavity exuding dark fluid, a dripping chasm. A wet chuckle escaped his lips, before he sucked in a ragged breath. "But it won't be quick like Malsurg. Oh, no; it will be inch by glorious inch." The skin at the edges of his wounds twitched and curled, preparing to fix his broken body. "Like solving a human puzzle, only, backwards."

Drayvex surged forward in a hot flash of temper. Writhing black tendrils shot out from his form, Saydor's careless threat sparking a wildfire reflex.

As the tendrils found their target, Saydor brought up his hands, erecting a barrier at the last moment. Drayvex punched straight through, refusing to be denied the agonised screams of the festering worm who thought he could lay his hands on the girl that was his and live. Saydor's eyes widened as the attacks connected, caught off guard by the sudden shift in gears.

"You mean, like this?" Drayvex floored the demon. Pinning him to the ground, he unleashed attack after attack, black tendrils curling around muscle and sinew, restricting and corrupting the tissue with his own personal cocktail.

The Demon Master hissed and writhed beneath him, eyes blank and staring as Drayvex played surgeon. Shoving his hands deep inside, he gripped something warm and soft and felt it disintegrate as he squeezed.

Risking a glance behind him, he zoned in on Ruby's location, and his own insides constricted. She was mere feet away from the portal. Any moment now, she would touch it. Gruesome images flashed through his mind.

It's over, his calculating subconscious offered.

Two demons on either side of her tensed to spring, no longer interested in watching her walk to her death, provoking ripples of excitement from those nearest.

If the portal didn't burn her from the inside out, the demons would rip her to pieces. Yes, it's over, he deadpanned in response.

*

Ruby found Drayvex from across the space. He was going to win. And she was going to die.

A laugh that sounded like a sob bubbled to the surface. The hell beasts on either side of her tensed, fixed on her like a cat on a lame bird. A bird that jumped every time her strings were plucked.

It didn't matter. As long as the Earth was safe, she could take it like a warrior. Couldn't she?

She didn't want to die.

Ruby focused on the demon again, her demon. He was looking at her. Time stopped.

She didn't want to die, but she wasn't afraid.

She slipped her hands into her pockets, and jumped as they brushed something cool. The pyramid.

*

Saydor quivered beneath him, lashing out with putrid claws, aiming for his eyes like a trapped animal. Drayvex swatted them away, feeling a restless frustration building inside him. He couldn't protect her, not this time. He was going to lose her.

He lashed out with a closed fist, smashing it down into the face that was still, impossibly, staring up at him with pained, sadistic relish. The demon was getting his kicks out of watching Drayvex squirm.

"If I can't have her, then neither will you."

Ruby reached towards the portal, her arm stretching out to touch it in a slow, trance-like motion. The demons around her prepared to spring.

Drayvex knew that he had to let her go. Let her die, kill Saydor and restore equilibrium. Laugh in the face of any vicious, damaging rumours that would talk of his filthy affiliation with a mere human. Protect his reputation as Demon Lord.

Yet, as he watched her fingers inch ever closer to her death, the world around him stopped.

Let her go.

As her life hung by a thread, he felt feelers of his own power push out impulsively towards her, his instinct to catch her kicking in, as it had many times before. Everything that happened next seemed to unfold by the skin of their teeth.

Ruby reached out, inches away from the kiss of death. Drayvex raised a barrier around her, almost chopping off her fingers in the process. Demons bounced off the barrier, launching backwards not a second too soon. It stopped her in her tracks, and as he wrapped folds of power around her, enshrouding her within, he put layer upon layer between her and the damaging things from his world.

Drayvex vaguely wondered if he could still kill the amped Saydor, with half of his power directed elsewhere and a body that felt like it was melting. She would be the death of him. Any moron with eyes could see that.

He didn't know why he couldn't bring himself to cut her loose. Surely, she was more trouble than her worth to him. What he did know, though, was that the shit had just hit the fan.

As this bitter thought occurred to him, he was hit from the side by a whirling dervish of blades. The hissing, spitting Demon Master barrelled into him, giving him less than a second to respond.

Drayvex absorbed the onslaught, conserving precious power. He could take the hits. Saydor had already dealt his worst. And as he moved in closer, eager to finish the Demon Lord off, Drayvex moved in kind. He smashed the Demon Master with relentless blasts, saturating him with black, destructive energy.

His stunned nemesis lay trapped in unrelenting waves of dark power. They lapped over him, each blow reverberating through his entire form, turning him a deeper shade of puce. His screams cut off as he choked.

As Drayvex struggled to continue to produce waves of power, his mind was with Ruby.

Without warning, Saydor disappeared in an explosion of green. "I had no idea that the great and terrible Demon Lord could be so selfless," said a scathing, disconnected voice in the rising green dust.

Drayvex tensed, the urge to rip Saydor into a thousand pieces searing within him. That's right, he sneered to himself, *run*. I'm coming for you.

"Tell me." Saydor's face appeared in the green clouds as he leaned in close. His voice was a soft rumble, his flaming eyes fixed on Drayvex's. "Tell me why."

Drayvex was incredulous. It would be funny in any other situation. He supposed his reputation was just that notorious. "You poor fool," Drayvex mocked, spitting pieces of tooth onto the ground. "You think because you're about to die, I'm going to share my darkest secrets with you? Please. Don't hold me to your own baseborn standards."

That did it.

As Saydor lunged for him, Drayvex brought up his claws. Saydor landed on them stomach first, snarling like a rabid beast, long scythes bursting through his back.

Oozing green feelers closed around Drayvex's throat, more venom seeping through his skin. This body was failing him. He could feel himself coming apart, dissolving into Demon Lord soup. Every spasm of pain that erupted from his core made it harder to focus.

His vision flickered, liquefied parts of himself catching in his constricting throat. Still, he didn't need a physical form. Drayvex considered that while he was being strangled, watching the demons surrounding Ruby work themselves into a frenzy from an upside down viewpoint. He watched them swarm, crawling like insects over the spherical barrier of his making.

Saydor was weak. If he could get inside his mind, this would be over. In a vapour form, he would no longer be vulnerable, and Saydor would be just weak enough to allow him inside.

The Demon Master's feelers continued to constrict his throat, two more snaking out and wrapping around his wrists. Drayvex gave an involuntary shudder as something inside him spluttered and died—flooded with junk, unable to heal worth a damn.

Underneath the moving wall of demons, Drayvex could see small squares of exposed barrier. It flickered at a dangerous rate, its power source waning along with his consciousness. A sensation of bitter frustration rose up and smothered him. But then, if he gave up his physical form, the barrier would fall.

Of course. Of course it would.

Saydor grimaced in a vain attempt to grin through his pain. His quick eyes did not miss the glances. "If I can't have her," he echoed, his own blackened eyes sliding to the commotion by the portal, "then neither will you."

The barrier flickered. He was still going to lose her. In the helpless moments that followed, he couldn't breathe, dared not move while the thinning sheets of power around her spluttered, hanging by a thread.

For the first time in his life, he knew fear. And it struck him to the core.

*

It was like being in a fish tank. A fish tank walled with crazed, flesh-eating monsters.

Ruby took in stifling breath after breath, her limbs shaking. Drayvex was going to die protecting her. She was going to die a useless burden, and Earth would be left at the mercy of a maniac. This was all her fault.

She could see through the crawling masses surrounding her, through the tiny windows of the moving walls, opening and closing. The force that held them back was dying. That force was Drayvex.

Curling her hand around the cool pyramid in her pocket, she squeezed it in her fist. He was going all out for her, and it tore at her heart. This wasn't what she'd meant when she told him he owed her.

Well, he would not die for her today.

Ruby ripped the little black pyramid from her pocket and looked at it, holding it up in the demon-smothered gloom. The barrier that separated her from the demons also separated her from the portal's pull. Now that she could think and move of her own free will, the answer was obvious. She was holding it in her hand.

Krick had said that the pyramid absorbed power. If she could cut Saydor off from the portal, make Drayvex's job that little bit easier, then she had to at least try.

She stared into the portal's depths from behind the flickering wall, pyramid in hand. It was the one section that the demons couldn't smother. The part that touched the portal.

Ruby took a sharp breath, and then sprang for the wall of the bubble. Her hand wouldn't cross the barrier; but the pyramid would. Gripping the pointed tip with squeezing fingers, she inched the object out, until the flat base was touching the swirling red portal. The pyramid stopped almost immediately, as though the portal was a solid wall. The tip was poking through the barrier.

Ruby keened. Her fingers had been that close. What would have happened had she touched its swirling depths?

It took her moment to realise that nothing was happening. The portal and the pyramid remained the same.

No. This had to work. Her breath caught in her throat. Why wasn't it drawing power? What—?

Ruby stopped.

'*You have to feed it.*'

Power.

'*The key is blood.*'

Moving slowly, Ruby slid her palm over the pyramid's pointed tip. Then she pushed. She gasped as the point bit into her hand, but didn't stop. Within seconds the black pyramid was warm under her touch. Hot. Sizzling hot. Ruby hissed through her teeth, fighting the urge to withdraw her hand. Blood dripped from her palm to the damp earth.

The portal flashed in a blinding red, stinging her eyes, and then dulled.

Blinking, she scanned the space around her, then broke into a weary smile. The red string that had linked Saydor to the portal was gone.

*

The portal was in its death throes.

"*What* is this?" Saydor hissed, body stiffening. His face morphed into an expression of pure outrage. "What are you doing?"

Drayvex reeled. It had to be Ruby. Which meant that she was using something of his that he hadn't given her, in ways that he hadn't showed her, that as luck would have it, just happened to work in their favour.

Saydor had lost his grip. Drayvex could see it in his eyes, feel it slackening his hold. Drayvex lashed out, power screaming through his veins out of nowhere. Fuelling him with strength he didn't know he had. A current of undiluted power washed through him, spreading outwards.

Saydor jerked backwards, stiffening, eyes bulging as though he'd touched a live wire. His feelers retracted, before launching straight towards him again in relentless pursuit. Drayvex responded like for like with steel resolve, launching what power he still possessed in a tirade of attacks.

The little vixen. It had to be the black crystal. He'd pissed her off and then she'd taken it to spite him. He didn't know whether to congratulate her on her sheer bloody nonchalance, or make her hold the thing that would now be seared to her skin indefinitely. No one had ever stolen from him and gone unnoticed. No one.

"I'm going to tear that little bitch limb from limb."

Drayvex felt a heat sear deep within. No. You won't.

As the demon shot forward, Drayvex increased the force around him. He compressed Saydor, causing his blood to fizz, his veins to tear at the seams.

The air became hard and crushing, and still, he ramped up the pressure, until the bloated body he targeted was almost at breaking point.

The demons surrounding them had become silent and still. Saydor buckled, stumbled. Seeing his moment, Drayvex went for the kill.

The look in Saydor's eyes as Drayvex floored him told him that he was finished. Sensing an end, he pumped blast after blast of searing power into the body on the ground, hearing bones snap and internal organs explode.

The moment he fell still, Drayvex stopped, and took in the specimen on the floor. Saydor was wasted.

Ignoring the searing pain in his skull, he turned to the mass of surrounding demons, glaring at them with silent rage. "Get your worthless hides back through the portal," he snarled. He didn't bother to raise his voice. He didn't need to.

The demons sunk down low to the ground, and one by one began crawling back through the dilapidated portal in miserable terror. Drayvex watched the first few with mild satisfaction, knowing that they would all pay for their betrayal. His previous tweak to the portal would refuse them return access to Vekrodus. But not until they were inside.

At long last, Drayvex turned to Ruby. He motioned at her with a claw and waited as she crossed the wasted land between them, her steps stiff and slow.

As Ruby stopped in front of him, he directed the full force of his waning influence on her, doing what he should have done in the first place. She may have been under influence, but she'd left the park of her own free will.

"Wait here," he asserted, looking deep into her eyes, planting his request within her pliable subconscious.

She gazed back with wide eyes, doubt creasing in the corners as her mind tested the intrusion. They softened as she accepted his terms. She looked down.

Drayvex followed her gaze. It was the black crystal, just as he suspected. He raised his eyebrows at her, questioning her with mild amusement.

Ruby had the good grace to flush. "You started it," she said, surprising him with her voice.

Drayvex fought a small smirk. Oh, Ruby. So out of your league. "Give it here."

She looked down and then back up at him. "I'm not sure I can."

His smirk broke through, despite the pain, tickled by this. "That so?" He'd suspected as much.

She scowled at him. "Is it over?"

Ruby looked like he felt. "Almost," he said, the grin slipping from his face as he turned to deal with the vermin responsible for all of his troubles.

Darkness bred within his empty heart cavity, its missing counterpart undoubtedly filling like for like at its separate location.

Saydor glared up at him from the ground, hatred burning in the pits of his eyes. But there was also a gleam of something more. Something *vindictive* shining in their corners. That would not do.

Drayvex very much wanted to extinguish that flicker of spirit. To take great pleasure in breaking it. He wanted to leave Saydor crippled and blind in the dark, before wiping away the stain that he had left behind on the two planets. Time was not on his side.

"Well, well, well," he uttered with cold indifference. "I do believe we've been here before." He strode over to where Saydor lay sprawled in the mud, stopping when he was right above him. "If memory serves, you were lying at my feet then; a broken mess, waiting to be scooped up by my minions and disposed of." Drayvex tilted his head and smiled with all the remaining arrogance he could muster, savouring the moment with vicious appetite. "You seem to like it down there."

"Drayvex."

He ignored her. There was no room for mercy. It was not in his nature. "When I am done with you, you will be no more than a smudge on the memory of demonkind. Your legacy will be erased, your memory disposed of; discarded with your bones, which will be stripped bare by those you consider to be beneath you. You will be tossed back into the fetid pits you were born in. A nothing, just like when you first entered the world."

Saydor's eyes gleamed through his pain, teeth bared. "I always get what I want, Drayvex," he spat, his hand shooting out with the remaining vestiges of his energy.

Drayvex stiffened, realising his mistake. Hissing, he erected a hasty barrier behind Ruby's unprotected back.

Too late. Drayvex turned, just in time to see the stinger pierce deep into her neck.

Chapter 33

⁂

*D*rayvex watched the blood drain from her face, suspended within a state of disjointed inertia. This wasn't happening. Not now. It had to be some sort of sick fucking joke.

The clinical part of his mind knew that this *was* happening, whether he accepted it as fact or not. It was the part of him that never switched off, and now, it fed him undesirable details as he studied her. The prominent veins in her neck, thick and dark around the submerged base of the stinger, as the poison was forced inside her. It spread down her neck in a black trail, branching out like a tree as her blood mingled with the toxins. The blood would thicken and clot, becoming a dark mixture of toxic sludge, too thick to pump, useless to her body.

The demon behind her hissed, rattling the armoured plates of its scorpion hide in an agitated display. It snatched its tail back, indignant at having being used as a weapon.

As the stinger tore free, Ruby jerked against the force. Her eyes rolled to the back of her head, and she swayed on her feet.

Drayvex felt the precarious spell he'd fallen under smash.

As Ruby dropped dead weight, Drayvex shot forward, plucking her out of the air. All thoughts of blood lust and revenge gone, Drayvex sank to the ground and tried to fix the gaping screw up in her neck. He worked through a number of solutions in his mind, each one falling at the first hurdle.

Her blood would be thick. As long as the poison hadn't reached her heart, he could use his own stronger venom to destroy the other. He fingered the wound. He would then be able to suck his own venom out of her bloodstream.

Drayvex held her, dripping his fangs freely over the bloody mess of her neck. He stopped. It wasn't enough. The damage was too much.

He groped around in desperation inside his head for something—anything—that might save her. His own broken body screamed at him in protest as he continued to push it beyond what its capabilities. He couldn't focus.

Ruby stared up at him, her eyes glassy and unfocused as he gripped her in a useless way, as though he could keep her in this world through sheer force.

She's human, interjected the voice.

And?

She's dying. It's what they do.

Drayvex seethed. Not unlike the process of splitting the soul in two, he couldn't help but feel that he was now two different versions of himself, trapped in the same moment.

He whipped his head around, already knowing what he would find. Saydor was gone. He hissed out in frustration, an angry rattle that sent the lingering demons exploding in clouds of red. The ground split with an almighty crack, spreading halfway across the site.

Of course, Saydor had escaped. Attacking Ruby had been the perfect distraction. And the act of striking out at Drayvex's newly revealed weakness would have come in at a close second only to his desperate need to survive.

Drayvex gouged holes in the ground, ignoring the sharp, spreading sting it brought from his own weakened state. He could deal with pain. As a demon, he could endure any number of atrocities without losing face or nerve. The fact that he was physically unravelling was now a distraction that he welcomed, albeit an inconvenient one. But having Ruby slip through his fingers after everything that had happened was worse than anything Saydor had intentionally inflicted.

Then it came to him. The thought pierced his consciousness, blooming like a beautiful but deadly flower. It was almost overwhelming. He could change her. As a pure-blooded demon, he was the best chance she would ever get of having a successful demonic transition. All he had to do was bite her.

His saving grace began to circle the drain, fading as fast as it had appeared as he considered the consequences. He would be damning her. A one-way ticket to an eternal Hell. She would eventually shed her humanity like a second skin, and then the real battle would begin. Willingly become a heartless creature of the dark, or sacrifice her sanity fighting the change.

No, Ruby didn't belong in his world. She wasn't cut out to be a demon, and she wouldn't thank him for it. Then there was only one thing left to do.

Shelving temptation, he stood with her in his arms, pushing himself beyond his limits. The world around them swayed and blurred as his screwed physical form pushed back. Drayvex willed it into line, forcing it to respond with the dregs of his energy, and then started for the portal.

In the past, Drayvex had played out Ruby's death in a hundred different ways, back when he'd thought that she was the plaque he could purge. He'd even tried to enjoy it. It was nothing like he'd imagined.

He stared down at Ruby's lifeless form as he crossed the muddy waste, watching her slip away from him for a second time. A violent frustration burned inside him, putting the venom that was liquefying him to shame. Everything this girl had ever made him feel was smothering him. Memories, fractured pieces from his perfect memory jarred him with their tenacity. He couldn't stop them.

The urge to have his wicked way with her in the tavern.

The strange impulse to save her from the fire.

Fury when she was kidnapped on his watch.

Her open rejection when he'd gone back to pluck her from her dying planet. The restless torment of the days after. He'd been unable to sever that last thread that tied them together.

Drayvex fixed on the portal across the empty grounds, their destination set in his mind. He made a good effort to kill the senseless human impulses working their way through his system, knowing that they would not help her. He knew exactly what would.

The closer he got, the more he felt a nagging at the back of his mind—that selfish, self-serving instinct that kept him alive at all costs. It was protesting at his reckless decision, warning him. Under normal circumstances, he would listen to his better instincts. But Drayvex had finally given in to madness. Totally and completely. It fell on deaf ears.

As he approached the portal, Ruby began to convulse. The wound in her neck continued to bleed, staining them both with a dark coalescence of fluids. Where she brushed against him, her skin was icy to the touch. She was running out of time.

Drayvex placed his fingers on her neck, sending the dregs of his waning power flowing through her body like a current.

As his power seeped into each individual cell, her body began to shut down, slowing to move and perform at a fraction of its normal speed. That would buy them both some time.

Drayvex stood before the portal, staring into its depths. It was strong now, too strong to be openly advertising its free use for all. Its very existence was a dump on the porch of those who controlled the portals and their usage. What use was power without control? It had to be destroyed.

Ruby was silent and still in his arms. Her physiology moved at a fraction of its normal rate, but even that wouldn't stop the inevitable. At some point, her fragile human heart would give out.

Looking up at the gateway, he stared into the swirling void, allowing the desired location to fill his mind, to tease at his senses. As it briefly flashed emerald, he stepped through.

When he stepped out on the other side, everything had changed. The air was stagnant and heavy, the atmosphere suffocating. Drayvex was glad he wouldn't have to breathe it for long. Surrounded by green, this planet groaned under the weight of its towering trees and overgrown plants.

Whichever way this went, he had a grim feeling it would be over quickly.

His truce with the Nagur had been voided the second he stepped onto their world.

He made a slight adjustment to the unconscious form in his arms, then reached out one hand towards the portal. Summoning all of his remaining will, he pushed through the waves of fatigue lapping over him, his entire being protesting against his actions. No more, it begged as he rifled through the portal's immense depths. Have some goddamn mercy. But Drayvex had no intention of stopping now. Defeat was not a word in his vast and complex vocabulary, and so he would finish what he'd started. He used the deep, pulsing anger still reverberating inside him to strengthen that resolve; used the destructive things that were tearing him apart to fuel what little power his dissolving insides could still summon.

When he finally found his mark, he pulled. The Lapis Vitae ripped from the portal, shooting straight into Drayvex's outstretched palm. Without the stone, the portal collapsed, the pane of light dropping and shattering into fragmented pieces.

As crackling fingers of raw, unrestrained power shot up his arm, he realised that he'd directly touched the stone. Shit.

Caught off guard, he recoiled, almost dropping Ruby. The dark, blistering power of the stone jolted straight to his core, its raw essence exalting him in his diminishing state. Drayvex felt his current form slip, along with his corrupted resolve. Dark essence buzzed through his veins, drawn like a moth to a flame to his demonic nature, enhancing it. Encouraging it. It brushed away his inner turmoil; the pain, anger, bitterness. The gaping chasm of impulsive desire. Anything remotely related to Ruby. It was almost euphoric, having it all burnt away, like being unburdened. This was what he'd wanted all along. The power surge he'd craved.

A muffled thud sounded on the ground, scattering his thoughts. Distracted, Drayvex looked down at his feet. Ruby was sprawled amongst the tangled carpet of weeds, partly obscured by a wild mass of overgrown plants. He couldn't recall letting her drop. Then again, it was getting harder by the second to justify his reason for being here on this hag-infested planet.

As the earlier spell he'd cast to slow Ruby's heart trickled away into the atmosphere, she began to convulse once more. Her body jerked and contorted, the poison continuing its path unhindered. A thick white foam spewed from her mouth with each sharp movement.

Drayvex stood and watched Ruby's death throes through double vision as the Lapis Vitae pulsed with seductive ecstasy in his grip. The power was that of ancient demonic heritage. As a Demon Lord, it was like rocket fuel in his veins, and it embraced his true nature with immediate effect.

A familiar nagging prickled at the back of his mind, fighting the change. That annoying voice that insisted he was making a mistake. It had been present when he'd bitten Ruby in an alleyway, and when he'd dropped her coin into the acid lake around his fortress. Scrabbling for purchase, for himself, Drayvex wondered if this was what it was like to have a conscience.

Suddenly, he stopped dead. The silence that hung in the warm, sticky air was both sobering and alarming. It sliced through his dark euphoria, and as the stronger *self* won out, it crippled the other. He couldn't hear Ruby's heart.

Fighting his natural instinct to cling to power, Drayvex opened his hand and let the stone drop to the floor.

The moment he lost contact with the Lapis Vitae, everything inside him shifted. The power he'd acquired ripped from him with considerable force, leaving him with the sensation of someone having pulled the plug on him from within. When the stone hit the floor, he brought down the force of his steel-lined boot on top of it.

Drayvex scooped up Ruby and restarted the steady current of magic flowing between them. She was dead, he knew this. He'd killed her in a moment of weakness. However fragile his rational state of mind, this was something that could not be denied. For what he had planned, though, there remained a small window of opportunity between life and death. He hoped to Hell that he could still use it.

The stone coated the ground at his feet, no more than expensive dust in a primitive, undeserving world. Something inside him cringed as he turned, heading deeper into the undergrowth. He would regret that later.

The Nagur had been around for hundreds of years. They were vicious creatures, and his father's beef with them had cost him on an enormous scale. They enjoyed the lengthy solitude Drayvex's smart but fragile truce had bought them, only having to deal with outsiders when the occasional screwball decided to drop by uninvited. Today was one of those days.

Drayvex dragged himself through the twisted marshland, seething as he walked. Saydor had made a colossal error in judgement. He would chase him from world to world if he had to. One way or another, that lowlife would pay for everything he had done.

The sharp, keening anger that lay beneath the surface drowned out the worst of his physical pain, back now that the stone no longer supplied him with its power. Maybe he would track down a raellorb stone to bring the cretin back again and again, giving him leeway to be creative with every drawn-out death. The possibilities were endless.

Drayvex stopped and eyed the sheltered alcove. What looked like a large, muddy green boulder took up most of the immediate space. A thick layer of scum covered most of its visible surfaces like a skin, almost completely hiding what was underneath. It was an unspectacular object in a dull, green landscape. But Drayvex knew better than to dismiss it.

"Knock, knock," he growled under his breath, heading towards the large rock. Repositioning Ruby to slash at the moss, he revealed what was underneath in one swift motion. A dirty silver door gleamed at him, confirming his suspicion. This was it.

Drayvex stepped through the door into a dim cavern, his demonic instincts reacting to the strong scent in the air. The deceptively large space within was basic, with little to no clutter. Various items were pinned to the walls; leathered hides, bones, handcrafted weapons. Shrunken heads of varying species dangled at intervals from the low ceiling, and as his eyes dropped, they were drawn to a long table positioned in the centre of the room.

He stalked over to it and lay Ruby on top, careful not to break contact with her.

"Rise and shine," he called out, loud enough for his voice to carry right to the back of the cavern. The long silence that followed only served to heighten his already taut nerves.

He looked down at Ruby and studied her with a critical eye. He didn't know how wide this window of opportunity was, nor how dead was *too* dead for it to work. This had to work.

"I know you can hear me, witch, and I don't like to be kept waiting." It was a well-known fact that nagur did not like to associate themselves with their spell casting derivatives. In truth, baiting and angering one's enemies had always been a tactical response, a knee-jerk reaction that gave him an advantage in a fight. Baiting a nagur when you wanted a favour, though, was less smart.

Drayvex was about do something rash when someone responded to his demands.

The rattling breath of ancient lungs reached his ears, the sucking of rank breaths of air. The stench in the cavern intensified, almost overpowering to his sensitive nose, and as his eyes cut through the musty darkness, they focused on the hunched figure that limped towards him in the gloom.

"Well, well. This is a conundrum," muttered the slowly advancing figure, muddy eyes gleaming with vicious glee. "I'd heard that hell was freezing over, but I didn't quite believe it."

Drayvex felt his claws sharpen as she spoke, his fangs extend, her voice grating against his meagre self-control.

As the nagur approached the table, Drayvex found himself studying the repulsive form before him. Small and hunched, her clothes were no more than a patchwork of scraps, some recognisable as pelts from species he knew. Underneath the makeshift clothes, a distended stomach was visible, standing out against the rest of her bony form. Her skin was withered and cracked, her face long and pointed, with large yellow eyes just visible beneath the net of grizzled hair.

"Hell will have no fury in comparison to mine if this girl does not live," he said, hearing the edge to his tone as the creature met his gaze. "Make it so."

The nagur made a wet sound, somewhere between a hiss and a suck, and Drayvex tensed, anticipating an attack.

The gaze between them remained unbroken for a full minute. Then, out of nowhere, she cackled. "The Demon King, felled by a slip of a mouse. How the mighty have fallen."

Drayvex ignored the jab and continued. "Fix her," he said in a low voice, attempting to keep his cool, "and I will give you what you most desire." Hag.

The nagur narrowed her large eyes to a squint, before lowering them to the table. She made a short grunting noise, placing her hand on Ruby's ankle.

She broke away again almost immediately. "This girl is well and truly deceased. Her body is critically damaged and cannot be repaired with a hex. Now get out. Stop wasting my time before I lose my temper and remember that we're supposed to be at war."

Drayvex sneered, unperturbed by the witch's idle threats. Even in his greatly weakened state, he would be more than a handful for the nagur in a fight. "I know she's dead," he snapped. "And I have no interest restarting the war. I'm talking about *filenos*."

The Nagur's eyes grew wide as they snapped back up to his face. "You?" she asked sharply, a clawed finger stroking the table under her hand.

Drayvex simply stared back. "What do you most desire, nagur?"

The creature paused, her expression darkening. "You look like him, you know, beneath that tenuous human veil you think conceals you. Like your plague-ridden devil of a father. Just the sight of you makes my blood boil with ancient loathing."

Drayvex tensed, preparing to unleash everything he had left. If he couldn't bribe her, he would make her comply.

"You act more like *her*."

He faltered at the unexpected turn. He had no idea how to respond to that.

She laughed, short and sharp. "You're not what I expected, Demon Lord. Okay, fine. I will save your wench. You fully understand the terms, I take it? And the consequences?" That last word lingered on her shrivelled tongue, a taunt.

He knew the consequences, as well as any demon with access to ancient spells. But what he was about to sacrifice had never been done between

348

demon and human. A sliver of his soul. A piece of him, in her. Yet, in that moment, one single thought drove him: Ruby had to live. "Do it."

The creature flashed a sly smile back at him, rubbing a clawed hand up her bony arm. "Done." Her voice lowered to a rattled purr. "As for what I desire most …" She left her sentence hanging, pausing to take another rasping breath. "Nothing will bring me greater pleasure than to watch you live with the consequences of your actions."

Drayvex waited for that selfish, self-serving voice in his head that always knew best, but for once, it was silent.

Chapter 34

When Ruby had first come around, she'd lost her mind.

She stared at the lifeless figure in the bed, tracing the prominent veins under the pale, translucent skin. She'd spent hours just watching her chest move up and down, lost days taking in the stranger with her mother's face. Eventually, she'd had to take a closer look.

Both she and her mother were medical mysteries. Her mum had died. She knew this; she'd watched it happen. Felt it shatter her world. Ruby herself was a different matter entirely.

Ruby slid out from between the sheets of the thin hospital bed, putting her bare feet to the cold tiles. Her gaze was drawn to the neighbouring bed.

Approaching the bed was simple. Making herself take a good hard look at the figure within its folds was much, much harder.

Wires and tubes ran the length of the bed, connecting to the blinking machines they were hooked up to. The woman in the bed was pale, but the dusting of freckles on her face and arms stood out in bold contrast. Her face was lifeless, gaunt, but the shape of it was unchanged, achingly familiar. Sandra had always said that she had cheekbones to die for. The face of a model. Her hair was wild and untamed, with stray wisps jumping out from the pillow at various angles. Something that Ruby had been able to tease her about, even on its best days.

Ruby felt a single tear trickle down her cheek as she stood, held in place by the conflicting emotions that coursed through her. It was too much to hope for, and she didn't dare hope.

Something clicked behind her. Jumping, she spun to the source.

A tall nurse bustled into the room, pushing a trolley. She hummed a toneless melody as she walked, scanning a clipboard that she'd propped up on its surface, lost in her own thoughts.

When she saw Ruby, she stopped. "Oh, Ruby," she said, her eyes filling with warmth. "Are you okay, hun?" She tucked her pen behind one ear.

Ruby laughed, a confused sort of sound that sent her thoughts spinning. She *was* okay. She was absolutely fine, and she had no idea how in the hell he'd pulled it off. She traced a finger over her palm, looking again for the marks she knew should be there.

"You can go home today. Isn't that great? The doctor will be around in a bit to give the okay."

Home. She sucked in a breath, memories teasing at the edges of her conscious mind. Where was that, exactly? She looked back at the nurse and smiled for her benefit, the need to be alone with her thoughts surfacing.

As the nurse nodded at her and went about her business, Ruby probed at her tender neck. She remembered bits and pieces. Fragmented moments of consciousness amongst the darkness and the burning pain. And Drayvex.

Drayvex. One word, one name with a hundred memories attached.

Her memories of that day seemed alien now, like someone else's troubles as she recalled them, safe in this hospital ward. But they were vivid and raw and there was no denying that they were all too real.

Ruby had called out to him. They'd won, and yet she was losing him. She could see it in his changing features, the tangible darkness descending over him. She could feel the widening distance that it put between them, and it terrified her. But she couldn't move. She had forgotten how.

"Drayvex," she'd managed. She had wanted to tell him that it wasn't worth it. Had tried to tell him that she was scared, that she just wanted to feel safe again. She never got the words out.

She'd known it that was bad from the moment they'd met eyes. That was when she knew that, for all his efforts, she was still going to die.

Somewhere before the world had faded to darkness, Ruby had found an iota of bliss. A strange comfort in the knowledge that he did care for her after all.

Ruby glanced at her mother, sleeping peacefully in the bed next to hers. After a moment's hesitation, she shuffled over to the foot of her bed. For the umpteenth time, she grabbed the clipboard and thumbed through the doctor's slanted scribbles, looking for clues as to what was going on.

A moment longer, and Ruby had to admit defeat. She sighed, slipping the clipboard back into its pouch. Her mother was in a coma. And she, Ruby, was being discharged later today because there was *nothing wrong with her*. She just couldn't see how he'd managed to pull it off.

Ruby perched on the edge of the bed, and with fear coursing through her, she took her mum's hand. Smiling, she breathed in a deep, cleansing breath. Regardless of hows, Ruby was grateful. And when the dust settled, she would make sure that she was truly living, not just getting by.

Ruby sat on the bed, her legs swinging as they dangled over the edge. Today, she was not a patient but a visitor. Tomorrow, she would find somewhere new to call home.

Standing, she stepped over to the window and leaned her arms on the sill, the sea of twinkling city lights taking her breath away. She had missed these views. She gazed out and up, towards the full moon, her thoughts weighing heavy. There was still so much she didn't know. Had Drayvex recovered, too? Would she see him again, or had he put her behind him? Did she *want* to see him again?

A flash of red caught at the edge of her vision. Curious, she looked down for the culprit. Ruby did a double-take. It was a flower.

She stared at the bloom, stunned. A large red flower, shaped like a teardrop. It looked exotic, and yet it was familiar to her. As she took the object in her hand, she felt butterflies batter the walls of her stomach.

Her heart jolted as she considered the gift, a gift that had not been there a few hours ago. Ruby smiled, unable to stop herself. She supposed she would see him again, should the opportunity arise.

Next time, she would be prepared.

Epilogue

Since returning to rule, Drayvex had discovered many interesting and useless ways of smoking out ex-Demon Masters.

He had also discovered that hatred had a broad and colourful spectrum of shades, ranging from grizzled grey to unholy black death. And Saydor had triggered them all, one by one.

Drayvex glared down at the map, scanning the expanse of miniature holograms that represented a scaled-down Vekrodus. He would have to face her again, eventually. It was only a matter of time. That would be a fun conversation. 'Ruby. You look well. By the way, the demon that killed you to spite me? He's lost to the wind. Could be anywhere, so watch your back!'

Saydor would, at some point, discover her all over again. A living, breathing human. That was a problem.

He reached down and touched the point of the little single-spired Tower, feeling a strong hatred burning him from within. It had been a while since that day. Longer for him, but on Earth, a mere month. Of course, he'd seen *her* every day. After all, Ruby visited her dear mother every day without fail.

As plans of petty destruction began to take form in his mind, he sent a blast of power down his finger towards the Tower. It exploded into little pieces, showering the map with debris.

The mother had been a stroke of genius, if he did say so himself. Not only had it given him the ability to check on Ruby at regular intervals, it also gave her reason to believe that her patience would eventually be rewarded.

You gave her *false* hope, genius, sneered the conceited voice at the back of his mind. She'll never forgive you.

Drayvex dismissed the unwanted thought, but not before his mood plummeted. One problem at a time was enough. He glanced at the large tubes behind him, eyes falling upon the slight figure suspended within the largest.

As quickly as it caught his attention, he disregarded the body. Right now, Ruby's damn mother was the least of his concerns. Saydor was going to regret ever crossing him. He swore it on everything unholy.

About the Author

Rachel Hobbs lives in soggy South West Wales, where she hibernates with her bearded dragon and her husband. By day she is a dental nurse at a small local practice. By night, she writes.

Her debut novel SHADOW-STAINED is the first in a dark fantasy series for adults, inspired by her dark and peculiar experiences with narcolepsy and parasomnia. She's since subjugated her demons, and writes under the tenuous guise that they work for *her*.

Fuelled by an unhealthy amount of coffee, she writes about hard-boiled monsters with soft centres and things that go bump in the night.

You can connect with me on:
- http://www.authorrachelhobbs.co.uk
- http://www.twitter.com/rhobbsauthor
- http://www.facebook.com/authorrachelhobbs
- http://www.instagram.com/authorrachelhobbs